# THE WAGON TRAIN TO THE STARS WAS IN TROUBLE. . . .

"Target our phasers," Captain Kirk said, "and prepare to fire if that drone fires on us. Chekov, provide pinpoint coordinates to the upper left."

"Left . . . got it."

"Spock, are we broadcasting?"

"Yes, sir. The drone is unresponsive. It believes it has found its quarry and won't release."

"Boost the signal."

"Proximity range in thirteen seconds, sir," Sulu said, tipping his shoulders as he turned the ship. "Drone's firing on us." Spock watched his console instead of the gigantic crawling monster on the screen as it approached, then dipped below the ship's saucer-shaped primary hull. "Drone is tractoring on our en̲̅_____ing section. Five minutes to phaser-critical."

Tensely Kirk l̲̅_____ the fact that they_____ erful drone's chosen ta̲̅rg_____ the Expedition ships. Give us room to ma̲̅n̲̅e̲̅u̲̅_____."

# STAR TREK®

# NEW EARTH

## BOOK ONE OF SIX
# WAGON TRAIN
# TO THE STARS

# DIANE CAREY

**NEW EARTH CONCEPT BY DIANE CAREY AND JOHN ORDOVER**

**POCKET BOOKS**

New York   London   Toronto   Sydney   Singapore   Belle Terre

An *Original* Publication of POCKET BOOKS

POCKET BOOKS, a division of Simon & Schuster Inc.
1230 Avenue of the Americas, New York, NY 10020

A VIACOM COMPANY

STAR TREK is a Registered Trademark of
Paramount Pictures.

This book is published by Pocket Books, a division of
Simon & Schuster Inc., under exclusive license from
Paramount Pictures.

ISBN: 0-671-04296-3

First Pocket Books printing June 2000

10 9 8 7 6 5 4 3 2 1

POCKET and colophon are registered trademarks of
Simon & Schuster Inc.

Printed in the U.S.A.

# Chapter One

DISTANT NIGHT, the most distant. Today, a giant's finger of tractless lingering haze dusted space deep cobalt blue, painting the otherwise ink matte of weeks past. Everything changed day by day, even space itself.

Or perhaps it was only anger.

Prowling the central command deck, surrounded by a raised walkway that supported all the consoles and monitors that showed him the universe, Captain James Kirk bedeviled his starship's forward viewscreen with a punitive glare, as if he could mentally brutalize what he saw into submission.

"Red alert," he ordered, "again."

"Captain," Lieutenant Commander Uhura broached from the communications post, "we never stood down from the previous one."

Kirk ignored her. "Get the owner over here right now. Sulu, detonate those shots."

1

"Trying, sir."

The starship's bridge pulsed with activity. Colored lights winked, and soft mechanical noises sang in the background, a self-driven symphony of never-ending background music that could seem either comforting or nerve-racking, depending upon the construction of any given peace or panic.

Today, Kirk let his nerves go ahead and rack. Somehow it was a message from the ship that she would act out his will, that he was still in charge.

"Mr. Spock," he asked, "is that drone automated or manned?"

On the upper deck walkway, watching the main screen like a cat on the hunt, the starship's first officer was as much comfort as Kirk would get on this mission. Sharp-eyed and dynamic, standing out on a bridge otherwise manned by humans, the Vulcan posed a narrow form particularly imperial in the new Starfleet colors of brick and black. His slick black hair, cut in the style of banks and points that now was famous in the Federation, caught a band of light from the red-alert beacon, which also framed the triangle of his left ear as he turned. "We're not certain whether it's manned, sir. Sensors pick up no life signs, but may be fouled by the industrial machinery on board. Some of Mrs. Webb's factory ships do have security guards stationed with sensitive data files."

"Then we can't blow it up—yet. Invasive maneuvers, Mr. Sulu, get between that drone and *Oregon Trail*. Double shields port, right now."

"Port double shields, aye," the steady helmsman answered. Kirk was glad Sulu had come on this mission. Even though the course was essentially straight out into the middle of nowhere at noteworthy speeds, the helm at the hands of Hikaru Sulu somehow behaved just a thought better than at anyone else's.

The reassuring repeat of orders gave a sense of control to an uncontrolled situation. The starship moved forward through a magnificent funnel of spacefaring ships, every size and construction, that now moved aside for her. The view from here was eerie—dozens after dozens of ships flooding past, heading back as the starship headed forward. At the helm, Commander Sulu hammered coordinates and traffic directions into his computer console, sweeping the flotilla away from the danger point.

Though only a few seconds of pause lay before him, Kirk stole those moments to commune silently with the great entourage of ships he was here to lead. Huge Conestoga-class dormitory ships, with their bird-beak bows and bulbous living sections, plowed past with deceiving grace, each pushed by brilliantly conceived devices designed just for this journey by Engineer Scott—two detachable "mule" engines, huge rocks of unadorned muscle that could tow or push at fantastic ratios. Thus driven, the big people-mover ships were incarnations of the first iron horses steaming out toward treacherous frontiers, over scorching deserts, windy plains, and frozen mountains, hoping they'd make it to the other side.

Sprinkled among the Conestogas were private yachts, tenders, industrial drones, the mercy ship, the garden ship, the governor's VIP transport . . . What a sight. More than seventy ships, clustered in one area of space. Even after five months in space, it was shocking to look at them all, moving together in a great flock. Kirk was used to being in space, but alone out here, with his one powerful vessel, and the family of crew.

Though the crew of four hundred had always seemed bulky as ships' complements went, Kirk had found new epiphanies in the past months, leading a convoy of over sixty-four thousand colonists to a promised land—a land they had promised to themselves and were determined to settle, a dream they themselves had conjured and hammered into shape.

Here came the coroner ship, sedate and dignified in its promise to do whatever sad jobs came its way. Kirk tried to ignore the passing of *Twilight Sentinel,* but her presence off his starship's port bow jolted him back to the cold fact that he was facing a tragedy in the making and if he made the wrong decision, that ship would be full of bodies.

He pressed his hands to his command chair and pushed to his feet as the privateer ship *Hunter's Moon* slid past, her scratched black and green dazzlepainted hull gliding by at what seemed like arm's length. There, in the open space as the privateer cleared the viewscreen, was the tortured Conestoga *Oregon Trail,* being assaulted by a drone ship that had lost its mind. The functional-ugly drone, with its retractable docking claws all out, clutched at the Conestoga like a headless insect. Its flashes of torch phasers, several time brighter than they should be, crashed across the hulls of both free-floating vessels. Sparks danced into space, clouding the view. If those torches cut through the Conestoga's hide, this malfunction could quickly become a disaster.

Around him, the starship's refitted bridge glowed with the scarlet hue of red alert. In his misty mind, Kirk sometimes expected to see this place as it once had been, with its rows of etched black screens, the red rail, muted carpet, and grade-school colors that had seemed so crisp and happy. The refit had made the bridge more technical, more cold and metallic, but under the skin she murmured to him that she was still that old ship of his many adventures, the sturdy grand dame that had serviced the Federation so dependably. She recognized him despite the change, and he felt more at home by the hour.

At the engineering post, the convoy's senior engineer, Montgomery Scott, turned his iron-gray head and looked at the drone ship on the main screen harassing the Conestoga. Irritably he reported, "That damned box has sealed all its hatches now, sir. The hull's electrified and it keeps evading grapples. Nobody can get inside while the shields are up. The thing's gone completely raving."

Spock turned again. "Captain, I estimate eleven minutes to critical overload of those industrial phasers at this enhancement level."

Kirk flattened his lips. "Nothing compared to what'll happen when I get my hands on whoever enhanced them. Ah—Captain Kilkenny."

"Kilvennan," came the correction. "Michael."

On the upper deck, just coming out of the turbolift, was one of the privateer captains, in fact the captain of *Hunter's Moon,* which had just sailed past. Escorted by Lieutenant Chekov, with shaggy long hair and a musketeer beard, Michael Kilvennan was everything James Kirk imagined the captain of folklore to be—a mold that, ironically, he had never quite fit. Kilvennan wore a brown turtleneck and a belted sheepskin vest, setting him instantly apart from the starship's crew in their fitted blood-red uniform jackets and black trousers. In fact, the privateer captain looked uneasy standing next to the perpetually tidy Chekov.

"You better have a word with Mr. Chekov here," the privateer demanded. "Beaming me off my ship without permission—"

"We don't have time for permission, Captain," Kirk told him sharply. "And I have emergency authority." He jabbed a thumb over his shoulder at the scene on the main viewer. "That one of your drones?"

"My mother runs the line of trailing industrial drones," Kilvennan confirmed, watching the action before them in space. "Helen Kilvennan Webb. She works on the CP *Crystobel*, but our family lives on the *Yukon*. She's the one who should be here. Those drones trail after the commercial pilot—"

"Like little ducks," Kirk nodded. "You'll do for now. *Yukon*'s under medical quarantine."

"I'll 'do'? Just because Mr. Chekov's handling Expedition security doesn't mean he gets to yank people off their own ships and haul them around the fleet."

"Yes, it does. Your mother's drone is attacking one of our passenger ships. I need to know what's on it right now and whether I'm free to destroy it if I have to."

Kilvennan scowled. "Who cares what's on it? Blow the damned thing up!"

A voice entered the argument from the upper deck. "Captain, you can't!"

Kirk turned—so did everybody—to the future colony's young governor as he raised a hand from where he stood next to Scott. An idealist's idealist, Evan Pardonnet was a man for whom youth provided a shield against the digs that picked away at beliefs and dreams. He had planned this massive one-stroke colonial movement, overlorded its every development, and bristled at the Federation's inclusion of Starfleet into the mix at the last minute. James Kirk had cast away his mantle of admiralty and once again put on a captain's hat, and accepted command of the *Starship Enterprise* to go into deep space, escorting and guarding the greatest colonial project in United Federation of Planets history.

Easy on the drawing board. Reality was a picker bush. For five months Kirk and Pardonnet had wrestled over who had authority to do what. In a crisis situation, should the colonists look to their fleet captain, or to their governor? Was there time for a committee meeting? The governor now argued his point in his usual way—passionately.

"Mrs. Webb's line of drones," he protested, "is manufacturing things we'll need almost immediately to set up a decent first year on Belle Terre! We've got to protect it!"

"Blow it up," the owner's son repeated. Kilvennan seemed relaxed, but his eyes were fixed on the ghastly scene playing out in space, the drone ship carving plates off the *Oregon Trail*'s weakening blue side. "Webb Three's a manufacturing plant making subassemblies for industrial goods. Kitchenware, that's all—"

"Our ovens, ranges, refrigeration units!" The governor clenched and unclenched his hands until his palms were red. "Filtration systems, hydrators, dehydrators, waste-recyclers—we need those, Captain Kirk!"

But Kilvennan stood his ground. "What good's that stuff if you let it kill three thousand colonists?"

Kirk swung to him. "What kind of phasers has that thing got, Kilvennan?"

"Ah . . . level-six cutting torches, I think—"

"How'd they get up to level three?"

Pulling his hands from his pockets, Kilvennan

bumped forward against the bridge rail. "Level three! That's impossible!"

"You're looking at it."

"Those are supposed to be level-six industrials, defensive at short range to deflect meteors! Cutting phasers, that's all!"

"Captain Kilvennan," Spock interrupted, "if your mother's had her phasers enhanced, she's in violation of Belle Terre Colonial Expedition statutes."

"And," Kirk firmly finished, "she'll be held criminally responsible for any deaths caused by that drone."

Kilvennan met him with a gale-force glare. "Who in hell do you think you are, making a charge like that? If those phasers are enhanced, they'll overload! Don't you think we know that?"

Meeting the other captain's anger point for point, Kirk snarled, "Is there any living person on board? Anyone at all?"

"Nobody. Webb Three, Four, Six, and Nine are all completely automated. My parents run them by telemetry from the CP."

At the comm station, Uhura had her hand to her earpiece. "Sir, Captain Briggs is hailing from the Tugantine. Should he move in with *Norfolk Rebel* and pry that drone off the Conestoga?"

"Not even the Tugantine's engines could break that drone's tractors," Kirk calculated. "Not under fire, anyway. Tell him to stand by."

Scott poked at his engineering controls and scowled. "The drone's tractored itself directly to the Conestoga's hull, sir. There's not two inches between them now."

Irreconcilably prowling the command deck, Kirk seized the problem and applied his pure will to it. The chilling sight of the factory drone chewing at a ship with three thousand passengers on board—they might as well have been watching a cougar gnaw the leg of an elephant. Was there anything more frightening than a machine that had lost its mind?

Even through the gap of space between him and the Conestoga, he sensed the shrieks of fear, the huddling in horror, the confusion and desperation aboard that dormitory ship. He felt in his bones the painful thrumming of vibration from attack as it ran through the skin of the ship and up through the feet of those people and into their shuddering limbs. They were scared. He felt that. They needed him. He felt that too.

The bridge was all lit up with "windows" out to space. He saw all that was around them, all the ships of the Belle Terre Colonial Expedition, the thousands of civilians standing side by side with their spouses and children, watching what he would do next to save their neighbors, depending on him and judging him based upon the coming few minutes.

He hated an audience. Missions could be handled. Shows were messy.

Were they all thinking about the good old Earth they'd left behind, sinking into a gemlike backdrop, likely never to be seen again? Or were their minds on the planet they were heading toward, another Earth with clear skies and gleaming oceans, continents flushed as if they'd just been kissed?

Kirk was jolted as the last few ships cleared the way. The Conestoga *Lakota,* with her warp mule engines driving like Hadrian's elephants. The industrial ship *Macedon* towing an iceberg—their water source in space. The huge *Olympian,* repository for thousands of micro-scaffolds growing body parts for cryo-freeze. The coroner ship *Twilight Sentinel* with her elegant purple hull and white lights, the dairy barge loaded with real cattle and real cowboys. Wreckmaster Briggs moving his Tugantine out of the way. Finally the Starfleet combat support tender *Beowulf* skimmed past the starship and flashed her running lights in a good-luck salute.

*Beowulf* was the last of the Expedition ships blocking the way. Now the Conestoga *Oregon Trail* and her bulldog attacker stood alone on the vista of space, glowing in the airbrushed light of a sun they were passing, and Kirk was at center stage.

"Nine minutes to overload." Spock's baritone voice pretended emotionlessness, but that was a lie.

"Captain," the governor pressed, "I know what you're thinking and I don't like it. The colonists are depending on those drones. Webb Three's the only one manufacturing appliance subsystems. The Webbs have spacedock facilities, computer components, all sorts of things critical to our setting up a viable spaceport in record time! Please don't fire on their factory drone!"

Ignoring him, Kirk turned to the privateer captain. "When did you first notice its erratic behavior, Mr. Kilvennan?"

"It's Captain Kilvennan, and my mother's sensors noticed the rogue at the same time you did, *Captain* Kirk."

Suddenly ferocious, Kirk snapped, "Don't get provoked with me. I'm having a bad week and I'm not in a good mood."

Though Kilvennan visibly boiled under the skin, he offered helpful information. "My first mate wondered if maybe the lightship's signal scrambled Webb Three's autonav. I told him I didn't think we were picking up a signal yet from the *Hatteras*."

Spock turned to him. "We've been receiving a phase-distant homing signal from the lightship for nearly four days, Captain Kilvennan. Only this morning it finally went to proximity one. The lightship uses extreme-range sensors to gather information, then broadcast them to anyone who might need them."

"Not now, Spock," Kirk preempted. "We're not sure what set that drone off, but no stray signal's going to change level-six torches to level-three disruptive phasers. So somebody's been tampering. Now the ship's gone rogue and it's trying to cut up a people-mover with three thousand passengers on board."

Governor Pardonnet sweated as he watched the Conestoga on the main screen. "Can't we have one day without an accident?"

"This is no accident," Kirk rejected. "If it were just a malfunction, that drone would've snatched one of its own line of drones or some ship close to it. Instead it went right for the *Oregon Trail*, ignoring ten other vessels in its way."

Before them as the starship drew cautiously nearer, the chunky manufacturer ship, with its thick arms and pods extended like claws, assaulted the helpless Conestoga. Flashes of torch phasers, five times brighter than they should be, brightened the flanks of both vessels. At the helm, Sulu settled down to concentrate on moving just the starship now that the rest of the Expedition ships were out of the way.

Kilvennan asked, "Can't you fry its autopilot with a microburst?"

"As you pointed out," Spock answered, "enhanced phasers are quirkish. A burst might set them into critical mode."

Hearing their voices as if detached by a thousand

miles, James Kirk gripped the back of his command chair as the starship pulled closer, narrowing the distance between itself and the crazed drone. The Conestoga loomed so large on the screen that he could count its hull bolts.

"When it flew off on its own," Kilvennan offered, "my mother contacted me and told me to broadcast commands in our private code when it came past *Hunter's Moon,* but it wouldn't accept. Instead it passed right by the other ships and went for *Oregon* and started opening up."

"Seven minutes," Spock reminded.

Kirk almost snarled at him to quit counting, but held back. "Chekov, go down to auxiliary control and use the battle targeting computer to take a pinpoint firing fix on that drone. Contact us the minute you've pulled it up."

"I'll be there in thirty seconds, sir!" Chekov brushed past Kilvennan and plunged into the lift. With a hiss he was gone, and the young privateer captain stood alone on the aft walkway.

"Mr. Kilvennan," Kirk summoned, "would you come down here and take his post at weapons and navigation."

Startled, Kilvennan stepped back. "Nah, you don't want me. Never even been on a starship's bridge."

"And I've never been a privateer. The seat's right here. You're the one who wants to blow it up, and I need somebody to push the button when I give the order."

Making a decision he didn't like, Michael Kilvennan stepped down to the lower deck, grumbling, "Bet you haven't heard the word 'no' in twenty years." He slipped into the nav chair next to Sulu and tried to make sense of the multilights on the board before him. "Why don't we just blow it up now? Why wait?"

"We've got to get it off *Oregon Trail's* hull," Kirk said, "or it'll rip a hole in that ship the size of a gymnasium. There's Chekov's tie-in. He just connected."

Pointing at a grid on the right side of the board, Kirk moved around to Kilvennan's side, feeling compact and chiseled in comparison to the lanky hired gun with his long hair and rugged clothing.

"You're in my way," Kilvennan accused.

But Kirk didn't move. He paused in midstep, fingertips of his left hand poised on the nav console. He was looking up at the science station.

The ultimate of verticality, Spock continued to look down at him as if they had all the time ever made. Had they both stopped breathing? Kirk felt the eyes of Scott and Uhura, who knew them both so well. Governor Pardonnet was watching him too, but in a completely different way. So was Kilvennan.

"It *did* go straight for the *Oregon Trail*," Kirk murmured. "Didn't it?"

Spock peered at him. "The ID beacon?"

Kirk slapped the helm with a flat palm. "Try it, Spock! Sulu, shields down!"

"Our shields, sir?" Sulu asked. "Oh—of course! Shields down, sir!"

"Phaser overload on the drone," Spock ticked off, "within six minutes."

Six minutes, and the factory drone would blow itself up without help.

"What's going on?" Kilvennan asked.

Spinning to face the main screen again, Kirk quickly said, "Something must've told that drone which ship to attack. That means specific signal identification!"

"And that means programming," Scott punctuated.

Suddenly they were all milking their consoles, concentrating on prying that dangerous drone off the skin of the Conestoga. Again Kirk took his spare two seconds to empathize with the people on board that dorm ship—emergency evac drills, abandon-ship procedures, waking the children and fitting them with EV units—

And Uhura sitting up there at her post as if she were just a switchboard operator, showing none of the fabulous power of action she possessed as the Expedition's drillmaster and safety tsar. Were her drills coming to good use over there? Would lives be saved?

"Sir," she called, "Mr. Chekov signals he's ready."

"Have him stand by." Kirk's voice was gravelly with anticipation. He wanted to shoot at something. "You heard that, Kilvennan?"

"Still trying to figure out these lights. Don't count on me."

"Right there." Kirk pointed at an amber control grid. "That's the important one for you."

"Got it."

"Spock?"

One wrist pressed to the edge of his board, Spock pecked at the controls. He frowned, dissatisfied. "I'm unable to shut down the Conestoga's beacon by remote. There's some sort of signal refusal."

Cranking around, Kirk grasped the back of his command chair. "Ship to ship, Uhura, quickly. *Oregon Trail*, this is *Enterprise*. Shut down your ID beacon immediately. That drone is homing in on your code."

"*Enterprise, Captain Trautner. We figured that out, but our beacon won't neutralize. It's locked up. It'll take hours to purge the system. That thing's cutting through our hull!*"

"Evacuate passengers to the other side of—"

*"And shut the hatches. I did, but if it breaches the hull in the wrong place, we'll have a pressure detonation. Can't you blast it?"*

"Negative. The explosion would take out your port quarter. Keep working on that signal. Spock, broadcast the Conestoga's signal anyway. Maybe we can confuse that thing into letting go if it gets the signal from two sources."

Kilvennan looked up. "Why are you dropping your shields?"

"If we don't," Scott answered, "the drone won't be able to tractor onto us and it'll go looking for the Conestoga again."

Kirk's shoulders bunched under the uniform jacket. "Target phasers."

"About time," Kilvennan reminded, his hand poised over the firing control.

"Bring the ship to—"

"Captain, *please!*" Governor Pardonnet's brown hair flopped forward. "We'll be cooking over open fires for a year while we rebuild that infrastructure. There's got to be a way to neutralize it—"

"You're going to have to let me finish a sentence one of these days, Governor." Kirk gave him a mellow glance. "Mr. Kilvennan, target our phasers and prepare to detonate the beam, and only the beam, if that drone fires on us, understood? Chekov'll provide pinpoint coordinates on your upper left."

"Left . . . got it."

"Spock, are we broadcasting?"

"Yes, sir. The drone is unresponsive. It believes it has found its quarry and won't release."

"Boost the signal. Overwhelm the Conestoga's signal with the same code. Blast that thing in the ears. Pull in close, Sulu."

"Proximity range in thirteen seconds, sir," Sulu said, tipping his shoulders as he turned the ship.

Almost coming out of his chair, Kilvennan snatched a quick breath. "It's breaking free of the Conestoga!"

Sometimes victory could be horrifying. The angry drone ship, with its claws extended and its mechanical mind focused, clunked free of the dorm ship and turned its attack on the starship. Moving closer and growing larger by the millisecond, it was on them in instants. The starship jolted suddenly as it was struck by a phaser hit. Even a level-three phaser at this nearness could deal a bad blow. If it hit a nacelle—

"Firing on us," Sulu mentioned casually.

Spock watched his console instead of the gigantic crawling monster on the screen as it approached, then dipped below the ship's saucer-shaped primary hull. "Drone is tractoring on our engineering section. Five minutes to phaser-critical."

Tensely Kirk lowered his chin and digested the fact that they were now aboard the powerful drone's chosen target. "Mr. Sulu, bear off from the Expedition ships. Give us room to maneuver."

"Room to blow up, you mean," Kilvennan openly stated, and met Kirk's glare fearlessly.

"Target the drone's shield assembly," Kirk gnashed to him, "and fire, right now."

Kilvennan's hand went to the amber grid.

Phasers lashed from the starship's underbelly to the drone now clamped to her engineering hull. On the main screen now was a view of the drone latched freakishly on. The phaser cut a fiery line across the gap, struck the drone's shield array, and the array disintegrated. Only a scorched bruise, smoking and sparking, remained where the assembly had been mounted on the drone's bow.

"Drone's shields are down," Spock confirmed. "It's still compromising our hull. Opening fire now . . . four minutes thirty seconds to critical."

"I'll take care of it." Kirk took Kilvennan by the arm and yanked him out of his chair.

"What—" Kilvennan tripped on the steps leading to the upper deck.

Kirk dragged him the rest of the way, kicked open a maintenance trunk, fished around, and pulled out a magnetic oct-shank cyclospanner, a heavy hand tool, cast in traditional black ore, that only saw use about once every decade but was the only one for the job when it was needed. It was the right shape, and didn't conduct.

"Spock, beam us over there right now."

Kilvennan wrenched his arm away. "You crazy?"

"You're coming with me, like it or not," Kirk told him. "You know your way around inside that thing."

"Beam over there four minutes from critical? You're nuts! I'm not one of your crew to order around!"

"In that case, when I come back I'm arresting your mother."

"Hell—you mean when *we* get back."

"Spock, the guidance-control section, right now!"

Beside Kirk as the buzz of transport filled their ears, Kilvennan stripped out of his sheepskin vest and dumped it on the deck. "Shoulda stayed in Chicago!"

# Chapter Two

"THE GREAT Captain Kirk, and this was the best idea you had? Drag me into this steam oven and get me killed for a shipload of pots and pans? I didn't sign on for this!"

"You signed on to protect these people," Kirk said as Kilvennan led the way, crawling through the low-slung bowels of the factory drone. "Keeping them from starving or freezing once they arrive on the colony falls into that category. That means making sure your mother's business succeeds in supplying these parts. Keep moving. Three minutes thirty."

"Not that sure of the way. Haven't been in one of these—it's been a while. Don't work in the family business anymore."

The drone's mighty engines roared in their ears. Instantly drenched in sweat, Kirk paused only a moment to strip out of his uniform jacket. Kilvennan didn't wait for him.

What a place. A knot of sweaty metal and sputtering vents, this kind of ship was never meant to be crawled through, but only worked on from the outside in some nice safe pressurized bay. Braying madly around them was the high-pitched *pppew ppew* of the torch phasers, screaming their way to overload. Their yammer almost peeled Kirk's skull inside out. The drone wasn't insulated for sound. There wasn't supposed to be anyone inside. There was only air in here because the machinery was designed with air intakes for coolants, and not necessarily good air. The drone also had artificial gravity, because the units it was building would have to work on a planet's surface.

Fifteen seconds of crawling brought him and Kilvennan to the bow section. Pausing before Kirk, Kilvennan pressed his hands to his ears for a minute, looked around to get his bearings, then started to climb. Up through the complex of cables and grafting equipment, somewhere, was the cutting-phaser housing and the firing coupling.

"Still say," Kilvennan shouted, already panting, "we should disengage it from the hull, get off, and blast it. We're not gonna make three minutes. Take forty seconds just to break the flow."

The harsh climb now leveled off to another length of crawling. Tight quarters. "Then climb faster," Kirk insisted from right behind.

Wet tendrils of black hair strung down against Kilvennan's neck. "Whoever convinced you to come out here anyway? Take a starship out of retirement, lead a bunch of private ships and people-movers? Take sixty thousand colonists and their whole support system a zillion light-years into space to settle a planet that's hardly been explored? Why would Admiral James T.

Kirk leave fame and fortune on Earth and become a captain again to lead a mangled mess like this has been so far?"

"For the chance to crawl through a broiling metal box with a hired gun. What else? Move faster."

"All these months in space and nothing but trouble all the way," Kilvennan muttered. "Disagreements over everything from traffic patterns to cargo distribution, conflicts of authority between the privateers and Starfleet, two Conestogas hit by Rocky Nebula spotted fever or the Pioneers' plague or whatever it is—"

"It's not funny, Captain." Kirk scowled as his knees began to ache against the hard-shelled crawlway.

"Hell, no, it's not," Kilvennan shot back. "My little sister and my son both have the damned thing. Funny? That lung flu hits children the hardest. We've already had two teenagers die of it. Now my two kids stand to lose their dad for a shipload of subsystems, thanks to you."

"We both have bigger things to worry about than our own skins," Kirk reminded. "The disease has spread to a third Conestoga."

"What?" As he cranked to look at Kirk, Kilvennan's right arm folded under him and he stumbled. "But Dr. McCoy ordered a quarantine of the two Contestogas! How could it spread?"

Fielding a kind of ricochet of guilt at not having any magic wands, Kirk stole a precious second to wipe his sleeve across his forehead. "Quarantine didn't work. We're considering extending it to medical personnel too. Less than two minutes. Move, move."

"But Maidenshore told us— Ow!" An electrical charge snapped through Kilvennan's left thigh. He jolted hard and slammed down on his right side, clutching at his stinging leg.

Kirk reached forward and caught Kilvennan's ankle. "What'd you just say?"

"Vermin protocol's active! The rat-zap just bit me!"

"No, before that. You said 'Maidenshore'—*Billy* Maidenshore?"

"Yeah, what about him?"

A grumble of nearly forgotten irritation burst up in Kirk's chest. There was a name he hadn't expected to hear again. "Big man, big mouth, enough charisma to choke an opera audience?"

"That's the guy. He's on the *Pandora's Box*."

"Impossible. He's in jail."

"No, he's here."

*"Pandora's Box* is listed as commanded by a Captain Blaine and owned by someone named William Relick."

"That's him," Kilvennan said. "Uses aliases to avoid the media."

"How do you know that?"

"Friend of my parents'. Says he's had a lot of bad press because of politicians who want to ruin him. He's done a lot to keep *Yukon*'s passengers calm in the crisis. Everybody likes him. My mother does, for sure. Don't you even know who's on this convoy?"

Kirk's voice had a built-in scowl, no matter how he tried to shield it. "I thought I did."

"Sixty-four thousand people—guess you couldn't memorize them all. Do you know him?"

"Well enough to have put him away for interstellar racketeering."

"Since when are you into local law enforcement?"

"Since he had my private shuttle stolen." Now thoroughly consumed with the will to squash this latest trouble, Kirk gestured ahead with the cyclospanner. "Keep moving. I suddenly have a new reason to live."

All they could do was ignore the rat-zappers, tuck their legs and elbows close to their bodies, and keep crawling. By the time they got to the right section, both men had burning bruises along their arms, legs, and sides.

Kilvennan's shaggy hair plastered his forehead and picked at his eyes. His brown knit shirt, sweated into a sop, provided the only relief from the snapper burns. "Should be along here somewhere. This drone's one of the older ones. Don't know the tech very well . . ."

"It'll be in this direction." Suddenly recognizing the layout, Kirk angled off to their right, the cyclospanner clunking in his hand with every crawling stride.

"What if you're wrong?" Kilvennan called after him. "We don't have time—"

"When I was seventeen my father got me a summer job on an industrial freighter. It had the same kind of cutting system. This looks familiar."

Coming up in front of them was a sizzling, stinking mass of scorched coils and a huge blackened area of bulkhead. The destroyed shield array!

"Over there!" Kilvennan pointed through a web of cables. "Jesus, it's red!"

Raw overload pulsed through the side of the drone, turning the metal itself rosy with energy. A brief shuffle, and Kirk crouched before the phaser-torch relays.

"Same basic components," he assessed quickly. "Different arrangement. When I get the spanner in there and interrupt the Sherman-Kelly flow, you give it your family's emergency shutdown code." He bared his right arm and shoved the cyclospanner into the gap between the firing linkage and the coil housing.

Kilvennan shielded his face with one hand. "This how you got famous? Backing people into corners and twisting until they squeal?"

"Forty seconds," Kirk counted. "Are you thinking about your children?"

The privateer's dark eyes grew clever. "If I comply, no charges against my mother."

"No deal." Intense and uncharitable, Kirk winced hard all the way to his jaw as electrical activity rushed past his arm, buried to the elbow in the housing. "If your mother's been enhancing her phaser capacity, she's going to be held responsible. The Expedition's going to make it to Belle Terre if I have to push it there. I don't hear you squealing."

A huff of frustration blew from Kilvennan's nostrils. "You son of a bitch . . . E-shut down, Webb GCX Trident Obstruct-Michael."

The cutting torches burped, and the whine of harassment suddenly evaporated. Around them, the drone ship stopped its relentless pulsing and went to neutral engines. The hum of the tractor beam faded with a miserable groan. The whine of overload faded away. The red metal cooled toward ugly gray.

Relieved, Kirk slumped a little. "That was close. As soon as Spock confirms the power-down, he'll beam us out of this sauna."

Instantly exhausted, Kilvennan let his throbbing head drop back against the coolant tubes. "You're a bully, Captain Kirk."

Feeling his sandy hair going dark with perspiration, his face russet and blotchy, Kirk retrieved his burned arm from the housing. His forearm was scorched with a dozen electrical burns. His white knit sleeve smoldered. The cyclospanner thunked to the crawlway grid.

"And don't you ever forget it," he piped.

# BELLE TERRE COLONIAL EXPEDITION
## PRELIMINARY MANIFEST OF SHIP PARTICIPATION
### (TO BE REVISED UPON ADDITIONAL ENTRIES)

NOTE: MANIFEST DOES NOT INCLUDE PRIVATE VESSELS WITHOUT PUBLIC DUTY ASSIGNMENT

SOURCE: OFFICE OF THE GOVERNOR, COLONY BELLE TERRE PROJECT

OCCULT STAR SYSTEM, SAGITTARIAN STAR CLUSTER

AUTHORITY: UNITED FEDERATION OF PLANETS COLONIAL MAGISTRATE

OFFICE OF SETTLEMENT

| SHIP NAME | CLASSIFICATION | OWNER/AUTHORITY | MASTER |
|-----------|----------------|-----------------|--------|
| YUKON | CONESTOGA | UFP LEASE | BATTERSEY |
| OREGON TRAIL | CONESTOGA | UFP LEASE | TRAUTNER |
| LEWIS AND CLARK | CONESTOGA | PRIVATE | MAITLAND |
| MANDRAKE ANACHRONAE | CONESTOGA | PRIVATE | RAMPION |

| PROMONTORY POINT | CONESTOGA | UFP LEASE | HARVEY |
|---|---|---|---|
| NORTHWEST PASSAGE | CONESTOGA | UFP LEASE | BURCH |
| HAMPTON ROADS | CONESTOGA | PRIVATE | NICKLE |
| COMANCHE | CONESTOGA | UFP LEASE | GEGLIO |
| LAKOTA | CONESTOGA | CORPORATE | BRANCH |
| SACAJAWEA | CONESTOGA | CORPORATE | KATT |
| COLUNGA | MULE ROUNDHOUSE | GRAYMARK ENG. HQ | M. SCOTT |
| HUNTER'S MOON | ENFORCEMENT | PRIVATEER | KILVENNAN |
| ROYAL YORK | ENFORCEMENT | PRIVATEER | GILLESPIE |
| ZAVADA | ENFORCEMENT | PRIVATEER | SHEPPARD |
| RATTLESNAKE | ENFORCEMENT | PRIVATEER | SUNN |
| POLYNESIAN | CONESTOGA TENDER | UFP LEASE | MARKS |
| MABLE STEVENS | VIP TRANSPORT | PRIVATE | CHALKER |
| AMERICAN ROVER | PATHFINDER | PRIVATE | SMITH/GLASS |
| | | | J. Carpenter, Spec. Agent |

| SHIP NAME | CLASSIFICATION | OWNER/AUTHORITY | MASTER |
|---|---|---|---|
| TWILIGHT SENTINEL | CORONER SHIP | PRIVATE | NELSON |
| BROTHER'S KEEPER | MERCY SHIP | STARFLEET LEASE | SKAERBAEK |
| PANDORA'S BOX | INDUSTRIAL | PRIVATE | BLAINE |
| CRYSTOBEL | COMMERCIAL PILOT | PRIVATE | WEBB |
| WEBB ONE-NINE | FACTORY DRONES | CRYSTOBEL | AUTOPILOT |
| MACEDON | COMMERCIAL TOW | CORPORATE | WALTERS |
| IROQUOIS | INDUSTRIAL | CORPORATE | ISRAEL |
| RED BARN | CATTLESHIP | CORPORATE | KEJ |
| QUINCY B. HOBBS | CATTLESHIP/DAIRY | PRIVATE | SEMPATI |
| NORMANDY | FARM SHIP (BOTANICAL) | PRIVATE | MAXMILLIAN |
| UNCLE JAKE'S POCKET | HOTEL VESSEL | PRIVATE | DURANT |
| NORFOLK REBEL | TUGANTINE | PRIVATE | BRIGGS |
| KALEONAHE | MINE SHIP | PRIVATE | FOLSTER |
| FOGGY DEW | DAIRY BARGE | PRIVATE | MEKO |
| HEIDI | RANCH BARGE | PRIVATE | DVORAK |
| ANNIE B | RANCH BARGE | PRIVATE | FORSMARK |
| CHARGER | EQUINE STABLE | PRIVATE | BROWN |

| | | | |
|---|---|---|---|
| BLACK SWAN | GARDEN SHIP | PRIVATE | GAINES |
| OLYMPIAN | ORGAN LAB | UFP LEASE | GUE |

## UFP OFFICIAL ESCORT

| | | | |
|---|---|---|---|
| IMPELLER | CUTTER | STARFLEET | MERKLING |
| ENTERPRISE | STARSHIP | STARFLEET | KIRK |
| REPUBLIC | CUTTER | STARFLEET | DESALLE |
| BEOWULF | COMBAT SUPPORT TENDER | STARFLEET | AUSTIN |

<u>ADDENDUM:</u> BE AWARE—THIS IS ONLY A PRELIMINARY I.E. PARTIAL MANIFEST. UNTIL TWO (2) WEEKS PRIOR TO LAUNCH DATE ROSTER IS OPEN FOR ADDITIONS AND DELETIONS. COMMANDS MAY ALSO CHANGE.

<u>NOT LISTED:</u> SINGLE-FAMILY PRIVATE VESSELS, MULE TENDERS, RUNABOUTS.

# COMMAND DUTY ROSTER—FIRST AND SECOND OFFICERS

Senior First Officer: SPOCK, Cdr.

Duty Station: Starship <u>Enterprise</u>

## RESPONSIBILITIES:

All ships' manifests.

Licensure and qualifications.

Customs, warrants, liens.

Letters of Indemnity, contracts, clauses.

Insurance, special interests.

Charters, Port Risk Policies.

Builders' certificates.

Clearances, releases, registries.

## SECONDARY:

Coordinate with Lt. Cdr. Uhura, Chief Safety Officer.

All safety drills, communications.

# COMMAND DUTY ROSTER—MASTER OF THE HOLD

Chief Inspector and Chartering Broker: DANIEL MERKLING, Capt.

Duty Station: Starfleet Cutter <u>Impeller</u>

<u>RESPONSIBILITIES:</u>

Payload manifests.

Coordinate all baggage masters.

Warp trim.

Stowage.

Obstructions.

Coordinate with Federation Bureau of Shipping.

# COMMAND DUTY ROSTER—STRESSMASTER

Chief Inspector: RAY AUSTIN, Capt.
Duty Station: Starfleet Combat Support Tender _Beowulf_

## RESPONSIBILITIES:

Oversee all lines, cables, antigravs, clamps, fittings, gates, doors, coamings, straps, hitches, bolts, restraining gear, cargo nets, storage hammocks, bulkheads, gammonings, hydraulics, magnetics, mesh, gangways, fusion welds, corrugated bulkheads.

Oversee above for space-emergency tolerance.
Retrofit all ships for universal docking collars.

# COMMAND DUTY ROSTER—REARGUARD

### Senior Readguardsman: ANTON (Tony) DeSALLE, Capt.
### Duty Station: Starfleet Cutter Republic

## RESPONSIBILITIES:

Rearguard coordinator.
All recruiting and training of reserves.
Policing of restricted areas.
Flexible response.

# Chapter Three

*Cluster Z-80, Sagittarian Stellar Group*
*United Federation of Planets Catalogue: Star System*
   *"Occult"*
*Planet Four: "Belle Terre"*

"HOLY SMOKE, Dogan! You're always in your own world! Wake up! We have red alert!"

Ah, double-deep space. Demonic possession for the frustrated few.

The survey scout's deck smelled from overworked sensors and burned circuits. Broiled boards all over the deck, cluttered with tools and cable parts, same as always. Nobody minded doing the work, but nobody cleaned up either. Normal enough. Helm on standby, manned, no tractors, engines idle, thrusters zero, weapons cold, artificial gravity nominal, life-support green, cargo doors shut, hatches clamped, spark blinds hanging on the consoles, radiation sheets draped here and there with armholes gawking open, so on, so on, so on. So why the red alert?

Over there, trembling on his stool like a bug on a griddle, the twitchy analyst cranked around from his sensor displays and barked, "Dogan! Come here!"

"Clam up. My head's drummin'."

A deep sucking breath—clears the skull like a wire brush. Good long suck on the pipe . . . this was a good pipe. Teakwood, Tidewater tobacco. His last pinch or two of the old broadleaf.

Mitch Dogan trundled out of the narrow companionway, thinking about old wrestling holds. He'd sure do some of 'em different if he had the past back for a couple minutes.

The red-alert panels flashed in his face. His own voice, high-pitched and gravelly, banged through his skull worse than the warning alarm. His bathrobe dragged behind him, picking up bits of dirt and metal shavings. The undercooked feeling of getting rousted in the middle of the night churned his stomach. He tried to reconstruct the dream he'd been having when they woke him up.

At three feet two, with arms as thick as his chest, he was like three barrels strapped together, with feet. Still drowsy, he shuffled along the circular ramp that went all the way around the bridge. Up here on the ramp, he could be at eye level with his crewmates. They'd built it for him few years back. Sure made a difference.

He paused just starboard of the main screen and communed with a worn poster showing an exaggerated flicker-animate picture of himself, eyes flaring, arms flexed, lips curled back, red hair up like a zombie, short legs twisted, with Anchorhead McHale squished between his knees. Mitch "The Barrel" Dogan! New

Chicago's answer to high-yield neutronium! Hoot! Hoot! Hoot!

Ten years ago, yeh. The glory days on Altus IV, suckin' tourist credits to the tune of raving crowds, living on company-bred prime rib instead of cold rations. Oh, yeh! Them was the days!

Eh, anyway, a sports figure's career is always short, no pun intended. But them really was the days.

While Dogan rubbed away the cobwebs, the agitated science analyst finally had enough and slammed one coiled appendage on the ramp behind where the command chair used to be before they swapped it for a used low-gain generator. "Dogan! Pay attention to work! The quake moon's mass is changing! It reads hollow inside!"

"Slime down, smart boy," Dogan waved a thick hand. "Anybody seen my eyedrops? Marvin, did I leave my eyedrops on the helm? You didn't stick 'em someplace I ain't gonna look for a million credits, did you, you skinny bottom-feeder?"

The helmsman shrugged over his knob of a shoulder and scratched his big square chin. "Roib put some on his toenails."

"I know you're lying because he ain't got toes."

"What're you wearing your robe for?"

"I got a chill—what'd you care? Holy smoke, somebody turn off the stinkin' alert bell! Who turned that thing on anyway? I didn't even get a chance to go to the head. What'd we have red alert for, hanging here in the middle of nothing, can't even move a hundred meters because of Gamma Night?"

Emil Pashke, busy at his cartography station, pointed across to the science array. "Roib made us turn it on."

Dogan grunted. "Him again, like a hangnail. Roob,

you punk, listen to me. You ain't trained right. You wake me up at zero—what is it?—four hundred lousy hours, and what you got to tell me is a moon's mass is changing right while we're looking at it? Three years running this pothole tank around the survey beat and you still ain't got a clue what rises from hell when some insensitive spud wakes me up from my beauty sleep?"

Roib's three pool-table-green eyes rolled, then settled into a scowl. "The mass . . . is *changing*."

"Every couple of seconds, yeh." While the rest of the crew waited to see what would happen, Dogan abused his eyes with a knotty knuckle. "We got this Class-M planet, we got nine moons, nice pretty little star system, newly catalogued star, and the Federation making big bets on whatever we tell 'em next. The Fed wants this system surveyed for a new colony, the farthest away ever, and we send 'em a survey that says the biggest moon is slipping in and out of its own mass. Then they put us in a paper room and feed us applesauce, no cinnamon. Why don't you stand up and do 'Swan Lake' for us. Eh? Marvin'll dance the girl's part. Eh? Eh?"

Laughter boomed around the crew at Roib's expense. Dogan scratched his beard and took bows, blinking now that his eyes weren't stinging so much. Around the bridge, the only active screens were the local ones, about a third of what the bridge had to offer. These "windows" showed whatever the short-range sensors could pick up, not much more than the crew would see if they looked out a porthole. No magnification, no enhancement. When the sensors woke up at Gamma Dawn, they'd be able to count the cells on local fauna down there on the new planet, but not till then.

When the stir died down, Dogan turned away from

the frustrated analyst and looked at the bored quartermaster. "Hey, Grady, call the galley and tell that toothless wonder of a cook that if he don't defrost some of the meat we hunted down on that funny brown planet two months ago, I'm gonna come down there and introduce him to a whole new way to fry flesh. And tell him I'm tired of mushrooms. No more mushrooms. Throw'm right out."

"But I like mushrooms," Grady rebutted, leaning on his elbows and yawning.

"Yeh? Let's have a party. We'll wallpaper Grady's rack with mushrooms. Roob can reach both ends of the deck at the same—"

"Dogan!" Roib screeched. "Work! We have to notify Starfleet!"

"Starfleet? What'd you want to tip off those prima donnas for? They'll just laugh. I bin an independent contractor for longer than mosta those bootlickers been alive." Dogan lumbered to that side of the bridge and peered Roib right in the eyes. Well, two of them, anyway. "Ever since I known you, kid, you think every blip on the scanner is something new and exciting and it never is. You always keep thinking you'll find the big wonder. Forget it. We're a survey unit. Everything we do is dull. Get used to it."

Roib's shuddering dropped away, replaced by annoyance. His voice lost its chime. "Being around you, I'm already used to dull."

"Whatever you're reading, you made a mistake," Dogan insisted. "You don't have spatial bodies this dense that are hollow inside. You don't have 'em. Got it? Baby physics. There ain't no such thing."

"How do you know *I* made a mistake?" Roib cranked around on his swivel-stool, his top three limbs sweeping across several dynascanners, then back again to isolate key readouts. "Look at the mass here, and now look at it *here*. They're different!"

"Mass don't change. Maybe you was dreaming. Do people from your planet, do their eyes actually close when they sleep? Did you glue your eyes open or what? Maybe you slept through that class."

Roib settled all four of his shoulders. "I didn't build the instruments. This is what they say. I checked them. I calibrated them. I recalibrated them. They still say this. Here . . . let me point them at you and see if they say 'thickheaded lox.' "

While the crew laughed, Dogan accommodated by blinking his reddened eyes at the numbers on the screens. Sure enough, they read fluctuating density on the moon in the middle.

"Yeh, that's what it says," he muttered, unconvinced.

"You see?" Roib squawked. "The quake moon is actually vibrating! The core is supposed to be hollow, yet it's dense, yet there are quakes, volcanic activity, and plate movement! And the mass keeps changing!"

"It can't," Dogan insisted. "None of that fits together. Just get used to being wrong this time. When Gamma Dawn lifts the sensor blackout, we'll move in close to the moon and prove you're wrong. Then I can get back in the sack and finish squeezing out Anchorhead's lungs."

"Hey, Dogan!" Chuck Lindsay interrupted from nav/tactical station.

Lipping his pipe to the other side of his mouth, Dogan turned. "Yah?"

"Would you please explain to Emil that we *can't* move during Gamma Night? Not even ten kilometers so he can see past the second moon? All the time he wants to move a little at a time and I keep saying it's too dangerous. Tell him he's gotta just wait."

"Emil, we ain't moving. I ain't taking that kind of a chance, feeling around on thrusters without no sensors in a solar system full of debris and projectiles, asteroids and dust. We been through this before. The only way to move in Gamma Night is by dead reckoning and hope the navigation ain't even slightly off. It ain't worth it. There's nothing out there we can't look at in an hour, when Gamma Night lifts. You gotta just wait."

Emil Pashke's dark brown face braided into a sneer. "I hate neutron stars. If we didn't have Gamma Night, we coulda been done with this job a year ago. Everything's twice as long. Ten hours out of every thirty, stuck without sensors, feeling around . . . something that far away screwin' us out of so many hours . . ." The cartographer went on grumbling into his console, but only the console listened.

Dogan snorted and glanced around. Nobody but Roib was excited about the short-range screens. Outside, not far from where the survey ship hovered, immobile during Gamma Night, the newly claimed Federation planet of Belle Terre hung in space with its butter-yellow sun way beyond it. Out of direct sight were six of the planet's nine moons. From here, out the "windows," three of the moons, including the largest one, could be seen standing in a row like chorus girls. The middle one was giving Roib a nervous attack. All the others were too small to get any attention.

Pretty good entertainment, that moon. The whole solar system was littered with moons and projectiles and every kind of junk that provided dangers for a ship trying to set up satellites and markers, trying to map the rich quarry of minerals that were here for the taking.

While all the other moons were ordinary rocks running around in space, the moon in the middle bubbled and smoked with some kind of quakes and plate movement, some kind of constant volcanic activity. And it was dense, much heavier than size suggested it ought to be. The funniest part was that the core read hollow.

Now what? Send back a long-range message saying the moon's mass was changing every once in a while? Hope somebody believed it? No chance to explain themselves? No two-way communication? Yeh, that'd go over.

It couldn't be hollow. Physics didn't allow that. Until today, they hadn't moved in close enough to take serious readings, to find out why a dense body read hollow. Today they were going to get answers, and kill the silly rumors.

Except Roib was over here having a fit over mass changes. No way, no way.

"Gamma Night's flippin' the numbers around," Dogan said. "Gotta be. Pretty soon the blackout'll lift and we can move in close and pin the data to the mat."

"Get that pipe away from me," Roib snapped, waving a tentacle. "It smells worse than the circuits."

"It ain't lit."

"Smells anyway."

"You're just mad because the moon ain't changing."

"It *is* changing. The orbit-wobble alone—"

"Squid, there are nine moons." Pressing one stumpy elbow to the console, Dogan gripped his pipe. "Their orbits could affect each other. They're shifting all the—"

"I checked that!" Roib's chicken-egg eyes flared. "None of the others are wobbling! This isn't my first week, Dogan! I checked—"

In a sharp fit of calm, Roib interrupted himself, put all his limbs on the edge of the console and pushed back out of the way, leaving the board free.

"Check it yourself," he said.

By now everybody else was watching them. Why not? Nothing else to do till Gamma Dawn.

Dogan adjusted and readjusted the dials on the information coming in from the very limited sensor readings. Before him, a half-dozen screens flickered and struggled.

"Mass and density alternating every couple of minutes . . . Doppler shifts confirm . . . yeh. What I thought. It's a mutant." Ragged laughter roared from his throat. "Hey, Wayne, Lindsay, everybody—holy smoke! A mutant moon!"

"Hollow core," Roib said. "I told you."

Dogan shrugged. "The data *says* that. It can't *mean* that. Get the difference? Don't look at me smug like that."

"I don't have a smug look."

"When your snorkel goes up over your top ear, that's smug. Don't give me that's not smug. I know smug."

Roib, beyond arguing, knew what he saw. "What was it you said about our work's being dull?"

"I never said no such of a thing."

"Contact the outpost at Meridian. Tell them. Send them this new information."

Dogan gave his analyst a couple of moments to be terrified that he wouldn't do it, then let him off the hook. "Soon as the blackout lifts. But you gotta put your name on this weirditude, cuz I ain't."

Roib's excuse for a smile appeared. "Communiqué from your survey ship, your name goes on it. It's automatic."

"You're a lucky spud." Turning his compact body again to peer at the unenhanced picture on the main screen, Dogan scanned the shifting clouds and green seas of Belle Terre. Looked a lot like Altus IV, except for the green. Nice landmasses too, a couple of big ones, three small ones, and a spice of islands all over the place.

"Ain't that a pretty planet?" he commented. "We'all gonna live there someday, once the colony gets rollin'. I'm gonna start a wrestling club. You all gonna work there. Marvin, you can be the timekeeper. Roib's gonna scalp tickets. He'll get 'em comin and goin'. Emil's gonna draw all the posters. Lindsay and Wayne—"

"We wanna be bouncers," Wayne piped. "I wanna beat up troublemakers. Get some scars. I got no scars to show the dames."

"I wanna audition the dames!" Grady called out.

Chortling, Marvin scratched his dangly gray mustache. "What're you gonna be, Dogan?"

"He's the ref!"

"Ref and proprietor *and* the guy who auditions the dames!" Dogan crowed.

"Then I get to fit their sarongs," Grady said.

"Why not?" Wayne pulled a radiation sheet off its clip and drew it around Grady's chest. "You'll look good in a sarong!"

As the crew cheered and Grady did a kitten dance across the lower bridge, Dogan proclaimed, "We're gonna have some times! Parties and prize matches and auditions and a grand opening every Christmas!"

"And picnics?" Roib asked, all his eyes narrowed, making him look like a cartoon butterfly drawn as happy. "In a garden?"

As the other men cheered, Dogan patted the analyst

on one of the shoulders. "We'll do it all, Roob. When the good times come again."

Together they basked in possibility's glow, wondering what the future would bring to this brand-new star system with its unusual moon and that habitable planet just out of reach.

The bridge fell quiet and entered a dreamlike condition, no lights or buzzers, the red alert now resting, few systems bothering to work during the blackout, and nobody had much to do. Couldn't move the ship or study much, no sensor readings to pick at, only yesterday's data to sift through. If only there were a starting bell and a couple of ugly sweaty meatheads crashing in the middle of the deck, this would be heaven.

Ten seconds later he was bouncing across the lower deck like a medicine ball. All he saw was feet, fingers, and spark sheets. Carpet grazed his cheek. Only the beard saved his chin from a bad rub burn. He landed with his barrel-shaped arms sprawled at his side and his stumpy legs poking up on the platform that had once held the command chair.

He raised his head. "What the hell . . . meteor?"

What happened to his eyes? They stung and didn't work. Vents began to whir and suck at the gouts of smoke pouring from several system outlets. Couldn't be good.

"Somebody tell me somethin'," Dogan demanded. He rolled onto his stomach, put both wide hands under his chest, and shoved. His short body levered up and his head bobbed into a stratum of gray smoke. "Somebody tell me somethin'!"

"Got hit!" Grady's unbodied voice called.

"By what?"

"Don't know."

Crawling up onto the ramp again, Dogan moved around to the middle of the ramp, to a point where he could see every station, now that the smoke was clearing. "Put all the local screens on. Let's look out there."

"We'll only be able to read line of sight," Wayne pointed out, but they knew that. He always did that when he was nervous, overexplaining what they already knew.

"What's with the screens?" As the smoke thinned, Dogan cranked around and around, looking for a screen that worked. Every monitor flickered with static or struggled with an indistinguishable mass of color and shapes. None could focus or settle. "Try the direct hoods. Somebody tell me something."

"I've got some feed coming in." Roib peered at the only screen that showed crowded space, which was the hood of his direct feed. "It's a ship!"

Short legs spinning, Dogan crossed the ramp and blinked into Roib's hood, the only clear view of near-space. Outside, not fifty meters away, hung a mustard-colored ship the shape of an old-fashioned house key. About sixty feet, maybe? Not very big. A third the size of the surveyor. Hard to judge, though, just by looking. Sensors were on, but offered crazy distorted numbers. He checked just to check—the other ship was ten feet long, unarmed, the ship was eighty feet long, carrying cannon, four feet long with—nah, no point looking at the sensors. Just use the old eyeballs.

"Holy smoke . . . Whose ship is that? You ever seen that design before? Who makes a ship that color? Makes me want a chili dog . . . You seen that shape before? Anybody?"

No takers.

"Did we have a collision or what?" Dogan pressed

on. "When did space get so small that two ships gotta bump?"

"In Gamma Night," Roib said, "we can't tell how close we are to other solid objects. Maybe they came in for a look at us and then they didn't know how close they were."

"Lindsay, hail 'em. Tell 'em to back the hell off. We're on a legitimate survey and they're inside our primary maneuver zone and if they don't back off I'm gonna have to throw the barrel on 'em. I don't want to get bumped again. Can you get a reading on it? What kind of a ship is it?"

Roib squinted all his eyes. "I still got Gamma blackout here . . . can't get clear readings. But it looks like a one- or two-man fighter to me. Maybe one-man. Linds, what do you think?"

"Never seen no fighter like that."

"Didn't ask if you recognize it, I asked what you *think* it is."

"I don't know what I think it is."

"Thank you."

Dogan stomped across the ramp to the tactical station and tried to pull up a catalogue. "Gimme ship to ship."

"Okay, go."

"Hello, this is Captain Dogan, Federation Survey Ship *Kensington Taylor.* We've got a limited survey warrant giving us exclusive territorial license in this star sys—"

A deafening boom ate his words. The ramp under him tipped, then dropped a foot. Dogan dropped to meet it, this time landing on a knee and an elbow. His meaty paws served as perfect platforms and he was back on his feet in an instant.

"Talk!" he ordered.

"They're shooting at us!" Grady shouted. "They didn't collide with us—they were shooting!"

"Phasers?"

"Not phasers," Roib said. "Some kind of troto-glycic energy arch. I can't trust these readings, but I think he's armed about ten times better than we are! Dogan, do something! He's powering for another hit!"

"Clean up!" Dogan bellowed. "Feet on the mat! Gamma Night, no sensors, odds against us! Hot damn, we're cookin' now! Full shields up! Battle stations!"

The robe snapped from his shoulders and roiled to the deck as Dogan thumped along the circular ramp. Grady yanked the fight poster down. Behind it was a battlefield tactical display that hadn't been active in years. Spark blinds and radiation sheets crashed back in the hands of Lindsay and Wayne and splayed to the spark-scorched carpet. The crew scrambled to remember skills they hadn't used since basic training, to man stations that had been on standby for more than three years.

Another strike from the mystery ship sent the *Taylor* heaving and layered the deck with a blanket of sparks that poured from the underlying electricals.

"There go the cargo pressurization ducts," Grady moaned. "Teratogenic supply feed's ruptured too. He means business."

"We got electron drain in the containment grid!" Wayne shouted. "I gotta take care of that myself!"

"Go," Dogan allowed. Wayne disappeared down the emergency chute to the engine room. Dogan held on to Roib's chair post and shouted over the whine. "Who's the tactical officer?"

Grady and Roib gawked at him. Lindsay, Marvin, and Pashke gaped at each other.

"Well, I know it's not me," Lindsay said. "Emil, wasn't it supposed to be you?"

"I don't remember," Pashke countered. "We never got shot at before. Grady, ain't it you?"

"I'm the mate!"

"Oh, yeah . . ."

"You sure it's not you, Linds?"

"I'm the quartermaster. Maybe it's Marv."

"Marv's on the helm," Dogan interrupted.

Roib swiveled into the discussion while the mustard ship pivoted on his little screen and came around for another strafe. "I think it's still Snyder."

"Lot of good that does," Dogan said. "He died two years ago."

"He's been doing a good job," Grady muttered. "I say we let him keep it."

"Lindsay, you cleaned the weapons ports last month, didn't you? You be tactical."

"Me?" Lindsay's bony face dropped its color. "You want me to *shoot* at somebody? I'm an engineer!"

Dogan felt his own features crumple. "Learn fast!"

A new blast scraped the underside of the surveyor, sending the surveyor into a disk-spin. Dogan's next words, whatever they would've been, were licked away by centrifugal force. He got his piglet-shaped fingers around a rail strut and managed to hold on until the thrusters sang and the shrieking autograv system tried to regain stability. In his periphery he saw Marvin fighting with the helm to take manual control. His face twisted, but ten seconds later the ship stopped free-spinning across space.

"He sure does mean business," Lindsay choked when

he could speak again. "That one smashed our starboard—no, it didn't . . . yes, it did—thruster's gone. I was right the first time. I oughta learn to listen to myself."

"Call Wayne," Dogan said. "Have him fix it."

"From inside?"

"Tell him do his best," Dogan ordered. "Forget the secondary screens. Concentrate on the main screen. I gotta be able to see this bugger if I'm gonna tackle him."

While Roib and Pashke both scrambled to do that, Grady shouted, "Send a distress signal!"

"It wouldn't get 3 kilometers in Gamma Night. Why'd you even say things like that when you know better?"

Grady held out an imploring hand and explained, "At least get one ready to send. Then all we have to do is punch a button when the blackout lifts."

"Mmm, yeah, okay, long as you're reasonable . . . How do I do it? I never sent one before."

Roib didn't turn from his board, but called, "Deep Space Prospecting Emergency Code Sierra-Zero-Sierra and your personal ID clearance."

"Can you do it for me?"

"Only if you're dead."

"Tell 'em I'm dead. I don't care!"

Roib turned his tennis-ball eyes at Dogan and nearly wept. "Why are they shooting at us? They must want my quake moon! They know I've found the wobble and they want credit. I told you the moon was important!"

"I'm gonna get him behind the knees." Dogan heard his own voice as if from another room. He tried to sound confident. They didn't buy it. That was a power-packed ship out there. The surveyor was a lamb being

circled by a hyena. A distress signal was no more than
a formality at this extreme distance. The nearest outpost was months away at warp four. Rescue was a mirage. If they didn't take care of themselves, nobody
else would.

"Grady, we got anything on the starboard thrusters?"

"Not a damn thing."

"Flood some energy through there anyway."

"Energy? But we can't *use*—"

"He'll read the flow and won't know we're crippled.
Never let the other guy know you're tired. It gives him
confidence."

"You're crazy, but . . . flow confirmed—"

"Now turn us to port, using the aft and port thrusters
on reverse."

"But that move doesn't make any sense."

Marvin shook his head. "I'm not even sure I can do
it!"

"Yeah, I know. Try anyway." Dogan sneered an evil
grin at the attacking fighter on the main screen. "They
*loved* me in tactical class."

"Here he comes again," Grady warned.

"Phasers at three-quarters," Dogan ordered.

"Is he trying to kill us or just drive us off?" Pashke
asked. "What if he thinks he owns something around
here? Maybe it's his moon."

Roib turned colors. "It's *my* moon!"

"It's our moon," Dogan confirmed.

Lindsay looked around and asked, "Why you got the
phasers scaled back?"

"I don't want to kill somebody if he thinks he's just
defending some rock and he thinks it's his rock."

"It's *my* rock," Roib muttered.

In the grip of tension they watched the struggling

main screen as the mustard-colored ship wheeled its long bow around and speared toward them, coming in close.

"Look at him," Dogan barked. "He can't measure distance any better than we can—hold on!"

At the last instant the fighter strafed their starboard side with its flashing white weapon. The surveyor jolted severely, but there was no significant reading of power loss, and no alarms lit. The fighter had hit systems that were already damaged.

".Yah!" Dogan howled in victory. "Keep him off balance! Make him waste energy! Yah! Yah!"

"Beautiful!" Grady shouted. "He guessed wrong!"

Dogan launched his truncated body forward and clasped Lindsay behind the knee. "Shoot, Linds, point-blank! Destroy his hips! Go! Go! Yaaah!"

Lindsay's shoulders hunched over the weapons controls while the enemy ship was still in short-range. The surveyor buckled sharply under them, but this time the jolt wasn't from an attacking strike. It was instead the surveyor's own phasers built up and suddenly releasing one gut punch.

On the screen, red streams bolted from the array and joined the two ships in a deadly pirouette. The mustard ship's long bow heaved upward as if it'd come up on rocks. Then it just kept going up, up, and all the way over. Even from here, even without sensors, they could see the other ship shudder violently.

"Direct hit!" Pashke gasped.

The crew cheered. Dogan crowed, "Haaaah, that one gave him the hippy-hippy-shakes! See, boys? Technique wins over strength every time. Keep varying your moves, that's the trick. Make him waste energy!"

Sweating and grinning, Grady cast him a sustaining

glance. "We gotta get a mat back under you again someday, Barrel."

Dogan indulged in a wink of gratitude. "When the good times come again."

As his words worked on the men during the brief rest from attack while they gathered for another strike, he tried to think reasonably about solving the problem before it got any worse. Why were they being attacked? Nothing like this had happened in three years of surveying in this star cluster. They hadn't even seen another ship for a year and a half—and that was just passing in the distance.

"We got no reports on hostiles coming in here, do we?" he took a moment to ask. "What about those last dozen communiqués I didn't bother reading? Did anybody look at 'em?"

Grady's gap-toothed grimace met him as the first officer shook his head. "Wasn't nothing about hostiles. I don't know who this guy thinks he is, but he's packin' for trouble. He's overarmed for his size."

"Maybe not for his space force, whoever they are," Dogan corrected. "We got no way to judge. When you don't know the other guy's manager, you gotta deal with what you see."

"Maybe he's not a space force," Roib suggested nervously. "Maybe he's a rogue or a mercenary."

Dogan wagged his head in thought at a new idea. "Let's go off a couple hundred kilometers and see if he leaves us alone."

Emil Pashke turned, worried. "That's taking a big chance with the sensor blackout."

"Just go slow," Dogan warned, "but do it quick."

Pashke's flat lips almost disappeared, though he made no comment. He hunched to his controls.

As they pulled back, the stunned yellow fighter grew smaller on the screen. Many seconds passed. They watched, unable to take any action. Firing weapons would be guesswork as the distance expanded. Only ultra-close range could possibly make for anything better than a lucky hit. He was done trusting to luck.

"Batten down, everybody," he ordered, determined to fill the uneasy silence with something, anything, even if only his own rough squawl. "Fire up the intermix in case we gotta go to warp. Tell Wayne to check the deuterium flow. Secure the driver coils and EPS power distribution."

"This is insane," Roib stammered. "We've never fought a real battle! We're surveyors!"

Dogan sneered at the negativity. "We gotta remember how to be efficient real sudden-like. We're all trained. We'll go by the book."

"We never read the book!"

"*My* book, desperado. The Handbook of Mitch Dogan. Like this from Chapter Two—when he shoots, aim right at the weapon stream. Ignite it in space before it gets to us."

"Shouldn't we hail again?" Roib asked. "Find out why he's doing this?"

"I don't care why he's doing it," Dogan proclaimed. "Keep your bloodshot eye on his weapon port, Linds. Don't look away. Don't sneeze."

"Don't get an itch," Grady added.

Lindsay's eyes watered. "Cram it!"

Nearer and nearer the other ship surged, gaining speed with every meter, until it was racing down upon them, ports glowing and some kind of attack wing spread wide behind what Dogan guessed to be the pilot's cockpit. Through a darkened floral arrangement of coated plexi windowports he imagined the face of the pilot who was after them. Was it a face he would be able to understand? Would it have eyes? Did it breathe? Did it have an ex-wife in Beta Aurigae it was still in love with?

"He's serious, Dogan." Grady grimly studied the rapid approach. "Look at the angle."

"Yah, I'm gettin' the idea." Dogan stomped halfway around the ramp to show that things had just changed. "That's it! If he wants a turf war, he's gonna get one. No sympathy! Let's blow this no-good bum from now to September! Double shields front! Lindsay, full phasers! Arm photon torpedoes!"

"We haven't got any photon torpedoes left. We used 'em all to clear asteroids."

"Good. No complications. Just phasers. Never cross your feet. I like it. How're those thrusters?"

"We got port side, aft and forward. Starboard's a corpse."

"Turn the bow just a little bit to starboard so he doesn't come down that side again."

They stopped asking questions and just did what he said. That was better. He saw their perplexed eyes racing to him and away again. Here came the yellow ship, running for their port side, which Dogan was now teasingly presenting. Sure, the other guy thought he'd already hit the starboard side, which he had, and could be baited to the port side.

"Okay, here's the strategy," he began. "He's coming in. When he gets to pretty close range, we're gonna enable the forward and aft thrusters and we're gonna do it quick and mean. Linds, keep your hand on that firing control."

"He's packin'," Grady warned. "Coming in hot! Look at those energy ports glow!"

"That's our guts you see glowing out there." Lindsay's voice quavered with raw and undisguised fear. "He means to kill us."

"Get ready," Dogan snapped, and met Lindsay and Roib's terrified eyes with an eager glower he hoped would be reassuring. He gave them a pretend growl and flexed his barrels.

"Here he comes!"

"When do you want me to shoot?" Lindsay quavered.

Dogan launched from the ramp and slammed flat on both feet to the lower deck. "Put me up on your chair!"

Lindsay spun out from the tactical seat at the helm, scooped Dogan up under the arms, and hoisted him feet and all onto the chair. Dogan took the weapons controls himself, and fixed his small eyes on the approaching fighter as it changed angle slightly to bear down on them.

Closer, closer . . . they could see the bolts in the yellow plates when Grady broke. "Dogan!"

"Keep your underwear on," Dogan growled, and kept ticking off seconds. "This is gonna be a photo finish."

The other ship wasn't taking any chances on missing. He was coming in low, trying to avoid the surveyor's phaser array, but he could only avoid it so much. If he wanted to shoot at that speed, that angle, he'd have to come into the firing cone. Any second now.

Dogan tried to think like a fighter pilot—no, no, wrong, guessing would get them killed. Do what you know and know what you're doing—

"Dogan, Dogan, Dogan . . ." Grady's teeth were gritted, but sound still came out.

The enemy was nearly upon them, couldn't have

been more than two hundred meters and closing. Any second they could reach out and grab him. He was holding back till the last instant and so was Dogan.

Roib let out a senseless squawk as the yellow ship's weapons ports glowed blindingly and let loose on them at point-blank range.

"Lateral thrust right now!" Dogan shouted to Marvin, and leaned on the weapons controls.

The surveyor ship skidded sideways like a toboggan on an icy hill, moving a critical two meters—just enough to be missed by the point-blank energy blast from the other ship. At the same instant, Dogan fired the phasers, but not at the other ship. Instead, he aimed directly at the ball of energy blast coming at them. The salvo, whatever it was, detonated.

While the survey ship and its shields were more or less a cocoon-shaped bauble presenting its rounded side to the blast, the fighter was pointed and flat-edged and coming right at the wash. Eruption blanketed both ships.

Dogan felt his block-like body flip off the chair, felt his feet leave the cushion, and had a detached idea of the faces of his astonished crewmates turning like billiard balls, bonking off each other and spinning toward the corner pockets. A drop in cabin pressure stole the air from his lungs. Rivets popped and spewed past his ears as if he'd ruptured a bee's nest.

He bounced off the port roof, bunched into a knot, and landed on top of the environmental-control console, wedged between the scanners and the keypads. The whine of emergency manual override told him that somebody other than himself was still conscious.

With a push from one elbow Dogan rolled across the keypad and dropped to the deck. Gravity still working, at least.

Beside him, a knotwork of spirals and coils, Roib blinked in shock.

On the main screen, a fireworks of sparks and glowing hulk of the attacking fighter powered out of control, spewing fuel and atmosphere, driving headlong into the moon.

Dogan heaved himself to his feet and wobbled up to the ramp in a cowl of smoke. Around him, his crew shook themselves. One by one they came upright.

He spiked both arms into the air beside his ears and jumped up and down in a victory dance.

"Waddya know!" he crowed. "We lived! Yah! Yah! Yah!"

"Yah! Yah!" The crew shook themselves and joined him in a ringside hoot and holler.

Roib crawled to the edge of the ramp and wrapped one limb around Dogan's cylindrical ankle. Dogan looked down at the science analyst who'd given them something to fight for and said, "Told you the good times would come, squid. Now you got something to tell when we get settled down and build ourselves a town. You got a real space story to tell. What'sa matter? You scared or what? We won!"

Roib shuddered, regained control, swallowed a couple of times, then blinked.

"What's a photo finish?" he asked.


A million pieces of shimmering matter raced to the nearest three moons within thirty seconds, traveling faster than natural objects ever could. Sharp-edged debris sprayed into the golden volcanic flow. The quake moon sputtered and blushed as if accepting the gift of passion. Blast-driven, the debris bored into the moon's crust as effectively as industrial drills, blowing away plumes of ejecta a mile into the cloak of space around the moon.

Dogan saw the difference. An unnaturally brilliant lime-green fan of active matter, looking more like the neon blaze of an exposed warp core than anything volcanic. Green? What was that? Some kind of reaction with whatever that fighter was made of?

Everyone stared at the sight. Even damage control went waiting. Before them the Fourth of July opened up as the brilliant blue sparkles changed happily to crystal green, and then to a completely unexpected and unexplainable sunset red.

Green to blue . . . to red?

Stayed red, too. Didn't fade or lose its inner glow, but sprayed past the surveyor ship and continued out into space without losing a bit of light or potency. How could that be? The cold of space alone . . .

"Hey, spud," Dogan began, "you getting a reading on that stuff?"

Back at his station, Roib vultured over his equipment as the sensors accepted readings of the material blowing into space. Gamma Night was lifting. The sensors were beginning, sluggishly, to work again, to pick through the veil and distill information again.

He blinked and blinked. Seemed like he couldn't believe what he saw. Then a sudden suck of breath made everybody look at him.

"I found it!" Roib suddenly gripped the edge of his board with four of his limbs. Every eye except the back one was fixed on his readouts, and the back eye spun with excitement. "Dogan, I know why the moon's changing mass! I know why! I found it! That explosion, it ruptured the crust! I've got it! I'm not wrong! I'm right! Is the Dawn up? Can we send a message?"

Dogan waddled to Roib's side, but from down there he couldn't see the scanners that mattered. "What's the matter with you? Whatcha see there?"

"Dogan . . ." Grady's voice was soft, so quiet that everyone heard it. The single word, in that tone, cut through the reawakening sensor noise and the hiss of vents and attendance to anything Roib had just discovered.

Before them on the forward screen, a great shadow came to blot out the vision of the quake moon, a gargoyle-gray form eating up their view of some miracle they didn't yet understand, something worth dying for.

With only enough time to lower his hand to Roib's limb still coiled around his ankle, Dogan thought absurdly about taking a final breath just for the sake of dignity, but never got the chance.

The gargoyle shadow swallowed them, blanking out their screens so their last moment was dark except for the skyline flicker of bridge equipment, as if they were passing a city on some unapproached planet's nightside. Dogan's eyes focused on the forward screen as it cleared in one corner. The quake moon was no longer way over there. It was right here, inches away.

Life pods? Was there time?

The hull ruptured as jagged volcanic rock cleaved the ship into sheets. Heat poured through the torn skin. Dogan felt his body blowtorched and his bones begin to scorch. Through the instant of mindbreaking pain, he thought about the good times and understood that he'd lost a pretty decent crapshoot.

# Chapter Four

"THE APPROACH is a Kauld battlebarge! He pulled the science ship into the middle moon!"

"Are you sure it's Kauld? Your readings could be—"

"We should go for reinforcements!"

"At this distance? We could never escape. See if there's a place to hide. Is he blazing us?"

"Not yet. Still on an approach triangle, on the other side of the middle moon. They blazed the surveyor ship and dragged them into the moon's surface."

"Then maneuver into the Blind, quickly, before they notice us. Use the time to blend for Ulwen. Is there anything at all? Any signal?"

"Nothing . . . blend reads only melted debris. I'm very sorry for this, Shucorion. I'm sure it was my fault."

"Dimion, this was my own poor judgment. I should never have let him volunteer. He was always too anxious to be first. This is my fault. Garitt, keep us very still. The battlebarge may yet not see us. Make no emissions. Dimion, keep looking for Ulwen. I'll look also."

Cryptic, as conversations often became on board a fighting vessel. Around the two men standing at the strip-screens on the cylindrical deck, the rest of the operative crew watched from overhead and both sides, held in place by the constant centrifugal spin of the tube-shaped ship.

Shucorion, avedon of this Plume, battled a grisly surge in the pit of his gut. From a hiding place behind a veil of astral dust they had watched the unlikely success of the alien surveyor ship against their better-armed and faster Savage. They had hidden effectively, not even bothering to activate the gravity cyclons, relying instead upon the rotation of the ship to keep them on their feet. They had expected Ulwen, in his Savage, to do the fighting for them today, but Ulwen had failed.

Interested only in their own fighter's assault on the surveyor vessel, they hadn't watched the rest of space. Now a Kauld Marauder was nearly upon them.

In the Blind, they still had a chance. The Marauder might not see them. He assumed the worst. His people had picked and picked at details for many generations, discovering ways to maneuver in the Blind. Hyperaccurate charting, unlimited patience, enduring work. Only this had given them their one advantage over Kauld in space. They could move, when Kauld could not.

But the Blind would rise soon. That would be the end.

Color drained from his sapphire complexion, leaving his cheeks papery. This annoyed him. He had always been on the poorer end of a poor civilization, and listened hungrily as his mother told him that his wealth came in good cheekbones, demonstrative eyes, and the brew-brown depths of his hair, which he allowed to grow until a long plait drained down his back to his waist. He had never seen the attraction she showed in her eyes, except in appealing pictures of his father which she relentlessly held before him as he grew from boyhood. The dark lashes making a striking ring around crescents of air-gray eyes, the fresh blue complexion and the sly intelligent smile—he hoped he looked like his father to others, but he had never seen it in himself.

Self-consciously he rubbed his face to bring the sensation back.

At the pilot station, nearly upside down overhead, Garitt craned his neck and manipulated his controls to move the Plume deeper into the Blind, and glanced at Shucorion every few seconds. The other men didn't look directly at Shucorion either, trying to keep up an image of working while their leader made his decision, but it was all lies. Garitt, at least, was being honest in his eavesdropping.

Shucorion recalled for an instant how odd this way of life had been when he'd first come to space, living on the outer walls of a specialized drum forever turning. Now he was used to it, accustomed to walking on the wall, to speaking upward at others, and to the constant scent of repairs and paint. Near his left knee, the bulkhead strut had just been all welded and painted after the last encounter, that incident with a rogue Kauld Marauder, and gave off a strong scent of chemical bond. If they died today, he'd miss that smell.

They hadn't even known a battlebarge was in the vicinity, or they'd have avoided it. All they could hope to do now was hide from it with their navigating skills, draw the cloak of their own relentless work over their heads, and huddle in the sensor silence. Troubling.

As he stood with Dimion against curved bulkheads the taupe of weathered stone, he glanced around at the crew. Each man in his monocolored jacket or tunic or shirt was a dot of color different from the man next to him. Their faces were tight blue patches as they listened and waited, their eyes dots of concern and readiness. Only the instruments made any noise or movement, flickering in patchwork bits of light against the paint-swatch tunics and shirts and jackets.

They were entranced by their avedon's way of thinking at times like this. Shucorion was accustomed to that, their listening, their curiosity, even the sometime fear in their eyes. None of them had ever challenged him yet. They could leave if they didn't want to be here with him. Anyone could leave at any time, and in the past some had left, but these ninety defenders had stayed with him for many turns and no one made noise of leaving.

Some stayed, he knew, because they enjoyed being free of the disasters that constantly befell their planet. Space was better than earthquakes and tidal waves. Others, though, stayed because of Shucorion and what they believed about him. Their trust was a sharp pinch.

Very upsetting, to have a Kauld Marauder so far out, but he knew why they were here. They were beginning to defend this little star system with its big happy habitable planet that had never been claimed.

"They're defending that planet already," he said aloud, "before they even put a stick on it."

"Then it's true?" Garitt asked. "They mean to build a fleet base there?"

"It's true. For the first time in the history of either of our races, one of us is moving off our homeworld. It means the end for Blood if Kauld establish a base outside our system and put half their fleet on it. They can build freely on another planet, and we're finished."

His honesty clearly upset the crew. The truth was better swallowed whole. Along with it was the sauce that Blood could never hope to prevent such a base. Kauld could build it, and there was nothing that could be done to stop them.

Why was that acute-sensor light blinking? It never blinked. Not that one.

He stepped closer and squinted into the readout cylinder. "Dimion . . ."

"Unbelievable." Dimion kept his voice low as Shucorion peered over his shoulder at the critical screens. "How could a Series Two Savage be destroyed by a scanner ship? A scanner ship!"

Obliged to answer the unanswerable, at least to sound as if he knew, Shucorion shrugged and continued looking at the factors in the cylinder. "They tricked him somehow, maneuvered him into obliteration. Dimion, what is this data?"

"A scanner ship . . ." Dimion agonized. "Nothing but a surveying vessel."

"Not by the vessel," Shucorion said. "By the skill. They fought not with power, but with cleverness. They were relentless. Even with level-nine damage they continued to stand firm. Where did these figures come from? Do you see this?"

"What kind of people are they?" Garitt interrupted. "Who stands firm against something they can't beat?"

Frustrated, Shucorion took Dimion by the shoulders and turned him toward the data cylinder with the funny figures. "Isolate these. Do it now." Then he turned to Garitt to retire the persistent subject. "They stood against the impossible and they won. We've never encountered people like this before. Even the Form-less went away when they found out about the conflict between Blood and Kauld. But that scanner has been here far longer than we expected. They stayed and stayed, picking through the cluster, always studying, never growing frustrated, never lonely, never lost inter-est . . . they never engaged in any kind of conflict, yet at the first challenge they meet a trained savage with Series Two primary armor and manage to destroy him! They could've run away and come back some other time, stronger. Instead, they stood their ground against enormous odds. It was an insane thing to do, and yet they won." He paused, shook his head, suffered a little longer. "I should never have sent Ulwen to strike them."

Dimion shook his head. "I should've advised you differently. At least he died working—" His instru-ments clattered then, drawing him back to the security of work. However, this refuge was to slip away imme-diately. "Avedon . . . these figures . . . I make no sense of them. They're . . . core content ciphers . . . spectral band . . . blast ignited . . ." He shook his head, com-pletely confused, and apologetically added, "Of course, I'm not a geological engineer. You're the only blast technician Blood have in space."

"Let me look."

Shucorion leaned over the numbers, the symbols, the machine's digestion of chemical compound, clastic lev-els, and all the other signals that spoke of those sparkles and shines.

"I think the survey ship broke through the moon's

crust," Dimion told him, unsure. "Some kind of matter blew out. It changed color, but the heat activity never left it. Are the readings wrong?"

Wrong . . . wrong? Wrong . . . could they be?

Or were these the numbers and symbols that would cleave the future apart in favor of Blood?

Think. Think. Harder.

The symbols played through and the screen went to neutral, waiting for someone to tell it what to do. Drymouthed, Shucorion could scarcely find his hands to work the controls, then could scarcely recall how to do it. *Think.*

"Dimion," he stammered, "show . . . the numbers again."

Confused, Dimion hesitated a moment as if afraid this might be a joke or a ruse, but finally came to do as he had been asked.

The information rolled and rolled. Clastics. Compounds. Blast results. Chemicals. Reactorants.

Shucorion's heart began to drum. Could he believe his own eyes?

"Show them again."

Completely baffled, Dimion huffed a breath as if to speak, then changed his mind and simply ran the information a third time.

As the data played its lights across his paling face, Shucorion sank onto the seldom-used stool, which luckily was right behind him because he didn't look, and gripped the handholds on the cylinder rack.

"Again."

Dimion pressed the controls and turned the cylinder slightly to make the readings come still another time. "What are you seeing in them, over and over?"

Shucorion strained some moisture into his mouth.

"Something only a blast technician could possibly understand. Something . . . wondrous."

Was that his voice? Were those his hands?

Here he sat, wishing the stool had a back so he could slump. He was staring at the impossible. *Impossible!*

"Impossible," he whispered. "Can this happen? All at the same time? My mortal enemy is about to build a base on a planet that . . . This changes everything . . ."

"What is it?" Dimion begged, bending low. "What do the numbers mean there?"

Shucorion stared into the cylinder, his feet and legs tingling. "A gift has been laid at my feet . . . I *am* chosen!"

For the first time his eyes left the numbers and fixed upon Dimion's diffident gaze. They looked at each other, Shucorion digesting his amazement and battling the sudden changes that must occur to everything he had ever assumed, Dimion quite frightened to see that battle going on.

"Avedon! We're being flashed," Garitt interrupted. His eyes were crimped and fearful as he looked up. For the first time he looked truly afraid. "Kauld have found us."

# Chapter Five

## Industrial Yacht *Pandora's Box*

"JIMMY."

"Billy. I had to see this with my own eyes."

"Big as life."

There he was. The latest boil on the backside of a generally sterling career. Well, sterling in the eyes of history, anyway. So far.

James Kirk came to a halt face-to-face with Billy Maidenshore, quite literally the last person he ever expected to find lurking in the hindquarters of the Belle Terre Expedition.

"What is this?" Billy Maidenshore spread his hands to receive Kirk and the captain of *Pandora's Box,* Felix Blaine, two of Kirk's security guards, and two of the Expedition's private detectives. "Don't tell me you've got more trumped-up charges to lay on me, Admiral?"

Kirk studied the other man's face for a few lingering seconds, deciding whether or not to speak at all. "It's 'captain' for the duration."

"Why don't they just call you 'sledgehammer'?" Billy asked, smiling in a particularly confounding way. "These methods of yours, they got no finesse. How'd you get aboard a private ship, 'Captain for the Duration'? This could be taken for unlawful entry. I don't suppose you have a warrant. You didn't the last time."

"I have reciprocal jurisdiction," Kirk told him. "Until we arrive at Belle Terre, I'm the local law enforcement."

"Doesn't mean you can make up the rules, does it?"

"I'll ask the questions, Billy. First, didn't I put you away? Or did somebody drop the key?"

"They dropped the ball." Maidenshore's gray eyes twinkled and his metal-shaving hair gleamed from its latest visit to the onboard salon. "You tried, sledge, you tried. But like so many before you, you got all caught up in the victory and slipped on the follow-through. You had no case. You had no proof, no justified cause of action, just like you had no warrant for search and seizure. That's because you acted rashly. Me, I stayed calm. And here I am. A man like me, you can't just whisk under the rug."

"Why'd you register under a false name?" Kirk incited.

"Why stir up trouble? No sense getting you all flustered as the Expedition was launching. You had your hands full. Supplies, fuel, cargo, policy and procedures, protocol compliance, mission goals, expenditure forecasts, operational priority ... operational chain of command, disease control, weapons coding ... seventy-plus ships moving through space, providing one hell of a tempting target for a raiding party . . . why should I add one more little worry to your list?"

Kirk narrowed his eyes. Maidenshore had just given an almost perfect rundown of Expedition command responsibilities. There was a clue in there. Somewhere.

"You slipped through my fingers once, Billy," he warned. "I won't let you do it again. This is my expedition and I mean to have order here."

Maidenshore laughed and pressed a manicured hand to his chest. "These aren't Starfleet ships, Jimmy. Blaine here and the others, they're not Starfleet captains. Not just bush pilots or bus drivers. They've got their own way of doing things. Everything's volunteer on this expedition. All these captains and crews, they've got stakes in this. They're not used to being bossed. Haven't you figured that out, all these problems you've been having for the past three months? They're resisting you, pal. You're better than Broadway, the way you think of yourself."

"How'd you get out of it, Billy? We had a collection of charges against you the length of your leg."

"Nothing to get out of. I never did anything wrong. I just contracted to move some things around for some people, on a modest commission. The charges were bogus. They don't put innocent people in jail." He struck a stage-worthy pose and gnashed, "At least not smart ones."

"If you're so innocent, why are you using an alias?"

"Popular and successful people always have enemies, y'know," Maidenshore said airily. "I mean, you should know, more than most, right? Admiral James T. Kirk, big hero, adventurer, famous . . . don't you have any enemies?"

Kirk chafed, but managed to keep it under his uniform. "What're you doing on the Expedition? Why would you suddenly drop everything and sign on to a no-return expedition?"

"You should ask? You confiscated everything I was planning to stay for. My future was all tied up with that shipment. You took it away, just like magic. Why did I come? Because I'm flexible. I came for the opportunity! A whole new world, new frontiers, new challenges . . . It's been real good. I fit in here. I help these people. I'm a very generous type. This is perfect for me, out here, with all these people who didn't know what they were stepping in. Sickness, hunger, fear . . . who else can give them comfort? You? That dreamy young governor? Nah, they need a father figure. You shouldn't be so surprised to see me on the Expedition. After all, you gave me the idea. Remember?"

## Three months earlier

"I think you'll like Evan Pardonnet, Jim." Councilman Howard Tanner, United Federation of Planets, heeled back in his chair. "He reminds me of you in some ways, not the really obvious ones. He had this idea to just get up and go, with a whole colony all in one swoop, set up a spaceport city complex and build, completely on their own, a new Earth. No preliminary outposts, no scouting other than the basic stuff, just pick a planet they could live on way far out, and just go. They petitioned the Federation Council for support and we liked their pioneer moxie. They've elected Pardonnet their governor."

"Pioneer moxie," Kirk tasted, and glanced at Leonard McCoy. "They've given it a name."

"You still hold the copyright," the doctor commented. "What planet are they going to, Councilman?"

"They've picked a solar system we call 'Occult,' " Tanner explained. "It's got a flicker distortion when viewed from here. There's a planet out there, nice one, that's practically Earth all over again. Temperate climate on both hemispheres, couple of nice big continents, ice caps, blue water, the works. They call it 'Belle Terre.' "

"Belle Terre." The words rolled around in Kirk's mind. He pressed a hand to his Starfleet-issue powder-blue trousers and felt as if he were fading away. "Beautiful Earth. A Class-M planet nobody else has claimed?"

"Nobody around wants it, I guess. Maybe there's nobody out there who can live on Class-M."

"What's the problem then? Why'd you send for me?"

"The area hasn't been extensively scouted. Only a ship or two, freelance. The only outposting we've done is to put a lightship on the edge of the sensor-dark area. We just don't know what's out there and the Federation was uneasy about supporting a colonial effort in an unscouted, uncleared, unoutposted area, so we withdrew. The colonists threw a fit. They said they didn't want an area that was already laid out and cleared. They want to carve the wilderness for themselves. They're real fighters from the heart. They just wouldn't be put off, not even when the Federation Colonial Bureau decided to withdraw support and Starfleet protection. The colonists said fine, hired themselves some privateers to protect them, and mobilized to go anyway. They've got seventy-two ships so far, to move sixty-four thousand colonists. They've come up with a whole new way to move themselves. Conestogas—huge passenger warehouses in space. They have no engines. They're moved by detachable mule engines, independent power plants that can tow at impulse or warp speed. Your friend Montgomery Scott helped develop them. They were the idea of one of his students, so he sponsored the development."

"Scotty," Kirk muttered. "And I don't suppose he gave you any other ideas?"

"So," Tanner continued, "what could we do? Send them off into ultra-deep space with no support? Just some rat-pack privateers to fend for them? How would that look? I convinced the Council to allow for one starship and a couple of tenders, like a CST and a cutter, maybe. They agreed . . . but only if you lead the expedition, Jim. James Kirk and the *Enterprise,* back together again. Gives the Belle Terre Expedition a ring of credibility."

"Spock's captain of the *Enterprise* now. Why don't you ask him?"

"We did. After all, it's his ship now. He said he'd go, but only with you in command. We agree. We think your reputation alone will protect the Expedition to a considerable degree. Listen, why don't you meet Governor Pardonnet, and let him give you his pitch. He's pretty infectious."

"Not to worry, Councilman," McCoy spoke up. The sun came in the window over the Jefferson Memorial Rose Garden and glinted on his otter-brown hair, picking up buried threads of gray. "I think Jim's already infected. Am I right, Jim?"

Kirk tilted his shoulder and peered at him caustically. "For a middle-aged clairvoyant with terminal speak-out-of-turn-itis."

"Why don't you give me a gag order? You've been a captain long enough."

"I'm an admiral, Doctor."

"The hell you are. The uniform's an admiral."

After indulging in a little grumble in the back of his throat, Kirk shifted back to the councilman. "Howard, you're not expecting me to stay out there with these people, are you? I'm not the colonist type."

"No, no, you'll be rotated back as soon as they're anchored on their planet. We'll send a frigate out to patrol the area. This is just for the initial transit. Just get them out there alive. It's far, though, Jim, six months at warp six, and the Conestogas can only go warp two. That makes it a nine-month one-way journey, then six back with a starship. Are you game? A new mission in deep space? Or have you given all that up for the admiralty?"

"You know my reputation," Kirk reminded. "I never give up. I'll do it, Howard, but on one condition."

"Ouch! The last time you said that, you made the Council release a whole planet to some guy who— ah, never mind. Let me get my legs braced. What's your condition?"

Kirk glanced at McCoy, wearing his washed-out medical suit, and at his own clothing, a cloud-blue flight suit with sewn-on slippers instead of boots.

"My condition," he parried, "is that you get me out of these pajamas and into the new uniforms slated for next year."

Tanner's face turned into a jack-o'-lantern.

"Deal!"

McCoy leaned forward, pressed his elbow to a knee, and eyed Kirk as a mouse eyes an Australian brown.

"The new uniforms," the doctor appraised. "Jim, I always knew that someday your power and influence would be used for good instead of evil."

"What answer did you offer the councilman, if I may ask, Admiral?"

Standing peaceably in his own shapeless blue flightsuit, Spock was waiting for them as Kirk and McCoy emerged from the UFP Bureau Building on the grounds of Starfleet Headquarters. Together the three walked down the curved brickwalk toward the shuttle pad, and Kirk felt the prying eyes of both his friends, Spock wondering what he'd said and McCoy poised to analyze what he was thinking.

"Don't be a sorcerer, Spock," Kirk commented. "I know when I've been cornered."

"I've no idea what you mean, sir."

Kirk paused, gazing down the slope to San Francisco Bay, where the Golden Gate Bridge was enduring its yearly paint job. Workers in antigrav weather suits floated around the bridge like fairies on a garden trellis. The enormous suspension bridge seemed ever to be reaching, holding its own for centuries, so people could get to the other side. Sunlight decorated the artful grid of cables and made him think of bigger things.

"A new star system," he mused. "New planet. Fresh, young . . . untamed. I wonder if they know what they've laid out for themselves." After a moment he blinked. "What do you know about it?"

"Common knowledge only," Spock confessed. "I know the Expedition has arranged for two rather large high-warp robotic supply barges at the perimeter of the roughest area, the sensor-blind phenomenon. They're counting on those barges to resupply them with food, fuel, power packs, medication, and other amenities to reinvigorate them and support their travel through the roughest quarter of the voyage. All this assumes the two barges will arrive safely, which is a fair assumption, given known risk factors."

"Oh? But you don't know anything about it."

Spock offered only a vocal shrug. "I also know the Belle Terre planetary system has a single star as well as a large scrubber planet which serves to clear the area of asteroids and other dangers, much as Jupiter serves us here. Therefore the combination is particularly alluring. Most such star systems are already occupied."

"What's the big deal about a single star?" McCoy asked.

"Lone stars are actually unusual, Doctor. The greater majority of stars are binaries. They may loop at great distance, but they're moving in direct relation to each other, such as the star system nearest to Belle Terre, which is a relatively active binary. We call Belle Terre's single sun 'Occult,' and the nearby binary 'Whistler' and 'Mother.' Other than that, I know relatively little about the Expedition project."

"Whistler? Mother?" McCoy blustered. "Who picks these names? And are they getting bored with their job?"

"The UFP Agency of Stellar Cartography and Cataloguing picks them," Spock said. "Since names like 'Gemini' and 'Romulus'-'Remus' were already taken, the binary was named after other famous people. Occult was named because Gamma Night causes the sun, from our perspective, to go dark at regular intervals, rather like an occulting navigational beacon."

McCoy peered at him. "Remind me to explain to you what 'rhetorical' means again."

Breaking off his communion with the bay and the bridge, Kirk turned to Spock. "You'll come with me, Captain, I humbly assume."

Spock clasped his hands behind his back, as he did when he wanted to pretend he hadn't already made up his mind. "In fact, Admiral, I could not make a selection until I knew of your decision. Whether the *Enterprise* remains here or leads the Expedition rested wholly upon your decision. Certainly I would decline such a mission otherwise."

"But you won't decline it now?"

Spock gazed at him hopefully. "Then you'll go?"

Kirk swiveled a little and looked at McCoy. "Should I just keep him in the dark?"

"Why not?" McCoy rocked back on his heels. "He's so comfortable there. . . ."

"I, Doctor," Spock continued, "will accompany the *Enterprise* on her new mission on one condition."

Kirk buried a grin. "More conditions."

"Yes, sir. I have suggested to the admiralty that an admiral's authority is not necessary on such an expedition as the Belle Terre project since there will be no Starfleet armada of ships of the line. I suggest removing myself to the role of first officer, and that you once again assume the mantle of post captain."

"The decision seems to have been made for me."

McCoy waved off the impulse. "Before you accept, Jim, you know it'll be a giant headache. You won't be just leading the way, no matter how splashy that sounds. You'll have to set up C and C, conjure up a duty roster, disseminate judgments, arbitrate disputes, try to get freewheeling private captains to fly in formation, not to mention handling privateers who won't want to listen to a Starfleet authority. You don't strike me as the trail-boss type."

"Doctor," Spock flouted, "the admiral has never shied away from new challenges. Why would you expect him to do so now?"

"Because this isn't his kind of challenge. He's always commanded crews who knew what they were signing up for—Starfleet crews, who understood they were putting their lives on the line. Most colonies start small, after space has been secured and studded with outposts. That's why the military goes first into the wilderness and establishes forts. These colonists don't have any idea what unout-posted deep space is like. They think they're rowing across a nice calm pond. The area they want to settle hasn't even been thoroughly scouted. Just because there's been no sign of trouble doesn't mean there isn't any trouble. Jim, you know what it's like to go across a swamp—the water looks peaceful and still until you step in. Then you find the alligators and snakes. I just don't see you as having an interest in a colonial operation."

Kirk started walking again, gratified to have them both here with him, for he was admittedly unsure of his next few steps. "I not only have interest, Bones, but from the first moment I heard about Belle Terre,

I never had any intention of letting them leave without me."

He let them drop back a few steps to imagine what he meant, to concoct in their minds whether he had been manipulated to be here today or whether he himself had done the manipulating. He wasn't about to clear the air. Some things were better murky. There would be a Starfleet presence on the Expedition after all, and it would be the *Enterprise*, with the crew of choice, and it would be him.

"It won't be easy," McCoy warned. "Or even pleasant. These people are in for some surprises. They're only looking at the pretty picture."

Kirk almost looked back on his career, to the ugly moments, the terrible losses, the pain and sacrifice, but somehow those seemed clouded to him now. He tried to put faces to those who hadn't made it back, but only heard a choir of encouragements.

*That's what we died for. Go out, and make our lives worthwhile.*

Before him, the bright blue water of the Bay rippled toward the ocean, drawing him forward.

"To get out in a ship again," he murmured, "be part of something fresh, something young, a true adventure, not just a life securing the benefits of past accomplishments . . . I want it. I need it. And I'm going. You're both going with me."

"Me?" McCoy protested. "Do you see the word 'sucker' painted on my back?"

"No," Kirk said, "but I did see your name on my active-duty roster this morning."

"Now, look—"

"No arguments, Bones. I need Spock and I need—I seem to need my shuttle. Where's my shut-

Diane Carey

tle?" They reached the end of the walkway, crossed the avenue to the shuttle pads, only to find the tree-lined waiting area completely empty. "You left it here, didn't you, Spock?"

"Yes, I did." Spock stepped out onto the tarmac, made a little circle, and looked mildly annoyed.

"Not another one," McCoy grumbled. "How many is this?"

"Three. Three shuttles!" Kirk threw both hands into the air. "I've had it. Three private, coded shuttles stolen in two weeks! What's this base coming to?"

"There has been a rash of security breaches at high levels," Spock mentioned. "Apparently it has something to do with an interstellar cartel which exacts skyrocketing prices from Starfleet contraband. Someone seems to delight in harassing the admiralty."

"Oh? Well, they're not dealing with the admiralty anymore. Now they're dealing with Captain James Kirk. Bones, get out of my way. Spock, give me the details."

"What is this? Who do you think you are, boarding my ship like this!"

"I'm Captain James Kirk. Security, over there and over there. Get into that hatchway. Check every compartment. Clear out the crew and passengers. They're all in custody as of now."

Jim Kirk felt a surge of vigor as he strode past the confused captain into the hold of the twelve-hundred-foot deep-space freighter, with his starship pulled up abeam. This was his first mission back in space in quite a while, and the ship's too. Of

78

course, they hadn't had to go very far yet, not for this one.

"That's my shuttle, right over there." He led the way past the ship's befuddled crew to a line of parked shuttles, some private, but several obviously Starfleet design that had been chopped or painted. "They've sprayed over the admiralty seal. I can see it right here. All right, you people," he began, speaking loudly enough that his voice echoed in the enormous hold, "I'm confiscating all the cargo here. All of you are under arrest for—"

"Hey, hold on!" A new voice interrupted him, with essentially the same sentiment as the captain's protest, but a higher pitch and a bigger insult. "All right, everybody stay calm and we'll clear all this up. Who's in charge? Who are you people?"

Striding forward from the bow section was an impressive man with a silver coif, an iron-black mustache, engaging gray eyes, and a particularly aromatic blue-leaf cigar. Clicking quickly behind him was a woman, several months pregnant and wearing a velvet suit and too much makeup, and two followers who could only be described as yesmen.

Kirk turned fully to meet the newcomer. "I'll bet you're Billy Maidenshore."

"Really?" The big man wheeled to a stop in front of him. "What does that make you, champ?"

"Captain James Kirk, Starfleet."

"And I'm Santa Claus. What're you doing stopping a private freighter? Everything here is due in the Orion cluster in two weeks. You're putting us behind schedule and we've made promises."

Stepping closer and ignoring the drip of despise

from the woman's glare, Kirk declared, "These are stolen goods."

"You've got the burden of proof," Maidenshore charged stubbornly. "All this cargo is here on commission or consignment. Perfectly legal."

"Where are your bills of lading?"

"Where's your warrant?"

"I don't need a warrant. We're in Vulcan space and they've given us carte blanche for confiscation."

"That won't stick in UFP jurisdiction and you know it."

"Really?" Kirk mimicked. "What's in these crates?"

With Maidenshore and a gaggle of wide-eyed transport crew following him, including the suddenly silent captain, Kirk motioned for his Starfleet guards to pry open one of the large crates on the starboard side.

"That's my private art collection," Maidenshore said with a tone of protest.

"Not anymore," Kirk told him. "Everything here will be held pending investigation. We're cleaning you out, Mr. Maidenshore."

Though his face was red with controlled fury, Maidenshore chuckled. "I like a stubborn jackal, I really do. How about a whole box of my favorite cigars? Toastmaster Monsoon Blues, grown only in the rain forests of Eminiar Nine. They only put out seven thousand of these a season, after the spring rains. I'll see that you're buried in them. Let me light you one up."

"Why, thank you." Accepting the dubious gift, Kirk let Maidenshore light the fresh cigar, then dropped it and put it out with his boot. "You're under arrest, Mr. Maidenshore."

The other man's eyes crinkled. "Got charges on you? In the pocket next to the warrant?"

"Interstellar racketeering, for a start. Tampering with Starfleet property, grand larceny, petty larceny—"

"This is Vulcan space. I've got a deal with them."

"Oh, I think the Vulcans will comply with me this time. Don't you, Mr. Spock?"

Lurking in the back, behind several of the helmeted security squad, keeping his alert eyes on the process, Spock stepped forward. "I can virtually guarantee it, sir," he offered.

"Mr. Spock, allow me to introduce Mr. Billy Morningstar."

A puff of cigar smoke, the impressive man's expression finally changed. "Shore. Maidenshore. Get it right."

"Oh, I'll get it right where it matters," Kirk promised. "But guess what—it'll be somebody else's problem after today. I'm remanding you over to the local Starfleet authority, who will remand you further to the UFP Bureau of Criminal Investigations on Starbase One. Then," he added, turning to glance at Spock with a particular satisfaction, "I'm heading to open space. I wash my hands of your kind, Mr. Maidenshore. In a few days, I'll be far away from you and everybody like you."

Maidenshore nodded almost hypnotically, with cruel bravado. "You won't be going so far away that you can't be found by certain determined souls, I bet."

"Bet all you like. I'm going farther than anybody ever has, with the possible exception of . . . well, me. I'm going with the Belle Terre Expedition, and I'm leaving you behind to face the music. Spock, come with me."

Billy Maidenshore watched the Starfleet officer stride away and had no choice but to let him go. A moment later he was holding up his hand to keep his two attendants from doing the wrong thing. He waved them back. They sank away without a word. Probably choked by intimidation at the sight of Starfleet uniforms. Weaklings were like that. Had to do their thinking for them.

As Maidenshore watched the rakish Starfleet hero enjoying himself, cracking open crates up and down the hold, the woman in velvet shivered to his side. "Billy, how'd they find us?"

"I don't know, but somebody'll pay for it. Bastard's confiscating the mother lode."

"Are you going to show him the records?"

"What do you think the records are for, Lucy? To throw him and everybody else off. Why else keep any?"

"This shipment was going to make us tycoons in four star systems." She lowered her voice to a whisper and hissed, "And you know those people—they'll come after you! What're we going to do now?"

"What do you mean 'we'?" Maidenshore stuffed his cigar between his teeth and watched Kirk ordering his goons around.

"If I get a chill—" She pulled a hotpack from an insulated pouch and pressed it to her throat. "This baby's gonna come early, I just know this baby's gonna come early."

"Better hang on to it till after your trial. Maybe your mother'll help you out."

"It isn't funny. That man was serious. Did you see his eyes? Somebody's been bribed. We better find out who it is."

Maidenshore nudged her out of his line of sight as he watched Kirk and the Starfleet men smashing the control boxes on magnetically sealed crates. "Quit whining. I'm trying to think. The goddamn motherlode . . . how do I replace two years of collections?"

Her big eyes scoping Kirk from across the hold, Lucy shivered and shook her head compulsively. "A lot of people are going to go down for this."

Irritated, Maidenshore squared his shoulders. "How does that affect me?"

Lucy stuck her hand into his elbow and pulled. "Send me someplace, will you, till it's all over? Someplace warm, at least."

"Go where you want. Angus, get over here. Over here, this way. Don't look at them, stupid, what if they can read lips? Look at me."

"Billy, cut it out!" Lucy hurried after him as he met Angus at the far end of the row of mismatched runabouts.

"Get the bills of lading." With his legendary residual strength, Maidenshore took Angus by the upper arm and crammed him into the side of the shuttle in question. "Get the *right* ones, got it? If you make another mistake, I'll dig out your heart with a nail file. Have you got this?"

"I got it, Billy. What'll we tell the Orions?"

"You tell them nothing, nothing. We're not finished yet. People are going to kiss my feet."

Lucy came around to his other side. "Please, Billy, I'm getting flushed. Tell me what to do."

Maidenshore bent over Angus, staring into the other man's face and thinking about how much uglier he could be on a moment's notice. "This is the last screw-up in the western galaxy for you, bubbles. You get my lawyers up here, all six of them, including Shapinski's little pointy mustache. He's about to get a real time-consuming hobby that—Lucy, get away from me, you're crowding my elbows here. I don't like to be crowded."

"Don't joke around," Lucy shrieked. "You scare me when you talk like that. I'm your wife!"

Leaning his wide shoulders as if to engulf her rounded form, Maidenshore rancorously asked, "Where's it written? Think back."

Horror rose in her eyes, abruptly, like a light going on.

Cruelly he turned his back on her and pressed Angus harder. "Either those pencilnecks get this Starfleet yokel off me, or I know what I'm gonna feed to the Orions when they show up and ask for their cargo. Is any of this getting through your leathery skull?"

"It's in, Billy," Angus choked. "Shapinski and Van Duzen, they're a good team, they didn't never let you down before—"

"Billy, talk to me," Lucy whispered urgently. "You're kidding, I mean, you're just kidding. We been together eight years. I run two-thirds of this business!"

Maidenshore paused and peered down at her. "Did I marry you? No. What comes next, it's going to take sophistication. Charm. Things you lack. Be grateful you got eight years."

He turned to walk away from her, but found his eyes caught on the Starfleet bigwig prancing around the deck, giving orders to uniformed jumping beans. "Y'know . . . that reminds me. I never promised the Orions any *particular* kind of valuable cargo, did I?"

Frantic, Lucy dug her sculpted nails into his arm. "Billy, you have to talk to me!"

"Quiet, quiet." He waved his cigar near enough that Lucy had to back off a step to avoid being burned. "I think I found a loophole here. Let me just think about this arrangement for a minute . . . yeah . . . yeah. Angus, come here. Get me information about this colonial business the sledge over there talked about."

Lucy pressed a hand to her forehead. "This whole thing is making me sick. Take me home, will you? I hate spaceships."

"Go where you want," he said. "In about ten minutes I'll have a whole new plan. In this business you've got to be flexible. That's what I do best. That's why I always win. It's why you lose."

"Quit talking that way!" She struck him with a tiny pointed fist. "I'm sick, you hear me?"

"Yeah, I hear you." He took her elbow and turned her in the direction of the Starfleet team. "Right over there? See? Those needleheads'll take you to a nice warm cell. Better start thinking about getting yourself a lawyer. Where I'm going, I won't need complications. Angus, let's crack."

*"Billy!"*

"Tell her to be quiet. I'm thinking."

## Belle Terre Expedition

"Then it was Billy Maidenshore after all?" Spock asked as Kirk strode back onto the bridge like a fox into its den.

"In person. I don't know how he wheedled out of those charges, but when I get back I'm going to find out. Whatever good it'll do, with him out at Belle Terre. He's here because of me, Spock, I can feel it. I saw the mockery, the vengeance in his eyes. He takes me personally. Just what I wanted to do . . . jump-start a Garden of Eden by providing a built-in serpent."

"Maidenshore is a minor racketeer at best, Captain," Spock assured. "Surely you won't allow his presence to curdle this experience."

"No, I suppose not. He just strikes me as a symbol of all the lowlifes and petty troubles I was trying to leave behind. McCoy was right . . . now I have all new troubles."

At the navigation console, Chekov swiveled to them. "Sir, as chief of security, I should've been more thorough in screening the passenger manifests. This is my fault."

Spock tilted his head in that warning way he had. "That was not your responsibility, Mr. Chekov. That was for the governor's office. This is a civilian operation, based upon nonjudgmentalism and the precepts of economic and cultural freedom."

Sulu turned halfway around from the helm. "It's not the first time civilians didn't understand the problems of travel in deep space. I wouldn't worry, Captain. They'll get over it."

"That's right, sir," Uhura bolstered from the comm station. "The governor's just found himself in the middle instead of at the top for a change."

Letting himself sink into their comfortable presence here, Kirk absorbed the support, and their presence at their old duty stations despite overwhelming command postings. They had each asked to serve their Expedition posts with the starship's bridge as their headquarters. He knew, though, that they each spent a full second watch running their assigned overseerships—Chekov with Expedition security, Sulu organizing all the helmsmen and pilots, Uhura on safety and evac, Spock coordinating all the first officers and their respective duties. Like him, this was the place where they could relax from all the other pressures.

Somehow being here was better than being in a bunk someplace with music and a book. Only Scotty was missing, and only because he couldn't run the vast engineering concerns of the Expedition from one station. He'd been moving about so much that Sulu had been forced to give him carte blanche on runabout movement, even within the complex, collision-tempting stacked-and-packed fleet formation.

"Captain," Chekov broke into his thoughts, "do you want me to put surveillance on this man?"

"I could monitor *Pandora's Box*'s communications," Uhura offered. "Even onboard communiqués."

The offers, not exactly by the book, took Kirk by surprise. "I . . . don't think we have due cause."

But he looked at Spock for an opinion. A moment later they were all looking at the Vulcan.

"If Maidenshore, shall we say, 'beat the rap,' " Spock began, "it becomes our duty to accept the decision of the legal system and allow him his chance at building a new life. Ideally, participants should be able to leave the past behind and begin anew."

"Are you suggesting," Kirk needled, "that we should

assume the best about a man who somehow silently gathered a fortune's worth of contraband and slipped it past even border cutter and municipal treaty in four sectors before we found it? I think I'd rather assume the worst."

"As you wish. Certainly your instincts are superior regarding the criminal mind."

As Chekov and Sulu grinned silently and turned back to the helm, the aft turbolift hissed and a new voice drove away the unfinished conversation.

"Captain Kirk!—good, you're back."

"Governor," Spock responded, sparing Kirk the bother. "Good morning."

Was it still morning? All this before lunch?

"Yes, thank you." The colony's exuberant head of state, organizer, chief advocate, and first-line cheerleader bounded down from the turbolift. Evan Pardonnet was barely thirty years old, narrow-faced and large-eyed, a good four inches taller than Kirk, with a crop of thick heroic brown hair, scrupulously neat, and an air of nervous sincerity. "I've had a grievance filed against you by the captain of the *Pandora's Box*. He says you beamed aboard and harassed the ship's owner without proper clearance."

"I don't need clearance, Governor," Kirk reminded. "I *am* the clearance. After four and a half months I thought we understood each other on that."

"For the first three months, we did. But lately—we've practically tested a new disagreement every day. Don't forget, Captain, we didn't want the Starfleet escort. You were more or less foisted upon us at the last minute. We were perfectly satisfied with the private protection."

Kirk glanced at Spock and modified his tone very

carefully before turning to Pardonnet. Mellow, mellow. "And you seem to forget that you're the senior official of a nation that doesn't exist yet. It won't exist until we debark on Belle Terre. Until then, this is a fleet. My fleet."

"It's not working that way," Pardonnet said. "This isn't your average colonial settlement that takes twenty years to get rolling. We're already rolling. We're not going somewhere to be a colony—we're *already* a colony. We've got everything from cowboys to metallurgists to sanitation engineers to architects, and all the raw materials to let them do what they do. With our factory ships, most of the construction for a whole spaceport will be ready to assemble upon arrival. We already have everything any other major city complex has. After all, we're not going halfway across the galaxy to dig in the soil and raise goats."

Spock seemed puzzled by that, or at least pretended to be long enough to stir up trouble. "Agricultural colonies have been a staple for steady expansion, sir."

"I've never understood that template," Pardonnet rebuffed. "Why does anybody need to go five hundred light-years to have a farm? We're going to be a critical port city almost instantly. We'll be a diplomatic and cultural hub, a literary mecca, a science center, headquarters for adventurers and entrepreneurs—anybody who wants to come and pull his weight. The Federation has never seen the likes of us before. You're trying to run this operation as if it's just another military mobilization. It's not. I know what you're doing and I appreciate your commitment to us, I really do, but—"

"That's a dangerous 'but,' " Kirk anticipated, "out here in the middle of unprotected space."

"The 'but' is that we'll be filing for independent Federation membership with planetary nation status almost immediately. That's never been done before. I have to protect our individuality so no one in the Federation can say we relied on anyone but ourselves or asked anybody else to foot the bill. We're committed never to leech off our neighbors . . ."

As the governor went on speaking, caught up in his laudable goals, Kirk realized that the governor was using his strong beliefs to overcome his lack of confidence in himself. That was one of the traits that made Evan Pardonnet's exuberance tolerable—he had more faith in his dreams than he did in himself, and let his dreams lead.

While the governor spoke, Kirk's eyes strayed to the forward screen. He'd caught sight of a movement there that he didn't like. Which ship was that, breaking formation and moving off by itself? A melon-shaped vessel, one of the older ships, with a handle-like foil running around its aft end, had veered off from the flotilla pattern.

Internal alarms rang in his head. Was something wrong over there? Loss of power? Control?

Without moving more than his eyes, he connected attention with Spock, who shifted one foot and slightly turned his body toward Kirk, yet in such a way that Pardonnet couldn't see that concerns had left the noble speech still going on.

"We don't want some agency offering grants," Pardonnet proclaimed, "or subsidies to skew the results of ingenuity. There won't be any cruisers telling us what we can't take out or bring in. If somebody wants to build a porch on his house or a landing tarmac on his property, he's not going to have to tithe the government to buy a permit."

"I like that idea," Kirk shoved in, but he had now connected eyes with Sulu and Uhura. To Uhura, he tipped his head slightly forward, eyes crimped a little at the corners.

Quietly, Uhura put her earpiece up and, keeping her movements small, peppered the communications board with one hand. A voiceless communiqué. *Problem over there? And do they know about the gravity well we picked up this morning?*

"There'll be no monoliths on Belle Terre, no Department of Settlement telling people where they can and can't live or who they have to hire. That's the kind of people who are on this convoy, Captain, not the kind who signed up for a set of rules and regulations."

Keeping his eye on the straying vessel, Kirk tried to remember the name of that ship as he placidly warned, "Governor, you're having that same conversation with yourself again."

Flushed, Pardonnet faltered and held both palms up in self-deprecation. "I know I do that, I just want to do what's right. These people are determined to be free of authoritarian forces. It disturbs them when Starfleet barges in on private property. They look to me to insure their dreams don't get off on the wrong foot."

Abruptly put off, Kirk didn't hide his insult. "I don't suppose they mind Starfleet barging in on the lung flu crisis aboard the *Yukon* and *Promontory Point.*"

The young governor pressed a foot up on the bridge step and grimaced. "Don't be that way, Captain, when you know what I'm talking about. We've got something really unique here, a true first-time thing . . ."

*Mandrake Anachronae.* That was it. A ship full of historic reenactors who studied ancient history and enjoyed the fun parts of reliving it. They left the blood, gore, starvation, and sickness to the pages of textbooks and enjoyed the chivalry, honor, jousting, swordplay, and fantasy that remained unrotted in this age of clean toilets and physicians who were more than glorified whisperers.

So what were they doing moving off on an unplanned trajectory?

Kirk had one eye on the *Mandrake* and the other on all the rest of the Expedition ships, moving off in a long flocking formation visible on several small screens around the bridge. A stab of fright raced through him, as it did sometimes in the middle of the night when he was supposed to be sleeping. He'd come out here to escape the fears of sedentary life at an admiral's desk, and found himself in a swarm of other, newer fears, and these new ones all had real people's faces on them. Look how many ships there were . . . . and how few Kirks.

*I'll have to talk to McCoy about having an eye installed in the back of my head.*

How close would the *Mandrake* stray to that gravity well? Had they paid attention to the warning bulletin this morning? Or were their sensors just too weak? Since the suction of a well couldn't be accurately measured with standard sensors, no one, not even Spock, could predict its behavior.

Kirk caught Sulu's eyes again—not hard, because Sulu was already anticipating a move and was watching. With his fingers, Kirk made a motion of *four. Change course. Mark four.*

Slowly, imperceptibly, the starship moved off to port, following the straying *Mandrake*. Kirk crooked his index finger where Sulu could see it. *Be ready to throw traction on them if we have to.*

Sulu touched his board while Pardonnet continued.

". . . and we're worried about mandates and statutes thundering down from On High and sending us the bill. It means, and again I'm sorry, that I have to keep you at arm's length if I can. Can you understand?"

"We understand perfectly," Kirk countered. "It's why you couldn't set up shop within conventional Federation territory. The mandates would follow you. You want to make local decisions."

Rolling his eyes in relief, Pardonnet nodded and shrugged in a consummately fallible and savvy manner. "Right . . . and . . . well, we also want to go far enough out that if we completely screw up, we're not going to hurt anybody else."

"Commendable," Spock offered.

Still without a clue that anything else was going on, Pardonnet accepted the compliment with a grace both humble and uncollapsible. "Well, we know how big this trick will be . . ."

"Unfortunately," Kirk added quickly, "you're going to have to put up with an increasing amount of organizational tyranny if things don't get better. The series of malfunctions has yet to be explained, a rampant viral disease has two Conestogas quarantined, there are mutterings of dissatisfaction around the Expedition—the colonists are hardly speaking in a singular voice. I, however, have very singular orders. I intend to get you to Belle Terre if I have to strap all of you down and carry you there. Your captains and their passengers are going to have to comply even more strictly in the next few weeks. We'll have to prepare for Gamma Night."

At mention of the impending phenomenon, the governor's expression changed. He glanced from Kirk to Spock and back again. "Why would a period of sensor darkness necessarily change the way we're operating the fleet? We just go on through it and stop every night."

Kirk motioned to the helm. "Mr. Sulu? Would you mind?"

"My pleasure." Sulu pivoted only one shoulder toward the governor. He was still moving the ship on a pie-shaped course away from the Expedition flock, though Pardonnet hadn't noticed the change. "Gamma Night is a navigational phenomenon caused by a neutron star and a black hole which are orbiting each other. Though we'll be traveling nowhere near this anomaly, its effects are far-flung in the region engulfing the Sagittarius star cluster, and therefore the Occult star system and the planet Belle Terre."

"I know that's why the star Occult got its name," the governor mentioned. "Because it seems to flicker. We'll have to adjust our spaceflight schedules once we settle on Belle Terre. I'm no pilot, of course."

"That's all right." Sulu offered a trademark smile. "As a spaceport, your whole colony will have to learn to live with the resulting physics. It causes a period of 'nighttime' for all ships' sensors for ten hours out of thirty-two. Communication becomes spotty and dim. Movement of ships is done while virtually blind. Warp speed is unthinkably dangerous. Of course there's no point moving at impulse, so you might as well heave to and wait it out. . . ."

Sulu was speaking to the governor, but doing two other more important duties—keeping Pardonnet distracted, and piloting the starship in proximity of a gravity well—and as the well's draw became something he could feel in the controls, his conversation fell away.

One hand on the tractor-beam controls, Chekov

shook out of his silence and took over. "The only way to move is by dead reckoning. If navigation is even slightly off, the results may be disastrous. The only way to detect vessels out of line of sight will be inaccurate readings of electromagnetic output. Vessels in the vicinity can be viewed, of course, by simply looking outside—"

"By which time they're right on top of you," Kirk threw in, just to hurry things up. The distress light was going off on *Mandrake*. He looked to Uhura. She nodded.

He crooked his finger again, and Chekov pressed his tractor-beam controls. *On.*

"Ships' routines and watch schedules," Kirk continued, only halfway attending his own words, "will have to be altered to maximize efficiency. A standard round-the-clock watch schedule is pointless. There's no sense, for instance, in having your most experienced helmsman on duty during Gamma Night."

"This is the kind of thing I mean." Pardonnet held out a beseeching palm. "Why can't you just let the individual captains run their own crews their own ways? They'll put anybody they want at the helm."

"Because a flotilla isn't a free-flowing colony." Kirk let himself breath again. *Mandrake Anachronae* had stopped moving sideways, and began a sluggish turn back toward the Expedition. She'd been stuck at the bank of the gravity well. While not in danger of being sucked in, she had been the equivalent of aground—stuck, without the strength to pull herself out. A little tug had brought her out.

Now, what had he started to say?

"Uhura and all the watch leaders," he recovered, "will have to make changes in the emergency drills, be-

95

cause more people will be asleep during those hours. Mr. Spock will be coordinating all the first officers on ships' status. Mr. Scott will have to keep a strict eye on power levels and general condition. We're only as fast as the slowest ship. If we have to take someone in tow, that slows down the whole fleet. Slowing down invites more trouble. And I won't split us up."

Answering a signal from the other ship, Uhura pursed her lips and wrinkled her nose. A shrug—and she waved her hand, then pointed at the forward screen in a motion he understood. *All's well now. Watch.*

Under her own power again, the *Mandrake* was pausing in space. A shimmering golden plume vented from her exhaust ports. Kirk drew a sustaining breath. That explained it. Being an older ship, she didn't have the advanced filtration sytems of most of the other vessels. She'd had to bear off to vent her core waste.

Connecting gazes one more time with Sulu to make sure the *Enterprise* stayed between the *Mandrake* and the well until the Expedition was past the phenomenon, Kirk stepped around the command chair and approached Pardonnet in what he hoped would be a brotherly manner, or at least be taken that way.

"Your colonists have been acting as if they're on some kind of vacation," he said. "That led to disorganization in loading processes, treaty violations, conflicting stowage diagrams, infectious failure of over a dozen OUS capacitors—a hundred little mistakes that Mr. Chekov and Mr. Spock had to iron out before we could run smoothly. Now we're out here, and your colonists are getting even more indulgent as things get harder."

"They're trying to keep their spirits up," Pardonnet submitted. "They're not experienced spacefarers."

"No, they're not," Kirk said with a sigh, and the extra eye still on *Mandrake*. "Spacefarers are used to doing without. The ideal is to arrive with a significant portion of your fuel and supplies still in the tanks. You won't be doing that. That means I have to keep tighter control, or you won't arrive at all."

"The dream of Belle Terre is to go so far away from established bureaucracy that people like you simply can't reach us. We want a chance to set up a system based on true individual rights of decision and property . . ."

As the governor went on, Kirk fogged out briefly to note Sulu's choreography. *Mandrake Anachronae*'s less-than-graceful return to the flow of the Expedition train had to be adjusted to keep her out of the wash from the organ lab *Olympian,* but also keep her from bumping the iceberg being towed by *Iroquois.* Almost there . . .

"Don't get me wrong," Pardonnet continued, "the Federation's done fairly well, bumping along under its big net of regulations, but nobody can fly in a net. It keeps us safe, but at what price? Sit around being safe until we die off?"

Kirk blinked and finally gave all his attention back to the governor. If that wasn't the oddest thing he'd heard in a while—when had the maverick James T. Kirk become one of the establishment?

"If I don't keep control," he said, "we could find ourselves with anarchy. That's not the kind of freedom you want, is it?"

Pardonnet straightened his shoulders in defiance. "What we want is to go into space to live our dream, not to be another rung on James Kirk's climb to glory."

Snapping his attention also back to the Pardonnet,

Spock visibly bristled. "That's most uncalled for, Governor."

"Sir," Sulu spoke up, his features animated, "if Captain Kirk's ego were hurt, he could commit suicide by climbing to the top of his medals and jumping off. He's not here for glory."

"Thank you, thank you." Quieting each with a brief contact, Kirk mildly admonished them with a genuine rush of humility. "I think we understand each other." He looked at Pardonnet. "You breathe too much fire, Governor. There's nothing all that wrong with the way we old-timers do things, is there?"

"There are some things wrong," the young man defended. "If we're not passionate and vigilant, the Dark Ages can come again. Freedom can die."

"Governor Pardonnet," Spock put in, "you misinterpret the Federation Council's decision to assign Starfleet to the convoy. Our participation is a gesture of sworn duty to protect citizens in space."

Pardonnet's expressive features flared. Suddenly his voice got a tinge of resentment, his eyes a spark of savvy. "Oh, I *know,* Mr. Spock, why the Federation's suddenly so interested in giving us Starfleet protection. We shocked them by signing up privateers and plowing ahead even after they withdrew Starfleet's support. We were moving to Belle Terre without plundering our neighbors' pockets."

"Governor—" Kirk held up a hand, and fielded away the temptation to blurt out that they'd just averted a possible disaster and only experience had done it.

On the other hand, why crow in a barnyard?

Pardonnet talked without bothering to breathe. "We're not wishing for paradise and forcing somebody else to foot the bill. We're going out to build paradise with our own sweat. The Council knows we don't need their help, and they're terrified of being left behind. That's your job—be here when the future happens, so they can say they were part of the most ambitious success in Federation history. You're their figurehead."

Sensing the eruption of his personal defense team again, Kirk deliberately backed off a step and nodded passively. "Very well, Governor. I'll exercise some discretion next time. I had reasons to investigate one of the owners because of a . . . mutual experience."

"Are you sure that's not just your suspicious nature at work?"

"Oh, yes it is," Kirk admitted. "My suspicious nature is always at work."

To his credit, the young official dropped the expression that got him to this point and changed his manner. "Maybe we really do understand each other. Thanks for listening. I'll tell the owners that you were very gentlemanly about this. Permission to, ah . . . whatever you say when you duck out."

Kirk nodded lightly. "Permission granted."

A bit awkwardly the governor walked through the ensuing silence and onto the accommodating turbolift. The silence remained until the lift doors closed, then a few seconds longer, until they all knew the tube was cleared.

Then it blew.

"What a brat!" Uhura squalled. "I never heard such idealistic puffery! No respect for authority at all!"

"No sense of circumspection," Sulu agreed.

Chekov nodded and held up a demonstrative finger. "No finesse!"

Spock folded his arms and surveyed Kirk with one of those comfortingly annoyed expressions. "One would hope he might have reviewed your service record before carrying on so."

With a shrug, Kirk let his shoulders relax and stepped up to the command chair's podium. "I'll get over it."

"Captain," Uhura mused, half-grinning, "you've just been accused of being a glory-grabbing bureaucrat by a juvenile history-hound. Don't you have anything to say?"

Kirk settled back into his chair and crossed his legs. "Yes, I do," he announced. "I like him."

# COMMAND DUTY ROSTER—MEDICAL

Designated by James T. Kirk, Adm.
Belle Terre Colonial Transit

Senior Project Medical Officer: LEONARD McCOY, Cdr.

Authority: Surgeon General, Starfleet

Duty Station(s): Enterprise, Starship NCC-1701, Kirk
Brother's Keeper, Mercy Ship SCCM-778 Clevenger, Capt.
Skaerbaek, Surgical Treatment; M'Benga, General Practice
Twilight Sentinel, Coroner Ship SCCM-99, Satchell, Capt.
Rochea, Chief Coroner

## DIRECT RESPONSIBILITIES:

General health and welfare, vaccination, dispensaries.
Life support systems, life pod integrity.
Exercise program and facilities.
Dense rations, potable water, galley inspection, hydroponics, dairy.
Troop space, living space.

SAR teams, HazMat teams.

Coordinate medical diagnostics, dispensaries, treatment, surgical procedures with

General Practitioner aboard Mercy Ship.

Coordinate above with all medical officers.

## INDIRECT RESPONSIBILITIES:

Coordinate with Drill Chief: life pods, EVS units, evac procedures, life support, rations, emergency medical evac and transport.

---

## COMMAND DUTY ROSTER—EMERGENCY PROCEDURES

Project Emergency Drillmaster: UHURA Lt. Cdr.

---

Report to: Spock, Cdr., senior first officer

McCoy, Leonard, Cdr., safety, SAR, HazMat

Duty Station: Communications, NCC-1701

## DIRECT RESPONSIBILITIES:

Coordinate all watch leaders and emergency duty rosters.

Devise and direct safety drills for atm. contamination, hull breach, unfriendly contact, fire, collision, abandon ship.

Communications: devise visual pennant system, coded audio system, coded signals, networks, frequencies, tolerances, process for emergency traffic notification. Disseminate all coded procedures to first officers, communication officers.

Coordinate SAR and HazMat teams.

# Chapter Six

## Coroner Ship *Twilight Sentinel*

A SOLEMN SHIP, a funeral home in space. The *Twilight Sentinel* provided the Belle Terre colonists with one of life's oldest and saddest necessities. She was their Boot Hill, their Oak Crest, their Sunset Valley. She was the celestial cemetery where the departed could be discharged for burial in space, or stored to be interred on the new world where their families would live out their lives without them.

She was a purple-hulled transport, flickering with tiny white lights, a piece of the night sky floating in elegant repose. Here there were dark burgundy draperies, devices of all known religions, private booths, viewing areas, a pleasant little café, a library, even a children's play pit. The owners wanted Belle Terre's citizens to feel comfortable here, to not mind coming if they had to or wanted to.

The aft end held an off-limits morgue, coroner's lab, and crematorium. Midships, sepulcher vaults, both occupied and not, lined long quiet corridors. The occupied vaults had imitation stone faces with etchings like historic gravestones, truly lovely and homey in their way, telling the needed stories, and the ship was indeed sweet as potter's field.

Yet, somehow the designers had made a hopeful, forward-looking place here too. Near the bow was a plush lounge area, divided into more private conversational cloisters by mini-grottos of tropical broadleafs, ferns, and stone fountains. There, along the ship's curved forward section, were floor-to-ceiling windows framed in carved mahogany. It was as if the old craftsmen of a simpler time had put their stamp upon the stars and nebulae of open space. People could commune with their passed relatives and friends, then move forward and sit together, gazing at the future out those windows.

Jim Kirk had squirmed more at the idea of coming here than he ever had at beaming into the sweltering drone that was about to blow up. This was an entirely different kind of squirm. He recalled it from his visits to the chapel on *Enterprise* to comfort crewmen who had lost mates in the line of duty.

He had never been good at that. Action, yes. Comfort, no. He never had the words. All he could do was provide his presence and hope the captain's aspect eased the process along to a livable end.

Today he stood with Spock and Scott in the midship corridor, providing that presence for the families of two teenagers lost to the lung flu, and three people who had died in the drone attack.

"How many have we lost total now, Spock?" he asked, very quietly.

Spock watched the families milling among the draperies and plush couches. "This bring us to a total of fifty-nine deaths since leaving Federation space."

"Fifty-nine," Scott muttered. "Let's hope it holds."

A moan of agreement clawed up in Kirk's throat. He strode away from them a few steps, hands clasped passively behind his back, fielding nods of sorrowful greeting from passengers who met his eyes, and hoped not to attract more attention than just low-key respect and gratitude that he'd bothered to appear. He didn't really want to speak to these people. They had each other. What could he say to them? We all went into space to start a new life, and you're saying a final farewell you never counted on. That's space travel. We warned you.

Hmmm . . . better not.

Turning again, he paused for a moment, looking at Scott in the new Starfleet uniform. The engineer stood prouder in this uniform than the previous design. He'd always claimed the old ones were making him color-blind. But then, Scotty always looked durable and fitted, no matter what he was wearing. Age had peppered his hair and brought on a thick iron mustache to brighten his toothy flyboy smile. He wore the years well, along with the fire-red shirt under his darker blood-red jacket. Somehow Scott had always been older, even back when he was younger.

Spock, on the other hand, was ageless. The white command-status turtleneck framed his angular face and offset his slick black hair and Vulcan ears. The belted garnet Fleet jacket and black trousers made him seem even taller and slimmer than he was.

Kirk could only hope the outfit also provided that effect for the stockier build of a mariner who wasn't thirty anymore. He felt as if it did. He'd felt more polished in this uniform than he had since the old days in his command golds.

Today he needed to feel in control, to sense he looked commanding to the people watching him. Because he wasn't. He hadn't prevented those fifty-nine deaths from accidents and malfunctions and sicknesses. Could he prevent the ones that were on the way, between here and Belle Terre? Could he jump that high, run that fast, stretch his arms wide enough to protect seventy ships full of innocent people?

Spock was approaching him, and paused casually. For a Vulcan, he did a good casual. "Is everything all right, Captain?"

"I don't like this place," Kirk admitted. "I can't stop it from existing, and that bothers me." He took Scott's arm, pivoted him and pointed to the bow section. "Let's go forward. Walk through those people so they can all see that we're here. Then I want to leave."

Escape, he meant. Only nodding, Spock began the stroll, which Kirk and Scott had no choice then but to accompany. The three made their way through the velvet Victorian couches and stone grottos, shaking hands, murmuring sorrows, and accepting greetings, and Kirk measured every face, doing his best to remember each person. He knew he couldn't hold on to those identifications, but he wanted to try. He pretended to know the people who clasped his hand, recalled some of them, truly knew very few. They all knew him.

By the time the three of them paused before the forward viewing windows, hovering over to the side in a kind of polite solitude, Kirk's hands were cold and trembling. He glanced back over the mourners like a nervous bird. The Expedition was passing a nebular cloud which seemed close, but in fact was light-years away. Even so, it dominated the entire expanse of the port-side windows.

He put his hand on his jacket collar and tugged down to relieve his tightened throat. "I feel like I'm going to a hanging. My own."

Though Scott stayed away a few steps, near the opposite windowframe, Spock came around a little at Kirk's side, to partially face him while not closing off his view of the people who were still meeting the captain's eyes for a sad, passive communion.

"They don't blame you, Jim," he said.

Uneasy, Kirk couldn't stop a smile. "Quit reading my mind."

But the assurance warmed him some. He turned to gaze out the viewport at the nebula's crawling gases, but his eye strayed. Instead of the nebula, nature's true grand performance, he found himself staring out at mankind's grand performance . . . a fleet of ships he was leading.

There were so many of them, following each other, bunched in Sulu's traffic pattern that kept them in order and safe from collision or other mishaps. So many lives inside the shells protecting them from the vacuum of deep space, and they were all depending upon him and his command of the million details that had gotten them this far and would hopefully get them the rest of the way. Flexible response, stowage diagrams, cubic bale capacity, palletized load units, capstan shackles, arbitration clauses, lists and demands, memos and cries for judgment—his mind spun with it all as he looked out at all those ships.

"I was surprised," he mentioned, "when I scanned the officer manifests for all those ships. Remember what that was like? Seeing all the familiar names among the unfamiliar ones? You don't realize how many acquaintances you've gathered over the years. Tony DeSalle, commanding his own Starfleet ship now . . . Senior Geologist Ben Childress, one of those lithium miners we got in trouble with all those years ago . . . Thomas Meer, Ele'en Aka'ar's second son . . . I sponsored his application to the Merchant Space Service. Jamie Finney and her husband, two kids . . . and Lieutenant Bannon! That kid who hit me once."

"He *tried* to hit you," Spock reminded, amused.

"Did y'deserve it?" Scott asked.

Kirk shrugged. "Of course."

"Thought so. Even locked in deep space," Scott said, "we touch many lives in our travels."

"This from Commander Montgomery No-Artistic-Expression-Allowed Scott." Kirk smiled again. "I have to admit, it's been good to have you and the old crew to depend on during all this."

"Careful how you use that word 'old,' sir."

"You'll never get old, Scotty. You'll just ferment."

The chief engineer chuckled and scottished, "Go' that right."

Though Kirk started to say something else, his mind suddenly cleared as, before him, the *Crystobel* and *Macedon* changed position, resulting in their parting before him like theatrical curtains. He found himself gazing up at his queen.

Siren intoxication filled him, as if he could reach out and touch her, trace the bolts on her patchwork plates, tickle the call letters, kiss the witch.

There, just above his eye level, rising slightly over the mismatched flock, was his *Enterprise*. From here he could look up to the underside of the starship's dish-shaped primary hull, seductive and available, lit by the ship's self-illumination system. Here in deep space, only the soft gold vapor from the nebula provided any other light, and that was on the other side of the ship. She made a dove-gray silhouette, backlit by the nebula, forelit by the funneled light of her own hull lanterns. Her swan neck and main hull, struts and nacelles shone like the body of a quiet Lipizzaner.

He loved to see her from outside, and burned the vision into his memory. She had more than sturdiness and beauty, more than strength, even more than the elusive subliminal consciousness that makes sailors sure a ship is alive. She had a fathomless dignity that tethered him to her, and always would.

"Sometimes it startles me," he quietly spoke, "to find out that other people feel the same about their ships as I do. It's easy to get arrogant, with a ship like her."

At his sides, Spock and Scott provided him their presence, but neither said anything. In his periphery he could see the glint of pride in Scott's eyes, and the solemn respect in Spock's.

When his communicator whistled, he ignored it—the first time, anyway.

Only when Spock touched his arm did he break from his conversation with the starship and spring back to his job. "Kirk here."

"*Sulu here, sir.*"

Kirk turned again to look at the ship, as if he were speaking directly to her and not really to Sulu. "Problem?"

"*Possibly. Uhura just called from the* Yukon. *Dr. McCoy's beaming over right now. They've got some kind of riot going on among the passengers. Something about the lung flu medication.*"

"Does she need backup?"

*"No, sir, she wants to handle it herself, using the emergency procedures she developed. She didn't even want to disturb you, but I felt something like this should at least be reported."*

"Very well, Mr. Sulu. I don't suppose this critical emergency requires me to beam back to the *Enterprise* immediately? I hope? To stand by? Just in case?"

*"Oh . . . why, yes, sir, yes it does. Thank you for asking. We're barely holding our own."*

He took Spock by the arm and started pulling. "Then I'm coming right home. Kirk out."

## Conestoga *Yukon*

"Hold those people back! Where's the security team from the *Impeller?"*

"Right here, Commander!"

"Report to Commander Giotto on the main deck. Doctor, what about the hold? They've got sick people from three ships laid out down there, and people from all three Conestogas want to come and tend them."

"They're going to have to hold back their altruism. I want medical personnel only. Hey, you, get away from that hatch!"

What was all the shouting about? Michael Kilvennan stepped out of the transporter vestibule on the Conestoga *Yukon* into a hive of shouts and clatter, demands and accusations that gave him an instant shiver up the spine. To his left, Lieutenant Commander Uhura was snapping orders to security teams who were holding groups of passengers at phaserpoint. To his right, Dr.

McCoy held a padd and checked items off on some list or other while more security men made sure nobody got to him.

"What's going on here?" Kilvennan demanded. "What's everybody so worked up about?"

"Michael! Over here!"

In the chorus of shouts and accusations, fist-waving and orders, he needed extra seconds to find his brother's face in one of the crowds being held apart by guards. At twenty-two, Quinn Kilvennan was tall enough to wave over the helmets of the meaty guards, though when he tried to push through he received a nightstick in the shoulder. His buffalo plaid fleece vest disappeared and his winter camouflage sweatpants came up; then the whole patchwork disappeared into the flock of irrational passengers.

" 'Scuse me, Doctor." Kilvennan pushed past McCoy and got to the crowd in time to prevent his brother's getting hit again, but the guards wouldn't let him through. "Quinn, don't fight the guards!"

"They won't give us the medication we brought with us, Michael." As he righted himself, Quinn's usually ivory face was russet with fury, his dark hair in a flop. Who was this stranger? "It's not theirs to confiscate! Josette and Ian are still sick and now Mom's starting to get dizzy."

"How are Stefan and Mae?"

"Oh, Stefan's sorry he ever married into the family and Mae's threatening to divorce you. How do you think they are? They're scared and tired!" Quinn pointed across the crowded deck to McCoy. Quinn the poet, the bard, the storyteller, the devout fellow of faith thinking about priesthood today was maniacal and unfamiliar. "Starfleet says there's not enough medication. They've got it, but they won't give it to us!"

"Can't believe that," Kilvennan countered.

"Ask him!"

"Dr. McCoy!"

Leonard McCoy craned at him over the considerable shoulders of a guard who was pushing two passengers away from another group. When the way was cleared, the doctor crossed to him through a keenly felt Starfleet presence.

"Captain Kilvennan," McCoy began, "you should've stayed on *Hunter's Moon*. This Conestoga's quarantined. How'd you get past the beam shield?"

Kilvennan shook his head, surprised. "Shield wasn't up. Took it to mean the quarantine had been lifted. My wife and kids are here, you know."

"Yes, I know. Uhura! The beam shield's been dropped. Do you know anything about that?"

Lieutenant Commander Uhura pushed past a wall of security uniforms and joined them, scanning Kilvennan with an exotic but critical eye. "We dropped it to beam Captain Merkling's security team in, but it was supposed to go right back up. Sulu's falling down on the trafficking job."

"Or somebody's tripping him," McCoy commented. "I'll bet my medical bag his board shows the shield's up." He turned to Kilvennan. "I'm sorry, Captain, but you have to go under the quarantine now. Your ship will have to do without you."

"Unacceptable," Kilvennan replied. "I run a privateer ship with a small crew. Got the picket duty."

"Your mate will have to take command," Uhura smartly said. "Even a privateer ship has a command line, doesn't it?"

113

He cocked a hip and worked up some insult. "'Even' a privateer ship?"

"Then they'll manage, won't they? You'll have to stay here."

"And no moving about between the decks," McCoy added.

"No moving between decks?" Kilvennan protested. More rules and regulations on ships that were supposed to make their own? "What is this, a prison ship? My family's below!"

The doctor's brown awning of hair cast a shadow over his eyes as he lowered his chin in a fatherly manner. "Captain, we're trying to keep a bronchial viral infection from spreading. Why can't we get some cooperation?"

"There's a rumor going around that you have medication but you're withholding it. True or not?"

McCoy's vibrant eyes glanced around, deeply troubled. He lowered his voice. "There's a critical shortage. Part of the medical stores have been contaminated. Some of the uncontaminated medication's been stolen. It's showing up here and there as contraband, but people are giving it to children who aren't very sick or who aren't even sick at all. We're trying to confiscate it and distribute it to the most severe cases first, including, I might add, your sister and your son. Can I count on your cooperation?"

Just like that, he wanted cooperation? Around them, the shouts and protests of the passengers proved that nothing would be that easy between the citizens of the new colony and Starfleet officers assigned to escort them. Escort, not overlord.

Yet, McCoy and the other doctors had been working tirelessly on the medical problem, Kilvennan had to admit. At least, that had been the outward appearance.

"What about the medicine you do have?" Kilvennan asked. "Are you withholding it?"

"We're withholding it," McCoy admitted, keeping his voice down, "because we need a base for synthesization. If we don't have any, we can't make more. What's making people so angry is that we have to give it to some test cases in order to develop a vaccine, which we need as badly as we need treatment. It's no good to cure part of the population if the disease keeps spreading. Eventually it'll outspread the medication we still have. I need enforcement. Are you here to help or not?"

The deadly statement drilled itself home right through the atmosphere of anger and fear on the open deck. Kilvennan scanned the frightened and angry people, his friends and neighbors, folks he would know for the rest of his life once they reached the new planet. On a whole planet, sixty-some thousand people wasn't very many. Somebody here would probably marry his daughter someday.

But he couldn't promise McCoy that he would unconditionally enforce rules just because Starfleet said he should. He had to find another way past this ugly moment.

"At least clear me to go to my family," he implored. "How long is this quarantine going to last?"

"We don't know yet!" McCoy flared with frustration. "We could handle all this if people would calm down and quit competing for attention. I can't treat them if I have to waste my time keeping them from infecting each—"

An eruption of fury drowned him out as Quinn Kilvennan broke through the security line and plunged forward, his hands driving at the throat of a security guard.

Trying to shove through crowd that surged after his brother, Kilvennan shouted, "Quinn, no!"

The guard's nightstick came up again, but Kilvennan was there. His shoulder plowed into his brother's rib cage, driving both of them off the guard. Together they crashed into a support strut as their neighbors jumped out of the way. Kilvennan felt his head ring off the strut and winced, clamping his eyes shut as stars rolled around in front of them. No—no time to fade out. He forced himself to open his eyes and deal with the throbbing of his skull. Familiar faces tumbled past as he unknotted himself and felt around for Quinn. There he was.

"Don't hit a Starfleet guard!" Kilvennan pulled his brother upright and held him by both arms, feeling the anger course through Quinn's body like electricity through a circuit. "What's the matter with you?"

"They're authoritarian murderers!" Quinn's young features twisted into an ugly mask. "Let go of me if you're not gonna fight them!"

From the crowd, Tom Coates's booming lumberjack voice carried over the general squabble. "Give us what you promised, McCoy!" Coates stepped through and helped both Kilvennans to their feet, but his motions were harsh, even threatening.

Wincing again as his head pounded, Kilvennan stood back to look into the faces of his brother and neighbors. What was wrong with them? Their faces were flushed, eyes ringed with red. Tom Coates was more like Santa Claus than a union boss—what was going on?

Before he could speak, the whine of phasers broke behind him. Instinctively he drove his brother and

Coates backward, down, out of the line of fire. Around them, dozens of people collapsed into a moaning heap.

"Killers!" Quinn raved.

Desperate, Kilvennan held him down and shouted. "No, no! It's just light phaser stun! Stay down!"

Rising from the heap, Kilvennan turned to Dr. McCoy and the security squad, and the half-dozen phasers now aimed at him. On the other side of the deck, a sheepish crowd of passengers now huddled, afraid they'd be stunned too. They were right.

"Don't shoot!" McCoy barked, grasping the arm of the nearest guard. "Captain Kilvennan, can you contain your friends?"

Heaving with exertion, Kilvennan started to shake his head but stopped when it hurt too much. "Don't know—they're acting strange. Quinn, you stay down or I'll knock you down myself! Tom, goes for you too."

"Don't order me around, Michael," Tom Coates roared. "My kid needs treatment! We have to turn back while there's time to get home before people start dying!"

Behind him, a pressing throng came forward again and shouted their agreement.

"Turn back?" Kilvennan repeated. "Who had ever said anything like that? Let me try to handle this, will you? Because this mess isn't doing it."

Coates's enormous paw came out of the crowd and grabbed him by the collar. "We didn't want Starfleet along in the first place! We hired you and the other privateers to protect us! Start doing your job!"

Kilvennan squinted at Tom, at the fist knotted into his collar, at his brother's pale lips and ringed eyes, and thought of his wife and children, in their quarters below on this Conestoga. Were they in the same condition?

"How 'bout if you stay here a minute," he ordered, in a tone he usually only used on his own crew.

Would they listen? Would they hold back until he could figure all this out? If they didn't, eventually he wouldn't be able to stop the guards from stunning them all and incarcerating them for inciting a riot. Law? Rules? Nobody was that sure what applied here in space.

Back at the Federation, everybody knew what the laws were. Out at Belle Terre, when they arrived, they would set up a court system and establish new laws of their own. Out here in space—nobody had every talked about that. The governor and Captain Kirk had wrangled back and forth since the Expedition left Federation space, and still the answers were fuzzy. What was the jurisdiction here?

Holding his hands up in a passive manner to the guards, Kilvennan made a silent bet that the guards would let him cross to Dr. McCoy without shooting him down. "Doctor, there's something else going on," he warned. "These people don't act like this, even when they're worked up. My brother's practically a monk, and I've never even seen Tom Coates work up a sweat."

"How can you say that about everybody here?"

"I can say it about my brother and Tom. I've known Tom and his wife Lilian most of my life. Something's wrong. Could that virus have symptoms you don't know about yet? Affect their behavior? Make them agitated like this? Look at their eyes. No blood in their lips. Even if they're angry, would they all have the same look in their faces?"

McCoy scanned the fuming crowd, held back by guards with phasers, and the groaning mass of people who had been stunned. He stooped beside a dazed passenger, pressed the man's eyelid up, and peered into his eye. "Hmm . . . Commander."

Uhura reappeared from a hatchway. "Right here, Doctor."

"I think we may have a medical reason our peaceful evacuation of a deck turned into a riot. I want to take one of these people back to the *Brother's Keeper* and run some tests. Can you keep the peace here?"

"I'll keep it if I have to tie them all down and tickle their children. All right, you people, order has been restored, is that clear?" With her queenly presence casting a distinct damper on the waves of rage, Uhura motioned to the guards. "We will now continue the *peaceful* evacuation of decks four and nine so they can be sterilized. Any further incidents will result in arrests and charges."

"Here." Kilvennan stepped away, and when he came back he was dragging Quinn. "Take my brother. He tests great."

"Are you flipped?" Quinn heeled back. "Turn myself over to these tyrants? They'll dissect me!"

Kilvennan pulled him close, got him by the back of the neck, and made him pay attention. "You'll live through it. I'll handle things here."

"Liar! You're never here!"

"Take him." Burying his anguish at the sight of his brother in this foreign condition, Kilvennan roughly handed him to the two nearest guards. "Doctor, I want to see my family."

McCoy snapped his fingers at the hatchway guards. "Clear him through!"

"Mae? Mae!"

Kilvennan jogged past three fistfights and two arguments in his family's corridor on the giant people-mover *Yukon*. The innards of the Conestogas were brilliantly designed, with four- and six-person family units that had fold-in sleeping racks and modest communal living areas with some games and a café. They'd all known the lifestyle here would be spare and that was the price they were willing to pay for several months. This way of life was hardest on the littlest kids, who just didn't understand why they'd given up their lawns and trees and planetside playgrounds, their own rooms and unlimited choices for dinner for a really weird set of bunk beds.

Teenagers had a hard time getting off by themselves. Adults were crammed together into a mutual living environment where decisions had to be cooperative and where cooperation frequently meant giving in or being quiet. Not easy for a bunch of people who were going off to find elbow room and a chance to freewheel. Living like bees wasn't in their nature.

Relief plunged through him at the first sight of his wife—anything could happen when a couple was separated in space. Even to see her each time gave him a thrill, but especially now.

He was relieved, until Mae ran to him and lathered him not with an embrace but with a crack of her hand across his face.

"Where've you been!"

Kilvennan dropped back a couple of steps. "Are you flipped? Why'd you hit me?"

"Oh, I don't know!" She pressed a hand to the side of her head, the cloud of wild auburn curls squeezed between her fingers. She wore only a long red GO DRAGONS T-shirt that picked up the flush in her cheeks, and a pair of fuzzy slippers somebody gave her as a going-away present. "The whole ship's been a nightmare all day, Michael."

"Something funny's going on. Where's Mom and Stefan and the kids?"

"Where's Quinn?" Mae threw up both hands. "What're you doing here? You broke the quarantine! Now you have to stay. What about the *Moon?* Can Troy run the ship in these conditions?"

"Didn't you just hit me for . . . never mind. How's Ian?"

"He's had a fever all day and a cough all the way down to his toes. Why won't they give us the medication?"

"Dr. McCoy explained the problem to me."

"I don't want to hear it." She stalked away, back toward the quad unit.

Kilvennan blinked. "You don't want to hear it? Mae, listen—"

"Ahoy, Kilvennans!"

Just at the door of their quad, they both turned to see Billy Maidenshore trundling elegantly toward them, patting others on the back and glad-handing his way down the corridor.

"Billy!" Mae hurried to him. "How'd you get in through the quarantine?"

"There's a breakdown in the beam shield," the big man said, giving her a juicy hug. "I can only stay a minute or two or they'll get wise. How y'been?"

"Awful," Mae said.

"Weird," Kilvennan added.

His wife sank back against the door's edge and gazed into the place where their children struggled just to breathe. "I wish we'd never come. Lilian and Tom are talking about turning back while we still have the chance . . . before we get too far. . . . Nobody told us it was going to be like this. How can we stand it all the way?"

His chest constricting, Kilvennan watched his wife's misery and feared to tell her how much worse things yet could turn, that they were approaching the halfway point, that Gamma Night would soon enhance their burdens and lengthen their voyage, that the belt would have to be tightened even more. How could he talk to her in this state? With her mind flicking like a candle?

"We've got our dreams and our plans, Mae, honey," Billy Maidenshore told her, rubbing her shoulders with affection and concern. "You're one of the strong ones, you'll make it through, all the way to our new planet. You and the Coateses, the Brocks and Sawyers, you're the tough kind that makes it. All you need is a little help along the way . . . and I think Uncle Billy's got you covered."

He glanced up and down the corridor, then stepped just inside the quad and pulled a med hypo out of his suit pocket.

"Take it, quick. Three cc's for each child, five for adults. It's for you and the Coates family. I've got enough for three other families too. I'm working on getting more."

"What's that?" Mae demanded. "Billy—the lung flu medicine? Oh—oh!" She plunged forward and clamped her arms around him, pressing her face to his chest.

"Sweetheart," Maidenshore crooned, "think I don't know what my pals need? Keep your voice down, hon."

"Wait a minute," Kilvennan interrupted. "That's contraband. You're the one who's been stealing it?"

"Michael, who cares?" Mae wailed. "It's a miracle!"

Maidenshore frowned and sighed a wounded sigh. "Stealing? Skulking around? Does that sound like the Billy Maidenshore you know? It's being contrabanded by the people who stole it."

"How do we know it's not you?" Kilvennan asked again.

"Because if it was me, Mike, think, think—I'd be selling it, wouldn't I? I'm *giving* it to you. I've been using my resources to track it down and buy it up, so I can pass it along. Why shouldn't I do what I'm able to? I'm making sure the people I care about get it first."

Uneasy with what he saw, both repulsed and magnetized, Kilvennan shifted on his nerve ends. "Billy, the hospital ship needs that formula in order to make more."

"They've got enough for that." Maidenshore looked him square in the eyes. "They just want it all. You know how Starfleet is—they want all the balls in their court. You're not turning sacred on me, are you, Mike? With your own kids and your little sister in there, dying maybe? Now, I've got to get out of here before that beam shield goes back up, so I need an answer. What kind of a guy are you, Mike? Know a good thing when you see it? Even if Starfleet has it, somebody'll get this first. Why not you?"

"Why not us?" Mae's eyes, beseeching, swung upward. "Michael? . . . Why not us?"

# Chapter Seven

"FLASHED BY a Kauld battlebarge?" Shucorion peered upward at Garitt's instruments. "You must be mistaken. The Blind is fouling your intake."

In the time necessary for the data to be checked, their final chance of slipping into the silence of the Blind withered away. They stood now in the position of the little survey ship, caught out of the darkness by a more powerful and unconquerable enemy.

"Definite now," Dimion confirmed Garitt's readings. "All systems are clearing. The flash . . . it names you personally! From . . ."

These pauses were aggravating. Shucorion's hands were cold now. "Who is it, Dimion? Speak up."

Abruptly Dimion's wide shoulders drew tight. He seemed to shrink from his normal massive size to a withered shell. He struggled for breath. His lips hung open several seconds. Crimped and desperate, his eyes turned to Shucorion.

"Battlelord Vellyngaith!" he blurted. Immediately he scoured his panel strips again. "I must be wrong. . . ."

"Vellyngaith!" Shucorion gazed at the flickering image as the concave vision screen tried to draw in enough data to make a picture of the approaching battlebarge. "Vellyngaith . . . on that ship?"

"No," Dimion protested. "I must be wrong."

"Flash them and ask."

Garitt gripped the two sides of his pilot station. "We'll be giving our position away. We might still—"

"They already know we're here," Shucorion said.

Sensible words added tension while Dimion sent a message that might be their last.

"The barge flashes that Vellyngaith is on board," he finally said. "The barge is the *Tonclin*. Does that sound right? Have you heard anything about Vellyngaith on a battlebarge named that?"

"They might be trying to frighten us," Garrit suggested, his hands icy on the piloting station.

"It's too late to check with Core Command. Battlelord Vellyngaith . . . and he claims to speak and not fight?"

"So he claims. This can't be good. A battlebarge has three times our vigorants. His kinetics alone are over—"

Shucorion held up a hand. Dimion stopped speaking, clamping his lips upon the words that might've come next.

"He must've found out," Shucorion murmured. "He must know about the . . . why else would he flash? If he knows, we're finished."

His men watched him fearfully. To them, he was

babbling. Perhaps he had cracked. Of course, they couldn't possibly know why he was behaving this way. Should he tell them?

"Stack everything," he ordered, forcing himself to think about their survival for a few more minutes. "Prepare for a fishtail run in case he attacks. Load the drain margins and propulsion undercasters. Lock the tow bolts and buckle them. Activate the dynadrive. Garitt, stitch our way out of this system. We'll get away if we can."

"Avedon," Garitt responded from pilot bench. From his posture they could all tell that Garitt was ready to fight. He was like Ulwen had been, always volunteering to be first, determined to get a job done faster as if that made things better. Work solved everything.

Shucorion believed that also, but in the past few minutes he had watched Ulwen die at the hands of unexpected skill. The crew would be less likely to want to surge ahead this time.

Throughout history there had been a few tales of Blood pilots escaping from the more aggressive Kauld Marauders, but never from a battlebarge. Unlike the men around him, Shucorion entertained the idea briefly, a song of heroism and impossible events, but sense quickly returned.

"If there is a way out of this, I'll have to be more clever than Vellyngaith," he said aloud, "not stronger. I must be something he cannot estimate, like the unknown ship we faced."

Quietly afraid, Dimion paled to vapor-blue. He remained hunched over his strip-panel, his eyes fixed on the pictures and numbers. "It's said Vellyngaith can charm his enemies into poisoning themselves."

When Dimion looked up, Shucorion offered him a little smile. "I won't eat anything."

A loud *crack* rang in the inner skin plates of the Plume. Dimion's thick body jumped. "What was that? Did he strike us?"

"No. Structural fatigue." When Dimion gawked at him in a stew of nervous anticipation, Shucorion added, "I *was* a mining engineer."

This seemed to ease Dimion's terror somewhat, and when the flash sang again he was capable of checking it. "Vellyngaith wants to speak to you."

"Yes . . . now we'll see if he knows. Put him through."

Anticipation strangled any other words as the communications system clicked and hummed to collect signals as the Blind waned. As it came every day, the fading of the Blind offered new chances, although hiding would not be one of those. Stealth was only possible while the sensor intakes were masked.

A tremor rolled through his stomach at the sight of the people's mortal enemy. The Kauld men, with their feathers and beads, always seemed to be flaunting their wealth, showing off the fact that they had time to decorate themselves. Vellyngaith's features were dark azure, his hair the startling silver of sunrise, his squared eyes and once-broken nose from that famous incident were a kind of shock in themselves. The famous battlelord's appearance was well known among Blood and no surprise, but somehow seeing him now and knowing he was so very close by caused Shucorion a strong and unsmotherable reaction of cold in his gut.

*"You are Shucorion,"* Vellyngaith said. *"Avedon of Plume Savage Ten."*

Rather than confirm what they both apparently knew, Shucorion studied the vision of his people's archenemy. "Why are you speaking to me instead of attacking? Is this a trick?"

*"No. I have a truce for you."*

Shucorion's stomach twisted. To begin with lies?

"Why would you have anything for me?" he asked.

*"You're known among Blood Many as one who tries new things. When I saw your ship approach the foreign surveyor, I knew it must be Shucorion who would risk coming this far."*

"I took no risks," Shucorion denied. "We've known the surveyor was here for many months. It was time to drive them off."

*"I agree."*

"Obviously, since you destroyed them."

*"May I come aboard your Plume?"*

Beside Shucorion, Dimion gasped audibly, enough to be certain Vellyngaith had heard it even over the incompatible communications flash. Above and around them, the other crewmen were chokingly still at the beguiling request. Never before in all history had any Kauld battlelord approached any Blood in this way. Not battlelords or anybody. Never had a Kauld come aboard a Blood Plume or any Blood vessel as anything more than a prisoner.

Very rare, prisoners.

Mute with astoundment, Shucorion could barely breathe, much less answer. For several moments he didn't try. There was only one reasonable answer—Vellyngaith must know about the middle moon. He must've seen the glowing matter and known how to read the numbers as Shucorion had. He was coming with no truce, but with a final threat.

That had to be it.

Vellyngaith waited without repeating his outlandish beckoning. He understood what such a possibility meant to a Blood avedon.

Yet there was a grinding respect due so high an official, even in the enemy fleet. Pressure.

"Come aboard?" he tasted. "Come aboard . . ." When repeating the incantation didn't help him see a clear way out, he asked, "Why did you destroy the scanner ship?"

*"To keep them from knowing,"* Vellyngaith said.

Shivering under his tunic, Shucorion leaned forward without taking a step. "From knowing what?"

*"Whatever they were here to discover. We must keep them from knowing anything about our star cluster that might encourage them to come here."*

Perfectly irritating. Not a bit of snobbery. Simple statement of facts.

"A moment of privacy." Clicking off the communications link himself, he folded his arms and continued to gaze at the screen, which now showed Vellyngaith in silence, waiting for an answer. To Dimion he asked, "What do you think?"

Dimion's complexion had faded still more. He whispered as if Vellyngaith could still hear. "This can't be good."

"Don't take the chance," Garitt agreed. "There's risk in it."

"It's against survival," Dimion said, shored up by Garitt. "Tell him to go away."

"Do you think he'll go?" Shucorion asked. "If we fight, he'll kill us. If we run, he'll chase us and kill us. We can't hide without the Blind. If I meet with him, let him say what he wants. He may still kill us, but we will have a fighting chance to kill him first."

"You're not thinking this can be good, do you?" Dimion interrupted. He grasped Shucorion's elbow fiercely this time. "Are you thinking that way?"

"No, of course not." Shucorion tugged out of the grip. "However . . . is there less risk in speaking with him than in telling him to go away and hoping he will actually go?"

"Hope is a bad idea," Garitt agreed. "But speaking to him is a risk too. What should we do?"

Shucorion took a step away, to a place on the curve where he could be more or less perceived as standing alone.

"Until now," he contemplated, "Blood Many held our own in the Elliptical Wars. Those times are over. The Formless have given us the terrible gift of dynadrive. The Elliptical Wars are finished. Now we have the war that will never end, until Kauld defeat us eventually. We Blood are the poorer force, the weaker force. We have no time now to rest and rebuild. Vellyngaith knows he possesses the superior power. If he knows that, why would he approach us with some kind of passive offering? Now that I know about . . ."

He stopped himself from telling them, and paused to think about his own words, to scour his logic for flaws. What did Vellyngaith know?

"I must find out what he knows," he continued. "This time, I'll have to take the risk over the hope."

"Only you would think that way," Dimion uttered with both admiration and apprehension. "I don't know how you do it. No one else can think the way you do."

"You know my past," Shucorion reminded. "I may be the only one again."

Dimion quivered. "But what if this borders on recklessness?"

"No, no, no. I simply have two bad possibilities and I have to pick one. Keep everyone working. Be careful not to hope. Let me speak to him again. Are you ready to make history?"

# Chapter Eight

ON DECK SAVAGE, between the rows of fighters resting upon the curved skin of the ship, waiting for deployment, Shucorion stood with Dimion and six other armed guards, all brandishing their armor and hand weapons. Two of them held punch-grenades, primed and glowing.

In the ten transfer caskets, all ten of them, red-hot shimmering energy scrambled and roared.

"He has a squad of ten, Avedon," the deck guard, Derron, reported. He turned to his own squad of guards and ordered, "Double-load!"

Shucorion made no countermand. Derron was right to take precautions, even to the point of handing Shucorion a weapon to hold. Each guard now held two weapons, and each of those was double-loaded. Ten Kauld could never get out of here alive. Not all ten.

When the hot caskets began to cool, the ten clouds faded back and revealed the sweat-glazed forms of Battlelord Vellyngaith, two Foilsmen, a full Marksman, and two Bladers. Interesting diplomatic corps.

Each Kauld wore a heavily padded purple jacket, buckled at the waist, and padded skintight trousers that looked uncomfortable. Unlike Blood, they all wore the same color. Uniforms. A wasteful and frivolous convention. Only the beading on the shoulders and down the fronts of the uniforms was different, made of shells and polished stones from the Kauld planet. Who had time for such ornamentation? Every boot had a feather dangling from the front, just below the knee, and they all had more feathers plaited into their hair. No Blood ever had so much time to frill.

Shucorion suddenly felt very plain. He stepped forward a little, so Vellyngaith would see that he wasn't hiding behind his men.

The great battlelord, famous in two civilizations, came forward too, as if there were no weapons nor any other soldiers in the hall at all. His eyes fixed upon Shucorion and never shifted. He was shorter than the legends said.

"I thought you were the man who takes risks," Vellyngaith commented, nodding at the bristle of guards.

"You're wrong," Shucorion told him. "Rumors exaggerate. Especially rumors that flow between the Blood Many and All Kauld. Say what you came to say."

The Kauld battlelord gazed at him as if they had known each other much longer than these few seconds. "Alliance," he proffered. "I knew Blood would not listen. I thought you might."

The entire deck dropped to complete silence. Even the soft whisper of the Plume's engines and ventilation seemed suddenly to lose its breath.

"Alliance," Shucorion repeated. "Alliance . . ."

"Yes."

"Why?"

"It has become necessary for us to join forces. Kauld and Blood will be stronger together."

"We could've been stronger together a thousand years ago. Why today?"

As he heard his tone take a bitter edge, Shucorion interrupted himself. Under the burning eyes of the Kauld squad and of his own deck guards, he gathered his inner strengths and continued. Would Vellyngaith tell him if he knew about the moon?

"Since the Formless gave us dynadrive," Shucorion said, "we have no rest from the eternal conflict between us. With starspeed, we can reach each other's planet any time. We will never rest again. Kauld have every reason to rejoice and no reason to offer a friend's hand to us. Yet you come today to speak with me, at a time when alliance makes no sense for you. True?"

"In the way you mean it, yes, it's true."

"This is mystifying, Battlelord."

"I took information from that ship before I destroyed it. We have translated it now, and it speaks of trouble for us all." The elegant enemy paused, realizing he wasn't being believed.

Not a good start, to begin with a lie, Shucorion thought. He knew Vellyngaith had been monitoring the survey ship's transmissions for months and clumsily translating the messages.

Vellyngaith let a few seconds slip by, then spoke bluntly. "New people are coming to this cluster. They call themselves 'Federation.' "

"And you just dragged their representatives into the moon," Shucorion snapped. "Many have prodded around this cluster. Prinda, Meram, the Formless—all have passed by this star system for one or another reason. Bad strategic location, unremarkable properties, too far-flung, or wrong for their bodies somehow. Why do you bother to destroy a little scan ship out by itself?"

"You sent a Savage to attack the scan ship too, Avedon."

"I wanted only to drive them out. It wasn't in my plans to destroy them."

Vellyngaith narrowed his deepset eyes. "Were you squeamish about killing them?"

"Killing them would not have served me yet. My plan was to drive them off, strand them in open space, and let them limp away. They would have reported to their people that they found hostility here and were violently driven away. Then they would have left us alone. Now that you've destroyed them, their people will come searching for them. You, Battlelord, have sent an irresistible flash to Federation and beckoned them here."

A gritty silence fell between them. The battlelord's eyes hardened as if there were a real chemical change occurring, so strong were his emotions. His hands clenched. His guards raised their weapons a few inches, drawing upon subtle signals from their leader. His lips pressed and worked. Despite the overture of approach, Shucorion felt the cruel vibrations of pure animosity.

"I had not thought of that," Vellyngaith admitted when he could speak again. "You have an interesting mind, Avedon. However, my actions change nothing. The information from the scanner ship told of many horrifying things. The size of Federation, first of all—according to the records, they are enormous! Far more immense than you can imagine. Your people and mine have been locked together for generations and always will be, but we have always lived in a great empty ocean. Now the ocean is crowding. The scanner ship's log tells us that Federation is coming here, now, as we speak today, in a great single movement of ships. They mean to settle this planet."

Shucorion pointed at the wide viewing portal at the end of the Savage deck. "That planet?"

"Yes."

"But you Kauld . . ."

"Yes, my own people have a plan to build our first off-world base there. So you know about it?"

"Everyone knows about—" Shucorion's mind began to spin off a simple answer to a very complex possibility as he realized what Vellyngaith had just said. Yes, everyone knew that the Kauld were planning to construct a huge military base to house their entire force, to replace the facility that had served them through so many Elliptical Wars. Ambitious—and fantastical in its providence. They were building it off their world!

Instantly he couldn't contain himself. His hand once again flew toward the vision on the screen. *"That* planet?"

Control yourself! Don't give anything away! Don't laugh.

He clamped his lips shut and fought to drive the raving delight from his face. Sober, sober, don't give it away. He knew they were planning to build off their world, but on this particular planet?

"Seems," he struggled, "inconvenient. . . . Why . . . would Kauld bother to build a fortress away from your world? How could you defend your world?"

"With starspeed we will be able to defend." Vellyngaith turned suddenly gaunt in the face, as if this observation disturbed him. "With all these changes, we must all start thinking in a more interstellar way, Avedon."

What kind of answer was that? Kauld were not known for their philosophy.

"Are you," Shucorion prodded, "prepared to build there soon?"

"We're making preparations. This is the first time for us to move off our planet. We are forced to do most of the building in established facilities, then move the constructed parts. And, of course, you Blood would rather we failed."

The critical moment had arrived. Shucorion's next claims would be the hinge upon which the future would turn. *Yes, I would prefer failure, if I didn't know what I know today.*

Moving slowly, Shucorion forced himself to pace as if in thought, as if changing his mind.

"I would rather you failed," he stalled, thinking hard. "A Kauld installation of significant proportions, outside of our binary system, would be troublesome for Blood. It would be our end."

"You were here to look at the planet, weren't you?" Vellyngaith asked candidly.

Guarding his expression, Shucorion faced him and handed him his deception back in a new form. "We could never hope to stop your constructions, Battlelord. Both our races are weak with repeated conflict through the generations. You can barely expand, and we could not possibly stop you."

Vellyngaith nodded. "We want to expand, but it is difficult while in the middle of conflict that will never rest from now on. We can build an installation, put our army there, and spend the next years destroying Blood. Or you and I, today, can make history."

Shucorion smiled, letting a hint of his overwhelming delight spark through. "We've already done that, Battlelord."

"Yes, though more can happen," Vellyngaith said.

"You can join me, as a signal to your people that things need not be destruction between us anymore. We could destroy you all, or all of you can live under our hand. Life is better, I think."

Oh, this was too much. Shucorion folded his arms. "What do you want? Why offer me this?"

"Because Federation is coming. It changes everything."

"How does it change everything?"

"If they build on that planet before Kauld can make our installation, we will never have the strength to dislodge them. Federation is soft and warm and harmless . . . until you cut it. Then it is all claws and teeth. Both Kauld and Blood should be concerned that Federation be kept away from here, or we will undoubtedly be under them."

True, then. Vellyngaith didn't know what the sparkles in space meant. He hadn't analyzed them correctly. Otherwise he wouldn't still be talking about wanting that planet.

Was that possible? Was Shucorion the only man in space who possessed the specialized knowledge to decipher those readings? The surge of realization nearly made him laugh, an eruption which he managed to catch back at the last second. *Astounding!*

"There's nothing essential for them on that planet," he pointed out carefully. "It hasn't even any name."

"They have named it. In their language they call it 'Belter.' "

"Belter . . . What does that mean?"

"We have no idea what it means," Vellyngaith said.

"Why would they build there?"

"According to the recorder library of the scan ship, they seem to do things just to do them. They come to live on planets where the air and water are right for them, and even tolerate extremes of temperature."

"What do they do on these planets?"

"Live on them, apparently."

"Leave their homes without a reason?"

Vellyngaith's squarish eyes widened. "Adventure is their reason. Wanderlust."

"Adventure . . ." Shucorion squinted at the word, shook his head, paused, tried to imagine such a wild unessential goal, then shook his head again. Wanderlust? *Wanderlust.*

"To us it seems frivolous," Vellyngaith confirmed. "But they do it. We have come to believe, if we interpret their messages correctly, that Federation has conquered planets far-flung for light-years around their primary star system. If they're coming here, we must all learn to think differently for the first time in our history. You, Shucorion, among Blood, are the one who thinks differently."

Cautious before his own men, Shucorion made no claim to that accusation, remaining noncommittal and silent.

"You're right," Vellyngaith went on. "Kauld and Blood have battled each other to weakness. Before dynadrive, the years of separation between cycles gave us a chance to rebuild and face each other again with strength, but those periods of rest are gone forever. If Federation settles here while we are still weak, this will be their space by the time of the next cycle. They'll overrun both of us. The time for fighting between us will have to be over. I am surprised too. Necessity is a hard bargainer."

Shucorion gazed at the other man's piercing eyes in their squarish frame of silver lashes. "Are you lying?"

*Are you pretending not to know about the moon?*

Vellyngaith made no oaths. "Federation will bring a

139

thousand fighting men for every Kauld and Blood man, woman, apprentice, or infant. We must establish our installation on their chosen planet, so they decide not to come here at all. Unless we work together, we will be their next conquest."

Unpleasant, these new ideas.

Shucorion nodded, mostly to himself. "Killing each other *was* getting a little dull. . . ."

"We saw no other way," Vellyngaith said. "Now the other way has found us."

Disturbing, to get words from your enemy which seemed completely truthful. Strange, odd, unbalanced.

"What do you want?" Shucorion asked forthrightly.

"I want you to carry a message of cooperation to Blood Core. We must work to discourage Federation from coming to our star cluster long enough for my people to build our army fortress. Then, Kauld and Blood can embark on a future that will not leave us all dead and our planets barren. I believe that you, Avedon Shucorion, among your people have the nerve to do this."

Without waiting for further discussion, Vellyngaith cast one glance at Dimion, then gestured his men back to the transfer caskets. "Will you transfer us back alive, or shall I contact my barge?"

"You will go back alive," Shucorion promised. "If I have you killed in the transfer process, your barge will slaughter us all."

"Yes." Vellyngaith stepped into the first casket, and his men stepped into their own, until all ten were loaded. "Take time to think. You will come to the conclusion that this is not a risk. To show you that I do not lie today, you and your Plume will be allowed to leave this star system, no matter what you decide."

\* \* \*

"He went!" Dimion gasped. "You made him go! How did you do that? He's letting us live when he could sla—"

"He wants us alive," Shucorion said, "or so he tells me. He calls it 'time to think.'"

Lowering as if weak, Dimion sat on a Savage's landing strut and groaned. "Thinking is dangerous. He's trying to make us confused."

Shucorion folded his arms and looked down at him. Nearby, Derron and his squad watched their leader with undisguised nervousness. Some of the guards had rushed back to their posts to watch the Kauld battle-barge warily, to see if Vellyngaith's word turned out to be worth anything, but Derron and the primary squad would remain here to escort Shucorion back to the control core, where he would make his decisions known to the rest of the crew.

"He has succeeded then. I'm confused," he admitted. "Overtures of peace? Why? Dynadrive was the last curse for Blood. It eliminated the period of rest between wars. The Kauld were ultimately going to defeat us, because we would never again catch up to all their advantages. Now Federation is poking around, and suddenly the Kauld want truce? It doesn't make sense. There can only be one reason. Kauld want to build their fortress on that . . . on 'Belter,' while Blood go off to fight someone stronger. This is a way for them to keep us fighting while they rest and build their installation away from the disasters of our solar system."

"You're not going to do it, are you?" Dimion stood up, his legs shaking. "If they're willing to let us get away . . ."

"Nothing comes without a price, Dimion." Shucorion paced away a few steps, staring at the deck. "I've been thinking about the Blood Curse, our people saddled with a star system that brings us to war every few generations. And now this enormous change . . . and that moon . . ."

His mind spun. He pressed his knuckles to the sides of his head.

"Vellyngaith's forces are stronger, but not so strong that they need not keep an eye on the Blood Many. Now he conjures to spread us out, make us thin, weaker. But I see another possibility here. He doesn't know about that moon."

"What about it?" Dimion asked.

Shucorion almost told him, but held back. He was still locked in his own rocketing thoughts. "Is this an opportunity? Do we dare think in terms of trying something so radically new?"

Derron and the other guardsmen came around the ring to gather near him, to listen to what their avedon and Dimion were saying to each other. Shucorion preferred privacy, but how could he have it? They were all understandably curious, hovering here on the edge of destruction and having just made history. Shucorion felt their eyes and wished away those expressions of trust and near-worship. He had stoked his own legend in favor of his people, and these men were the truest believers. Many, like Dimion, had been clearance contractors who worked after every disaster, who took their refuge in that occupation, for there was always work. Without work, what future was there?

Instead they had come to space with him, to forge a new kind of future.

"I was like any other Blood," Shucorion mused, "until the one day when I got lazy and took a risk. That's all it was, you know, laziness. Yet things suddenly became better for me. You know the story. What if

I am the instrument of change for all our people?" Careful not to meet the eye of any man, to corner any individual into declaring belief aloud, he wondered, "What if a curse runs out with enough work?"

"What does that mean?" Dimion asked. "Are you saying you'll become Vellyngaith's ally? What if Core Command disagrees?"

"If they disagree . . ." Shucorion allowed his words to trail off as he considered more alternatives than most of his people would dare.

Disagree?

Almost immediately he made his decision. "I won't tell them."

His men stared at him. The risk bewildered them. Yet they were tempted by his example.

Quickly, to smother any idea that he was going too far over a line, he went on. "If I tell Blood Core, then they'll be forced to make a decision that should be mine, in a situation I invited to happen. If I take action myself, without consulting them, then the disaster will be my fault and Core will be able to claim truthfully that they sanctioned nothing I did. Vellyngaith won't be able to use my mistake against Blood, because no one will know but us."

Speaking for a crew of ninety, people who trusted him,

"You are favored among Blood." Dimion gazed at him in the way Shucorion hated and also relied upon. "You may be the one to turn the curse away."

Shucorion let a few moments pass, the new idea settle in. "We mustn't hope. But if things can change for us, Dimion, I may be the element of that change. If we can once turn the future in our favor, the Blood Curse might be broken forever."

This was a day for astonishments, one after the other.

The men around him freely showed their apprehension and with their silence gave him permission to get them all killed. None wanted to be the first to speak up against him. For a moment he took this as a testimonial, only moments later to decide that they had been ready to die in space together for a long time and that this was but one more step toward the inevitable.

Not today, though.

"Why would they bother to build a new fortress at all? As far as they know, they've won. They have star-drive, and they are stronger than Blood. That means they've won if they simply bide their time. Why embark on a massive movement of all their forces off-world?"

"Could they be trying to reduce potential losses by separating targets?"

"Possibly. Because their planet is more stable, they've always been able to house and train all their military people in one massive complex on the lower hemisphere of their planet, away from the rest of the population. With star-drive, they can be on two planets, put their fleet strength away from our star system, avoid the Ellipse disasters, and never have to rebuild their military base because of storms or quakes."

Frantic, Dimion gulped, "We can't let them build there!"

Shucorion put out a calming hand. "Things are not as they seem anymore. I believe, at last, the Blood Curse is lifting for us."

"How? Do you think we can stop them from building it?"

"No, no . . . not stop them. Everything is different today." Shucorion spoke slowly, intending to be completely clear, if not understood. "Today, I *want* them to build their base."

"You *want*—" Dimion choked on his own words. "But that's—that's—"

"Treason. I know." Ripples of amazement—no, even horror—broke and ran from face to face among the crew. No one knew what to say.

"The Federation surveyor has given me a template," Shucorion went on. "How gallant, how robust they were! I expected them to run. I would've run and come back later. They turned and stood their ground . . . even during the Elliptical War I never saw anything like that. I have to learn from it, or we'll fail. Dimion, get me all the recordings you can find that come from Federation's signals."

"Avedon," Dimion responded, exhausted and perplexed.

Someday he would have his answers.

"From now on," Shucorion whispered, "we will have to take the initiative. It's me, Dimion . . . it's my providence. I am gifted to break the Curse. I will meet their gallantry with stealth, their robustness with deviltry. And never again will I underestimate the people of Federation. So I must be clever. Find some way to keep them from coming here, long enough for the Kauld to establish their base. I want them to finish it. I want them to move their entire military force to live in it, as long as they do it on that planet. A beautiful planet."

Stepping away from them, he gazed at the view cylinder, showing a passive picture of the Kauld battlebarge flowing away in the greater distance, and the planet now called Belter by its Federation surveyors.

"Breathable," he murmured, "pleasant . . . doomed."

# Chapter Nine

"WE DON'T KNOW who's causing these problems. Apparently no one's going to volunteer, so let's start in another place. *Why* would anybody do these things?"

The *Enterprise*'s refitted briefing room was a rather unwelcoming place, despite the high design and futuristic materials, the black glossy table that wouldn't take a fingerprint, and the wide viewing ports curving along one whole wall. Every time Kirk came in here he wanted the old briefing room back.

The litany of problems besetting the convoy was taking on the din of a funeral bell. Every day there was something more, something else, something new to go wrong. Supplies had dwindled faster than anyone expected. Rationing had taken its toll on civilians who had never lived this way or had to deprive themselves. Kirk and his command team had been flitting from ship to ship, putting out "fires" that ranged from "let's turn

146

back" discussions to a mutiny on one Conestoga that Kirk had ordered to share its supplies with three other Conestogas.

The turn-back club was small, but growing.

Moments alone like this, with Spock and McCoy and nobody else, had become cherished and rare during this expedition. He saw McCoy less and less, with the doctor shuttling between the mercy ship and medical hot spots all over the fleet. Even Spock had his hands full coordinating all the first officers and keeping his finger on science concerns as well. He'd hardly seen Scotty at all, and Sulu, Chekov, and Uhura were so happy with their fleet assignments it seemed a shame to give them any grief. In deference to them, knowing they had their hands full, Kirk had forced himself to make all the decisions, even taken on more than he should, and the load was becoming oppressive. He needed advice.

Sign of weakness? Age? Maybe.

Glad to be doing something, even something menial, Kirk got a cup of coffee for himself and one for McCoy, who was seated in the middle of the absurdly large table. Nearby, Spock gazed out at the trail of Expedition ships spilling out in the darkness, mostly just shadowy shapes distinguished only by the hazy glow of a nebula they were passing.

"We know we've got some nefarious characters on this expedition," McCoy provided, "starting with four ships chock-full of itinerant privateers who won't let us have security clearance rights on their crew manifests. Anybody could be lurking around on those vessels. We've got shady personalities like Billy Maidenshore, Eli Samms, and others with even worse records who want to make a clean start, or say they do—"

"The instigators could be among the privateer captains themselves," Spock pointed out. "They have steadily resisted Starfleet authority, and if Starfleet remains at Belle Terre to patrol the Sagittarius Star Cluster, it could undermine their value to the colonists."

"All except Kilvennan," Kirk crisply claimed. "It's not him."

Spock tipped his head. "How do you know?"

"Just have a feeling."

Kirk blew across the top of his steaming coffee and inhaled the sweet aroma. If only he could crawl in there and let his muscles soak in the heat. "We've got to start anticipating trouble rather than just reacting to it. Bones, get with Chekov and cobble together a team skilled in terrain intelligence. Pull people from security, SAR, HazMat, and planetary specialists. Sulu could serve both as a captain and a botanical advisor."

McCoy nodded. "I'll do it, but what for?"

"If we run out of food, we might have to forage a passing planet."

Kirk buried an internal shudder. He didn't even like the sound of that, raiding some other planet, breaking off the main track, taking such an enormous risk. Even rationing was a better option. Suddenly he wished he'd talked himself out of even mentioning this to McCoy. Judging from the doctor's expression, the concept was as unwelcome to him as it was to the captain.

"Don't worry, Bones," Kirk assured, "it's a last resort. If we play our cards right, it'll never happen. Don't forget the passive measures—cover, concealment, camouflage, protective construction."

"All right, Jim. There's a new officer in Search and Rescue over on the *Beowulf* who'd be just right for this. I'm sure Captain Austin will let me borrow her."

"Good. And, Spock, we need more trained service

troops. Maintenance, supply, and evac. Choose people who can continue the duty when we reach Belle Terre and act as the landing zone control party. Have them phaser-certified. We might want armed reconnaissance. Train them to establish and operate communications signal devices, ground installations, and a matériel pipeline."

Turning from his commune with the stars, Spock paced inboard, away from the viewports. "I suggest putting Mr. Carpenter from *American Rover* in charge."

"Jack Carpenter," Kirk commented. "I remember him. He's everywhere, like chain lightning. He comes up with solutions before we ever hear we've got problems."

"Yes, he's been acting as chartering broker, finding space on various ships to shift ordnance, supplies, and personal freight to better facilitate warp trim."

"Maybe he's your saboteur, Jim," McCoy commented, sipping his coffee. "Somebody who's moving around from ship to ship all the time, access to secure areas, good general knowledge of mechanics and procedures—"

Kirk pondered that, then dismissed it with certain distaste. "I hate to think anyone who's been that much help could do so much damage. Carpenter and Captain Smith and Colonel Glass from the Pathfinders on the *Rover* have been on my A-list for problem solving since we embarked."

"See?" McCoy made a definitive gesture. "An evil disguise."

Kirk leveled a finger at him. "Don't tamper with my A-list. It's all I've got."

Sixty-four thousand civilians. Pushing down the butterflies in his stomach, Kirk tried not to show his nerves flickering. Spock's X-ray eyes could see them, no doubt, and he hadn't succeeded in hiding anything from McCoy in twenty years. Must be hiding from himself.

"What about the governor, Jim?" McCoy suggested. "Could young Sir Evan have some ulterior motive? Trying to make himself look good by refusing to give up or even think about turning back? It wouldn't be the first time a politician fiddled with events to make himself look good. He holds a high post, covets historical legacy, he's young, could be influenced by underworld powers—"

"Barry Giotto's already combed through that," Kirk dismissed. "It was the first thing we thought of. Evan Pardonnet's a decent young man. He doesn't want to be treated as if he's special. I also believe he doesn't see clearly that other people can be rotten under the skin. He's so can-do that he doesn't consider what could go wrong, or that some people might make things go wrong on purpose. He's suspected me all along of wanting credit for his project . . . I don't want credit. I want them to succeed. I'll do anything in my power to make that happen."

They both looked at him now. He was cracking like a melon. They sensed it, then saw it as they surveyed him now. Kirk felt the pressure give a little under their gaze.

"I've been privileged with a stellar career," he mused. "I've become a household word. People tell their children Captain Kirk stories at night. With every passing year, I get more aware of how many people are left out of those stories."

"That's how it always is, Jim," McCoy comforted. "Society likes a hero."

Kirk waved a hand. "There's something flawed about

it, though, Bones. Millions of people provided the resources we had at hand for our missions. Hundreds, thousands, even millions of lives sacrificed during events I've personally had a hand in changing, some of them my own friends and crew.... Captain James T. Kirk has absorbed the applause and gratitude that by rights I should be sharing with all those who've died in the line of duty, or been lost trying to establish colonies like this."

The sudden unbidden doubts he had never dealt with in his youth rushed in on him. Kirk shifted to sit on the edge of the briefing room's glossy table, to look out the viewports at the cut-outs of running lights streaming back into near-infinity. He'd never had these thoughts in those early days, in those high-flying times.

"Jim," McCoy attempted again, "everybody has doubts as they get older. I did."

"It's not doubt, Bones," Kirk told him. "It's guilt. I . . . I enjoyed myself too much. I should've been more aware of the ones who died breaking through the iron curtains, opening the gulags, establishing the mining operations, terraforming inclement planets, people living out their lives under truly ghastly conditions with nobody to remember their names or tell their stories."

"You were a soldier, Jim," Spock offered solemnly. "A soldier must keep his mental armor intact, or he will never make the hard decisions."

"Some of them were hard," Kirk accepted. "Sometimes in the night I can't justify things that happened, or the lives that were the price. I'm standing on those people's shoulders, not the other way around. So are the two of you. We owe them. We had to come on the Expedition to represent those lives and make sure there's more Federation in the galaxy, not less. That's why I'm here. I don't want the people of Belle Terre to *leave* the Federation. I want them to *lead* the Federation."

Mildly, showing the generosity of spirit for which Kirk so deeply cherished his friendship, Spock simply asked, "What would you like us to do, Captain?"

There was something in the Vulcan's timbre that drew Kirk back, a sense of hands-on, of right now, of get it done. Spock had that almost-smile on his face, the sparkle in his eyes, the crease in his cheek, as if waiting for Kirk to get over the squalling and do what he did best, because Spock knew he would.

Grateful, Kirk turned and gazed at him for a moment. "Yes . . . thank you both."

Slipping off the table he straightened up, drew himself back to immediacy, and faced the thousand problems in his pocket.

"We've been lucky so far. I don't mean to keep depending on luck. First of all, have Mr. Chekov keep a particular eye on Billy Maidenshore. I know—we'll be accused of harassment. So tell him to be subtle."

"Your gut at work again?" McCoy teased.

Kirk managed an unenthusiastic smile, but it didn't last. "Second, start long-range low-energy sensor sweeps, broad-spectrum, forward, aft, and abeam of the convoy. See what you pick up. If anybody's moving around out there, I want to know about it."

"Angus, come in here. Scan this place. I don't trust Kirk as far as I could kick him."

Billy Maidenshore enjoyed a long draw on one of his prize cigars. He couldn't light up a blue leaf anymore without thinking of Jim Kirk. Just one of those mind tricks he couldn't shake. He waited for Angus to scan the quarters for interference, listening devices, bombs, the usual.

"All clear, Billy." Angus turned off his short-range tricorder and tried to keep his fingers from their typical twitching. Billy didn't like to see the twitching. Whether the twitching was more annoying than watching Angus try to hide it or stop it—flip a coin.

"Okay, are you listening?" Maidenshore asked, the cigar clutched between his teeth. "I got a few things to say. I don't want to say them twice."

"Sure, Billy, I'm listening. You know we'd all do anything for you, anybody on *Pandora*, we'd do whatever you want. You took care of us, we'll take care of you."

"I'm counting on that, wiggler. I'm always watching you, remember that. I watch everybody. Here's the problem. Every time I set up a disaster, a good reason for people to get scared and stay that way, Kirk moves in and fixes things."

"You're getting what you wanted," Angus told him. "You're even more popular than the governor now, on *Yukon* and *Promontory Point*. You already got one more Conestoga going for you than you set out for. Isn't that good? Better, right?"

"Better," Maidenshore agreed, "but is it enough? When the time comes, will they listen to me, or will they listen to Pardonnet? I've got to make double sure the only voice those people pay attention to is this one right here." He pointed at his own throat and patted himself on the cheek. Another draw on the cigar got him thinking further. "Nah, there's got to be even more. The only good audience is a good and scared audience. You get people worked up angry, they act a certain way. You get 'em worked up scared . . . you can lead them over a cliff and promise you'll get them wings and they'll go. That's what I need. I need them so flustered, so shook, so afraid it's about to be them next . . . that they'll do anything I tell them to."

"How can you do that, Billy?" Angus stared at him, fascinated by the way Maidenshore's mind worked. "How do we make them that scared?"

"Could be anything," Maidenshore supposed. "Sometimes I don't know what I'm going to say until I say it. Like magic inspiration. It just hits me. The right thing at the right time. All I know is we've got to get control of at least one Conestoga, two is better, far enough out in space that Kirk can't bring the fleet along when we double back. Our friends'll be waiting to pick us up and take possession."

"Wouldn't it be great," Angus demonstrated, "if we could get *three* Conestogas?"

"A fortune," Maidenshore agreed. "But we can't get greedy the first time out. We better make sure that Kirk keeps his four Starfleet cutters out of our hair. That means they have to keep enough convoy ships with them that they can't split up. Why do you think I've been keeping my activities centralized in two Conestogas?"

Angus settled back and imitated Maidenshore's lounging posture. "I see what you mean. That makes sense. Our friends could handle maybe one starship, but not much more."

Both irritated and flattered by the mimicry, Maidenshore absorbed the adoration. "I tried being nice, y'know, Angus, I really did. I gave them what they needed, let them survive every malfunction, the contaminations, all the tricks, gave them the lung flu, then provided them with the cure . . . primed the pump in every way possible, so that when the time comes, they'll hear me and only me. But I can't get past Jim Kirk. This guy, he keeps putting out every fire. Just when I have 'em good and frightened, there he is. And there's that sappy governor, talking in patriotic lyrics, like that's real, like you can live like that. Those two, they keep upstaging me."

Angus nodded once, decisively. "They're upstaging you, Kirk and Pardonnet. I wouldn't let them get away with it, if I was you."

"You're dead right . . . dead right. Things have to change now, that's all I can say. I tried doing it the easy way, but Kirk won't play. Am I right?"

Closing one eye, Angus pretended to think for a minute, his gnarly face screwing up into three different expressions before he made his decision. "I don't see it no other way. You got a clear way of looking at things. What do you want to do next?"

Maidenshore relaxed back, sliding his hips downward until his head rested on the back of the chair and his legs were sprawled out halfway across the limited quarters. "Yeah. I need our people to be so scared of what's coming that they can't even imagine not turning around when I give the word. Angus . . . the time's come for people to start dying. A lot of them. A catastrophe. A whole Conestoga. Three thousand people. Whoosh."

"Tall order, Billy," Angus warned. "Big risk, to make something like that happen."

"Risky for them, not me." Maidenshore crossed his ankles, sucked on his cigar, and shrugged. "What else can I do? It's out of my hands."

## COMMAND DUTY ROSTER—PROPULSION ENGINEERING

Superintendent of Fleet Engineering: MONTGOMERY SCOTT, Cdr. Eng.

Authority: James T. Kirk, Fleet Adm.
Duty Station: Industrial Roundhouse Ship Colunga, ECC-989
Main Eng., NCC-1701

RESPONSIBILITIES:

Function and maintenance of mule engine propulsion systems.
General motive power, all ships.
Coordinate all engineers, disseminate equipment and assistant personnel.
Repair facilities and personnel.
Coordinate Wreckmasters Norfolk Rebel and Combat Support Tender Beowulf
as needed.

# COMMAND DUTY ROSTER—TRAFFIC CONTROL/TRANSPORTER COORD.

## Chief of Fleet Operations: HIKARU SULU, Lt. Cdr.

### RESPONSIBILITIES:

Fleet movement, train order.
Coord., all fleet pilots and helmsmen.
Traffic control, Rules of the Road.
Choreography of all beam traffic.
Security, all unauthorized beaming.

# COMMAND DUTY ROSTER—PATHFINDERS

Pathfinder Command: BROOK SMITH, Capt.
Special Ground Forces Command: JOHN GLASS, Col.
Investigations and Zone Control: JACK CARPENTER, Special Agent
Duty Station: American Rover

## RESPONSIBILITIES:

Zone Control.
Establishment of markers, signal devices.
Planetary exploration.
Security of immediate flight path.

## COMMAND DUTY ROSTER—TENDER/TRANSPORT MOVEMENT

Chief Fleet Coxswain: DAN MARKS, Capt.
Duty station: Conestoga Tender _Polynesian_

## RESPONSIBILITIES:

All small boat and tenders movement.
Shifting of mules, runabouts, pods on board and off board larger vessels.
Provisioning, all tenders.
Safety, all tenders and personnel.

COMMAND DUTY ROSTER—VIP TRANSPORT

Host: NED CHALKER, Capt.
BEVERLY CHALKER, Cdr.
Duty Station: S.S. <u>Mable Stevens</u>

## RESPONSIBILITIES:

Colonial Governor's transport.
Security and safe conduct for high-level dignitaries and guests.
Delivery of specialized technical data.
Host ship, Officers' Arrival Banquet.

# Chapter Ten

"CAPTAIN KILVENNAN, welcome back to the *Enterprise.*"

Over his shoulder, Jim Kirk heard Spock's mild greeting and knew he was being watched from the aft of the bridge again. Seated here in his command chair, he was usually protected as if in a bubble. He could feel Michael Kilvennan behind him, drilling holes in his spine from aft, while Governor Pardonnet hovered on the upper starboard side, signing a requisition for Uhura. No, Pardonnet wasn't looking at him right now—at least, not with his eyes.

Was Spock being sincere or just trying to grease the skids? Or remind Kilvennan of where he stood? More likely he was using the mask of greeting to warn Kirk of the privateer captain's presence.

Even before turning to scope the other captain's expression, Kirk sensed Kilvennan's insult at having to come here again. For Kilvennan and the other enforcement captains, the bridge of the *Enterprise* was probably an oppressive place. All the other captains had signed on with the idea of being led out into deep space. The privateers had signed on with the idea of leading. Then, at the last minute, once the finicky UFP Council had swallowed the idea that the Belle Terre Expedition would launch with or without official blessing, the Council had decided to insist upon Starfleet escort. They didn't want to look like spoilsports, but ended up looking like pushy parents instead, forcing the privateers to choke down admiralty authority. Governor Pardonnet had made them agree. They were stuck, obliged to let James Kirk or his command staff make every decision.

As he sat here, knowing Kilvennan was behind him, Kirk realized he could've handled this more sympathetically—or at least, more courteously. It would've been better for Kirk to have visited *Hunter's Moon*, and let Kilvennan rule the turf for a change.

Oh, well . . . too late.

On the walkway, Governor Pardonnet looked up at Kilvennan, sensed the tension, but didn't interfere. In his periphery Kirk saw the governor offer a nod of recognition to the privateer. It was good that he wasn't interfering. The governor didn't like to be here either, Kirk knew, preferring to separate the civilian and Starfleet authorities as much as possible, but some things required his presence whether he liked it or not. The line of separation had blurred more and more with every malfunction, every accident, contamination, or theft that plagued the Expedition. Starfleet had moved more and more into clear control. The privateers and even the governor himself had been pushed out of the enforcement command loop.

Once he couldn't get away with further stalling, Kirk swiveled his chair around. "Captain Kilvennan, I see you've been cleared out of quarantine."

"Yeah," Kilvennan responded drably. "McCoy cleared the whole Conestoga."

"I haven't seen his report yet. I hope this means the lung-flu problem is solved."

"Some parts of it are. The rest, I guess he'll have to tell you for himself. Me, I've got another problem. Scott cleared my mother of tampering suspicion. The phasers on the factor drone were enhanced, but not with my mother's code or Stefan Webb's, or anybody else authorized by Kilvennan-Webb. The access didn't cross-check with anything we recognized."

"A relief, I assume," Kirk offered.

Kilvennan stepped a little closer to the rail. "It is, but the charges you levied against my mother haven't been dropped. It's time to drop them."

"Not yet," Kirk disavowed. "There's an investigation pending. I intend to see it out."

Kilvennan flushed with anger. "My mother and her husband run an appliance industry, not an assassination service! We didn't have anything to do with that drone malfunction! What do you think that accusation is doing to my family?"

Keeping a grip on the command chair, Kirk stood up and faced him. No, that wasn't good enough. He let go of the chair and climbed the little steps to the upper deck, where he faced Kilvennan, aware that the two of them must make an odd pair of bookends indeed to the others who were watching.

"How desperate was your mother to get medication for your family?" Kirk bluntly asked. "It's possible she sent that drone out as a distraction while she arranged for the medicine to be stolen or contrabanded. Those events happened about the same time."

Kilvennan's eyes narrowed. "What are you really up to? Trying to smoke out criminals by charging innocent people and hoping the real thieves relax enough to try something else? I've heard you do that sort of thing."

Like a rock out of a slingshot, Kirk felt his own expression change. "I've been hearing things too. I've heard your children were cured first, along with selected families on the *Yukon,* even before they'd been treated by Dr. McCoy. Is that true?"

Chafing at the ring of truth, Kilvennan hesitated. "Contraband medicine was being distributed," he admitted. "What could I do? Stand by while our kids suffered? You wouldn't either. Nobody's that noble."

Unaffected by the accusation, Kirk stepped closer in a way he hoped was strict if not threatening. "I want to know where you got it."

Kilvennan refused to be intimidated—actually a pretty good sign. "From people who helped us. They gave it to us, they didn't sell it. I won't betray them."

"Instead you'll betray us all?" Kirk countered. "That's not what I expected of a man who's been hired to enforce the law, Captain."

"Spirit of the law," the privateer disclaimed, "not the letter of it."

The turbolift hissed open and interrupted the stand-off. At first Kilvennan didn't look to see who was coming, until his name was called by a voice he recognized. "Michael?"

A sheepish young fellow came out, pushed onward by McCoy. The boy wore camouflage trousers and a buffalo plaid shirt—a pioneer if ever there was one in the stereotype file.

"Quinn!" Kilvennan spun around and grasped the newcomer.

Behind them, McCoy got Kirk's attention, motioned at the younger fellow, and mouthed, *His brother.*

Something about the meeting let steam out of Michael Kilvennan. Kirk could guess what the younger brother must've been like on the *Yukon,* among all the other wildly feverish passengers. There'd been something wrong with them, something abnormal, McCoy had reported, and now Kirk chafed to get the whole story. There was a certain sensitive timing to a moment like this. He opted to wait a few seconds, give the brothers a chance to downshift.

"Feeling better?" Kilvennan asked.

Quinn Kilvennan shook his head, deeply embarrassed. "I acted like some kind of possessed soul! I didn't even . . . recognize myself!"

"Didn't recognize you either." His brother patted Quinn's arms, showing in every possible demonstration that he was forgiven for the messy behavior on the Conestoga, yet failed to massage the lingering humiliation in Quinn's eyes. "Everybody acted like animals, not just you. Thought Mae was going to crack in half. Did you see Tom Coates, roaring like a stuck bull?"

"Why would anybody do that to us?" Quinn's doleful eyes implored answers. He looked past his brother, to James Kirk.

Kirk raised his brows, and shifted his eyes to McCoy. The buck passed again.

"Atmospheric contamination," McCoy crowed, happy with himself. "And, Jim, there's no chance it was random or accidental. Nothing so formula-specific could be a malfunction. The adjustment was geared to elicit exactly the response we saw." He pointed casually at Quinn Kilvennan.

"What did you see?" Kirk prodded impatiently.

"Well, you know we put all sorts of atmospheric mixtures together for space travel. The air in our ships has antibiotics, vitamin supplements, corpuscle stimulants, extra oxygen, the usual things. Apparently the computer system for infusion tanks on the *Yukon* was fed a revised program, causing an intoxicant effect very similar to Zenite gas."

"Zenite," Kirk murmured. "How well I remember . . ." Sudden empathy for Quinn Kilvennan got him by the throat. He remembered that awful nauseous feeling of mindless anger. And what if McCoy hadn't found it soon enough? The drug-crazed citizens might've turned the Conestoga's minimal weapons on their innocent neighbors.

"Right," McCoy said. "You almost took that other man's skin as a souvenir of Stratos City."

Michael Kilvennan pulled his brother aside so he could ask McCoy, "Why didn't *Yukon*'s filter alarms go off?"

"The filter system was programmed to ignore the gas."

On the side deck, Governor Pardonnet sank into the nearest chair. "We've got to find out who's doing all these things, and more importantly, why."

"Out of sixty-four thousand people?" Kilvennan asked. "With so many scientists, mechanics, architects, and technicians, how do we find out who's doing things that are clever and technical? The skill to make them happen isn't exactly rare on this Expedition. We're towing our own hospital, factories, and labs, with resident geniuses in every one of them, for Christ's sake!"

Quinn put his hand on his brother's arm. "The Lord's name, Michael."

"Sorry." Kilvennan gave him a moment's attention, but turned to Kirk now, wanting a theory if not an answer.

Kirk, also in need of theories, turned to Starfleet's theory machine—Spock.

Spock came forward without bidding.

"Commander Giotto's detectives," he explained, "are investigating these problems under Mr. Chekov's strict eye. So far they've only managed to track down the causes, not the perpetrators."

Near Kilvennan, Kirk rubbed the knuckles of his right hand, aching to punch somebody. He felt his brows come down, lips press tight, and knew he was giving away his worries. "Yes," he grumbled, almost to himself. "It limits the circle of people I can trust."

In fact, that circle was just about all here, on this bridge. Scott was working on the mule tender, Sulu was off somewhere in the fleet, and Chekov was trying to iron out this very problem. Everybody else . . . his circle of confidence had grown small indeed. Having so few people to depend upon—the closing tunnel was chilly. Out in space almost all his life, with an ocean of admirers and a wall of accolades, a whole civilization depending upon his actions, yet a truly limited pool of real friends, and no family to notice, he suddenly felt isolated, chased by night terrors. The pool was shrinking.

"Who'd want to do this to us?" Governor Pardonnet broke into Kirk's thoughts. "Who would want to ruin our future?"

Before Kirk could stop anyone from posing an unpolished answer to a rhetorical question, McCoy had already turned and said, "Don't be naive, Governor. This mission can be seen as the first wave of a massive Federation expansion. Hell, that's how *I* see it. Lots of forces in the galaxy would like to see you fail."

"Fail we might," Kilvennan said. "People are talking seriously about turning back."

Evan Pardonnet looked up, and the flame of determination came back into his words. "We can't allow that kind of talk to take over our minds. We'll soon come into Gamma Night. We need to believe we can get through this together."

Drawing the center of attention back to himself, Kirk strode in front of the Kilvennan brothers and positioned himself between McCoy and the governor, but faced Michael Kilvennan. "You sure it's not the lingering effects of this contaminant speaking for them?"

"Dead sure," Kilvennan claimed. "I knew when they weren't themselves, and I know when they are. These people don't belong to you, or to you, Governor. You can't force them to stay if they decide to turn back. This isn't a Starfleet operation."

Kirk clamped his lips tight. He wanted it to be a Starfleet operation, wanted problems solved by being able to just give orders, throw his weight around, not be questioned. He'd never liked diplomats before, but was abruptly beginning to appreciate them. Tough job— holding someone's hand when you really want to break his arm.

"I won't allow the Expedition to split up," he vowed. "We're under mysterious assault. If we split up, I can't protect both sides."

"Could send the cutter back as an escort," Kilvennan suggested. "And I'll go with them too."

"Michael," Quinn hedged, "you sure?"

"If Mom and Mae want to turn back, I'm not going out to some dustbowl planet without my family. The other privateers think the same."

Kirk stepped to him, giving him that tigerlike glare which had served him so well in the past. "We need you to patrol the perimeter. Report to Captain Briggs or any of his sons on *Norfolk Rebel*. They're coordinating the outer patrol."

Defiant, Kilvennan shook his head. "I'm not reporting to your Wreckmasters. How long before one of these disasters takes three thousand lives and you can't catch it in time? Another couple of weeks, there's going to be a shortage of food. Think we haven't figured that out? We're willing to admit maybe this whole project was a mistake in the first place."

Pardonnet stood up. "You signed on to protect us. You signed a legal contract."

"What good is 'legal' out here in the middle of nothing? I've got kids to think about. When we get back to Earth, you can sue me."

Kirk moved slightly to his left, just enough to come between Kilvennan and Pardonnet, so that the privateer captain had no choice but to look at him, and only him. "Your assignment," he said, "is to patrol the perimeter. You're not officially deputized. You can be the chief constable, but you're in."

"I'm not yours to order," Kilvennan reminded, "or yours to promote."

"All the privateers will submit crew manifests to Lieutenant Chekov for a new security clearance background check."

Kilvennan shifted his weight. "Aren't you listening?"

Kirk didn't look at anybody else. He'd had his fill of committee command. Pick one opponent, one target, and deal with it. "Oh, I'm listening. I'm just not entertaining any talk of splitting up or turning back. Things aren't that bad yet."

"Not *yet*," Kilvennan repeated. "That's what we're afraid of. If there's an accident out here, it's not just a ship's crew, it's a three-thousand-person critical mass. We all know about your reputation, but you can't reach into the past and pull forward the power to keep together a caravan of sixty-four thousand people under conditions that are deteriorating. My whole family was put at risk when the atmosphere went bad on *Yukon*. How long before life-support goes out completely on one of those moving mountains?"

From behind Kirk, Spock offered, "Conestoga life-support is phenomenally reliable, Captain Kilvennan. All the machinery with the exception of shields is devoted to it. That's one of the benefits of Mr. Scott's independent mule engines."

"There've been a hundred little breakdowns," Kilvennan pursued. "Contamination grids rupturing, isolation compromised, half the lung-flu medication contaminated, hot things running too hot, cold things freezing solid, trouble with the sanitation systems—and you're going to take these people forward into Gamma Night?"

"These aren't accidents," Kirk said, determined to get that one point, if no other, across. "There's sabotage going on. Very possibly the criminals you're protecting."

"How can you possibly know that?"

Kirk couldn't help a miniature swagger. "I feel it in my gut."

Smoothly, Spock added, "The odds, in fact, against all these types of breakdowns, in this length of time, with this particular variety of equipment, are roughly eighty-nine thousand six hundred twelve to one."

Jabbing a finger over his shoulder, Kirk drawled, "He feels it in his gut too."

To one side, McCoy said, "Spock's gut has always had more decimal places."

Kilvennan folded his arms as his brother watched with a paling face. "Glad you can still laugh."

Growing even more grim, Kirk warned, "You can go to the perimeter, or you can go to the brig."

Did he mean it? He wasn't sure himself. A risky bluff if it was called.

Okay, then apparently he meant it.

Though neither of them really moved, somehow another inch closed between them.

"You agreed to protect these people," Kirk went on. "We're living under duress. By Federation law, that gives me the right to confiscate any ship, including yours. A privateer crew has to be able to trust its captain to keep his word . . . if you leave after promising to see us through, their trust in you will begin to erode. After that, it's just a matter of time."

He chose his words carefully, consciously trying not to frame a true threat, yet provide the kind of rumor that would get around. On the bridge, everyone's posture changed—subtle, small, but notable.

The silence ground like a mill, enhanced by the twitter of bridge noises in the background. Only when the whistle of the comm system broke through did Kirk allow himself to be pulled from the confrontation.

"Sir," Uhura interrupted, "Mr. Sulu's hailing from the *Normandy*."

Kirk turned. "What's he doing on—never mind. Put him through."

*"Sulu here, Captain."*

"Mr. Sulu, what are you doing on the farm ship?"

*"I was working on some shirtsleeve botany when a major hull leak broke in the hydroponic section. There's no time to seal it from inside, sir, and we've got five minutes until there's a total loss of crop. Permission to use phasers to seal the hull from inside."*

"Go ahead, your discretion. Contact us as soon as you know whether or not it worked. We'll send assistance if you need it."

Under the blood-colored jacket, Kirk felt his shoulders tense like warning sensors going off. Kilvennan was watching him, gauging his response, his every word, his tone and posture. The other captain knew, somehow, that he wanted to go out there, chafed to go, ached to go, that he hated leaving others to handle trouble. Torn between his desires and his responsibilities, he battled with himself while Kilvennan watched. The others were watching too, but he knew in some mysterious way that the privateer was the only one who really understood. Command had its viruses.

When he turned back to the immediate problem, he was careful to change his demeanor. Kilvennan was a captain, after all. This was one of the niggling problems for Kirk, who had spent his life in space as a captain, not as an admiral. In deep space, he had seldom had to deal with anyone of equal rank or better. Now he had more than seventy of his own species to deal with. Muscle and might wasn't working with Kilvennan. The mind of a privateer captain was a peculiar mechanism. Such men as Kilvennan were in that business because they didn't think anybody else was worth serving under. Every one of them had earned, usually the hard way, the respect of his crew. None of them were under assignment or orders. Brute force wouldn't work.

Thinking quickly, Kirk opted for an unfamiliar trick.

"I'll make a new bargain with you," he attempted. "You see us through to the lightship *Hatteras*. After that, go where you want. You can turn back when the *Republic* does, and go with them back to Federation space. I'll take care of the Expedition the rest of the way. Your parents, if they stay, your brother here . . . and anyone else."

Everyone was watching them. Moments ticked by.

Slowly, Kilvennan shifted again and unfolded his arms. His expression mellowed. He glanced briefly at his brother, who took hold of his arm in silent emotion. Kilvennan had been trumped. Kirk had used an all-expenses-paid power play and won without forcing Kilvennan to lose, letting him off with pride intact by leaving him a choice. No brig, no threats. A short-run solution.

A grin of irony tugged at Kilvennan's trim beard when once again he locked eyes with Kirk. "Bully," he derided.

Kirk felt his own expression change. Just the eyes, really. He winked.

Just so everyone else would know he wasn't gloating, he extended a handshake to Kilvennan, not at all sure it would be taken.

And he would never know. Behind him, the bridge jangled its electronic noises and a warning klaxon went off. Uhura's voice cut through a second time. "Sir, emergency call from Mr. Scott!"

She didn't wait for his order this time, but cued in the audio speakers.

*"Scott here! I'm aboard the* Comanche!"

Kirk dropped to the command deck. He knew that tone. "Nature of the trouble, Scotty?"

*"Imminent catastrophic explosion! Mule engine malfunction, got a mighty hot potato on m'hands, sir! Clear the other ships away from us!"*

"Stand by. Governor, Captain Kilvennan, get back to your ships and get them out of range. Mr. Spock, clear the *Enterprise* of any nonenlisted personnel. Red alert."

"Red alert," Spock repeated. "Gentlemen, the emergency evacuation transporter pads are on Deck Two."

Stepping aside for the governor to go first into the lift, Kilvennan cast a glance around the suddenly active bridge, where the lights had gone to emergency scarlet and the crew had already forgotten about him. As he took Quinn's arm and nudged past Dr. McCoy, he cast one final connecting look down to Kirk, who met his eyes for a last salute of understanding.

Kilvennan pulled his brother into the lift, and as it swallowed them, he jovially broadcast his opinion. "Give a man a new uniform and he thinks he rules the galaxy!"

## The Captains' Meeting

### October 31, 2272

"Ladies and gentlemen, just before we launch the Belle Terre Colonial Expedition, we at Starfleet Command wanted to be sure our officers and crewmen won't fade into the background during such an important expedition. Therefore, we went shopping. When you go looking for our personnel from now on, look for the new Fleet-issue uniforms. And since it's Halloween . . . I'll change my costume."

Indulging in a bit of stagemanship, Jim Kirk

stepped away from the podium from which he addressed the flock of captains gathered for the last strategic meeting before the Expedition's departure hour. This was it, the last time they'd see each other in a group. After this, they would be voices and numbers, communicating over chunks of open space, trying diligently not to collide or get in each other's way.

There probably wasn't any other occupation in the universe that would bring together so diverse a collection of men and women as the captaincy of a mixed flotilla. Each was doggedly individual in style and method, yet there were common goals and an instinctive mutuality of purpose that couldn't be trained in.

A yeoman came forward with a box, which Kirk opened, and from which he drew a spanking new brick-red uniform day jacket, trimmed in pitch black and iceberg white. The yeoman took the jacket and slipped it onto Kirk's shoulders, then settled it into place. Kirk winked the young fellow back and folded the diagonal chest placket closed himself, and flipped the brass toggle on the shoulder strap that held the placket up. Finally he brought the black belt around and snapped the delta-shield buckle.

Like his duty undershirt, the shoulder strap, the wrist bar, and the inside lining were crisp white, suiting his command rank, while the belt loops and placket trim were cannon black.

Cannon, glacier, and blood. The new uniform described Kirk's whole life.

With dry palms he touched the front of the jacket, ran his hands down the sleeves to the admiral's rank pin and service bars on the wrists, then lowered his arms to his sides. Suddenly he felt *dressed*.

As applause erupted and rang through the hall, Kirk was caught unexpectedly blushing. Despite his years of experience and his mountain of accomplishments, he felt deeply humbled, as if he were wearing the support of thousands who had sacrificed their lives so he could have this moment.

He gazed down at his long-wrought friendships—Scotty, McCoy, Sulu, Chekov, Uhura, and of course Spock; white was for senior command, for the sciences sky blue, medical services' fern green, security and engineering's gold, and dove gray for ship operations—

Traveling through another rite of passage with him, his old friends shined up at him as if they were all alone here today, having a private moment, promising him that they would embark with him on another spectacular adventure, danger and trouble and all, beating off the thought of strains that would come to challenge the new Starfleet issue, playing steward to thousands of hopeful pioneers who had no real idea of just how far they were going. No one could know who hadn't already been out there.

Kirk put out a staying palm to slow the appreciation, warmed by the smiles throughout the crowd. Even a couple of the privateer captains were grinning with cheerful envy through their don't-mess-with-us-but-we'll-wait-while-you-decide attitudes. He thought about their freewheeling life and fielded a bit of envy himself. They had no codes or regulations forcing them into prefabricated images. They and their rugged ships were archetypal symbols of the intelligent maverick. How would they deal with his authority, inflicted upon them by UFP edict during the last few weeks of a job they had accepted as theirs alone?

Could they see how worried he was? How long he had hovered here, in secure space, hungering for the dangerous life he had somehow survived? Could they tell he was nervous about reacquiring it? Would he remember how to do this? Was he still young enough to be reckless? There were a lot of lives depending upon him, more than ever before in a spaceborne operation. He'd watched whole planets die, and yet this somehow was a hundred times more disturbing. Did he still have the touch?

When the applause fell away, Kirk let the silence go on for several seconds, to saturate the room with sobriety for the task ahead.

"When we get out into deep space," he began slowly, "that's all there is. Whatever we take with us will be all we have. We'll have only each other to depend on. We're going to be passing through a very large desert and we're not sure what's on the other side. As the senior officer of Starfleet who'll be going with you, I promise we'll get you there or die trying. If anyone starves, Starfleet will starve first. If anyone's in danger, we'll be there first to share it. If anyone dies, we'll be the first to die. That is Starfleet's promise, and I'll be personally keeping it. My friends . . . let's go build a Beautiful Earth."

Snug as a hammock, battered to perfection, just slovenly enough to be user-friendly, the old privateer *Hunter's Moon* was hove to with the rest of the Expedition during an emergency situation. The ship was quiet—most of the crew were off watch, sleeping, and didn't know yet what was going on out in near-space.

Michael Kilvennan ignored the searching eyes of those who were up and aware. He didn't have answers and didn't want any questions. He had beamed off the starship without even knowing the nature of the emergency yet.

"What's happening?" He charged onto the weather deck and climbed the vertical ladder to the quarterdeck.

"Didn't you see it?" Engineer Sylvie Graves was already riveted to the three forward screens, showing a view of the volatile situation now developing. "*Comanche*'s mules are firing in two independent directions," she gasped, breathing in shallow gulps. Her short blond hair was plastered flat, making her ears stick out.

"Can't do that," Kilvennan opposed. "They're plugged into a single control system."

"Look for yourself. They're pulling the Conestoga's hull in two different directions. They'll peel the ship apart in a matter of minutes."

She was right both ways. On the privateer's dashboard of easy-view interconnected screens, black matte shapes with running lights bumped and jolted in unnatural movements. The bulbous shape of the Conestoga suffered the glow of overload on both its mule engines, casting garish lights on the people-movers' flanks.

Kilvennan's mouth went dry. "What're the odds of every failsafe crashing on two mules?"

Graves shook her head in disbelief. "Every failsafe crashing on *one* mule is impossible. You want me to call all hands?"

"Where's Starfleet? *Republic*? *Beowulf*?"

"They're both on rearguard, more than fifty minutes back. *Impeller*'s off looking for *American Rover*."

"Tugantine?"

"Twenty ships back, towing a disabled mule."

"Jesus." Kilvennan swallowed hard, then suddenly thought of his brother. "Start praying, Quinn . . ."

In space, with no sun to illuminate them, the ships of the Belle Terre Expedition looked like bunched-up stars themselves. Running lights—white, red, blue, and the occasional yellow—made identifiable patterns on the velvet curtain of space, some crossing in front of each other, making patterns without sense that looked more than anything else like Christmas trees in the dark. Not since the last Great Starship Race had so many ships been gathered in one close area. Beyond them, real stars, nebulae, and clusters glowed without a flicker.

From here they had an unblocked view of the endangered *Comanche,* its gourd-shaped side lit up by scene lights from its own mule engines, lights usually used for tractoring and towing movements and disengagement of the mules. Overlaying the scene lights was the terrible glow of overload—demolition cast a light of its own on both sides of the people-mover.

"What do we do?" Graves asked, her voice quavering.

"We wouldn't even be here if I hadn't come up to talk to Kirk,' Kilvennan said. "Let him handle it. He wants control. Let him have it. Maybe he can famous the problem away."

"He used to be famous. Now he's an echo. Closest he gets to his past is a wall full of medals."

"Pardonnet thinks that's why he came on the Expedition. To get back that old feeling."

"Has-beens are pathetic . . . oh, God . . ." A disembodied voice grumbled from below.

Kilvennan bent over, craned a little, and found his first officer lying on his side, peering into the open repair trunk, moaning every few seconds. "Troy? Are you on the deck?"

"Yeah ... yeah, down here ..."

"You all right?"

From the deck, First Mate Troy Augustine's voice was ragged and aggrieved. "It's making me sick. ..."

Bending a bit more, Kilvennan twisted until he could see Augustine's close-cropped Nordic hair and the direction he was looking into the trunk. "Oh, watching the direct feeds."

"*Comanche*'s thruster exhaust," Augustine groaned, "the direct heat index sensors. Those people, Michael ... they're dead."

The removable towing engines were an idea conjured up by Fleet Coxswain Dan Marks, then developed on a scale of dozens, within weeks, by Montgomery Scott. The independent mules were fundamentally simple, tug engines without a tug, with inboard generators and cooling systems, and each with a powerful impulse drive and its own warp core. They ran basically with on-off switches, and could be jettisoned almost instantly, or taken off and put in the roundhouse ship *Colunga* for repair.

So why weren't they being jettisoned?

"Syl, click on the comm system. Let me hear what's going on."

"Comm," she repeated.

A crackle broke sharply through the speakers, and Montgomery Scott's voice, broken by electrical interference, was mixed in with James Kirk's.

"*—overload on both systems—put up the Conestoga's shields to shore up her hull integrity.*"

*"That won't hold indefinitely. Scotty, why can't you jettison those mules?"*

*"They're hard-riveted onto the hull. Whatever happens to us, if you didn't have concrete evidence of sabotage before, you bloody well have it now."*

Troy Augustine jumped up from the deck, stumbling a moment on his bad knee. He scanned the upper screens until he found the one with the view of the *Hunter's Moon*'s upper starboard quarter. "Here comes *Enterprise*! Wow, she's close!"

Graves jumped to the helm as if to make an adjustment.

"Hold position," Kilvennan barked. "Don't confuse them with changes."

As the privateer held her ground, the starship skated over them at collision proximity, a huge black shape illuminated only by the sconce lanterns on her hulls and nacelles. Watching *Enterprise*'s lovely swan shape, cloaked in shadow and sprayed with funnels of frosted light from her own mounts, Kilvennan tried to imagine any maneuver that would change the fate of the shuddering Conestoga out there.

"What does he think he can do alone?" Graves wondered. "A Conestoga's heavy as a lead asteroid. Why aren't they signaling for help?"

"He could try holding it in place with traction while pushing against one of the mules."

"Won't work," Kilvennan said. "The other mule'll pull them into a spin. It's crazy."

"He's only got one ship."

"And I didn't come out here to wreck mine!" Kilvennan reacted. "Or to leave my kids without a father either. That wasn't the deal I made and neither did you." When they were silent a moment, slapped back by his venom, he asked, "How many passengers on *Comanche?*"

"Four thousand sixty at last count."

"God save them . . ."

Augustine's whole body shook. "Why isn't Kirk calling for additional thrust?"

Graves bit her lip. "Maybe because he doesn't want to up the death count."

Kilvennan whispered to himself. "Or because I told him we wouldn't come."

*"Kirk here. Scotty, we'll try to use our tractor beams to hold on to the Conestoga while we push against the starboard mule's outboard thrust at the same time. Direct pressure. How much time do you need?"*

*"Don't know that yet, sir."*

"He can't keep it up," Graves deduced. "He'd have to pull for three weeks till the mules run out of fuel."

In his mind Kilvennan could imagine what was going on, the bridge of the starship tense and efficient, Mr. Spock measuring Engineer Scott's activities with sensors, down to the five-hundredth decimal place, frowning the way he did when things weren't going well. Kirk prowling the lower bridge, his eyes never leaving the screens, cooking up idea after idea and having them smashed by reality, then cooking up more.

*"All ships,* Enterprise. *Plan is to shut down mule engines simultaneously. Chances are poor. Keep safe distance. Repeat, keep safe detonation distance."*

"See?" Kilvennan pointed out. "He knows. What good would it do for us to get ripped apart with them?"

Graves coiled her arms tightly around her thin body and bounced on her toes as her nerves began to fray. "I feel like I'm in a lifeboat watching thousands of people die in front of me."

Sensing it was time to give her something to do, Kilvennan forced himself to cough up an idea. "Sylvie, contact Kirk and offer to use his wide-beam transport to beam people off that ship and onto *Hunter's Moon*. We can cram five or six hundred into our hold and companionways. He can take another fifteen hundred."

"There are four thousand on that Conestoga."

"Other ships could come in for a second wave. Call, call."

Frantically Graves typed the message into her fingerboard, keeping the conversation from broadcasting on audio. It was enough the crew could see what was happening, never mind hear the disaster unfolding. Kilvennan wanted to keep his options to himself for the moment.

Soon a beeping response flowed through the comm. Graves looked up. "It's Lieutenant Commander Uhura, Michael. She says they don't dare evacuate. The sudden change in gross tonnage would cause the mules' thrust to work even faster on the hull. They'd get half the people off and the Conestoga would split in two almost instantly. There'd be no second wave."

"How do you suppose they figured out a thing like that?"

"Because Kirk thinks ahead," Kilvennan muttered, but no one heard him. "If one of the other Starfleet ships could get up here, they could provide thrust from the port side. Two ships working together could hold that Conestoga in one place while Scott shuts them down . . . maybe."

"Yeah, maybe." Graves was cautious of her tone. "They'd never get here in time. *Enterprise* still isn't signaling for assistance."

"What'd you expect him to do?" Augustine asked.

She glanced at him. "I expect him to order us to come over there and rip ourselves apart helping him."

When he tried to speak, to give them some kind of captainish wisdom about chances and choices, Kilvennan found his throat tight and his mind on his family. "He doesn't think we'll come," he murmured.

Only Troy looked at him. He didn't seem sure of what he'd heard. Or he was pretending.

Four thousand people were about to die in front of them. *Enterprise*'s valiant effort would go unrewarded. If wild mules were to be shut down simultaneously, it would have to be done with manual controls, right to the core mechanics. Even if a wizard like Montgomery Scott could manage to coordinate that with the Conestoga's engineer, it was a lot more likely there'd be a split second of miscalculation. During that second, with one mule shutting down and the other still under lateral thrust—*whoosh*—the Conestoga and the starship would go spinning off and rip themselves to splinters just from the raw stress.

Kirk was trying it anyway. What was he thinking?

Nauseated, Graves flattened her hands over her face and turned away. "Tell me when it's done. I don't want to look at four thousand floating corpses . . ."

Before them, the Conestoga's mule engines' exhausts burned white-hot, the fist-shaped engines themselves actually beginning to glow orange now as they pulled against each other, using the Conestoga as the rope in a scatheful tug-of-war. On the starboard side, *Enterprise* had her primary hull blunted up against the side of the *Comanche*, pushing forward while her own tractor beams pulled backward at the same time. She was trying to hold the Conestoga together all by herself.

What a bitter prospect—the whole Expedition forced

to surge forward, ship after ship, with bits of bodies and pieces of blown hull bumping against them like waves on a lake. Graves was right. Nightmare.

He fixed his gaze on one screen, where the bow of the *Enterprise* pressed relentlessly against the side of the Conestoga. Together in their death dance, the two massive ships shifted this way, that way, and turned on a changing axis in their wicked struggle, fixed together by tractor beams and thrust. What Kirk must be going through to coordinate an impossibly seamless effort—

"He's no bureaucrat," Kilvennan rasped. "Just look at them! He doesn't have to do this. . . . He's risking the ones he could save, plus the rest, plus everybody else. A bureaucrat would play it safe by beaming off two thousand and getting called a hero for saving who he could. He's not in this for glory—he's in this for believing in it."

As if his own heart were the vessel being pulled in two, he felt it hammer in his chest until the din reached his ears and he thought his head was coming off. He closed his eyes, shutting out the sight before him. His hands went out to his sides to balance his churning body.

Impetuously then, like a fever breaking, the tension drained away. His heart's thud calmed. His hands relaxed. His eyes opened. And everything was different.

"Only live once," he murmured. "Troy, call all hands."

Beside him Augustine turned and stared like a snowman. With abrupt enthusiasm he grasped Kilvennan and shook him bodily, then turned again. "All hands on deck! All hands!"

Sylvie Graves jumped high enough to plant a kiss on Kilvennan's cheek before rushing to disengage the holding thrusters and flush the propulsion system with power. "Impulse drive ready!"

"Quarters."

"General quarters, all hands!"

The *Hunter's Moon* thrummed to life around them, all the lights going to alert scarlet. In the aft decks, they heard the pummel of feet hitting the decks and the voices of startled crewmates barking for action. The engines hummed. The helm lit up.

"Troy, take the helm. Forward thrusters, midship."

After raising the alarm, Augustine came back bright-eyed and flushed. "Midship! What changed your mind, Michael?"

Kilvennan drew a breath, probably his last, and looked at the center screen. There, *Enterprise* stubbornly held the Conestoga together using tractor beams, thrust, hope, and the brazen tenacity of her captain.

"He did. He's not letting them down. I figure someday he won't let me down either. You can go forever looking for a captain who'll fight for your life like that. Sylvie, signal Kirk we're moving in to assist. Approach the *Comanche*'s port side, bow to. Let's get in there and do it or die trying."

"Hah!" Augustine charged the helm and jammed the controls. "I always wanted to die trying. Helm's over!"

# Chapter Eleven

"BATTLELORD."

"Avedon. I find honor in your willingness to meet with me again."

"Thank you for your sincerely delivered lie. Would your men like a meal? Warm drink?"

"We would never take such a chance."

"Neither would I. Perhaps you would like to sit."

"I would never sit in your presence."

"Neither would I in yours."

Shucorion smiled, rather genuinely. He understood Vellyngaith's reasons both for honesty and deception. There was some comfort in knowing they could not trust each other. At least their relationship, for mortal enemies who would under other circumstances tie each other's arteries, was forthright in its way.

The Blood guards and Vellyngaith's Kauld guards glared intolerantly at each other from across the half-cylinder of deck, weapons glumly buzzing, as their two leaders met in the middle of the curved deck on the Blood Plume's loading area. Remarkable, for Vellyngaith to come here a second time rather than demand a reciprocal meeting upon the battle barge.

But alliance was a new trick. No one knew the rules.

Intimidating. Shucorion was hardly the Blood's equal to the Kauld's greatest warrior. Not since the last Elliptical War had Blood possessed such a man, and that one died at the end of the cycle. He was still famous, but legends gained no ground.

"How is the building of your fortress progressing?" Shucorion began, hoping his question had a neutral sort of flavor.

Vellyngaith's strong face tightened, as if he had eaten something tart. "Preconstruction has begun. I am no builder. I can't judge."

"When can you begin working on the planet? Taking possession of it?"

"Quite a time, unfortunately. Like you, Kauld have never done anything off our homeworld. All our factories and facilities are geared for preconstruction. To build on the planet itself would take years of preparation. Everything must be built ahead, and transported in sections. Whether we will take possession before Federation arrives, or as they arrive, or never, I cannot yet tell." Vellyngaith paused, his eyes strained. His silver hair, slick and long, seemed somehow dull today. Perhaps it was the lighting. "I was told you have conditions," he said. "I shall listen now."

"I have conditions," Shucorion told him, "now that I know you were being truthful about Federation's movement to this area. The agreement, you must admit, was one-sided. Blood would go out and defend you against

new enemies, when we are the weaker side. I agree that
the Elliptical Wars are over whether we want them over
or not, now that we can move at starspeed. We either
learn to live with each other, or we will strangle until
one side dies. It is time to put an end, stand together
against a new enemy. But there must be balance."

Giving Vellyngaith a moment to absorb this and accept the proposal that was his idea after all, Shucorion
paced away a few steps, looked out a portal, and
viewed the vista of open space.

Addictive, this risk-taking! Some kind of narcotic.
Taste a little, taste more . . . if he didn't die, a bit more.
How long would his specialness carry him through risk
upon risk?

"I suppose there is no other way," he murmured.
"The only way our planets would stop fighting is to
stand against someone else." He turned again to Vellyngaith. "My conditions. You will send three of your Rul-
ing Forum to our planet as a guarantee."

"Hostages?"

"Advisors. And we shall send three of ours."

Vellyngaith blinked, seeming for a moment not to
understand the words. "I've never heard of such a
thing."

"I made it up," Shucorion said. "I also made up that
each side will give free access to all military technology schematics to the other side. We will know what
you have, and you will know what we have."

The battlelord's stony blue face took on a palette of
shock. "How will we know?"

"I'm not sure, but experience will tell us what to
think in time. That is what alliance is all about, Battlelord, or we will never trust each other. If you truly
want to call an end, there's no reason for us not to

know how each other's hardware works. If you want us to trust you, we'll all tell what we have, this is how it works, here is our dispersement. And . . . you will supply us with two ellipses' worth of antimatter for our dynadrives."

Behind them, the Kauld guards tensed so sharply that Vellyngaith had to slash his hand toward them to stand them back.

Shucorion moved a step closer, faced the battlelord squarely, and lowered his voice some. "I don't want Federation here any more than you do. But if you refuse my bargain, Blood will go away from you and take our chances with them. They may not kill as many of us and you might."

Lips parted, dark eyes crimped, complexion flushed purple, Vellyngaith stared at him. "Why do I need you so much? What do you bring in return?"

"You need me because I among my people am the one who can dare take a chance. You also need me because Blood navigation can lead you through the Blind."

He paused, watching Vellyngaith's expression. The Kauld battlelord's posture changed slightly enough to give Shucorion advantage. Kauld had strength, but Blood had cunning. Blood had survived through many cycles by outworking their opponents, by developing the one talent Kauld had never mastered. Kauld had come to believe that Blood were somehow mystical, that the black cloak of the Blind selectively protected them. Shucorion knew their success was only patience, science, simulation drills, and tricks like using the darkness to make weakness and cause illusions of strength. Tricks which Kauld had never bothered to develop.

"I will take those chances for us both," Shucorion said, "if you accept my conditions. You must give me a reason to believe you will never again turn on my people. A fleet to stop Federation will be composed of Blood and Kauld, but under Blood control. You will strike, but we will tell you where."

Vellyngaith's hard cheeks softened. He held back a punishing smile that made his soldiers shuffle with uneasiness. "Is there more? One of my legs, perhaps?"

"The new Kauld fleet," Shucorion went on, "when it is housed in your new fortress, will be twenty percent Blood."

"Twenty percent!" Vellyngaith nearly choked. "Avedon! You dream deeply!"

"If I am to believe that your fleet will not turn on Blood, then Blood must be part of it. Did you expect me to go out and defend against Federation while you build your fleet fortress and trust you not to use it against my planet? Battlelord, we will never know each other that well."

The eyes of the men from both worlds were fixed upon him. He felt every thought, every doubt, every suspicion as if needles pierced him. For a man of Blood, this was the hardest thing.

"Agree," he said, "and you will have time to take that planet. You will own it when they arrive. If we are true allies, then I will go out into space and find a way to cripple them, cause them to hold back, perhaps not come at all. What is that worth, Battlelord? For our new 'alliance'?"

# Chapter Twelve

## Conestoga *Yukon*

"WE WANT YOU and your security men off our Conestoga, and your starship out of our way. We're turning back before a disaster happens that you can't stop at the last second."

The situation had been fomenting for weeks aboard the Conestoga *Yukon.* Now a suspicious collection of troublemakers crowded in front of James Kirk, Spock, Dr. McCoy, Uhura, Governor Pardonnet, and Michael Kilvennan on the people-mover's green-carpeted park deck.

With more than three thousand passengers crammed aboard, each Conestoga virtually qualified as a town. This deck was the place designed to make them feel as if they weren't sardines in a can, even though they were. The park deck on each Conestoga was the only open space aboard, the only area not devoted to sleeping or private matters. Ferns and small trees were potted in brick containers, providing not only simple appeal but oxygen. The carpet on this particular Conestoga was a big flat jungle of printed banana leaves. A play area in the center provided a hub for pub tables around the perimeter, relief for frustrated parents with little ones who didn't understand the confines.

Today, though, there were no children scrambling on the climbers, nets, and tubes, no parents and grandparents clustered at the café tables with built-in cappuccino machines gurgling in the background and entertainment tapes at their fingertips. No one seeking a meeting place with friends or a refuge for private thought.

Instead, the deck today was crowded with grim adults. At the center of the forefront, instigating dissatisfaction in a particularly infectious manner—though not unexpectedly—was Billy Maidenshore.

Kirk wasn't at all surprised to see this latest irritant at the laserpoint of trouble. As he approached the passengers, he felt set apart, uniformed, magnetic, for he knew that Maidenshore was here because of him, to render a verdict the courts hadn't anticipated when they let this criminal slip through the legal loopholes. He knew also that Maidenshore had stirred his cauldron on this Expedition freely for many months while Kirk busied himself ignorantly with fleet details. Before him as he approached was his big mistake—or perhaps just a flaw of delegation. He hadn't been able, or careful enough, to look over the manifests himself, to scan the names with prior records. He had forgotten that the name and reputation of James Kirk could be a conduit for revenge. In his years of conquest and salvation, he'd made many enemies.

Standing with the latest shady character were several upright citizens, side by side with Maidenshore in suspicious companionship, many who had emerged as leaders on this particular dormitory ship. The Kilvennan family was here—Michael's frowsy little wife and his pious brother, at least—the well-meaning loudmouth Tom Coates with his wife, and many others who were familiar to Kirk by looks if not by name. Seeing them stand with Billy gave Kirk a shimmy of failure deep in his innards.

But what could he prove? How could he convince them they were listening to the wrong man? If Maidenshore had legitimately squirmed out of grand theft, embezzlement, and racketeering, it was Kirk's own fault for not pushing the charges personally. Since then, Maidenshore had been, annoyingly enough, a model citizen on this convoy. Among the sixty-four thousand colonists, there were unquestionably many with besooted backgrounds among whom Maidenshore was only one, yet seeing him here today, stirring up this crowd, didn't come as much of a surprise.

"You've made friends over here a little too efficiently, Billy," Kirk accused. "What are you up to?"

"What would I be up to?" Maidenshore spread his hands elaborately. "The same as all these other people. My business collapsed back on Earth, so I come out here to start a new life, take a chance, throw caution to the wind—"

"What're you accusing him for?" Pressing forward, Tom Coates challenged Kirk with his big lumberjack presence. "Billy's been helping us all along. Encouraging us, talking about putting our fears behind us, plugging forward never mind all these problems. He's kept us going this whole time!" As Maidenshore patted his arm and uttered shhh's, Coates grew red-faced behind his thick beard and bellowed, "Well, you have!"

"Meant every word," Maidenshore calmly declared. "And I mean it now when I say it's time to cut our losses. That accident with the mules on *Comanche,* that was too much, too close. We almost had four thousand people turned into little sprinkles before our eyes. There's more trouble going on out here than Starfleet led us on to believe."

"Starfleet never led anybody on," McCoy argued.

Uhura, at the same time, snapped, "You people were determined to come no matter what the odds."

Before anyone else could speak, Evan Pardonnet stepped between the two groups and appealed to the people who had been devoted to his vision until recent days. Everyone suddenly turned quiet in deference to this most ferocious advocate of principled expansion.

He used the silence to meet their eyes, connecting with each one of them before he spoke.

"Have you all forgotten our dreams?" he asked. "Our plans? We're going out to establish a new mecca. All of you would be founders of the future. Now, because of setbacks, you turn your backs on everything we've built? Everything we can still do together? We have a chance to show the whole Federation what real independence and freedom means. If you turn your backs," he finished quietly, "no one may ever come again."

So sincere were his words, so deep his gaze into the times that could come for them that they indeed could see it too, there, just beyond the next mountain. They had already moved a whole range together, just to be here today.

Kirk watched the dismayed faces of the pioneers, saw the undeflectable devotion of Evan Pardonnet, and felt himself charged with a very old feeling. He found himself just standing here, pressing down a grin of admiration, even gratitude. For a moment he almost hoped—

"We're making up our own minds," Maidenshore broke in, plowing over the near-miss. "That's the first kind of freedom. We've got this whole ship's company, plus another eighty-seven people from other Conestogas who want to turn back while the gettin's good. I got to admit changing my mind on the whole thing, I'll be the first to admit it. Nobody here wants to be the Donner Party of space. Nobody's in that big of a rush."

"Sorry, Governor." Mae Kilvennan spoke without a trace of sympathy, not like an intrepid pioneer, but like a mother who had just seen her children on the brink of tragedy. "We've elected Mr. Maidenshore our mayor. We're seceding from the colony until things are safer to bring our families out here."

Clearly wounded by the statement, Pardonnet murmured, "Seceding . . ."

"It's been months living like this, Governor," she added, then shook her head and didn't bother describing.

Pardonnet simply stared at her. His silence was far more poignant than any further plea.

"Once the track's been stabilized," Maidenshore took over, filling the gap of guilt as it rose, "I've promised to underwrite the expedition for any of my friends here who decide to take another shot at it."

The gaggle of families broke into applause. Very irritating.

"A particularly generous pledge," Mr. Spock commented, leaving a great deal unspoken.

There wasn't exactly approval in Spock's voice. Kirk glanced at him, but knew a dead-end street when he saw one. He turned to the *Yukon*'s commanding officer and asked, "Captain? Your intentions?"

Freight Captain Linda Battersey blinked as if she still had doubts. "Definitely I would prefer to stay with the Expedition. However, I'm bound by command contract to ferry these people wherever they want to go. If that means back to Federation space, that's where I steer."

"Understood." Again Kirk turned, this time to Michael Kilvennan. "You're going with them too?"

The privateer captain hesitated at being so bluntly questioned, then made a single unambiguous nod. "Right."

"I thought I'd changed your mind."

As Kirk waited for an answer, Kilvennan's inner struggle, if there was much left, showed only in a single flicker behind his eyes. When he spoke, though, the words had no waver. "There's not one man in a hundred thousand who's worth serving under," he declared. "You haven't changed my mind on that."

Kirk felt the stinging eyes of all the people around him, both friend and not-so-friend. He met none but Kilvennan's. "You made a deal to stick with the Expedition. Is this all your word is worth?"

"I didn't make any deals to die out here or sacrifice my family."

"What about the other privateers?" Spock asked. "Have they made their intentions known to you?"

Communicating that he couldn't read minds, Kilvennan simply shrugged. "We're not a club."

Evan Pardonnet made one simple and final appeal. "Please don't do this . . . don't give up before we've even begun."

Scanning the mismatched committee of spokesmen, about twenty people speaking for the thousands aboard Conestoga *Yukon,* Jim Kirk knew what had to happen but couldn't make himself like it. He managed to stiffen his facial muscles and not let the complications show in his expression. The next few minutes, hours, and days would pilot the future of the Expedition, of the colony at Belle Terre, whether it would indeed survive and thrive, and what mettle these people really had. Having second thoughts was normal enough— he'd had his share. Usually had to fight them. What these people didn't understand yet was the consequence of compromise.

Unfortunately, he would have to help them learn this painful lesson. Otherwise, they would never fully believe, or fully commit.

"Governor," he began, changing his tone of voice, "these people have the right to make up their own minds. You've been saying all along that personal choice is the hingepin of your colony. We'll let them go."

"You're kidding!" Pardonnet blurted. "After all your talk about holding us together by force if necessary? How it's not a colony, it's a fleet, and all that?"

"There's only so much anyone can do. If they want to leave, we'll try to keep them safe while they do it."

"This is a dangerous precedent, Captain! From now on, the minute we run into the slightest trouble, somebody'll want to turn back. And there's not even any guarantee that they'll get back safe."

"No," Kirk agreed, "but I can hedge the bet. Captain Battersey, you and your Conestoga are free to go. You can take with you a complement of anyone who wishes to transfer from the other Conestogas, up to the safe capacity of your vessel as determined by Commander Uhura here. We'll also assign the *Impeller* to escort you back. You'll have a Starfleet cutter to see to your safety. And I'll go one better—I'll send Lieutenant Chekov back with you, as a navigational and tactical advisor. Does that make you feel any better?"

The paled faces of the citizens mellowed, somewhat sheepishly. Applause broke out again, this time on Kirk's side. His sudden change disarmed them. Even Billy Maidenshore made a suspicious paddle with his hands that might in wild imagination have been approval. Was it?

The governor valiantly faced Kirk. "I disagree completely with sending the *Impeller*. The *Republic* is already scheduled to break off with the Expedition and head off on a tangent mission of its own in another week. . . . Now you're sending away another Starfleet ship? You're lessening the protection of sixty thousand people in order to guard one Conestoga that's breaking the pact."

"Not everything is numbers, Governor," Kirk told him evenly. "Uhura, you'll organize the transfer of anyone who wants to go with the *Yukon*. And notify Mr. Chekov he's being reassigned back to Federation space."

With an uncloaked sigh of frustration, Uhura said, "All right, sir, if this is how it has to be."

"Very well, carry on. Captain Battersey, Mr. Sulu will be in touch about pulling you out of the formation. Mr. Spock, let's beam off and get these people on their way, then get on our own. After that, we'll see what happens to our house divided."

## *Enterprise,* Mess Hall

"There's someone stalking this Expedition. It might be from inside or it might be from outside, but we're being hunted. We have to smoke them out, get a jump on them, force their hand."

"Or, Jim," McCoy pointed out, "you could just cliché them to death."

Jim Kirk allowed himself a chuckle at his own expense.

His breakfast got cold on the table before him. Only the coffee had merited any attention as he stared down into the black pool, one sugar. It was pretty to look at, comforting somehow. Open space, no stars.

At the officer's table with him, Spock, McCoy, Captain DeSalle of the *Republic,* and Captain Austin of the *Beowulf* sat in an uneasy gathering. This had originally been a farewell breakfast for DeSalle, but dissolved almost immediately into a strategy meeting. Unfortunately, the only strategy now was to hold breath and wait.

The *Yukon* was gone, heading back to Federation space, with the Starfleet cutter *Impeller* and the *Hunter's Moon* as its escorts. Sadness and a sense of failure permeated the Expedition, even though all the other ships were continuing on their way into the unknown, toward a shining planet that would be their new life. Breaking the pact by even one ship was taking a spiritual toll.

"I wish Chekov could've been here," Captain DeSalle mentioned as he picked at his eggs Benedict. "I would've like to rib him a couple more times before I veer off."

"He always has taken you personally for some reason," McCoy acknowledged. "Want to let us in on that?"

"Uh-uh," DeSalle declined, grinning. "Private backstory. Get him to tell you. Just one of those multifaceted episodes that occurred when Jim led a landing party and left us gorillas in command."

"I should never leave the ship," Kirk commented. "Every time I do, my officers end up with more 'backstory.'"

"They have to," Austin said. He found time while devouring his third omelet to eye his comrades teasingly. "It's the only way they can keep up with the old 'Shoot first and ask questions later' Kirk."

"I always ask questions first," Kirk told him. "But when it's time to shoot, shoot. Unfortunately, that's what we have to do until we get a signal."

"Who's going to send it?" DeSalle asked. "Merkling? Chekov? Isn't that a little obvious?"

Kirk smiled.

"Well, if it's them, and your perpetrators are with them, they'll think of it."

"What if we never get a signal?" Austin asked. "How long do we wait?"

"You don't wait," Kirk told him. "I do. You and the *Beowulf* will continue to escort the Expedition forward. *Enterprise* will hang back, with Mr. Spock's long-range sensors on narrow focus."

"Listening for a distress call?" DeSalle asked.

"That's right."

"How long?"

"Until my instincts tell me not to listen anymore."

DeSalle didn't like the sound of that. He pushed his plate away and frowned. "If you get one, we'll already be too far away to assist. Are you sure you don't want us to stay back with you?"

Kirk somehow nodded and shook his head at the

same time, grateful for the offer. "Yes, I do, but no, I don't. I'd appreciate the backup, but *Republic* has its own mission now. The critical mass of that blue giant in Pisces Zeta has to be analyzed and diagnosed if the Federation's going to take action on behalf of those three star systems around it. As of midnight tonight, your timeline tightens. You'll have to make warp eight all the way as it is. You don't have a few days to lag back."

DeSalle shrugged. "Suppose not . . . if we don't leave now, we'll have to adjust our course back in the other direction too. It just seems to me you'll be having all the fun while I'm off measuring gasses and spectral shifts."

"You might be saving the populations of four outposts and more than ten colonies with those spectral shifts, Captain," McCoy mentioned. "After all, that's more in line with a cutter's duty than what you've been doing on the Expedition."

"True." DeSalle slugged down the last of his coffee. "I have to admit, it'll be good to get back to one ship, one crew, and no civilians." He looked at Kirk. "I haven't envied you this duty. You've had to be an admiral whether you wanted to be or not. A lot of us have bet in the past that you never really wanted to be."

"It's not all it's cracked up to be," Kirk agreed through a grumble. "With people like Billy Maidenshore pulling these people's strings, the job's been less than appetizing no matter what rank's tacked onto it."

He almost confided in them. As a young captain, he used to fantasize about being admiral, running the operations of several vessels, a whole fleet, and what he would do that had been done before and that never had been done before. Only a few very limited times had he been called upon to choreograph more than one ship in a maneuver, and those had always been fighting ships with fighting crews who knew what was on the line. For this project, he had relinquished those admiralty stripes in order to be a captain again, because this was an independent operation, a milk run in which all the other captains would operate their own ships and all would go smoothly.

Hadn't somebody said that once upon a time?

No, he couldn't bring himself to speak quite that openly to other Starfleet captains.

All he could do in the next days would be to watch *Republic* sail off in a tangent direction, watch the Expedition flow forward on its way, and wait for a signal from behind that might never come.

"What do you think Maidenshore's up to, Jim?" McCoy prodded. "Assuming you're still running on that theory."

"I certainly am. Aren't you? He all but waved a flag."

"Captain," Spock reminded, "we must remain aware that Mr. Maidenshore was here legally and the *Yukon*'s colonists legally appointed him their spokesman. Starfleet has no jurisdiction regarding either party."

"Spock, how long have we been in space this time?"

"Five months, eleven days, sixteen hours, twelve—"

"Exactly." Shoving his plate out of the way, Kirk pressed forward on both elbows. "So much for jurisdiction. We're the law out here. Billy Maidenshore's up to something or he wouldn't have worked so hard to change the minds of all those people."

Austin bent forward to see past McCoy. "I don't know why you let him get to you, Jim. It wouldn't be the first time a corrupt carpetbagging hair-oil peddler decided he wanted some kind of public adulation and actually got suckers to vote for him by promising them whatever they want."

Kirk leaned forward a little more, and met him with a glare full of absolute agreement.

"And anyone who promises you everything you want," he stated, "wants everything you have."

## Conestoga *Yukon*

### Sixteen days later

"What's the signature, Troy? Recognize it?"

*"Huh-uh. Neither does the computer, except it says there are at least five distinct—they're shifting again . . . design's conventional, though . . . solid hull, contemporary power output, antimatter traces, relative size to average humanoid configuration, conventional thrust—definitely some kind of hardware, Michael, and they're now on an approach vector. Why wouldn't we recognize it?"*

Those were the funniest markings ever to show up on a screen. Flickers after vibrations, emission traces, then nothing. Then patterns of the flickers would wink again. Always patterns. Nonrandom.

Michael Kilvennan licked his cracked lips and grimaced. "I don't know. Unless the signature's being masked or . . . deliberately contaminated to throw us off. Transfer the telemetry readings over to me and let me take a look at those too."

*"Transferring."*

At Michael's sides, his brother Quinn and Tom Coates watched the computer screen in the Coates's quarters while Lilian was teaching school. For two and a half weeks Michael had been slipping to the neighbors' place during his off-watch hours to check with *Hunter's Moon* on their constant surveillance of the odd shadows. On-watch was no problem. The *Moon*'s crew understood something was up. No reason to pretend over there. Here, in the Conestoga with his wife and kids and other people's kids around, there were limits. Traveling with families—weirder than he'd expected.

At first the shadows had been only minor flickers, unevenly spaced, taken as glitches or distortions on long-range sensors. Ordinarily he would never have paid them any attention.

"Got a good eye, Troy," Michael murmured. There was no response from *Hunter's Moon*.

Tom asked. "What's that green haze?"

"Trouble, that's what. Somebody's trying to look like a nebula or an anomaly. Trying to look like something natural. A ship with regular emissions has to work pretty hard to make this kind of mess out of their broadcasts."

"Moving at sublight?"

"Yeah."

"How do you know it's a ship, then?"

"Because natural objects don't change course."

Tom Coates straightened to his considerable height. "Somebody's coming at us, is what you're saying."

Michael stood up. "I've got to get back to the *Moon*."

"You're leaving us?" Quinn gasped. "With something unidentified coming at us?"

"Can't defend you from here, Quinn."

"I'll go aboard with you!" Tom offered instantly.

"Better if you take care of the families."

"I will be."

"Fine, come on. Quinn, do whatever it takes." Michael stepped out of the Coateses' quarters and shouted, "Mae!"

Carrying an armload of toys and computer parts, Mae Kilvennan appeared at the open door of their own family quarters. She blinked twice at the set of her husband's face, then grimaced. "Oh, I knew it!"

Helpless, Michael shoved his hands into his vest pockets.

Mae didn't buy it. Dumping her armload inside the door, she stomped out, fuzzy slippers flopping. "How close are they?"

"Ah . . . how close are . . . ?"

She socked him in the gut. Pointy fist, too. "How close, Michael!"

"Well, if—we—stay on—this course . . . just let me get my breath—"

"I'll let you get your breath." She kneaded her fingernails into his sleeve and dragged him down the narrow companionway as Quinn and Tom Coates followed, glancing at each other. Mae planted her husband in front of the security defense locker. "Open it."

Michael gaped at her. "I can't override Battersey's authority by arming the passengers!"

His wife put her walnut fists on her hips. "They're not her phasers. They're ours. We have the right to bear arms. Hand them over."

He leaned forward and virtually put his nose to hers. "I thought you'd thrown away Governor Pardonnet's principles."

"I was an idiot to marry you," she grumped. "I should've married Toby Parker when I had the chance. He understood me. It's awful to admit your mother was right."

Her frowsy puff of hair, about the same texture as her fuzzy slippers, caught an orange sheen from a utility light directly over them and made little wedges of pink on her cheeks. Her enormous soggy-puppy eyes had a ridiculous ferocity as she poked the weapons vault.

Michael gazed down at her. She was nearly a head shorter than he was and twice as skinny, her knotted fists attached to sticklike balls of pollen ready to pop off and fly away.

"I love your eyes," he offered.

"Gimme my phaser, pirate," she demanded.

"Hm. I guess I love your big mouth too. Stand aside, woman."

Tom Coates shifted his thick body decisively. "Give one to Lilian too."

"Will I ever," Mae vowed.

From behind both Michael and Tom, Quinn choked up, "And me."

Michael met the men's eyes, confirming what until now had only been theory, hot wind, wild proclamations, and hopes fueled by tall tales. They were about to make their own tall tale here, pioneers in the true sense, defending their prairie huts and fire pits.

Using the skeleton-key override shared by all commanders on the Expedition, Michael opened the phaser vault and handed his wife a fully charged phaser rifle, and Quinn a hand phaser. He shook Quinn's hand and kissed his wife on the cheek. "Put them on heavy stun or you could punch a hole in the hull. Don't switch to full disrupt until you absolutely have to. Call Captain Battersey and Mr. Chekov and tell her and him that the decks are armed. Do whatever Chekov tells you to do. And hide the kids. And don't shoot the wrong people."

"I won't." With the conviction of a mother lion, Mae shouldered the phaser rifle and clicked it to heavy stun.

Quinn, though, simply stared at the weapon in his hand, shaking to the bone. Michael turned to him, watching the unhappy communion.

Tom encouraged, "Shouldn't we get to your ship?"

"Yeah, minute." Michael reached for the phaser in his brother's hands and clicked the weapon to stun. "It's okay, Quinn. Killing the bad guys to protect your family isn't against God's laws. Do it if you have to."

Quinn raised his eyes, passion and panic brewing together in them, drew strength from his brother's example, and forced a nod.

Michael understood this kind of fear. Facing the unknown enemy was far worse than knowing what was coming. To fight Klingons, there was a way to do it. Romulans, pirates, Deltan raiders—there were known manners of approach, and even if they had rogues with crazy methods at least their technology wasn't a mystery. Just as his lips parted to mutter a word of encouragement for Quinn, his communicator whistled.

He snatched it up and thumbed the activator. "What's wrong, Troy?"

*"Michael, get over there! Our glitches just went into high warp and they're heading right at us! They'll be here in eight minutes!"*

# Chapter Thirteen

"COME ON, Tu, move in, moron. Focus, focus . . . Uncle Billy's doing his part. I'm still important to you—you get me out of here . . . are you reading me?"

Make a deal, see it through, make the appointment, expect the other guy to be in place when he said he would. Simple.

Up till now everything had been deadhead simple. A matter of playing to the soft side of suckers. The colonists had fallen into his grip with a couple of favors and a promise or two. He told them whatever they wanted to hear, they slurped it up, then did all the hard work themselves and gave him credit. They wanted to believe in something so much that all he'd had to do was step in and proclaim himself the thing to believe in. Hand them a carrot, and they tilled the field and thanked him for the sunshine. Suckers.

For a while it had seemed like a problem that Sledge

Kirk had sent the *Impeller* to guard the *Yukon*. He'd warned Tu that the cutter was along. That made it manageable.

Now he was down to the wire.

In his hands Billy Maidenshore held the single-frequency transponder he'd been hiding for months. He had the gain turned up as high as it would go, a gradual process begun when the *Yukon*'s passengers had voted him their mayor.

"Mayor," he uttered. "Mayor Maidenshore. As mayor of this fine city, I hereby order you morons to *show up.*"

He shook the transponder. Were they responding? Picking up the signal?

"Billy!"

Maidenshore flinched and pivoted around. "Jackass, I thought you were that stiff Chekov, spooking around like he does."

Angus rushed to him and instantly did the only thing he did well—apologize. "Sorry, Billy, sorry, sorry! Are they here? Did you get the signal that they'll beam us off before the trouble starts?"

"You'll be taken care of," Maidenshore told him. "But it's your job to keep the organization tight, got it? Tell Mary and Dick and what's-her-name with the ears that our deal's about to come through. If they're not ready, it's their own problem."

"Dick got the lung flu."

"Idiot! We were supposed to take the medicine first, so we didn't get it."

"He was afraid to," Angus said. "Should I give it to him now?"

"Let him die. It'll be a lesson."

"Okay, Billy . . . somebody armed the passengers, did you know that?"

"Armed? You mean phasers?"

"Yeah! Somebody gave them phasers!"

"Who?"

"I don't know who! Musta been the captain, right?"

"No, I mean who's got the phasers? Security?"

"No, no, the passengers! The families, like the women and men and the teenagers, they got phasers now somehow. Are you working that thing right?" He seized Maidenshore's elbow. "They gotta come and get us out!"

"Get your hands off." Maidenshore slapped him back. "They should be sending me a confirm blip. Keeping their promise to beam me off as soon as they got here. Otherwise, I'll be stuck on this crap heap with the suckers when things get hot."

Though the room they were in was small, a coolstorage bunker for extra gangway hatches, inertial damper plugs, and scrubber-filters, he found the room to pace away from Angus's simpering face.

"All these people," Maidenshore began, "scrambling from day to day, trying to convince themselves they have reasons not to shoot themselves in the skull, trying to forget they're one more day closer to dying . . . even though they'd given the past five years to Evan Pardonnet, I sold them some snake oil and they swallowed it. Sheeple . . . just as happy believing in Fairies as believing in God. Half of them think their cats are telepaths."

He drew a long breath and sighed it out, enjoying his success and the ease with which he could manipulate weak minds. If they'd just been a little stronger, he'd never have gotten so far, so fast. What happened to them was their own fault for being so spineless.

"Might have to wide-stun the whole herd," he contemplated. "Knock them silly and ship them out iced. That'll be a mess. Quieter, though . . . no screaming. Yeah, I kind of like that better. You tell Mick and Charlotte and their boys to start the process. Just stun the grownups. Kick the kids into the hold or lock 'em in their quarters. Heavy stun can kill a kid. They're worth more than the grownups."

"What about the crew?" Angus asked. "Can I do the crew myself? I always wanted to slug that lady captain ever since she—"

"Do whatever you want, but soon. Tu'll be here any minute and all hell's breaking out. He'll be beaming me off first thing."

"You're beaming off?" Angus asked. "What about the rest of us?"

"What do you think? If everybody's stunned, somebody'll have to drive this hulk while somebody else puts restraints on the sleeping beauties. That's you and Mick and Charlotte and the whole gang."

"We'll be here?" Angus frowned, suddenly more nervous than usual. "We'll be on *Yukon* when Tu takes us into his space? And you'll be over there on his ship with him? Billy, I don't know if the boys'll go for—"

"What am I hearing?" Maidenshore interrupted. He cupped a hand to his ear and leaned toward Angus. "Are you saying you don't trust me? Is that the thanks I get? Keeping you by my side all these months? Making you rich?"

"Oh, no, Billy, it ain't that. . . ."

"I think I better hear something else pretty soon."

"Thanks, thanks, Billy, for keeping me and making me rich. Thanks for—"

Angus clapped his hands over his ears as the security alarm drowned him out.

Maidenshore looked at the door panel as if some signature might appear there to tell him—"Who's that?"

Angus's face turned to plastic. The pounding sound grew louder, then abruptly stopped and became the howl of a security codebreaker.

"Angus," Maidenshore began again, "waxbrain . . . did you screen for tracking signals before you came around me? Moron? Did you?"

"Yes, I did, I swear it!"

"Well you didn't do a good job of it, did you? Now we gotta do things the hard way."

The locked panel creaked, strained, and cracked open from the other side. In a swipe, the bunker suddenly filled up with unwelcome visitors, led by Captain Battersey herself and Lieutenant Chekov. Behind them were Mae Kilvennan, Lilian Coates, Expedition Chief of Security Barry Giotto, and six security thugs with *Impeller* patches on their sleeves.

"Don't move!" Giotto snapped.

Moving forward instantly, Battersey snatched the transponder out of Maidenshore's hand and held it up to a tricorder for analysis, which was over in about three seconds. "You were right, Mr. Chekov," she said. "This signal is going out in the direction of the incoming phantoms."

"Captain Kirk was the one who was right," Chekov said. "We have been watching you."

"How?" Maidenshore asked. "Never mind. I know how." With the heel of his hand he shoved Angus two feet back into a wall. "Incompetent moron."

"He might be a moron, but it's not his fault." Chekov pushed Angus out of the line of ire and nosed his phaser into Billy Maidenshore's face. "Captain Kirk told me to watch you. I've been tracking your two-band communicator."

The unit came up between them as Maidenshore shook it. "You can't track this! It's impossible!"

Chekov indulged in a swagger. "Maybe impossible for you."

"I checked it myself!"

"You didn't check with me. All right, you, who is it coming at us?"

Bottling his rage, Maidenshore poked Chekov's chest with a defiant finger and returned the swagger. "Listen . . . I won. You can't change that. Before long it won't matter to you one way or the other who they are. You'll never be able to report back to your captain. Your days speaking that excuse for English are over as of about ten minutes from now. Get your hands off me and maybe I'll tell my buddies out there to let you keep your feet after they cut out your tongue."

Chekov kept his eyes on Maidenshore, but tilted his head toward Captain Battersey. "We don't have time to move him to *Impeller.* Can you put him in your brig?"

Battersey fought a tumbling stomach. "We don't have a brig."

"Will he fit in a locker?"

"If we fold him."

Maidenshore shrugged one shoulder. "Put me wherever you want. Pretty soon, I'll be steaming in a hot tub on Aldebaran II and you'll be on an auction block."

"Auction block?" Mae blurted. "What does that mean!"

"It means Orions," Chekov snarled. He looked at Battersey, then at Mae. "Slave traders."

Mae's respiration accelerated to heaves so violent it seemed they might crack her narrow chest. "Slavers? Why! Why would they do that!"

"Orions do lots of things. They starve people by millions, force the survivors to work, deplete self-confidence, rule through terror . . . the usual."

"But why?" Mae asked again.

"And how do you know so much about it?" Maidenshore asked.

Chekov felt his throat grow tight. Revulsion set deeply under his skin. He thought his eyes would boil as he looked at the man who had caused all this.

"It's a Russian invention," he said.

His words evoked a shock of physical chill for everyone who heard them. All at once, reality burned itself a hole in their hopes.

"He was going to sell us?" Mae's big eyes got somehow much bigger. She charged forward toward Maidenshore, held back only by Barry Giotto, who stuck out an arm at the last moment. Though another guard clutched her phaser and wrenched it out of her hands, nobody doubted her ability to claw Maidenshore's face to ribbons with her bare fingers if she got any closer. Her voice escalated to a shriek as she squalled, "Sell me? Michael? Our children? Kids who call you 'uncle'? Four thousand of your *own people?*"

" 'My own people,' " Maidenshore mimicked. "Hey, I kind of like that. *My* people. Like *my* dog, *my* cigar. *My* shoes. Say it again, honey, so I can suck on it awhile."

"Unbelievable! I don't believe it!" She started to lunge at him, but at the last second veered to one side and clawed at Chekov's phaser. "Give it to me!"

"No, no, down, down, down—" Chekov held her back with one extended arm while raising his phaser hand high in the air. She almost got it. He had to turn full about twice, with this harridan digging at his shoulders, before he managed to press her back.

"Guards," Mr. Giotto ordered, and handed Mae Kilvennan off to one of the uniforms. "Go back to your family, Mrs. Kilvennan, or I'll have to restrict you to your habitat deck."

"Fine," Mae said, steaming at Maidenshore. "I'll still find some way to poison his soup!"

"Put him in an EVS locker," Giotto added to the two guards who had custody of Maidenshore. "Then round up his network. Start with this weasel."

"Don't hurt me!" Angus wailed. "He was gonna leave me here!"

As the guards, criminals, and angry passengers flooded out, Pavel Chekov shook his head warily, his mind going in ten different directions. Soon he was left in here with Captain Battersey, and out loud he complained, "We track eight different suspects, and still can't find the real trouble until he broadcasts a rogue signal. I'm losing my touch."

"Orions . . . they never come out this far. I guess the prize was worth it." Linda Battersey stared at the tiny sensor screen on the Orion transponder. Ugly blue blips crawled swiftly toward them at a speed they could never challenge. "Look, Mr. Chekov, I'm a great ferry captain. I can move anything from here to anyplace else. I can tow, lead, pilot, chart, load, trim, rig, and raft with the best of them, but I've never been in a battle in my whole career. Every transit's always been in protected, patrolled space. I don't have the first idea how to deal with Orions!"

Having no way to empathize with a private captain after spending his entire life in Starfleet, Chekov barely kept himself from an insulting shrug. "Put up your shields, keep your narrow profile to them, and always be moving."

"According to my license, I can't relinquish command to you."

"I don't want command," he chafed. "If I take it, I can't go around freely. I'm your tactical advis—"

"My crew's never done this before!"

He took her arm. "I will help you. Go, go!"

By the time Pavel Chekov and Linda Battersey reached the Conestoga's bridge, low in the nose of the people-mover, disaster was already striking outside. Five Orion Plunderers were roaring in on full impulse, spreading out to circle the Conestoga and her escorts. The *Impeller* and *Hunter's Moon* were trying to move between the Orions and the *Yukon*, but there was no good way to do it. What two mismatched fighting ships could do against five fanged serpents, no one could yet guess. Certainly they couldn't physically protect a dormitory ship several times the volume of either of them. Chekov stared at the multi-screens and tried to imagine whether there was enough junior Jim Kirk in him to really change what was about to happen.

If only he knew what was about to happen. . . . Billy Maidenshore had sold them out—or just sold them. What would Orions do to cash in their purchase?

Clearly the Conestoga was the prize. Already the cutter *Impeller* was taking the brunt of Orion scatter-cannons broiling their shields and returning the blows with phaser fire. But space was big, and two of the Orion Plunderers broke through between the cutter and the privateer.

"They threw another one on the *Impeller!*" Bishop pointed at the starboard screen. His voice was steady, but his face was a matte of pure fear, as if a dead man were still doing his job.

Slavers. By now, the whole ship's complement knew. Word spread all over, instantly. Chekov hadn't tried to stop the passengers from knowing exactly what they were facing. To know the horrors awaiting them would make these people fight fiercely. Shielding them from the truth was no favor. If the Conestoga was boarded by Orions, the people would have to fight in the corridors.

"Keep moving," Chekov recommended. "Ignore the mesh."

Battersey glanced at him, then ordered, "Full about. Keep us turning, Ted."

Ten seconds. Fifteen. Twenty.

Chekov held his breath as the Conestoga turned and the Orion ships, for some reason, moved out of the way. Why would they do that? Why wouldn't they move in to attack, just as they were firing on the *Impeller?*

"And why not the *Hunter's Moon?*"

"What?" Battersey asked.

He waved a hand. "I'm thinking. I don't like something about this. . . ."

His words were overrun by sharp snapping under his left hand. Chekov winced backward in time to see electrical blowouts erupt all over the bridge, driving the crew away from their controls.

"It's charged!" Bishop reported over the noise. "The mesh is charged somehow. Energy surge all over the ship—the shields are overloading!"

"Keep them up," Battersey ordered.

"No!" Chekov shouted irreverently. "Shut down, quickly!"

"Why?"

"Look at your gauge!"

"My God—shut down the shields!"

"What is it?" Bishop craned to see what Chekov had showed his captain, and his expression curdled when he saw how close they had just come to frying in space. Before Battersey could repeat an order she shouldn't have to repeat, Chekov pushed Bishop aside and hammered the shield controls. Instantly the Conestoga was without protection, but the snapping electrical assault fell off.

"The mesh must be some kind of conductor," Chekov decided as he bent over a sensor readout. "It turned our energy directly to heat! Of course! We're forced to power down, can't use our shields or thrust. . . . So that's how they capture ships! We have always wondered!"

"You've never been able to track them down?" Battersey asked as she hurried from panel to panel, shutting down vulnerable systems that were still active.

Chekov used the precious seconds to continue analyzing the spiderweb now burned into the skin of the Conestoga. "Orions keep to themselves, but from time to time ships from other civilizations disappear without a trace. No sign of wreckage, no emissions to track. They must tow their victims away. No one could figure out how they could capture powerful vessels without a fight. This is wonderful! Now we know!"

"You don't have to sound so happy about it," Battersey complained. "We're going to know, all right. Firsthand."

"How long was it before the burst made us shut down?"

"Let me look . . . thirty-one seconds." She groaned and shook her head. "I know what you're thinking. We can't get anywhere in thirty-one-second bursts. Unless we get that mesh off the hull, we're caught."

"It's burned in," he reminded her. "Melted through the exo-hull and embedded. We did it with our own energy. It cost them nothing, and us everything." He thumped his hand victoriously on the console, barely missing the enact buttons for the shield power grid. Didn't want to hit that. "This is perfect! I can study this and stop the Orions from what they do!"

Battersey stared at him. "Mr. Chekov, you're delusional."

"Not yet, I'm not."

His mind spun with the chance to defrock the Orions of some of their sneak and mystery, perhaps shut down their slaving operation by giving potential victims a way to defend. This spiderweb conduction device was damnably simple, but no one yet had survived capture and escaped to tell about it. Victims simply disappeared. The very few persons, spies or traders, who had ever come out of Orion space had either not known how they captured their victims or hadn't found advantage in telling.

Or perhaps the truth was simpler still—perhaps the Orions fiercely guarded their secret. It was possible that even most Orions didn't know how the slavers did their business.

Never, never before had a Starfleet ship been captured by Orions. Never had the Orions dealt with trained Starfleet officers. Chekov vowed here and now to be the surprise of the sector.

With *Impeller*'s crew working on the cutter and him aboard the Conestoga, there was a chance. He wished he knew Captain Kilvennan and the privateers better, knew what they could do, their talents, their shortcomings, their ship's abilities. The gap in his knowledge gnawed at him. On the screen, the black-hulled privateer ship valiantly fired upon the Orion ships, until two Orions managed to get into position and spewed a mesh around the *Hunter's Moon.*

Chekov watched with voyeuristic curiosity as the privateer ship's hull lit up with a crackle of energy—her own energy, being conducted directly back into her skin by the formfitting Orion mesh. The privateer's black and green hull was suddenly veined with burns, and she was forced to shut down her thrust, emissions, and shields. He could hear in his mind Captain Kilvennan rasping the fatal orders that would put them all in the hands of the Orions.

"They hit the *Impeller's* bridge!" Ted Bishop's call startled Chekov into turning sharply. "All the pressurization ducts are blown! I can see the twisted distribution pipes from here!"

As he joined Battersey at the starboard monitor, the captain scowled at *Impeller,* lying nearly helpless now, tangled in the conduction mesh. "He had to drop his shields," she said. "They hit her full out."

Yes, in place of *Impeller's* bridge was a blackened and cracked dome, spewing atmosphere and flashing as emergency lights tried to come on in the impending vacuum.

"Beam me over there!" Chekov flinched at the sound of his own voice. What idiot had said that?

Battersey straightened sharply. "What? You're leaving us?"

"The Orions will not hurt the Conestoga, believe me."

"Are you crazy? They're dead over on the cutter! We need you here!"

Chekov raised a staying hand to her protests. "Repel boarders. Use thrusters. Move out of the way as much as you can."

"We'll burn ourselves to ashes if we use the thrusters!"

"Thirty seconds at a time." He fed his own coordinates into the transporter relay and cued it for the wild maneuver of beaming from here to the *Impeller*'s transporter room. At red alert, the pads over there should be active enough to pick up a signal and zero in on his coordinates. It was only a little bit insane. "I'm ready. Activate transporter."

Battersey grimaced and shouted, "Ted, emergency beam!"

Wondering what Jim Kirk would do and getting the feeling this wasn't it, Chekov sucked one breath to sustain him. As if he could hold his breath in a vacuum—in his mind he heard Spock placidly explaining that such effort would only hasten the inevitable rupture of his lungs, etc., etc., Mr. Chekov. There might be no air left when he arrived on *Impeller*. As he dematerialized, Captain Battersey's bitter glare followed him into confusion.

# Chapter Fourteen

## Starfleet Cutter *Impeller*

"CAPTAIN MERKLING, where are you!"

His cry leaped instantly into the open gulf leading to space, sucked out with the hissing atmosphere left on the bridge. Life-support systems screamed around him. In minutes, they would fail, beaten by the enormity of space.

Overhead, the ruptured bridge dome gaped like a lanced boil, lips peeled away, edges seared by weapons fire. What was left of the air stank and fumed. Life itself fleeted before him as Chekov physically pushed the bridge door panel out of his way and squeezed through the demolished frame. Beneath the shriek of spraying damage and the murdered life-support system, he heard a cough. The single plaintive noise gave him power to continue.

A cutter was not a starship. Finding his way here from the tiny transporter room had been mostly luck. He'd simply kept climbing, veering up. Chekov hadn't been aboard a cutter for years. Decades—was it so long? Had he been a teenager? And only a visit then. Ridiculously he found himself counting the years one by one as he dug through collapsed matter, twisted wreckage that scarcely resembled pieces of a ship. Nymphs of smoke nearly blinded him, racing for the ruptured dome. He had seconds, not minutes.

His heroic effort landed him flat on his face, his right cheek scorched by a glowing piece of metal. If he'd hit the jagged edge, he might've lost his head. Luckily, instead, he found something. The body of the first officer.

Now on his hands and knees, he crawled forward against the sucking force from above. He began to count seconds. Three. Five. His eyes stung.

Another body—this one alive! He felt upward along a leg, a hip. Female, for sure. The sleeve—a midshipman. Engineer.

"Wake up!" he snapped, grabbed a handful of hair, and shook the girl's head. She moaned, then began gasping short breaths. "Get up! Your cabin pressure is dropping! Crawl that way! Open the tube!"

In a swirling gray fog he saw the flash of a fearful eye, but the girl pulled her legs under her and made her way past him as ordered. As Chekov crawled forward around the circular edge of the bridge, he heard the tube hatch creak open behind him.

Suddenly the helm stopped him. The helm, up here on the raised deck! What an impact it must have been!

He found two more bodies, though living or dead he could not tell yet. His fingers dug into their uniforms and he pulled for all he was worth, dragging them across the tilted deck toward the general area of the tube that led through the repair trunks to Deck Two. Smoke choked his brain. He could barely think. Should he go back? How many people were in the bridge crew of a cutter?

A blur of hissing, of dragging, and a final entanglement in arms and legs—a tumble down the tube into near darkness made his decision for him. The tube's ladder disengaged itself and thumped freely, tempting him to go back up to the nearly airless bridge.

Pulling himself up on the tilted deck, Chekov blinked his tortured eyes. Trembling fingers found the wall panel and punched the hatch closure. Overhead a loud clack, a sucking sound, and finally terrible silence broadcast the automatic shutting of the hatch. Locked. The bridge, and anyone left lying there, would find a cold fate.

"Mr. Chekov!"

Through his watering eyes Chekov strained to see, to confirm that the voice he heard was Captain Dan Merkling himself and not an illusion of damage noise. As Chekov's vision fought its way back, Merkling staggered out of the darkness into the tiny flicker of an emergency worklight, supported by the midshipman Chekov had slapped awake and a young lieutenant with a sooty face.

The captain's blond hair actually smoldered, his face reddened and blistered on the left side. He grimaced in pain and couldn't open his eyes.

"Orion Cossacks!" Chekov blurted simply.

"What are they doing out this far?" the captain complained, almost as a side note.

"It was Billy Maidenshore," Chekov informed. "Captain Kirk was right to have us monitor his activity."

"I can't see," Merkling choked. "Chemical spray. Fire retardant, from the smell of it. You saved our lives," he pointed out, almost casually. "Did you come with a boarding party?"

Abruptly inadequate, Chekov flopped his arms. "I am the boarding party. How many are here?"

Merkling sighed fitfully. "I don't know—"

"Five of us," the young male lieutenant filled in. He looked at Chekov. "Burnell, sir, life sciences."

Merkling nodded toward the young man. "Burnell pulled Grenski down the hatch after you got me and Molyneaux out. They hit us with some kind of armor-piercer. Luckily I'd already ordered an evac of the damage-control team. This young lady is Molyneaux. Grenski's on the deck—" Over his shoulder he called, "Verdicchio! Is he dead?"

Out of the dimness another youthful voice called, "He's unconscious. Breathing's normal, but he's not awake."

"Then it's just the four of us," Merkling said. "Mr. Chekov, I only have a crew of a eighty to start with, and we've had fifty-one casualties already. Bridge is gone, life-support is on standby systems, my first officer's dead, I'm blinded—Molyneaux, was auxiliary control ruptured?"

"Not before we were hit, sir," the girl gasped.

"Are you the communications officer?" Chekov asked her.

"No, I am," Burnell spoke up. Oh, yes—a clear speaker's voice, deep in spite of his age, nearly perfect enunciation, with an English accent.

"I'm an engineer's mate," Molyneaux told him, "spectroscopy apprentice. Are they going to sell us into slavery?"

Her voice squeaked, but her eyes never wavered in spite of the stinging fumes. She was a tiny thing, the perfect opposite of the six-footer Burnell, and despite the French name she was obviously very Asian. They were both hardly more than teenagers, both waiting for the officers to make decisions.

A moment later, another young one popped up behind Burnell. This would be—

"Verdicchio, biochemistry," the skinny boy reported. "Are they gonna kill us?"

"Don't worry," Chekov told him. "I have them right where they want us."

Was there nothing but children in Merkling's crew? Or had only the children survived so far? Sometimes that happened—senior officers tended to move to the front of ship action during times of emergency attack and were often the first to die. It was a strange hearkening back to the ancient ways of charging on horseback to meet an enemy, the days when huge numbers of officers fell first, leaving their youngest recruits to fend alone.

"The Conestoga's mule power and shields have been compromised by the conductor mesh," Chekov said, knowing it was his turn to report. "So has the privateer. We can't move more than twenty-five seconds at a time."

"Where do you get twenty-five seconds?" Merkling asked.

"It takes thirty seconds for the conduction to build up enough energy. I believe we can move in twenty-five-second leaps."

"And go where?" Molyneaux squeaked. "A hundred yards here and there?"

The skinny boy added, "It's not enough to get away!"

"It's not enough if you *want* to get away," Chekov pointed out. "We want something else."

Now he waited for the captain's decision. A half-wrecked ship, a half-dead crew, insurmountable odds. As the only Starfleet ship, the most considerable threat, the *Impeller* would be targeted for destruction, not spared to be sold. Her trained crew would not be allowed to survive into slavery. They were too much a threat. Knowledge could be a curse. The Orions would see it that way.

The children gawked and swiveled to their captain, expecting an argument. Captain Merkling waved a hand before his injured eyes, tried and failed to blink, then shook his head. "I can't choreograph a battle if I can't see it." He turned more or less toward Chekov. "Go down to auxiliary control. If the ship's maneuverable, take command. Most of the functional crew is below—I'll go to engineering and make sure you have power. I don't need eyes for that, all I need is hands."

"I will, sir!" Chekov promised.

"Molyneaux, Verdicchio, Burnell, go with Mr. Chekov," Merkling confirmed. "Do anything he says, no matter how crazy it sounds. Grenski, get me down to engineering. Mr. Chekov, ship's luck!"

"Don't worry. The good part about being doomed is it can't get any worse."

The children looked at him when he said "kint gettany verse" and took a second to digest his accent.

Chekov plunged into the auxiliary control at a run and skidded into the secondary helm. He snapped his fingers at the skinny boy. "You—Verdi—what is your name again?"

"Verdicchio, sir!"

"Ah . . . I think I will call you 'Scotty.' Do you know how to steer?"

"Steer? The ship? I'm a biochem—"

"What about weapons?"

"Oh, I, I, uh—maybe I—"

"How old are you?"

"Twenty-two, sir."

Chekov put his hands on his hips and scowled. "What are you doing on a fighting ship at such an age? Are you in a bridge crew or not?"

Verdicchio's narrow dark eyes flitted like a bird's. "I was delivering a Hollister assembly and helping install it."

"Hm. Wrong place, wrong time, eh? Sit at the weapons. Shoot when I tell you. Burnell, can you steer?"

They were looking at him the way he used to look at Captain Kirk. He ignored them as he keyed in the manual overrides and made sure all the systems they needed were getting power. Molyneaux blinked her feathery eyes and scoured the controls, trying to make sense of them. Burnell did better than the others, slipping into the chair behind the aux helm and activating it, though he couldn't bring himself to respond verbally.

Generally this was the least used place on any Starfleet ship. Auxiliary control was the ultimate backup bridge, small and unglamorous, double-shielded and not very comfortable. The forward screen was much smaller than the one on *Enterprise*'s auxiliary bridge, but there were four additional screens mounted on the starboard and port bulkheads to offer a wider continuous view of the crippled Conestoga *Yukon*, and the valiant fight going on between two Orion Plunderers and Kilvennan's *Hunter's Moon*.

The privateer, befouled in conductor mesh and patterned with scorch marks, was losing. Yet Kilvennan continued to fire his phasers despite taking most of the impact right back on his own hull. Empathy winced through Chekov—the inside of that privateer must be damnation unleashed. Even from here he could see ruptures in main coils, venting atmosphere, spewing fluids, and the awful flash of systems failures. In spite of all that, Kilvennan was still trying to shoot his phasers in microbursts. Each time the phasers fired, the conduction mesh snapped viciously, sending jolts back into the privateer's skin.

The *Impeller* looked dead from outside. The Orions would move in for the kill any minute. He had to show them that the cutter wasn't dead at all. He would do it by drawing the pack off *Hunter's Moon*.

Working the nearest panel, he tapped out a flash message to Kilvennan—*Maneuver past us.*

"Come here—" Chekov grabbed Verdicchio and stuffed him into the weapons seat. "Put your hands over here. Push buttons. Very good. You look good there."

"If we fire, that net'll fry us."

"No problem. It's nothing compared to the time we went to the Old West."

"Vest?" The boy glanced up at him. "You're taking this awfully well—"

Chekov shrugged. "Been in worse spots. All power to weapons. Never mind the shields."

Verdicchio stared at the Orion ships, which raced past after having nearly incapacitated three Federation vessels. "Maybe we'll have to surrender." His fearful eyes glanced to Chekov to see whether his suggestion might be taken.

"I have a plan," Chekov said. "Don't worry. Captain Kirk taught me *everything* he knows." He pressed his hands to the photon-torpedo controls. "Which for this situation adds up to nothing. . . ."

No point telling them the whole truth about Orions. Starfleet trained its young men and women to understand the possibility of death, but the prospect of life-long slavery in some brutal tract never came into the mix of what to expect. Sneaky, shy, and expert at covering their tracks, Orions rarely toyed with the Federation anymore, having long ago found Starfleet too stubborn and unremitting a force. Billy Maidenshore must have coaxed them out here with the promise of a huge capture. Chekov now found himself burdened with the weight of keeping them from their prize.

"Molyneaux, start counting seconds when we move the ship. When we get to twenty, make a noise. Verdi, get ready to fire phasers when I say."

Burnell looked at him, confused. "What are you doing?"

"Arming a photon torpedo."

"A torp? With phasers? It's suicide to use both at the same time without maneuverability!"

"Do everything I say," Chekov told him firmly. "I will call you 'Bones.' "

Poor Burnell's face crumpled. "What?"

"Every few minutes, you say, 'Dammit, Pavel, you can't do that!' "

"Uh . . ."

"All I need now is someone to tell me I am illogical. Never mind—I will do that myself. You—come over here."

Molyneaux, running on one breath and turning a couple of shades of green, stumbled to him. "Yes, sir?"

"This is the photon firing control. It is now armed. When I give the order, you will fire it. Do not hesitate."

"Oh, sir—"

"Not 'Oh, sir.' 'Aye, sir.'"

"Aye, sir . . . what can we do if we can't move the ship, sir?"

"There are always alternatives. This is nothing compared to the time I was in a bar fight. Klingons, outlaws, whiskey, chief engineers—I know what to do."

He finished arming the torpedo and hurried to stand right between the helm and weapons stations. He put one hand on Burnell's shoulder and the other on Verdicchio's. One of the Orion ships shot past so close he felt its wingtip on his cheek.

He started by squeezing Burnell's shoulder. "When I give Molly the order to fire the forward torpedo, you will move the ship forward. You see those two Orion ships right in front of us? You will go right between them. Understand?"

"Move the ship forward, between the two Orions . . . aye."

"You will have twenty seconds, no more. I want you to go forward at emergency one-fifth impulse."

Burnell's wide face turned pasty. "That's awfully fast, sir! I don't know if I can hold it with the ship in this condition!"

"All you have to do is go straight. You don't even have to turn! Yes?"

"Y-yes . . ."

"And you," Chekov plowed on, squeezing Verdicchio, "will fire phasers directly forward on my mark."

"Aye, sir, do you want me to target the Orion on the right or the left? I don't think I can hit both of them at the same time . . . I've never done this bef—"

Diane Carey

Chekov shook his head. "You will not be shooting at a ship. You will be shooting right down the middle." When both boys snapped to look up at him, he gave them his best wise-old-sage glance and firmly repeated, "Exactly down the middle. No questions."

They settled tensely down and even seemed to physically shrink.

"Aye, sir," Burnell muttered, "no questions."

"Sir?" Molyneaux interrupted. I'm reading something funny . . . an incoming signal on long-range. Wow, it's coming in fast!"

Chekov looked around. "Describe it."

"Warp six point one . . . emissions Federation standard, Starfleet signature . . . mass approximately two hundred thousand metric tons—"

"Ah, about time!" Clapping his hands once, sharply, Chekov almost startled Verdicchio out of his chair.

Molyneaux leaped out of her seat. *"Enterprise?* It's them? Coming to help?"

Chekov made a nonchalant expression. "Of course. What else would have that mass-to-thrust ratio? You see? I told you don't worry. You worry anyway. What is their ETA?"

"Oh—it's . . . thirteen minutes!"

"Won't be soon enough," Burnell mourned.

True enough. Thirteen minutes was plenty of time for the Orions to finish their job. Chekov pointed at Molyneaux. "Sit down. Back to business. Begin to count now! Verdi, forward thrust!"

Around them the battered *Impeller* thundered with residual power, all systems seeking energy sources wherever they could get them. Life-support howled in the bulkheads. Engine thrust pulsed like a fibrillating heartbeat. On the forward screen, a sense of sluggish movement made the view of the enemy ships and the privateer *Hunter's Moon* wobble in a spacesick way. Flashes of greenish yellow light showed them the Orion conduction mesh building up to suck energy out of the cutter and burn further through her hull.

"Five seconds," Molyneaux reported. Her hand was poised over the photon firing control.

On the screens, the Orion ships drew closer. The cutter was on a course right down the alley between the two Orions, though they didn't seem to notice yet that the cutter was moving at all. Likely they were concentrating on the privateer, which continued to dog them in spite of the conduction mesh gradually murdering it.

"Ten seconds!" Molyneaux gasped.

"More thrust," Chekov ordered. "Increase speed to one-quarter sublight!"

"One quarter," Burnell responded, numb.

"By the way, Mr. Spock, don't you think it's time Mr. Chekov got promoted? Yes, Captain, very logical."

As the cutter drew quickly toward the Orions, Chekov leaned forward and found himself wickedly grinning. A strange and unexpected change was showing up in his behavior. His chest no longer hurt with struggling breaths. His hands were calm, even warm. His thoughts were in perfect order. Everything seemed clear, even easy. As the situation grew worse and worse, he became more calm.

That had never happened before.

Of course, he'd never been in command before, had he?

Pleased to discover a talent he didn't know he possessed, Chekov congratulated himself at his level temper. He had an idea of what could happen, what might happen if everything went right, and had himself convinced this was the time to do something crazy and off the books.

Or was he just good at faking it? How often had Jim Kirk been faking it?

"Fifteen seconds!"

Without turning to her, his eyes fixed on the forward screens, Chekov ordered, "Fire photon torpedo!"

With a twisting expression, Molyneaux held her breath and punched the controls. The torpedo spewed out on a pin-straight trajectory between the two Orions, barely missing the privateer on the right side. In a flash, the cutter was past *Hunter's Moon*, using its burst of speed to race down the corridor after the photon torpedo.

"Follow it right down the middle!" Chekov ordered Burnell, making a slicing motion with his flattened hand. "Verdi, fire phasers! *Detonate the torpedo!*"

This was no time to have to repeat himself. Caught up in the absurdity of the order, Burnell plowed the cutter between the Orions just as Verdicchio fired the phasers.

Before them, at proximity distance, the photon torpedo erupted into a deadly plume, detonated on the run, without an impact. Since there was nothing to stop it, the destructive power blew forward, its sun-bright glare forcing them to look away.

"Open fire, direct starboard and port, full phasers!" Chekov shouted over the squeal of the emergency alarms breaking out all over the ship. "Brace for the wash!"

As the unshielded *Impeller* barnstormed through the turbulent detonation cloud, buffeted violently, the children fought the natural fishtailing and opened fire on both Orion ships as ordered. Fingers of energy corrupted the vessel around them, torturing them with waves of electrical charge. The torpedo had not only momentarily overloaded the Orions' shields, making them vulnerable to point-blank strikes, but also blinded them to the cutter's location.

"Twenty seconds!" Molyneaux called.

"Cut thrust!" Chekov called. "Cease fire!"

The howl of power fell abruptly off, leaving only a snap and flail of residual flow here and there. The ship became almost peaceful, and simply coasted on through the photon wash, leaving the crippled Orion ships turning dazedly behind.

"Severe damage, all systems," Burnell reported. "The net's almost melted through our exostructure. Another burst and the hull's going to start collapsing."

"What about the Orions?"

"They don't look so good," Verdicchio reported. "They're falling away."

Molyneaux turned. "But the other three are coming forward to meet the starship!"

Burnell's wide face crumpled as he looked up. The young officer's question, innocent in its wisdom, put a lance through Chekov's heart.

"But Captain Kirk doesn't know about that net, does he?"

## Privateer *Hunter's Moon*

"*Impeller* hit them while they were blinded! Two of them are retreating."

"Keep broadcasting, Sylvie, no matter what happens. Troy, keep striking at the other ones. Fire at will, all you can."

"Our hull's melting."

"Let it melt."

"Firing."

"I'll have to remember that one. . . ."

Sucking small breaths and dealing with relentless pain from broken bones, Michael Kilvennan clamped his left arm to his ribs and haunted the only working screen left on his quarterdeck. They were watching themselves die by bits. Or worse—maybe they weren't scheduled to die like the *Impeller* was. The privateers and the Conestoga were probably on the same list. Up for sale.

"Michael—I've got—I've got a . . ." Lying on the deck, Troy Augustine was barely conscious, bleeding from both legs, gashed in the side of his head, breathing in shattered gasps, but watching the secondary access windows on the direct feed. "Signal," he shoved out before coiling in a spasm.

"Thank God!" Choked by his own injuries, Kilvennan slipped to the deck on one knee, braced a hand on Troy's shoulder, and looked at the staticky little readout screens, no bigger than the palm of his hand. Even through the static, clear signals bubbled of a solid object racing toward them at a ridiculous speed.

Troy's eyes watered as he fought raw pain in his legs. "Who's that?"

"The cavalry, pal." Kilvennan patted Troy's arm in quiet victory. "Sylvie, thirty degrees down. Get out of his way."

"Then it's him?" Troy struggled, his voice cracking. "It's Kirk? He actually—got our signal?"

"Yeah . . . yeah, Troy, he got our signal, thank God. . . . Let's get out of his way."

"Michael," Sylvie Graves called from overhead, "the three other Orions are turning into formation to meet the incoming signal. The starship'll come out of warp right into that conduction net!"

Troy flinched and raised his head. "Hey—what—! Sylvie, do you see this?"

"What's happening?" Kilvennan dropped to one knee beside Augustine and peered into the casing at the direct feed.

Racing toward them at warp eight-point-seven—past their maximum safe cruising speed, but necessary to close two weeks' worth of distance—the red dot giving off the *Enterprise*'s identification signal had begun to draw out into a thin line, like taffy being pulled longer and longer. He squinted, confused. Why would a hard signal stretch like that? Malfunction?

As he was about to stand up again, check the readings against their damage, the long red blip changed again, cracking at its thinnest points, pulling apart as if a giant hand had taken a scissor to the ribbon. Four, five, seven independent blips slowly drew apart from each other. Eight. Nine.

Kilvennan felt his throat tighten. "What the hell . . ."

Above him, Sylvie Graves gasped at the readings. "The starship's structure is breaking up! It looks like the hull's falling to pieces!"

# Chapter Fifteen

## Enterprise

"ENGINES ARE at critical, Captain. Redline on all systems."

"Just bite on something and hold warp nine, Sulu."

Sulu didn't give a response this time. Speed was actually about to break warp ten. He just hadn't quite been given that order yet.

The starship raced at fantasy speed. Her engines whined angrily as the helm demanded a curved course at emergency high warp. Almost impossible. If it hadn't been Sulu handling her, Kirk would've been forced to order a reduction before turning.

He had to turn. He had to get there. Kilvennan's distress signal had possessed a pitiful whimper of desperation.

Spock was watching him. Kirk deliberately didn't

look up there. Yes, the ship might break apart. They'd accepted that.

She also might not. This was one of those moments when Kirk felt the bond with the *Enterprise* that proved they were both alive. This synergy of spirit and hardware could only happen to a man and a ship that fit each other just so. Beneath her sparkling refit, under her new hull plates and touchpads, the starship proved she was still his old stress-tested mate of many adventures. All the weak parts had been long ago hammered out of her, leaving the residual strength deep in her bones upon which he dared depend. No cosmetic appliance could erase the bones that made her the one and only *Enterprise*.

She would hold warp almost-ten on a curved course as she carried him deeply down and around the enemy's flank for a surprise attack from behind.

She would hold together . . . she would.

## The Orions

"What's going on? What am I looking at? Explain it to me, you greasy wad!"

Billy Maidenshore grabbed Tu's slimy muscular arm and yanked at him dangerously. On the screen they were reading the approaching starship, racing in at warp speed, but the readings were splitting up, breaking apart, splintering. Was it an illusion?

The Orions were turning, breaking off their attack on the Conestoga and the privateer ship to face the starship coming at them. The *Impeller* was faltering off someplace to starboard, suffering her horrible wounds. Kilvennan's privateers weren't fairing much better. The Conestoga was theirs, free and clear, except for that damned starship racing in!

"Can't you get away?" Maidenshore bellowed at the Orion crew.

"I may not have to get away," Tu said as they watched the screen. "The starship begins to break apart."

"How do you know that? Show me!"

Tu pointed at the large circular table-screen between them. "This is the starship on its approach trajectory. It broadcasts the *Enterprise* identification beacon. See how it separates . . . three . . . five . . . nine . . . separate blips now, where moments ago it was one. They are destroying themselves rushing in this way."

Maidenshore tried to understand, but alarms were going off in his head. One blip, moving at warp six, now nine blips spreading apart. Behind the Orions, the suffering *Impeller* and *Hunter's Moon* were nearly helpless, throwing only potshots. The sting had been almost perfect. The Conestoga full of fat civilians was all his, ready to go to the stockyard.

Now the starship plummeted toward them and Tu and the other Orions had turned to concentrate their spiderweb technology forward to capture it, and the starship was cracking up before it even got to them.

Was he born under a lucky star? *That* lucky?

He seized Tu's arm a second time, more fiercely. "It's a trick. He's faking you! Turn around, turn around!"

Tu's arrowlike orange eyes squeezed tight. "Human, release me and stop babbling! I will face my enemy!"

"I'm telling you it's a fake, you idiot!" Maidenshore roared, desperate to be believed. "He's tricking you somehow, somehow it's a fake, somehow it is!"

"My enemy blows his engines apart by pursuing me too hard," Tu roared back, "and you tell me this is magic? You know nothing about ships."

"I know about salesmen," Maidenshore insisted. "I

know about acting—I know about humans! Don't believe what you see! Do something unexpected, right now!"

"Stand back from me." Tu shoved him away. His many-fingered limb pointed at the table-screen, where nine clearly separate blips were swifting moving farther from each other in a scattered pattern, like water spraying. "The starship is breaking into pieces. Believe it. We win without firing a shot."

Unable to make a technical case, Maidenshore backed up against the curved side of the Orion pilot station. He knew a fake-out when he saw one, and he knew a sucker too.

Or Tu.

When his shoulders bumped against the curved wall, he felt the first hard shot hit the Orion ship—and hit it from behind, where nobody but himself thought it would come.

A direct hit to the engines. Even a landlubber knew what that meant. Not enough power for the shields. Fighting capacity in the dumper. Turn and run, or get stomped.

Tu cried out with surprise and fury.

Maidenshore mentally tried to make himself smaller for a minute, to avoid getting attention. The Orions were busy. That was both bad and good—it would give him enough time to cook up a fresh story.

## Hunter's Moon

"Could they have overwarped?" Michael Kilvennan's skin crawled as he watched the ugly splatter that a moment ago had been a single large-mass ship racing toward them at warp five. "I've never seen that happen. . . . Oh . . . that's brilliant."

On the deck, Troy Augusting gasped, "What's—what's happening to it! Michael, the whole starship's falling apart!"

"It's not a starship," Kilvennan said, strangely calm as he watched the screen. "Look at the propulsion meter. They're all equal. Every piece has an engine. Damn, that's smart! It's just a formation of shuttles broadcasting the *Enterprise* ID code! Shuttles flying at burn-out speed. Sucker's smart . . ."

Troy choked up blood and spat it out, then struggled to keep his burning eyes on the graphic displays. "Bunch of shuttles to face down three Orions?"

Clamping his arm tighter to his ribs, Michael pushed off Troy, ignoring his first mate's seizure of pain at the sudden movement. "Syl, get us the hell out of the way! Drop, quick! Leave the Orions' stern without cover, get it?"

Scarcely was the order out, scarcely had the privateer even moved, when phaser blasts raked through open space, grazing them at proximity range.

Half the privateer's quarterdeck was swallowed by black smoke. Choking, Michael dragged Sylvie away from the toxic cloud, and hit the manual vent control.

"What the hell was that?" Sylvie gagged over the whine of suction fans.

"Sneak attack!" Michael shouted. "Look!"

On their one remaining visual screen, the three Orion ships glowed and staggered under phaser fire from their aft quarters. Behind them, gliding now at sublight, the *Enterprise* was still firing at them, point-blank. The nearest Orion ship cracked in half, exploded from inside, then exploded a second time from even deeper inside. Probably the engine room.

"How'd he get over there!" Troy rasped from the deck. "He was—coming from the—other direction—"

"Kirk decoyed them with the shuttle cluster. In tight formation, the shuttles read as a single vehicle while *Enterprise* did an end run around them at higher warp. Pretty good . . . the Orions thought they were turning to face the starship, and ended up putting their weakest shields and thrust assemblies square into his sights. Nice move . . . he completely faked them out."

They fell to silence, watching in disbelief as the starship cut into the remaining two Orions. Mercilessly it cut the hull apart on the next closest slaver until the Orion attempted to veer off, but instead blew itself to a sparkle.

Unceremoniously the *Enterprise* turned on the third remaining Orion, while in the background the first two, who had netted the *Impeller,* raced out of the area, abandoning their last compatriot to the starship's unsympathetic punishment.

Michael slid to his knees beside Troy, with Sylvie shuddering over them.

"Did it," he murmured. "He did it. . . ."

They watched in numb relief as the *Enterprise* bore down like a rogue elephant on the single suffering Orion Plunderer and simply chewed it to pieces. The sight seemed brutal, and gave Michael Kilvennan a sense of viciousness in James Kirk that legend had somehow cleaned up with time. He thought of his family as he watched the last Orion ship being cut up by the starship's unbroken phaser stream. He thought of his wife and his little kids, his sister, parents, and gentle-hearted brother Quinn dragged off some incalculable distance and put in chains for the rest of their lives.

He watched those phasers, and was gladdened.

"Captain Kirk," he murmured, "I'll follow you anywhere."

The buzz of transporter beams sang like a choir through the main deck of the *Hunter's Moon*. Ten minutes had passed since the destruction of the last Orion and the escape of the other two. Jim Kirk materialized onto a heap of wreckage that had once been the privateer's main companionway.

The area was secure. Hovering nearby, the crippled *Yukon* and the sorely battered *Impeller* were flooded with damage-control teams and security squadrons from the nine shuttles that had provided Kirk's distraction maneuver. He knew what *Impeller* would do—whatever he ordered them to do. He needed to know what the colonists were intending. The best barometer for that answer was right here on this privateer ship—its captain, Michael Kilvennan.

With one hand on his holstered phaser, just in case of surprises, Kirk picked his way through the wreckage to the upper casement and climbed to the quarterdeck. There he found Michael Kilvennan leaning on a support column, picking at the fried helm controls, alone. Probably he had sent his crew down to their microscopic idea of a sickbay.

Ragged, dirty, and injured, Kilvennan looked up and met Kirk with undisguised relief. "Made it," he commented. He slumped back against the helm. "Didn't think you were getting the signal."

"We got it," Kirk assured unnecessarily. "So they were Orions after all."

Exhausted, Kilvennan managed a nod. "Slavers. How'd you know?"

Not willing to take much credit for that one, Kirk let

out a sigh that had been waiting about three weeks to come out. "Just an educated hunch. Are you hurt badly?"

Valiantly trying to stand a little straighter, which didn't work, Kilvennan coughed out the last gulp of smoke and pressed an arm to his middle. "Broken ribs . . . glad to see you."

Offering a mellow grin, Kirk let him know tacitly that he understood all the emotions involved in fighting to near-destruction and pulling a last-minute rabbit out of a hat. "I'm glad to see you too. What's the status on board?"

"Nine dead, about twenty hurt. Lost one of my family's best friends . . . Tom Coates." Kilvennan slumped at the sullen announcement, as if the hard facts were just now sinking in and he could be something other than a captain. "How'm I gonna tell Lilian and Reynold?"

"I remember him," Kirk obliged. "I'll speak to Mrs. Coates if you like."

Kilvennan let his head hang. "It's mine to do. His son's only ten. When I get my hands on Billy Maidenshore, his name and about five body parts'll be a lot shorter."

Awkward and inadequate to do the emotional cleanup after throwing his thunderbolts, Kirk let a few seconds pass in respect for the many dead and their family and friends who would endure the rest of the voyage without them.

"If there's anything I *can* do," he attempted, "you deserve all our gratitude."

"Worried about my first mate," Kilvennan wheezed. "Got some bad electrical burns. You were right about *Impeller.* The Orions concentrated—their attack on the cutter . . . gave me the chance to notify you."

"The Orions would've been monitoring the cutter's

signals," Kirk confirmed. "I didn't think they'd pay attention to yours."

"*Impeller* took the—brunt. Gotta give them—credit . . . sorry—hard to breathe." Though Kilvennan tried to continue his report, a spasm of coughing demolished his attempt.

"You'd better sit down." With gentle force Kirk took Kilvennan's arm and piloted him into a locker bench. Then he pulled out his communicator. "With your permission, we'll move your mate to the sickbay on *Enterprise* and bring a medical team over here for your crew. Relax, and excuse me a moment. Kirk to *Impeller.*"

There was a brief crackle of damaged circuits, then an almost immediate response. "*Impeller, Merkling here. Captain Kirk, I wonder if I have to tell you how welcome you are. You must've pushed the* Enterprise *into another record with that maneuver.*" Merkling's voice was strained and breath came hard, but to his credit he was trying to cover that up.

Kirk tried to keep his empathy from showing in his voice. "We're just the cleanup crew, Captain Merkling. You comported yourselves with exceptional bravery. I'll be forwarding commendations for your entire complement."

"*Whoever piloted those shuttles, I want to shake their hands.*"

"Her hand. It was Lieutenant Commander Uhura in the lead shuttle, maneuvering the other shuttles by remote autopilot, in case the whole ruse went wrong. What are your casualties?"

"*I'm still counting. At least twenty-nine dead, over sixty injuries. Relatively light, considering what hit us, grim as that is to say. My bridge is a wreck. Mr. Chekov took over at auxiliary control.*"

"How did he do there?"

*"Oh, he did some things I wouldn't have done, but I'm not complaining. He's got a command style no magic mirror could predict. Managed to disable two of the Orions even though we could hardly move. That's why we're here to tell it. When're you gonna push that maverick out of your nest?"*

"I'll take that as a recommendation," Kirk accepted. "Can you make warp speed?"

*"Yes, our core's intact."*

"Four?"

*"Possibly five, with some strain."*

"Then you can report back to Federation space from here. Make Starbase nineteen within—ten weeks?"

*"Ten weeks at warp four point five. We've already calculated it. I agree that's the best course for us. It leaves you shorthanded, though."*

Kirk winced a little at the brave offer. "No, no, Dan, you've done more than your part. We're covered. Captain Briggs of the Tugantine *Norfolk Rebel* and his Wreckmasters are on their way here. We anticipated having to do some towing and repair. *Impeller* was going to turn back once we reached the lightship anyway. You might as well go now. Get your ship and your crew back to the help they need. You have my authorization to break off duty on the Expedition. In fact, I need you to go back and report the Orions' activities in case they decide to try this with anyone else. This is the first time they've worked with a human operative. Usually they don't let anybody in."

*"I guess Billy Maidenshore's offer was too tasty to turn down. You've got your hands full with the Conestoga. They've got sixty-two dead over there.*

*Civilians . . . it's hard to predict how they'll take something like that."*

"They're pioneers," Kirk suggested. He met Kilvennan's sad eyes, though still speaking to Merkling. "The wagon trains that crossed the continental United States in the Old West averaged a grave every eighty yards. It's a hard lesson to learn so far from home."

*"Yes . . . Merkling out."*

Belting his communicator, Kirk still heard the conversation continue in his mind, captain to captain, misery to misery. "We'll have to make some quick repairs," he contemplated, "get those energy webs off your hulls and get all of you back to the Expedition."

"We'll be weeks catching up," Kilvennan sighed, then winced. "I assume they're not waiting for us."

Kirk shook his head. "I sent them on their way, with *Beowulf* and *Republic* as a rearguard, in case the Orions got aggressive. We'll repair your ships and catch up by the time they reach the lightship *Hatteras*."

"Mmm . . . going from the prairie into the jungle. Gamma Night."

"Yes, Gamma Night."

Kilvennan peered at him candidly. "You guessed right every step. The shadows were hostiles after all. They just looked like shadows."

Somehow taking a compliment at this time twisted Kirk's stomach. "Mr. Spock and Commander Uhura deserve the credit. They found the shadows beyond the sensor horizon and interpreted them."

"If they were beyond the horizon, how'd you know they were there at all?"

" 'Beyond the horizon' takes on a certain elasticity when Spock and Uhura get to work."

"Hmm . . . but the traces could've been completely

benign. Innocent ships on their own passage. What made you suspect?"

"Just my own despicable streak. If they'd been ships passing through, they'd have made better forward progress."

"How did you know Billy Maidenshore was the one to watch?"

"Until he orchestrated the *Yukon*'s turn back, I wasn't sure. When he suddenly changed his mind and decided turning back was the thing to do, everything clicked into place. And something else . . . as soon as you left, the rash of malfunctions completely stopped."

"Must've made you happy."

"It made me angry. I don't like to be manipulated."

"Doesn't sound like 'just a hunch' when you lay it all out."

"It was partly hunch, partly other things," Kirk said. "Spock and Uhura deciphered the traces you were picking up. With your ship as a relay, we got much crisper shadows. Spock was able to apply spectral analysis to the exhaust and decipher the mixture as most probably Orion. Once we had the identity, we pretty much could guess what they were up to. And who put them up to it."

With a scowl of resentment, Kilvennan pressed his lips tight with anger. "You were right about Maidenshore too. He was the broker."

That sounded good somehow, to have the fact stated right out after stewing in suspicion for so many months. "Yes," Kirk said, relieved. "Unfortunately, I couldn't confirm it until after you left the Expedition. He went from brokering contraband to brokering slaves. A whole Conestoga full of them. Three thousand people, plus your crew and *Impeller*'s. Orions generally pick slaves from battle-survivors they can capture. It's a relatively small pool. This would've been a monumental catch for them."

"Kind of a prickly idea you had, y'know," Kilvennan said with an ironic smile. "Using my family and all our friends as bait."

Kirk offered an almost teasing scowl. "They were turning back anyway. We had to draw out the perpetrators, or we were headed for a catastrophe on a metropolitan scale. Maidenshore was right about nearly losing four thousand people on the *Comanche*. If he'd kept on doing his tricks, eventually I wouldn't have been fast enough or clever enough to stop a disaster. All I could do was let his game play out as early as possible. Sometimes you have to walk into a blind canyon in order to find out what's waiting there to jump you."

"No, no—don't get me wrong." Kilvennan held up a scratched hand. "Not arguing."

For a moment Kirk almost let the conversation flow into uneasy territory. He rarely had a chance to speak privately to another captain, and when that did happen it was usually captains of Starfleet. The code of social murmurings was different in uniform. It had limits. There were things left unsaid, images to maintain, the mirage of perfection to polish, and his own reputation usually chasing him. With older officers, he got either fatherly pride or tacit bitterness. With younger ones, either hero worship or jealousy. He'd learned to sense those, and field them, but they always curtailed the conversation. He couldn't be completely honest. He had roles to play.

Here today, with Michael Kilvennan, a privateer who ran in other circles, the temptation pulled at Kirk to spill his thoughts, captain to captain, about the burdens they both understood, how the rungs on James Kirk's ladder to glory were made of the bodies of those who hadn't survived the assault. Pressing behind his lips was the deep compassionate blame every time someone thanked him, congratulated him, pinned another medal on him, of knowing more every year how many unlauded others had paid for his chance to stand on the podium one more time. With every passing year the glory became harder to swallow. What a joke that people thought he wanted more. They didn't understand that with every triumph, as a hero progresses from win to win, luck to luck, medal to medal, the cost in lives and risks also increased. Glory could be a souring ingredient.

Maybe the mistake after all was for a man to have already done everything by the time he hit forty.

"How's your ship?" he asked. "Did the strain of continually broadcasting your sensor scans back to us cause loss of firing power?"

"Some critical burnouts," the privateer said. "Worth it, though. Without the burnouts we might've done better helping *Impeller,* but you wouldn't have known to come. Lose some lives, save some lives—doesn't always add up. Everything's some kind of . . . tradeoff."

Impressed by Kilvennan's instincts, Kirk let himself believe the other captain knew what he was feeling and was giving him a gift. Perhaps they'd just had the conversation he needed so badly. Just had it inside instead of out.

He was rescued by the bleep of his communicator. *"Battersey to Kirk."*

"Kirk here."

*"Captain, I'm sorry. I'm just not set up over here for maximum security."*

Kirk tensed. "What's wrong, Captain?"

*"Billy Maidenshore escaped with the Orions. He must've had a homing device on him somewhere. With*

*our shields down, the Orions must've beamed him out of the locker. All we've got is transporter residue and some foreign traces of exchanged atmosphere. I'm real sorry, Captain Kirk. I know how you hate to lose, especially once you've won.*"

"Yes . . . I hate to lose. Some people do manage to be evil and never pay the price. Every now and then, a Stalin dies in his bed or a corrupt president retires in glory. Some scoundrels are never held accountable. Put it in your report, Captain, and see to your ship."

"*I will.* Yukon *out.*"

Kilvennan watched as Kirk lowered his communicator and indulged in a bitter frown. "Sorry . . . we just couldn't cover all the bases, I guess."

"Don't apologize," Kirk said. "We might never have seen any of these people alive again if you hadn't agreed to be our eyes. If we'd arranged for *Impeller* to do the broadcasting, the Orions would've picked it up and waited until *Enterprise* had moved on."

Kilvennan touched his bruised jaw. "Figures they'd monitor all the Starfleet frequencies. With me pretending to go along with Maidenshore, he didn't tip them off to keep tabs on signals from *Hunter's Moon.* It was a good plan. You had a sharp sense of what they wouldn't expect to happen."

"I appreciate your taking my orders," Kirk told him sincerely. "You didn't have to do that."

Dark eyes shaded, long sweaty hair making him seem like a half-drowned pirate, Kilvennan accepted the words with a companionable shrug.

"Told you before," he reminded. "There's not one man in a hundred thousand worth serving under."

# Chapter Sixteen

"STOP IT! Stop it! You people are idiots, strangling a valuable commodity! I'm still important to you!"

Billy Maidenshore felt the cold grip of death closing around his vision. The stale breath of his business partner curled his lips.

"How are you important?" Tu demanded. His claw still tightened around Maidenshore's jaw. "I am down by three ships! I go back in shame! Instead of a wealth of human cargo, I have only you to sell!"

"You—won't—be selling—anybody," Maidenshore choked. "Your own—dealers'll—kill you. Get your—pickers off me—and let me talk."

Tu shuddered with pure rage at this unexpected failure. He had been tempted, then tricked. The cost was enormous. Battling every wisdom, he dropped Maidenshore to the deck. "Then talk."

"Ugly savage." Maidenshore rubbed his jaw. "What

d'you take me for? This was my new mother lode. I've got a lot hanging on this. You think I'm finished just because you had to beam me out of there? You think I don't have a backup plan?"

"Tell your plan."

"Just a minute. Let me get the blood back into my face."

And time to think. Not a clue.

Backup plan, backup plan . . . He hadn't wanted to be beamed over here unless the Orions were winning, but Tu had homed in on him and snatched him out anyway. Here he was.

Possibility—stall, get enough time to disable this clunker, maybe ex-out all these plugs in their sleep? Gas them? Poison?

He looked around at Tu, at Ri, De, Mu, and the others on this one-room ship as they watched him. Exing them wouldn't be all that tough. They weren't so bright at anticipating somebody else's moves, or he could've beamed in here with a phaser and they'd never have seen it coming. Once they relaxed, he could easily shed them all.

Then what? Drive himself all the way back to Federation space from way the flip out here? Months in space with Orion food?

He'd never driven a ship in his life. There were always peons around to do those things for him. He'd spent all his years being smarter than the mice with menial skills, so they'd always done things for him. By letting people know he was smarter, he'd always gotten the benefit of the doubt. People always assumed he knew more, and they did things for him because of it. Get them to relax, then start pulling the strings until he had what he wanted.

Stall, mostly, was what he wanted right now. If he didn't get past the next couple of minutes, the Orions would kill him. Or worse, enslave him.

The Federation wouldn't do either of those things. The Federation would put him in prison, but what difference would that make? Any clown with two brain cells and a toothpick could figure out how to slip out of that. Two years, let them "rehabilitate" him, they drop their guard, and poof.

Best bet number one—get to the lightship and surrender to Jimmy the Sledge. Come up with something on the way.

He had, of course, no idea what was out there, no more than anybody else did. A lightship and a sledgehammer heading toward it. Tu didn't know anything either. Orions never thought of what was beyond their space.

Not so hard—he had a goal now. Later he'd get another one.

"Okay, here's the backup plan," he said when he felt the timing go sour. "You got high warp on this bucket, don't you?"

Purple skin blistering, Tu raged, "Of course I have high warp speed!"

Maidenshore spread his hands. "Turn around, then. Head in the other direction. Go around those stumbling bumpkins and out to that lightship. What're you afraid of?"

"We never go so far." Tu turned burgundy with both fury and fear. "How will we find our way?"

Maidenshore shifted from one foot to another and gave Tu a you're-stupid look. "What else in all the kazillion miles of nothing out in that direction is broadcasting a Federation signal? Follow it."

Tu caught the disparaging tone and reacted. "You tempted us out here, human! You gave us this undigestible loss!"

"Nah, nah, forget about those other ships. What do you care about them, anyway? Open your brain! Think big! Listen to Uncle Billy . . . Instead of just one Conestoga, how would you like to go home with, oh, say, ten of them? Uh-huh . . . that's what I thought. Put your helm over. Let's kick this pig."

# Chapter Seventeen

## Belle Terre

"So THIS is the planet they covet. 'Belter.' I don't see the usefulness."

Green-gold meadows of wild plants and twittering insect life made a glorious nest of nonconstruction around them. The rolling hills bristled with gold-topped flowers in great sprawling fields, shot here and there with a spear of blue or red, and millions of brittle stalks topped with brushy purple hats. Not very appealing for a construction engineer.

Good bedrock, though. And those mountains read of heavy ore.

Shucorion had never been on any planet other than the Blood homeworld. This place smelled different. No sulfur. No dust. No scent of redirected runoff.

And there was a breeze. Shucorion was more used to wind, if air moved at all.

"Look around, Dimion. Is this a place that makes a civilization cross a wasteland of open dangers? What would cause people to do such a thing when they're safe at home? If they already have safe place, why come so far, through such strife?"

"Our people have thought of moving from our world," Dimion commented. "In the depths of time, we thought of it. When we explored, all we found was All Kauld. We stopped looking and started fighting."

"Ever since, that has been the way." Shucorion paused to feel the ground with his foot. "We work and fight, then work again to fight again. Shallow to the bedrock. Good building land."

"Vellyngaith thinks so," Dimion commented.

"You're afraid of him, aren't you?"

Dimion nodded. "I would run if I could. Come back later with more fighters."

"You're very prudent. Vellyngaith is intelligent and strict. He also knows his own limitations and our advantage with navigation. He's not an arrogant man. The combination is deadly for our people. We have no one with such skills in battle. We have to fight him some other way."

"Why did you call to meet him again? We don't have to meet him so much."

"We do."

"But why? Every time, they could change their minds and slaughter us."

"And every time, we can edge nearer to advantage for ourselves. He needs us, our abilities, our skills."

"Why have Kauld not invented the skill to navigate the Blind for themselves?"

"They think it's mystical, what we can do in space. Of course, there's no magic about what we do. It's nothing more than science, patience, accuracy. Kauld have always been fortunate to do things quickly. They have no patience. Vellyngaith is an example." Shucorion smiled and added, "I must admit, I felt for him in his embarrassment. He overcame much to contact me."

Dimion strode at Shucorion's side another ten steps, then paused. "Do you like him?"

"Like him? *Like* him . . . I loathe him. He is Kauld. Everything I have always had to fight. They are an aberration of Blood. The same skin, the same hands, eyes, but different. They had the advantages of our binary stars, we had the disadvantages. All Kauld became strong in one way, Blood Many in another. We grew apart."

"If we were ever together."

"The scientists say we were."

"In the dimmest of pasts. Do you think they're right?"

"Yes."

Dimion shook his head and stepped over a mound made by insects that flew in a disturbed pink cloud behind him. "I can't see it. I don't see them in us or us in them. Why did you want Vellyngaith to meet us on this planet?"

"I wanted to look at the planet."

Behind them, six Blood guards strode in complete confusion. This business of going to a planet, some strange place, this itself for any Blood was bizarre. Going to meet with an enemy, just meet and talk? There was no suggestion in their past of this kind of behavior and from their glances Shucorion had the idea they were more and more certain their avedon's brain was slowly turning to feathers.

He had heard the whispers. Sensed the fears.

"I'm afraid too, Dimion," Shucorion admitted.

"Avedon," Dimion interrupted. He put out a hand to stop Shucorion from moving forward. No longer walking, they faced each other. "I'm wary of him. I'm frightened of *you*."

Although the words forced themselves out, Dimion suddenly could no longer meet his avedon's eyes. He looked down, into the flowers and insects, following one across the other as if the expedition mattered.

Shucorion said nothing. He stood still. The breeze tugged at his bound hair, wagging it between his shoulder blades like a pendulum. Terrible, the silence.

Over there, the six Blood guards had stopped and were squinting into the breeze, waiting. Gazing over Dimion's shoulder at them, Shucorion saw that they knew what was happening. Was Dimion speaking for them? How long had this been going on?

Dimion blinked and scoured his innards for courage. Usually courage wasn't Dimion's problem. Shucorion found the struggle fascinating to watch.

Dimion looked up, finally ready to speak, but his eyes were instantly distracted from Shucorion's. He looked instead over Shucorion's shoulder to the landscape.

"There they are," he said.

Shucorion turned.

Coming over a stony hill, cloaked and armed, were the Kauld battlelord and twenty soldiers. They could easily kill Shucorion and his little field of men. Twenty Kauld. Shucorion's chest constricted. He hadn't been cautious enough.

As the two groups drew near, Vellyngaith's anger showed in the flush of his face and the bitter set of his mouth and eyes. He stalked through the knee-high meadow. The flowers bent before him, cracked, and were crushed.

Drawing to a stop, Shucorion caught Dimion by the wrist and pushed him behind, then motioned for the other men to halt many steps back. Appearing ready to attack couldn't serve today.

Could it? Or could it . . . No, no, keep to the course set.

Vellyngaith's heavy boots carved a path to Shucorion. "More talk?"

Shucorion held his hands between them in a settling gesture. All his possibility for success teetered on this moment, on being able to control these few seconds when the risk he had taken might go sour.

"Battlelord," he began, "you know Blood never rest when there is work to be done. We have survived against your Kauld strength for centuries by simply outworking you. Yes?"

Vellyngaith scowled. "What about it?"

Resisting the urge to glance back at his own men and at Dimion, all of whom were about to be delivered the shock of their year, Shucorion drew a breath and held it. He kept his eyes focused on Vellyngaith's.

"To make your fortress ready all the sooner," he said, "we Blood will send five hundred skilled blast technicians, geologists, construction engineers, architects, and structure men to help you build your fortress. When you are ready to transport it to this planet, we will go with you. I will organize another thousand Blood workers to help you finish it."

The Kauld leader, famous for his canny assessment of his enemies, stared at him with narrowed eyes. Shucorion gripped his hand with the other to keep it from trembling. Would Vellyngaith believe that a Blood avedon would send tireless Blood workers to build a Kauld fortress, to house a Kauld fleet?

Complex, complex.

Vellyngaith shook his head. "I feel as if I am being somehow directed by you. Why do you offer such a wealth of resource?"

"Because these agreements will someday serve to protect the Blood," Shucorion said.

"Protect how?"

"By building your fortress with Blood workers, we will be able to finish much sooner and be ready to join forces against Federation when they arrive here. By the time Federation comes to threaten us, I want the Blood and Kauld cultures so intermingled that there will be no more incentive to shoot at each other. We'll slaughter Federation instead, and they'll stay away forever."

Like the fall of equatorial night, the Kauld battlelord's whole manner changed. Over it went.

"How?" Vellyngaith asked. "We know so little about them, their strengths. . . ."

Shucorion paused, pretending to be thinking, making this up a step at a time. Very strange, this business of trickery. He had to pretend to be falling for Vellyngaith's proposals, while pretending *not* to fall for them by demanding conditions and offering concessions. Like a game. But in the end, one or the other of their peoples would be destroyed.

"I'll go to their outpost," he suggested. "Meet them, and try to hurt them."

Vellyngaith shifted. "What outpost?"

"They have a monument in space, at some distance. Our navigators have discovered it."

"How do you know what it is?"

Shucorion shrugged. "We know a signal beacon

when we see one. . . . At this outpost, an encounter will be far enough from their worlds to be beyond help, and far enough from ours that they can't easily blame us."

He stopped talking. At some juncture, talking would no longer serve to propose, but only to confuse. He waited. Stood very still. Envisioned a vicious slaughter of an unwitting enemy who in fact was a tool against another enemy.

That fortress had to be built. It had to be built!

"In the combined fleet of the Blood and Kauld," Shucorion went on, "you will be the supreme military leader. I will be second."

"You *do* take risks," Vellyngaith uttered.

"This is no risk. This is a precaution. If you want our navigation skills, this is the only way. Your soldiers will answer to me. Mine will answer to you. The future is on us, Battlelord. Blood Many accept changes very quickly. We will throw in our lot with Federation or with you. This is what I want in order for it to be you."

Vellyngaith's expression neutraled almost to unreadability. He had regained a warrior's skill for not letting himself be deciphered during negotiations. Shucorion had absolutely no idea whether negotiation should be done this way, therefore had no expression to hide. Only his disgust for All Kauld needed to be cloaked. Throughout the generations of Elliptical Wars, Kauld had never allowed Blood a moment's rest from eternal squabbling. Only now that someone else was coming did they reach out.

As the breeze ran around and the cloud of pink wings stirred up by Dimion found them and swooped between Shucorion and Vellyngaith, the two factions might as well have been on separate moons. Was this chance falling apart? This delicate balance Shucorion believed, perhaps blindly, that he could strike? Had he taken one risk too many and destroyed his chosen status? Abused it?

His men's faith in him was crumbling. He had plucked too many pebbles from the stone.

Suddenly he was shocked out of his thoughts by Vellyngaith's step to one side. Was the battlelord positioning himself to strike? Lop off Shucorion's head?

The Kauld warriors backed away, as if to give room. Shucorion stood his ground. At least he could show his men that his wild actions had some root in conviction. If he died here, they would question their own curses.

"I agree." The battlelord's words came abruptly, and were abruptly finished.

Vellyngaith whirled around—that was why he had stepped to his side—and his cloak batted Shucorion's legs.

Without looking back at all, the Kauld contingent stalked over the ridge, into the thick overgrowth at the edge of the meadow, and disappeared.

"Did he agree?" Shucorion croaked after they were gone. "Is that what he said? Did you see him when I offered him Blood workers? His eyes were actually sparkling. Wonderful to make someone else so happy."

Dimion did not answer, and didn't approach him. He was looking at the ground again. The breeze picked at his unbound hair and blew it across the top of his shoulder as if to brush away dust.

This couldn't go on. Shucorion stepped past Dimion, who made no movements, and spoke to the six guards.

"Go back to the lander," he ordered. "Make sure the way is clear and Vellyngaith hasn't plotted an ambush."

Speechless, with trouble in their eyes, the guards didn't even make an acknowledgment. They turned like stricken children and stomped down the hill, forced to follow their hand-locators because they had no idea how to track their way through unfamiliar land. On the Blood world, nobody bothered to go to land he didn't know. There were always guides. No one explored.

Shucorion watched them go, then turned and did not think of them again. "What's the matter with you, Dimion?"

"He didn't kill you," Dimion murmured.

"Did you think he would?"

"I hoped he would."

Still Dimion didn't look up.

"Why would you want me dead?" Shucorion asked.

"To spare you from this. What you're doing. Avedon . . ."

Dimion hesitated, and visibly shuddered. His trembling hand came forward from his side, holding a charged glaze-blade.

"Avedon . . . I think I have to kill you myself."

265

# Chapter Eighteen

THE ENERGY KNIFE buzzed between them, its energy ready to arc as soon as it touched Shucorion's body.

"Dimion, this is unlike you." Shucorion kept his shoulders and arms relaxed. To tense could be a sharp error. "You've been with me since the night I discovered I was different."

Dimion shivered visibly, and pushed the glaze-blade forward half an arm's length. His face worked with inner sufferings making their way out without much resistance from him.

"I won't defend myself," Shucorion proclaimed, and thereby stopped all motions completely.

"Why are you doing these things?" Dimion rattled. "Helping them . . . giving us to them . . . will you wear beads next?"

The glaze-blade buzzed with unbalance as Dimion gripped it so tightly that his knuckles turned to white dots against his blue fingers. The weapon sang louder, fighting against gravity, as he raised it higher until the blade murmured near his own heart. His breath came in gulps. His eyes no longer blinked, but watered and suffered as he stared at Shucorion, watching his personal belief shatter.

"Dimion?" Shucorion stiffened. "What are you doing? Kill *me*, not yourself."

His voice a crumble, Dimion rasped, "You know I never could. This is all I can do. I can't live with these risks."

"Dimion . . . you're about to be very wrong."

Shucorion reached out, rather slowly, and caught Dimion's arm with both hands, pushing the glaze-blade upward against Dimion's shoulder. The weapon sang and cried in both their ears.

Dimion wept, "Kill me. . . . You kill me."

"No, no. Let go of it."

For a long time Shucorion had been the avedon of the Plume. Dimion was used to taking his orders. He let go of the glaze-blade and sank to his knees. Shucorion stepped back and glared down at him.

"I'm not working for Kauld. I'm playing a game. There are things you don't know. I have to make Vellyngaith believe that I want our cultures to merge."

Gasping with emotional torment, Dimion blinked up at him with one eye almost shut. "You don't want us to . . . to . . . ?"

"I'm no dreamer, Dimion. Eventually there will be only one planet. Blood Many will exist or All Kauld will exist. Not both."

"Then you don't think we can merge?"

"With them? Only if we kill every last one of the adult Kauld and raise all their children as Blood. Any other way is hopeless. There is no truce. He's making a myth. I told you that before."

"But I don't understand," Dimion whimpered. "You're helping them build a fortress that they will use against us. Promising him Blood workers! We'll dig our own tombs!"

"If I don't commit Blood workers and Blood soldiers, Vellyngaith will sense that something is out of balance. He knows the truce he offered to me is perfectly silly and all in his favor. What would he think if I accepted without conditions in return?"

Sinking deeper on his knees, Dimion's arms flopped to his sides. He continued to look at the flowers. "You take too many risks. I know you are the only one who can . . . but this is too many."

"There's a difference between taking risks and following a path laid out to be taken!" Shucorion kicked at the flowers. Why did there have to be flowers where buildings should be? "Vellyngaith thinks he's won. Today I have committed a thousand Blood skilled men and laborers to death, to *death*, all to make Vellyngaith believe for a while what I told him."

Sharply, Dimion looked up at him. "Death? Why will they be taken to death?" He blinked around at the innocent planet with its waving stalks and buzzing life. "Here? A safe planet with no disasters?"

"Their death is as certain as if I took this blade and cut their brains myself. Millions have died among Blood Many. A few thousand more . . . that will be the price of curing the Blood Curse. I would willingly die myself to lift the Curse. I may be the one who can break it."

He paced a few steps away, pressing his hand to his lips.

"What will confound us is if we ourselves end up in a conflict with Federation. I must forestall that if I can . . . and make sure it's Kauld who are forced to spread themselves thin."

"Why did you say you would go to Federation?" Dimion asked.

"Because Federation is the key to our future, the breaking of the Blood Curse."

Dimion's expression worked from frustration to bafflement. "We can't change our lot. We're born to a station, a place in the universe—"

"I know," Shucorion told him. "But if just one time we confront the haunting curse, stare the animal down . . . we can change our direction. I changed my own direction, didn't I? Why can't that happen for Blood Many?" He raised his fists to the mighty sky and called to the fresh white clouds. "Finally after generations of Elliptical Wars, Blood will have an advantage over Kauld! We've never had one of those before! If I can delay Federation, then Kauld will establish its fortress and most of their forces will be housed on this planet . . . firmly footed in the path of disaster."

"Disaster?" Dimion's eyes swiveled in confusion around the utterly peaceful landscape, the soft sky, the silky meadow, the vibrant soil, unscrubbed by quakes and floods. "How will disaster come to a place like this?"

"I won't tell you. That risk I will not take. Trust me when I say this . . . by the time Kauld recover, we will be the power here."

Staring down at the weapon in his hand, Shucorion felt unmanageable power bolt through his arms, as if he could cut out the brain of all his enemies with the toll of a few Blood lives.

"A thousand of our workers . . . that will be the cost of winning," he said. "But the win will be excellent, Dimion. And final. Now stand up. We have an assault to plan. Federation is coming. We will be in space to meet them."

In the darkness of the trees, sheltered from the bright sunlight and wide friendly skies of this undamaged world, Battlelord Vellyngaith fell to his knees in the grip of convulsive coughing. His men caught him and held him through the spasms, but theirs would come eventually, and he would be holding them instead, were he still alive. No Kauld warrior could get out of it.

This was the future. Coughing, spitting blood, the pain in his lungs, the shuddering of his heart would come to every Kauld fighting man.

Such a shameful waste. More ghastly than having to humble himself before the Blood avedon.

"Do you trust him?" Fremigoth asked him after the initial spasm had passed.

Vellyngaith winced at the moisture in the soil as it seeped into the fabric around his knee. Suddenly he was cold all over. He wiped blood from the corners of his mouth and eyes. "No, I won't trust Shucorion yet. The idea that he is digesting anything I say is nonsense. He's planning to destroy me and I'm planning to destroy him and we both know it. Yet we've decided to play this game because there's someone new coming. He's planning to betray me. I just don't know how."

As he began to relax, his lungs constricted and sent him into a fit of gasping—moisture, he needed moisture—

Fremigoth was before him now, pressing a respirator to the battlelord's face and infusing pressurized chemicals that Vellyngaith breathed hungrily. Around them, the other men waited, twitching and glancing at each other. This was their future. They knew it. Every one of them would cough out his own lungs eventually and nothing could be done to stop it. He was older than most of these men, and that would save them a little longer than it would save him, though fate was set as firmly for all here, and all the Kauld military men.

Even in the middle of his struggle, Vellyngaith managed to straighten his shoulders and raise his head a little, hoping to give them a feeble hope that they could suffer with dignity and die noble deaths. But they were not accepting his deception any more than Shucorion had.

He pushed away the respirator as his lungs opened finally and he could breathe almost normally. Eventually, the treatment would stop working. For today, though, he could breathe.

He stared at the respirator hovering before him in Fremigoth's hand.

"What can we do?" he said. "Tell Blood that we're dying? Tell them that every military man among Kauld carries a lethal dose of contamination? That we condemned ourselves by making experiments on dynadrive? That soon there will be no one to defend the innocent Kauld?"

"Someone like Shucorion might understand. He seems amenable to a truce."

"You are the physician, Fremigoth! You're supposed to make *me* understand first, and you haven't done that."

"I've tried," Fremigoth complained. "You don't understand science any better than I understand why Shucorion would truce with us so willingly."

"Submolecular levels and antimatter shifts? Cell desiccation and tissue fissures? I'm not a man of science. These are mysteries to me, that these things happen. But it's no mystery to me that Shucorion is not trucing with us. He's pretending."

"He is?"

"Of course. He knows I haven't told him everything. He's wondering why our home planet is all at once not good enough for us. He's right—it makes no sense to move if we have a perfectly good planet. Why would we build another base? To him, now that we have star-drive, all we Kauld have to do is wait, and we'll win. Blood can't prevail over us now, not with dynadrive preventing them a resting period. Neither of us speaks of it, but one civilization or the other will end up dead. Because of dynadrive, we must completely destroy Blood or they will destroy us. If they find out that all our military men are soon to die—"

His own voice drummed in his head. The truths, the ugly facts, the unavoidable fate were needles boring into his skin. Add to that the humiliation of having to approach Shucorion at all, and he felt he was convulsing his own pride away.

Still wheezing, he choked, "What can I tell him? Can I say that our army has condemned itself with experiments that caused leakage? We breathed in our own doom? That one day Fremigoth of the Physicians came walking in and told us we were all going to die? Can I tell Shucorion that we need Blood navigators to lead our fleet so we can face Federation soon, while we have the strength?"

Fremigoth had no mind for tactical matters and only frowned at Vellyngaith's words, not knowing what to say to make his battlelord feel better. "This is the way of nature sometimes. Sickness, mistakes, mutations . . ."

"Not even a battle," Vellyngaith miserated. "Soldiers should die in body-wrenching action. Battles, explosions, warfare. Not like this, not cell mutation . . . altered reality on the submolecular level . . . you've explained it to me again and again and still I can't envision the thing that will kill me and every one of my men. I always thought I would understand the thing that finally killed me, that I would be fighting it at the time. How can I fight this?"

With a shake of his graying head, Fremigoth said nothing more, but held the respirator in front of the battlelord for another lung treatment.

Lung treatments. What a pitiful way for a battlelord to live.

Vellyngaith pushed away the physician's ministrations and glared into the trees, through them, beyond them.

"Shucorion could see I was desperate. He would never digest such a one-sided truce. I expected him to come back with conditions, but he turned out to be more reasonable than I anticipated. Something about his agreeableness . . ." He turned to Fremigoth. "Does this thing affect our minds?"

Fremigoth scowled. "No, unfortunately. We'll all be aware to the last. We'll start losing men in larger numbers very soon."

"So early?"

"Some. More later. All of us by two cycles more."

In a bolt of fury and anger he shoved himself to his feet and threw off the support of his men.

"The misery of it! We had this star-drive! We were

going to destroy them and be done with conflict! Finally finished! Now we have this!"

"We have all faced death," Fremigoth told him. "All Kauld understand that conflict is the way for us and Blood Many. What else can there be but trouble and trial?"

Vellyngaith closed his eyes tightly and gritted his teeth. "My death is not the problem. I am the most lauded battlelord in seven generations. Didn't you see the fear behind Shucorion's eyes? Yet I am a loser."

"How can you say that, Battlelord? No one is as great as Vellyngaith in the eyes of All Kauld."

"Vellyngaith is a failure in the eyes of Vellyngaith. I am responsible for protecting All Kauld and I have not done that. Things are bunching up before me. Somehow I must kill all Blood and all Federation. Either I die a failure or I die a slaughterer, but I will die. And so will you. All of us here, and thousands more soldiers who were at the base that month . . . that horrid month when we lived in ignorance as a simple leak was marauding us, making us sick. All the soldiers we have. All we have!"

Around him the eyes of his men, their pity and stiff-jawed acceptance, caused him more pain than the convulsions and coughing and bleeding from the eyes. They were brave men, faced with the prospect of dying in a sorry and hopeless way.

Furious, he threw the cloth to the ground. The moist blood instantly attracted several tiny insects who lit and feasted. His eyes blurred as he stared down at the little gathering swarm of blue wings and happy pincers.

Blood. They were like those insects. Work, work, even when there is no hope. Work, until your enemy has no hope, until something turns your way.

"Nauseating," he grumbled, "to shame myself, to ask that Kauld and Blood join to keep Federation from gaining a toehold in our cluster. What a lie, Fremigoth. I'm not used to lying. For the army of the Kauld, though, we have no fear anymore. We are an army of the dead. All we can do is make sure there is an army of the young to protect our people when we're gone. We must build off our world, Fremigoth."

He gripped a low-slung branch from the nearest tree, lacerating his hands on the spiny bark, and shook it. The pain did not register except to sharpen his awareness. Above him, the tree's crisp silver leaves laughed.

"What if our mistake had been bigger?" he thought aloud. "We might've wiped out our entire race instead of just our military men. We must build a new place for the young and strong to be trained. Build a new army to replace us, in a place where another disaster like this will not threaten the populace. And I must make sure there is no Blood army and no Federation army to threaten All Kauld after we're gone. From this day on, I will work as hard as a Blood. I will be like Blood until I die."

Having made that decision, convinced himself that this was the best course, no matter how distasteful or against tradition, Vellyngaith drew a sustaining breath now that he could get one and stomped past Fremigoth and through the other men to lead them out of these woods with only one cursory comment that would echo in his mind for his remaining months.

"Life is butchery."

# Chapter Nineteen

"WHO IS THIS? Who are they? Tell me they belong to you!"

Tu of the Orions grasped Billy Maidenshore by one arm and shook him physically.

Maidenshore also gawked out the viewport on the Orion ship and knew they all had good reason to be afraid. They had approached the Federation beacon at the lightship *Hatteras,* ignoring hails from the lightship keeper, who demanded they identify themselves. Much depended upon their not identifying themselves. The lightship probably had limited analytical abilities when it came to ships, since that wasn't its primary purpose. Unless they told him who they were, the lightship keeper would have no way to identify them as Orions this far out.

Even now the lightship was beyond visual range.

Not so the twenty or more alien ships that had come out of Gamma Night and surrounded them.

"How did they come to us during the Dark period!" Tu demanded. "Who are they? Tell me now or die now! Twenty against two!"

He was mad. He'd been mad for weeks, always on the edge of slaughtering Maidenshore for no particular good reason. Only quick thinking and dangling that carrot had kept Maidenshore's neck in one piece.

Now he had to think fast again. He peered out the viewport at the flock of unrecognizable blue-hulled enemy vessels.

Obviously battle-oriented ships—small, quick, built for agility, lots of round or tubular construction, but maneuverable on an axis. Those weren't freighters or transports, or any other kind of utility ship. Even from here the weapons ports showed, and the size of the engine chambers displayed that thrust power was important.

Maidenshore digested every possibility and picked the one that worked for him. He looked at Tu and puffed up like a bird.

"Still think I didn't have a plan?"

"Liar," Tu accused. "Look at them! They're not hailing us!"

"They don't need to. I can signal them from a device implanted right here in the palm of my hand. See this birthmark? It's not a birthmark. It's an embedded signaler. Don't touch it. Still think I didn't have this all arranged? You don't understand humans."

*I meant for the ship to burst into flames. It's my burst-into-flames plan. Your head is falling off? All part of the plan.*

Doubt, suspicion, desperation played in Tu's excuse for eyes. Maidenshore had learned to read those milky orbs over the past weeks.

"I move my thumb just right," he went on, wiggling his fingers, "and it signals them, and they destroy you."

Thousands of light-years from his home, the Orion commander shuddered. No Orion had ever come so far or ever wanted to. He had come out of fear, out of temptation, and because Billy Maidenshore had seemed to deliver most of what he said he could, with only the little problem of Jim Kirk having come in to botch the success. The thunderous din of events spinning so fast around him had Tu by the face. Maidenshore just kept feeding him whatever he wanted to hear, or expected to hear.

"Let me go talk to them. You got a universal translator on this bucket? Give it to me and beam me over there. Once they find out it's me, everything'll be fine."

Assuming, of course, there was air over there. Right now that was his biggest risk. If he stayed here much longer, he wouldn't need to breathe anyway.

Threatened beyond reason, Tu and his men asked no more questions. They wanted action after weeks in space, heading toward a thready signal beacon from a Federation source, possessing no clear idea of what would come to them from this line of action, knowing only that they could not go home empty-handed. Maidenshore had found his salvation in their fear. By telling them only select parts of the truth, he had been able to manipulate them completely. All his life he had used the simple trait that, generally speaking, people didn't want to think for themselves. These Orions were no more a special exception than the colonists had been. The formula still worked.

*Incredible. They're beaming me over. I can't lose.*

A swirl of activity, a bubble of Orion transporter

technology, and Maidenshore was whisked from the cusp of danger to the unknown alien ship, the lead ship of the twenty surrounding them.

It was the wrong ship. At least the aliens weren't spiny blobs or some kind of wagging eyeball hanging from the roof. Human-looking, give or take some color changes. A little fast talking brought Maidenshore to the blue stooge running that ship, and pretty soon there was a docking maneuver.

And pretty soon after that, the leader of the alien fleet was walking toward him on some kind of curved deck.

"Who are you?" the perplexed leader asked.

"Depends," Maidenshore told him. "Who are you first?"

"I am Shucorion. Are you Federation?"

"Me? One of those plundering demons? Never!"

"Then who?"

"My name's Maidenshore. I came here with those two ships out there to head off the armada."

A strong-looking thug with dark brown eyes and hair like a mahogany bannister, Shucorion didn't even try to hide his surprise. "Armada? You mean the fleet from Federation? They come to settle in the cluster, we hear."

"Settle?" Maidenshore gave him a façade of affront. "Oh, you poor fools ... you've believed the lies, haven't you? I thought if I came out far enough, I could escape the misguidedness. I guess I was wrong."

"There is another explanation?"

"Is there! It's all a deception. All set up to deceive those poor people on the transport ships. They *think* they're coming out here to settle a planet, but it's all a lie."

"Explain further," Shucorion invited. "What about settling a planet is a lie?"

"All of it!" Maidenshore exclaimed. "That armada is led by one large fighting ship, two other warships, and four hired killer ships. They're bringing over sixty thousand slaves with them in transports. The story of settling a colony is all a ruse to get those people out here without a struggle. They've all been hypnotized, drugged into submission. All the tapes, all the broadcasts and emissions, files and logs are set up to fool the people on those ships and anybody else they run into. This is the work of the most corrupt, oppressive force in our part of the galaxy. They've destroyed or enslaved every planet they've come upon, and now they're coming out here to take over your star cluster. They're moving out here because they've raped and plundered their way across our side of the galaxy. You people, you're next!"

Shucorion pursed his lips in thought, his eyes fixed on Maidenshore. "Very passionate," he uttered. "These warships . . . they're strong? Powerful?"

Since he couldn't see any screens or displays, Maidenshore swung his hand in the general direction of out-there. "You saw those two ships I came here with? Those are Orions. They're the most powerful civilization in our part of the galaxy, except for the Federation. They're the only ones who've been able to resist Federation imperialism. But those Orion ships out there, Federation's finally got them beat. Those ships are nothing compared to the warships leading that armada out there."

"Federation ships are better than Orion?"

"See those two ships? We started with five. We went up against one—just one—Federation ship. Now we're down to this, and we had to run to live. Despite our damage, we came ahead at high warp to keep Starfleet from pillaging still another civilization."

"Starfleet . . . Starfleet . . ." Shucorion tasted the word. He seemed to digest quickly whatever Maidenshore said.

Better watch out for that.

"I came ahead to warn you. That's no colony—it's an invasion! By the time they arrive, they'll have all sixty thousand of those people brainwashed into fighting anybody for them. You'll be facing an army of hypnotized slaves."

Pausing briefly, Shucorion turned a little to look at another of his own kind, to share a silent communication before turning back to Maidenshore. "And you . . . what do you want?"

"For you to join us!" Maidenshore spread his hands in a welcoming embrace of all he saw. "Together, we can fight them! We already have an ace—see, they don't expect me to be here. They won't know you've been warned. If you can separate away the fighting ships, distract them, cut them away from the transports. Then the Orions and I can take the transports away. Maybe not all of them, but a few. Enough to wake them out of their hypnosis, maybe come back and help you keep fighting. I don't know—I'm not a military man. All I know is they have to be stopped from spreading the disease of enslavement to another part of the galaxy." He lowered his voice. "It is my *mission in life* . . . to stop this from happening to another culture."

Shucorion stepped back, not very obviously, and took in the vision of this rough-shaven man who had been through some trial, judging by his stained clothing and his ruffled hair. Beneath the somewhat tattered exterior Shucorion saw a man who had until recently been well fed and in some favor. Other than the tattering, this Maidenshore's clothing was expertly made, tailored, layered, and matched.

"A moment," he requested, and began to turn to Dimion for a short council.

Maidenshore nodded. "If you don't want to join me, at least get out of the way and I'll save your people myself."

Shucorion stopped turning, leaving Dimion confused. Instead, he held out his hand and pointed at the glaze-blade on Dimion's belt.

Without a word, Dimion unlatched the weapon and placed it in his avedon's hand.

Like a shot of energy arching between power sources, Shucorion drove the newcomer to his knees, engaging the glaze-blade's electrodes against Maidenshore's throat. The big man bent backward against Shucorion's grip, but could not fall away. His arms flailed to his sides. His lips fell open in a silent gasp at the sensation of energy threatening his artery.

His own mind burning, Shucorion leaned close to this new person, so close he could smell the interior of the Orion ship lingering upon the man's clothing. The glaze-blade sizzled in his hand. Through it he felt the thud of Maidenshore's pulse.

"Truth," he demanded.

A finger's breadth from dying, Maidenshore gasped a pitiful breath and fixed his gaze on Shucorion's. The Blood men watched. No one moved.

Maidenshore tried to swallow, but failed.

"I . . . I'm a criminal on the run—I came out here with the arma—the colonists. I made a deal with the Orions that they could have ten of those transports, but the deal went sour. I had to escape. The Orions are about to kill me. To save my skin I pretended to be working with you—I was going to turn myself over to Starfleet—until I saw your ships. . . . If you don't go along and pretend to be on my side, the Orions'll kill me."

"You are of Federation?"

"Yes," Maidenshore choked. "You—obviously—came here to—meet them— Why don't you tell me what you need? I know a lot."

Shucorion's eyes narrowed as tension set into his face. He felt the stares of Dimion and the other Blood men, wondering what their avedon would do with this person who had come out of nowhere. Was this another flash of his personal magic? This Maidenshore had come out of nothing, a man of Federation, who knew what was on the way here.

"I want them to turn back," he admitted.

Maidenshore grunted with effort as the pressure on his throat decreased a bit. "So do I. Except I want them broken up. What do you care if I take ten of those ships? As long as they go away? Right?"

"How will we know which are the fighting ships?"

"I'll tell you."

"And you will tell me how to get on board the Starfleet vessels?"

"Sure, we can come up with something."

"And what I can do once I get there to make them turn back? You will give me information that will affect them? You understand the way they think?"

At this, in a single sudden flood, the fear dropped out of Maidenshore's eyes. In spite of his being bent backward with a weapon to his neck, he became abruptly confident and met Shucorion's eyes without a flinch.

"Buddy," he gagged, "I understand them better than they understand themselves. And if you don't want to believe that those people will eventually dominate this cluster, then go ahead and use that thing on me."

Again, fortune worked on the side of a Blood, on the side of Shucorion because he dared to ask incautious questions. Out of the Blind a chance had arisen. Was it an advantage or part of the Blood Curse? He couldn't tell, until he acted upon this new turn.

He knew Dimion was watching and longed to explain to him. *If we are in a burning building, it's less risky to jump off the roof than stay in the building. Come with me. Jump.*

Clicking off the weapon, he brought it away from Maidenshore's neck.

"I will save your ... skin." He stood back, and handed the glaze-blade back to Dimion.

His chest heaving, the man called Maidenshore struggled to his feet and wobbled briefly, then brushed the wrinkles out of his sleeves. He gazed at Shucorion with a strange expression.

"Had to come across the galaxy," Maidenshore declared, "to meet a man I could respect."

## Enterprise

"Red alert. Advise *Beowulf* to go to yellow alert and stand by at the rear of the convoy."

"Aye, aye, Captain."

On the upper deck, seated at the science station, Spock turned and reported on the transfer of troubling data from way out there. "Sir, *American Rover*'s preliminary scans suggest massive external damage to the barges and to the lightship. Both barges have been hull-ruptured and the contents contaminated. Lightship's hull is intact, but these data are inconclusive."

Jim Kirk felt the shadows on his face from the bridge lights as the colors shifted to alert scarlet. Reduced lighting was one of the many ways the Expedition had been conserving power over the long weeks. "Our sensors'll do better," he grumbled.

Spock offered him a brand of sympathy. "Of course."

"Any word about the lightship keeper? What's his name again?"

"Sardoch, sir. Incoming life signs are variegated and inaccurate."

"Sir," Uhura broke in, her hand to her earpiece, "Captain Smith has sent a boarding party led by Colonel Glass and Mr. Carpenter to the *Hatteras* to investigate. . . . Sir, the supply barges have been hull-breached. Heavy damage . . . most of the supplies have been contaminated."

She sounded tired, perhaps beyond shock. The amount of bad news throughout this voyage had been oppressive enough without this one heavy slam. Only as she listened to the rest of the message did a flicker of hope come into her birdlike eyes. "Captain, they also say they have survivors."

A twinge of both hope and despair caught Kirk in the gut. That could mean almost anything. "Survivors? More than one?"

"Apparently, sir."

"Spock, was there more than one attendant at the lightship?"

"Only Sardoch, sir."

"Then I hope the *Rover* went in armed."

Both barges, contaminated. Kirk's skin tightened. All their reserve supplies and rations for Gamma Night.

The bad news meant an even harder voyage to Belle Terre. What had happened? There was no one else in this area of space for six sectors in any direction, no reports of territorial challenge, no spacefaring cultures, nobody to cause any trouble.

A lonely place, isolated and undisturbed, with a completely uneventful history, until now. A peaceful and purposeful journey through the velvet darkness of space. One direction, no course changes, no speed adjustments, just a stressless warp two all the way. What a joke.

They'd all looked forward to a boring voyage out to the *Hatteras.* Kirk had expected his biggest problems to involve the typical brawls and irritation that tended to break out when people unaccustomed to space travel were sardined into ships and told to sit down for a few months. His most likely problem would be the sheer boredom that came with traveling on ships.

If only. For weeks there had been nothing but bulkhead-to-bulkhead troubles. Just when he thought things were starting to go right, the lightship's signal had gone dark. That was eight days ago. Kirk had immediately dispatched *American Rover* to plow ahead, but at her top speed of warp four, she had just arrived yesterday. At warp six, the starship could be much quicker, but space was very, very big. The Expedition would be several more days arriving.

Uhura broke him out of his silent complaints. "Sir, Governor Pardonnet has beamed aboard. He wants to know why we're ordering the Expedition to stop."

"That's all I need," Kirk muttered. "Tell him to come up here. Contact the privateer ships and tell them to maintain alert. Have the other vessels go to alert status, but maintain speed and formation. Halt all beamings.

Command communications only. Mr. Sulu, break formation with the Expedition and let's get to the *Hatteras*. Emergency warp six."

Sulu glanced at him. "Warp six, sir."

By the time Evan Pardonnet arrived on the bridge, the starship was already a quarter of the way across the gulf between the convoy and the lightship. The convoy would take another day at warp two.

"Why are we getting a yellow alert warning for the whole train?" the governor asked. Apparently the yellow alert had caught him out of the shower. He was wearing a T-shirt and drawstring pants, with hastily pulled-on boots. One pantleg was tucked in, the other running free. "And why is *Enterprise* pulling away? I just barely got on board before they shut down beaming authority!"

Kirk prowled the command deck. "We've had a report from our pathfinders that the lightship and the stock barges have been violated."

The governor's young face took on a sudden age. "Violated? What's that mean?"

"Means attacked."

"My God, our supplies! They were supposed to be safe way out here!"

"We thought they would be." Kirk offered an apologetic glance that Pardonnet didn't take well. "You don't look good, Evan."

The governor grimaced and drew a nauseated breath. "Just indigestion."

"Have you seen the medic on *Mable Stevens* about it?"

"He says I'm still spacesick. Captain Chalker just sort of chuckles at me and winks at his wife." Pardonnet braced himself on the ship's rail. His expressive eyes were crimped with worry. "Are you sure about this? It's not just a collision or a miscommunication?"

"*American Rover*'s at the scene. They've recovered the lightship keeper, injured and unconscious. Their medic is stabilizing him, but they can't speak to him yet. They report they've scanned the barges and picked up residue of weapons discharge and that the supply barges' hulls have multiple ruptures."

"Oh, no . . ." Pardonnet's hands began to shake. "What if all the supplies are compromised? What if we have nothing left? We counted on the food and medicine to get us through, then give us a jumpstart on the planet. How are we going to get the rest of the way?"

"The hard way." A chill of responsibility ran up through Kirk's spine and cramped his shoulders. He was determined to keep his temper. People expected more from him than the other captains. This could turn out to be a critical moment for the whole Expedition and the Belle Terre project, if he didn't "handle it" right.

He approached Pardonnet passively. "You're not giving up, are you?"

Inconsolable, Pardonnet shook his head. "Starfleet never should've sent the barges ahead. They should never have been let out of our sight! We could've protected them."

"Governor, if I may," Spock intruded from the upper deck, "the barges show signs of high-yield energy torch residue. That is a sign of a major conflagration. Whatever happened to them would certainly have cost lives had it come upon unprepared Expedition vessels. With this warning, we have the chance to reinforce ourselves and fend off future attacks."

Confused, Pardonnet shifted his shoulders in discomfort and looked at Kirk. "What'd he just say?"

"He's saying the barges acted as a buffer between us and whatever force attacked them. We have the chance to fortify ourselves, rearrange our formation for optimum—"

"But what about all our supplies!"

"We'll have to do without them."

"Captain, you can't really expect . . . we can't . . ."

The end of that sentence withered before it came out. Pardonnet's hot face turned gray. He clamped his lips and fixed his eyes on the forward screen, hoping to see something other than what he knew must be coming out of the star-dotted darkness.

Attention instantly shifted from the civilian aspect of the voyage to the military. All eyes moved to Kirk, except Evan Pardonnet's. The governor stared at the wide view of space before them, and at the suddenly uncertain future.

"ETA, Mr. Chekov?" Kirk requested.

"Seventeen minutes at this speed, sir," Chekov answered.

A very long seventeen minutes.

# Chapter Twenty

"SIR, ACCORDING to the autolog, the attack occurred eight days ago."

"Just when the lightship beacon went dark."

Jack Carpenter from the *American Rover* renewed a few of Kirk's beliefs that Starfleet people weren't the only ones who could get things right. By the time Kirk, Spock, and Pardonnet arrived on the lightship *Hatteras,* the beacon vessel was already secure and stationed with armed guards from the *Rover.*

Not that there was anything left to secure from. Whatever attack had struck here was eight days over with, according to the cold and dried-up residue that could still be tracked and the hull ruptures loaded with frozen self-sealant.

Secure situation? Kirk's internal alarms said no. Trusting his instincts, he kept his hand on his phaser as he ran a glance along the line of unexpected occupants in the wide-bodied lightship. The usually empty signal vessel was crammed full of survivors, at least sixty of them. Aliens.

Right away Kirk noticed they were a handsome people, without mixed races. Obviously they were part of an isolated planetary system without much intermixing, or the intermixing had happened eons ago and was finished. Not unusual, but becoming less normal for the constantly fluid Federation.

This, though, wasn't Federation space. Things in this star cluster would be different, like the early days of his first five-year exploratory mission, where anything around any corner was entirely new.

These people were humanoid, a strikingly typical formation in nature. McCoy had explained it to him once, a while ago, when it mattered—evolution had discovered early that anything going against the stream needed the senses on one end and the propulsion on the other. Four limbs worked well because extra ones got in the way and fewer didn't function as well. Two legs were best. Binocular vision, a braincase, upright pelvis, knees, elbows, fingers, the beautiful opposable thumb that made technology possible . . . humanoid.

Humanoid, but not human. Their complexions were sapphire to smoke gray, their hair mostly in the brown spectrum, some bending back toward the red. Good cheekbones. They wore simple pants, soft boots, and belted tunics in blocks of solid colors. No badges, no pins, no bands of rank, just patches of crayon colors. All of them were male.

Somehow it was both comforting and disturbing to see the similarities. Kirk also understood, from sheer experience, that sometimes humanoids, because of their natural passion and intellect, could be much more brutal about destroying each other than destroying anyone else. He didn't know yet who they were, where in the equation of attack they belonged.

Outside, docked to the lightship, were two grim-looking supply barges, decimated. The amount of food-stuffs and supplies that could be salvaged would fit into a duffel bag. Not disaster, but the dawn of great stress for the Expedition.

"Any word on the lightship keeper?" Kirk asked.

"He's still unconscious," Carpenter said. "It's a blunt-impact head trauma, not a weapon injury. He got knocked around pretty badly."

"Remand him to Dr. M'Benga on the Mercy Ship right away." Kirk scanned the line-up of bruised, battered, weak survivors. Now, questions.

His shoulders knotted, aware of the accusing impatience of Evan Pardonnet, Kirk simply stepped to the lineup of aliens, picked one, and squared off with him.

"Take me to your leader."

"We are Blood Many. Things were changing all around us. We had made an alliance with our eternal enemies, the Kauld, but they betrayed us. We live in a double-starred system—you know what I mean by this?"

"A binary," Spock delivered to the Blood man who said he was in charge. "Your stars orbit each other. Though still very far away, suns are extremely powerful forces."

The alien leader's dark eyes lit beneath expressive brows. "We have gravity distortion and many natural disasters. Sometimes space bodies are pulled from their orbits and strike our world."

Spock looked at Kirk. "Such a situation would cause

cataclysmic disasters on a common schedule. Extra heat, tidal waves, thunderstorms, extinctions, high-level storms, and earthquakes."

"That's a pretty grim picture." Evan Pardonnet gazed with both sympathy and suspicion at the leader of the survivors.

"We have weather disruptions every few days," the blue-skinned man said. "Normal seasons are sometimes moved by months. We spend most of our time struggling to live another season. Droughts last for years. Sometimes we have no winter. Crops die, famine, ocean storms, slides . . ."

"And every few years, a war?" Jim Kirk broke into the conversation with his intuition ringing. He was determined to keep the briefing on the best track for what he had to do next.

"Then you understand," the Blood man presumed. "Technology came slowly, but it came. We could prepare for disaster better, store more food, build better structures, recover sooner. Soon we began to look at the sky and at the god which came eventually to ravage us. We discovered it was not god, but a second sun, and that it had a planet. We concentrated on space travel, hoping to go out and find a new place to live, or at least a place of rest. We fixed to the one glimmer of hope. When we went out, we found no rest. We found only quarrelsome neighbors. They wouldn't share what we needed, and they took what we had. Suddenly the wars started. As well as every other curse, we had war every few generations."

"How long was the interval between wars?" Spock asked.

"If my calculations are right, about twenty-four of your years. Sometimes more, sometimes less. Not only did we have natural disasters, but we knew the enemy was coming. We built bigger weapons and prepared, sometimes struck first, because it was inevitable."

"Who are these Kauld?" Kirk asked. "Are they different from you? What do they look like?"

"They look nothing like us. They wear decorations. Uniforms. Their skin is pale. They are weaker, because they don't have to work as hard. They have time to entertain. They read stories. And they eat too much."

Come to think of it, all these blue survivors *were* very lean. Unlike chronically hungry people, though, they were strong and bright-eyed. Their hair had luster. Possibly they were generations acclimated to subsistence living and had learned to thrive on very little. Explained the fact that having no food didn't bother them much. No air, though . . .

"What changed that brought you this far out?" Kirk asked, forcing himself forward.

"We were given a terrible gift. Star-drive."

"Warp power," Kirk confirmed. "Matter-antimatter propulsion?"

"Yes. The Formless gave it to us. They thought they were doing a good thing. I suppose it would be wondrous, for anyone but Blood and Kauld."

Kirk held up a hand. "I think I understand. With hyperlight speed, you didn't have to wait for a twenty-four-year ellipse to bring you together anymore."

"We knew we had to use it, because Kauld would. Now we must work even harder. And we have no recovery period. The brief hope of technology betrayed us. Now we have a continuous war, instead of war only when the ellipse brings Blood and Kauld near. Star-drive is a terrible gift for my people. The warfare will never end now."

Though he was boiling inside, Kirk kept his tone keel-even. "Oh, we've found there are as many ways to end wars as there are ways to start them."

The man looked at him. "We had to find a way, or there would be a single war until one side was finished. We made an alliance which no one enjoyed. I thought there was hope. But Kauld betrayed us. As soon as we made contact with your beacon ship, they attacked us, here, too far to run for help. Blood believed we had made a pact, an agreement to deal with the newcomers together. Kauld betrayed us. Our ship was crippled, your supply ships wrecked, my crew injured. We escaped to your beacon ship. I believe they think they killed us all, or they would have destroyed everything."

"Where's the wreck of your ship?"

"They towed it away. They'll use it."

"Did you come in a life pod?"

"Yes, a containment envelope."

"Where is it?"

"We had to discard it because of your beacon ship's boarding mechanism. They were incompatible."

"Yes . . . just a moment, please. Spock—" With a nod that brought him alongside, Kirk clasped Jack Carpenter by the elbow and maneuvered the young man far enough away that they could speak privately. "What about it?"

"As far as we can detect," Carpenter said, "he's telling some version of the truth. We won't know for sure until the lightship keeper wakes up, if he does. We don't have any of the lightship's logs."

They paused as Evan Pardonnet, pale and overwhelmed, came to listen.

"No records survived at all?" Kirk asked Carpenter.

"Nothing. It's completely missing. The whole bridge

is mostly gutted and part of it was sheared off, completely gone. Lucky a lightship's bridge isn't manned, or we'd be counting corpses."

"If we could find them."

Dissatisfying. Not good, relying on eyewitnesses. There were too many illusions, too many ways in the active galaxy for the eye to be fooled.

Kirk tried to remain clinical, since that seemed to be where the answers lay. "What's their general condition?"

"Bruises, a concussion, few cuts, one broken arm."

"That's it?"

"That's all."

Kirk looked at Spock for confirmation of what he was about to say. "Seems a little light for a ship-wrecking battle, doesn't it?"

"Well, they're tough guys," Carpenter reckoned, as if he'd already thought of things that were just now occurring to Kirk, which was entirely probable. "These are the most industrious people any of us have ever even heard of. They'd just been through a battle, had their ship hijacked, and were left for dead on another derelict. No hope for rescue from their own culture—they said nobody knew they'd come out this far. Any survival training I've ever had involves stabilize your wounds, sit down, and don't suck up all the air and wait for rescue."

Pardonnet wiped his hand across his sweat-pearled face. "What did they do instead?"

"Look around," Carpenter said. "They *cleaned*."

Kirk glanced at the interior of the lightship. "Now that you mention it, this does seem tidy for a war zone. . . ."

Carpenter pointed as he spoke. "They've cleaned,

sorted, fixed, mended, sealed all the cracks, labeled all of it, and even re-wove the torn carpet. In less than a week, they've done two-thirds of the necessary repairs to make this ship space-functional again. Can you believe sitting there weaving carpet when the odds are you're about to suffocate and/or starve?"

Although he usually liked a testimonial of valiant behavior, Kirk didn't warm up much to what he was hearing. "Guess I'd better start imagining it."

"Despite the failing life-support system and no food," Carpenter went on, "they kept working. You should see the lightship's freight hold. Everything's organized into piles, even though they didn't know what some things even were. They stacked the Kleinfeld coils with the charged plugs. Nobody who knew what they were doing would ever put those together."

"They demagnetize each other," Spock agreed unnecessarily.

Carpenter looked up at him and nodded. "Right, but since they look alike, these guys stacked them perfectly over in that closet. They hung up every piece of a garment shipment that fell out of its crates. They built hangers and racks out of salvage to hang the clothes on, then built armoirs out of damaged bulkhead material so the clothes wouldn't get dusty. They even catalogued the scrap that should've been jettisoned."

Spock offered a perplexed look and asked, "I beg your pardon?"

"They kept scrap?" Kirk simultaneously asked.

"Oh, yeah!" Carpenter declared. "We couldn't believe it. Their captain told me his people always keep everything. They never throw away anything because they never know when they might need it. And they work at using whatever they've kept. They really think about it. No doubt, they saved the lightship by plugging up all the leaks and cracks and repressurizing. There's just one thing we can't figure out, though."

"What's that?"

Carpenter shifted his weight thoughtfully. *"Why* would they work so hard? As far as they knew, they were going to die out here. There were only a couple of days' breathable air left in the day tanks, and no food at all. It's just luck you sent us ahead on *Rover.* They gave themselves a little more time by repairing everything they could figure out, but the drives were smashed, they were running out of air, they were waiting to die, but they didn't just sit and wait. Even the port-side engine's running again. Wouldn't do 'em any good without a way to steer, but it'll power up. That's how they had enough heat to keep alive, even though the work used up more oxygen. They couldn't work on saving themselves, so they worked on other things. They even repainted."

"Who would do that?" Pardonnet wondered. "Who would do interior decor in a life-and-death situation? Why use up the energy?"

"One way or the other," Carpenter confirmed with a cryptic shrug, "far as they knew, they were dead."

"Repainted," Kirk murmured, contemplating all he'd heard. His mind rushing, he looked at Spock. "Everybody dies sometime . . . they wanted to die working."

"Captain Kirk," the governor fretted, "what are we going to do now? Our supplies are gone, we're running low on the foodstuffs, fuel, medical supplies, and everything the barges were supposed to restock, and now we've got—what, sixty?—more men to feed and house and treat. What does that mean?"

"It means we buckle down and get ready for a hard,

hungry road." Kirk made sure his tone was as pleasant as he could make it. A hopeful ring was elusive, but he tried. "We'll have to use what we have instead of what we hoped to have."

"Some of the cattle, for instance," Spock suggested.

Pardonnet gritted his teeth, tormented. "Those animals are meant to seed whole ranches and dairies once we get to Belle Terre! We don't even have one head to a person!"

"Very small rations of protein will go a long way, Governor," Spock suggested. "Your husbandry specialists, I'm sure, will have suggestions."

"This is a disaster. . . ."

"It's a setback." Kirk glanced back at the alien leader, who was waiting patiently for whatever decision would be rendered. "An entire civilization based on grim resolution. Always recovering from one conflict while preparing for the next. Float away from each other, spend the next eighty-four years recovering, get ready to fight again . . . it's quite a story."

"We have encountered such things before, Captain," Spock reminded. "Eminiar and Vendikar, for instance. People learning to live with generational warfare, acclimating to what they saw as their only path—"

"It explains their work ethic," Pardonnet suggested, knotting his hands nervously. "Success and survival come through hard work, and that is *all*. Have to admire it—"

"Hard work is something you obviously don't shy away from, Evan," Kirk bothered to say, sensing the governor might need that muscle of resolution very soon, and right here.

Ignoring the compliment, Pardonnet asked, "What're we going to do now?"

"We're going to forge on."

"With sixty more mouths to feed? How can I tell our citizens that?"

"The only alternative," Spock suggested, "would be to remand the survivors to the custody of the *Republic* or *Beowulf* and send them back to the Federation."

"Possibly," Kirk considered. "At intervals of emergency warp, they might make it in a couple months."

"No—" Pardonnet put his hand on Kirk's arm, changing his mind very suddenly. He seemed to be getting a headache. "We can't do that . . . they're refugees now. This is their home space. We're trying to make friends in the Sagittarius Star Cluster, not enemies. We have to live there from now on."

Kirk felt his brow tighten. "We're not that sure."

Pardonnet looked up. "Of what?"

"Of anything he's said."

"Well, no, but . . . who'd make all that up? Neighbor relations is a local government issue. I'm the local government. You won't be staying on Belle Terre, but we will be, for the rest of our lives. You'll have to defer to me on things that affect our futures and not yours."

"It's my job to make sure you have a future," Kirk vowed. "Don't forget that."

Though his arms ached with tension, Kirk tried to appear casual as he strode back to the Blood man leader. He knew he wasn't fooling anybody. He wasn't trying hard enough. His posture was stiff, eyes hard and hot, his jaw set. He stood before the taller man and glared into the dark brown eyes, daring the bruise on the man's cheek to be a fake, a lie, a trick. "Did you know the life-support on this ship was failing?"

"Of course we knew."

"And that your activity would shorten your time to live?"

"Yes, we knew."

"Didn't you want to survive?"

"We try not to want."

Kirk paused. "Pardon me?"

"When we expect little, we're delighted with what we get. Wanting asks for failure."

Curious way of thinking. Thinly masking his sarcasm, Kirk commented, "You did very nicely considering you had a disaster on your hands. Everything but stenciling borders on the walls."

"Disaster is always coming," the Blood man said. "If we complain, bad events can always become worse. We ask your hospitality. Our men are very hungry and will consume much as long as we have it."

"I thought you said your people were used to living on a subsistence level."

"We eat when we have it. Don't you?"

An irritable grumble came up from Kirk's throat, not exactly an agreement, not exactly approval.

"We understand, certainly," the Blood went on, "that you will now be turning back. We know you must take us to your space rather than ours, but we are prepared to deal with this."

"You'd come back with us?" Pardonnet asked, plumbing the problem, not really comprehending the vastness they were talking about.

"We must. You know now that there are horrors ahead. Kauld will take you as a threat, the same as they take us. Your food supplies are gone now, and everything else with them. You must not go on into the Blind. You'll have to lie still for many hours out of every day. You've come here with so many people . . . and space is a terrible place to die."

Aggravating. The look on Evan Pardonnet's face was enough to start animal sacrifices by. Which wasn't all that far a possibility.

Unsatisfied by the half-answers he thought he was getting, Kirk resisted another urge to glance at Spock for confirmation that suspicion and doubt were orders of the moment.

Rather than making any commitments, he opted for the general. "We'll have our medical staff take care of your wounded. You'll be treated as guests, but you'll be under surveillance and your access to the passenger ships will be strictly limited until your story is confirmed. There are certain vessels from which you may come and go, others which will require escort, and still others from which you are banned. Do you understand all that?"

"Oh, yes. Our thanks."

"Very well. Prepare your people to transfer to the convoy. By the way . . . what's your name?"

"My name is Shucorion."

# Chapter Twenty-one

"THERE WAS a story I heard once, about a man who inherited his grandfather's favorite clock. He put it in his living room, and soon discovered that the clock made a loud TOCK TOCK TOCK all the time. He tried to ignore it, but eventually it was too much to take. He didn't want to get rid of the family clock, so he called his doctor and asked what to do. Should he get hypnotized? Should he get earplugs? The doctor told him to get five chickens and put them in the living room.

"Strange prescription, but doctor's orders, you know ... the man went out and bought five chickens. The cackling of the chickens was so incessant that the man couldn't take a nap or eat a meal. After a week of this, he called the doctor again, who told him to put two cows in the living room. He did that, and before long the cows' constant mooing and stomping was louder than the TOCK and the CACKLE.

"The man was going out of his mind. He called the doctor and shouted about the TOCK CACKLE MOO. The doctor told him to get a power drill and keep it running all the time. You can imagine how that sounded. Well, this process continued until the man had a TOCK CACKLE MOO BUZZ BARK YOWL RING HOOT JANGLE BONG.

"After a month of living like this, he called his doctor and bellowed that he was about to crack and blowtorch the whole house. The doctor said, 'Yes, you've reached tolerance. Open the front door and shove out everything except the clock.' In a blind rage, the man emptied his living room of everything that made noise except his clock.

"All at once—why, a churchlike peace descended! There was complete tranquility. The man was amazed that the grandfather clock had changed! It now only made a soft, gentle *tick tick tick.* He called the doctor and said, 'Sir, you are a wonder! The house is quiet now and I'm sleeping like a baby.' And the man lived happily ever after, with his grandfather's favorite clock ticking away peacefully in his corner."

"Is that the end?"

"Yes. That's the end."

"Nice story, Jim. What's your point?"

"The point is, I used to think running a fully operational starship in hostile space with a crew of four hundred was pretty hard work. After running this Expedition, it's tiddlywinks."

The bridge of the *Enterprise* was usually an oasis, its pool pliable and docile, with tame operations going on around its banks, managed by professionals who didn't need watching. Moments of tension came and went over the course of time, the dutiful doing of ship's business, the scramble for solutions, or the coils of battle, but those moments in the past had encompassed a few hours, then were done. The bridge always bridled back to its neutral condition.

Once upon a time. This time the hitch of tension had been tied an hour out of Federation borders and had done nothing but tighten ever since. No matter how deftly Kirk handled every trouble, the strife increased as new problems piled upon those just grappled, with the ones before never completely going away. Supplies meant for the colony were useless in space, and things that wouldn't be necessary on Belle Terre were critical for survival out here. Some people wanted to jettison the planetary stuff and others wanted to ditch space necessaries in favor of some illusion about getting to the planet faster. How many times could it be explained? There was no "faster."

These irritations wicked all the way to the top of the command line, even though they shouldn't and normally would never have made it through the scaffold of authorities under Kirk. Sometimes it helped if he made a personal appearance and talked some poor shipmaster off a ledge. Sometimes it threw acid on the flame. He felt the fabric of his experience and value as a unifying force become thinner and thinner as he spread it around.

Kirk came onto the bridge expecting to feel at home, and somehow failed in that. He'd awakened this morning with a sense that he wasn't doing all of his job, and a burning desire to do it. He knew where that came from—he'd taken to heart Evan Pardonnet's charge that these captains should be allowed to run their own ships their ways, because they weren't Starfleet ships and because the Belle Terre project was based upon individual decisions.

It sounded good. In fact, it *was* good. But a fleet is not a colony, not a free-flowing economy. Everything that happened here affected almost everything else.

"Good morning, sir," Spock greeted as Kirk strode around him on the upper bridge.

"Spock," Kirk responded, a little gruffly.

Spock's eyes followed him. He knew something was about to change.

"Uhura," Kirk began, "record this session and broadcast it to Captain Smith, Colonel Glass, and Mr. Carpenter of the *Rover*, and Captains Austin and Parker, and all control personnel. Also notify Fleet Coxswain Dan Marks to limit the movement of small boats and tenders from this point on. Call Dr. McCoy up here, and request that Governor Pardonnet and Captain Kilvennan join us also. And . . . have Mr. Giotto locate Shucorion and bring him here."

His voice was gravelly as he spoke. He didn't like to sound tired. Ideas that had been forming for the past several days suddenly spilled out in some kind of workable order.

When he turned away from her, Spock was standing right beside him. "Is something wrong, sir?"

"I've had this nagging feeling for about two days," Kirk told him. "The darkness has brightened a little now that Shucorion's here. We can see the picture now, whether it's pretty or not. Spock . . ."

"Yes, sir?"

"I wish you had gut reactions."

Spock raised that eyebrow, a barometer of his inner self. "Really . . . is your 'gut' reacting?"

306

"There's something that doesn't make sense about what Shucorion says. It's . . . too perfect a disaster."

"I beg your pardon?"

"His story. I can't tell if it's real or if it's been written. Shucorion wants us to turn back, and all around the Expedition people are muttering about turning back. You and Chekov, look for clues. There has to be something . . . something that doesn't fit."

Folding his arms, Spock pressed a hip to the console nearest him and commented, "Shucorion's presence and that of his men has had an enlightening effect. However, it has also summoned a dangerous apprehension among the colonists. While the concept of turning back was an isolated sentiment before this, there is much more talk of it now that we know of the Blood and Kauld conflict in the star cluster."

"I know," Kirk established, vexed. "I can order Starfleet people to contain their gossip, but there's nothing to be done among the civilians. Fear, Spock . . . it's the worst disease out there."

He glanced at Uhura to begin recording the message he wanted sent around the Expedition. When she nodded, Kirk looked forward to the screens, the helm, and so that he could see Spock at his side. Somehow it was easier to make a proclamation when he clearly saw the living element that would be affected.

"Now that we're traveling in Gamma Night," he began, "we have to change our entire way of doing things. We're having to stop for ten hours out of every thirty. Stop moving, stop drifting, keep visual track of each other, use cables or tractors to hold position with each other so there's no accidental colliding. We tried to manipulate this without any personnel or watch changes, but that hasn't worked. We've had six collisions and had to evacuate an entire Conestoga. Repairs are going slowly. If we have a second accident like that, we'll have to stop indefinitely until things are back to normal function. I'm not willing to lay off indefinitely. I'm afraid the time's come for the Expedition captains to bend their procedures. Mr. Spock, advise the first and second officers to rearrange watch schedules to put more experienced people on duty during travel hours. We'll run skeleton crews during Gamma Night, and everyone else will get eight hours' sleep. Every ship should maintain full security alert during Gamma Night, with a senior navigator in charge of monitoring position. All short-range sensors will be on, whether they do any good or not, and keep alert watch teams scanning the skies."

At the helm, where he had been using an auxiliary screen to coordinate traffic patterns for the coming day, Sulu turned. "Why, sir? No one can move during Gamma Night."

"*We* can't," Kirk pointed out. "Maybe someone else can. We've now seen concrete action from enemy powers. They've come out from under the table, but the lights are still out. We can analyze their attack methods, their weapons, strengths and weaknesses, and by the time they come again, we'll be ready. I'm also ordering all ships, with the exception of *Enterprise,* to shut down long-range sensors, thereby extending our short-range capacity. We may be able to talk to each other in limited codes. It also makes us less vulnerable to anybody who might take umbrage at our stepping into an area, because we won't be sending any attractive probe signals."

Chekov simply straightened and said, "We'll be ready, sir."

"Good." Taking the interrupting as a chance to step to the lower deck, Kirk tried to shake the feeling that he was being watched by everybody in the convoy all at once. "Uhura, mandate emergency evacuation drills on every ship. I want all personnel ready for quick transfer to another vessel."

"I've already laid that out, sir," she said, "according to each ship's manifest of personnel. They didn't like it much. They'll like it even less when we make them drill the procedure with a thousand people at a time."

"They'll have to get used to it. We know there are hostiles in the vicinity, if not in the immediate area. I intend to be ready. They'll be very happy if they ever have to get off in a hurry."

"Very true, sir," she allowed.

The instructions might've continued, but for the interruption of the turbolift. McCoy stalked in, with Captain Kilvennan and Governor Pardonnet at his sides.

Kirk signaled Uhura to cut off the recording. Something told him this wasn't going to be an all-personnel kind of moment. He looked up at the men on the upper bridge.

Michael Kilvennan was now the official spokesman of all the colonists, something to which he had been unanimously appointed with Evan Pardonnet's recommendation. Did that mean Pardonnet was losing confidence in his own influence? Maybe. At least the governor's ego wasn't in the way of his looking for solutions. Kirk wasn't about to get into it.

"Captain," McCoy reported, "the lightship keeper Sardoch has regained consciousness and he's lucid. Do you want to debrief him personally?"

Kirk peered at him. His senses clicked on. McCoy

seemed grim this morning, had something on his mind. "Has he said anything enlightening—allow me to rephrase that. Has he said anything I want to hear yet?"

"Yes, he pretty much confirms Shucorion's story of an attack of some kind, though he was injured at the onset and wasn't conscious though much of the incident. He says the attack occurred during Gamma Night, so he couldn't read who was coming in."

Perking up suddenly, Spock broke in. "The attackers moved in organized fashion during Gamma Night?"

McCoy offered a kind of shrug. "I wouldn't scour those details too closely, Spock. Sardoch has a head injury. His memory could be mixing up events. Without logs to back him up, it's just hearsay. He recalls Shucorion's men stumbling on board the lightship in bad shape, and then a series of thunderous hits on the ship while the Blood men were on board. Somebody was definitely trying to hurt them. Sardoch also recalls hearing talk of an ancient feud, but he wasn't sure of his memory on that one."

"Hmm," Kirk grumbled. No logs left on that chewed-away bridge. An unreliable eyewitness. "Well, I've got a few questions for him. Will he be all right, Bones?"

"Oh, yes. It's hard to kill a Vulcan. I've been trying to annoy Spock to death for years."

"It *has* grayed me appreciably," Spock conceded.

Kirk glanced at him, then looked back at McCoy. "Thank you, Doctor."

McCoy folded his arms, somehow doing it in a completely different way than Spock did. For Spock, the gesture usually signaled the end of an issue. With McCoy . . .

"Don't thank me too soon, Captain. I don't think you'll like what I'm—"

Just as Kirk faced the doctor to hear the new opinion, the turbolift behind McCoy swept open, emitting Security Chief Giotto and the unusual guest Shucorion. Kilvennan and Evan Pardonnet moved out of the way, both heading around to the port side, crowding Scott and the two young engineers he had brought here for bridge experience.

"Sir," Giotto announced. "Bringing Mr. Shucorion, as requested."

"Thank you," Kirk said. "Mr. Shucorion, welcome to the bridge. How are you?"

"Nothing bad happened today," the Blood guest responded.

"Really . . . well . . . good. Come on a little farther in. You don't have to stand in the vestibule."

"My thanks." The blue-skinned alien man came to the rail beside Giotto, decidedly rugged and elegant in his way, even though Giotto was particularly proud of his newly styled Starfleet jacket and tended to prance. Shucorion's simple clothing carried a kind of comfortable medieval economy that made its own stylishness.

*He's a lot like Spock that way. Silently draws the eye, dark and shadowy, obviously intelligent, but doesn't talk much. Every time he does talk, he really says something.*

"Your command center is a handsome place," Shucorion commented. "On our ships, everything is built in cylinders and we walk on the outer walls. There is very little . . ."

"Style?" Kirk supplied. "I'd like to see your ships someday. In the meantime, I have something to discuss with you."

311

Aware of McCoy still standing nearby like a kettle about to steam, Kirk stepped to the upper deck. He liked to be eye-to-eye with people he was about to scold.

"We're engaging in an activity that is nearly as old as our civilization," he said to Shucorion. "Gathering together, traveling across wide expanses to settle new lands, spread new ideals, seek new adventures—this is a time-honored drive among human beings. What you see around you is a descendant of the pioneering practices of centuries ago on our planet, a practice called the 'wagon train,' in which hundreds of people would strike off together into the wilderness. This time, we're reaching farther than we have before. What you see here is a wagon train to the stars, Mr. Shucorion. It's my purpose to make sure these people arrive and succeed."

Shucorion paused, sensing the not particularly veiled challenge. "Then we will grieve you all the more, when you are consumed."

Getting some version of what he was plumbing for, Kirk squared his shoulders and raised his chin. "You'll have to refrain from saying exactly that kind of thing from now on. You and your men have been spreading your story among our passengers. It's frightening our passengers and worrying our crews. I'm going to have to ask you to stop. If I have to confine all of you to Starfleet vessels, I'll do it."

Shucorion's dark brows tightened. "Telling the truth? This frightens them?"

Kirk offered a vocal shrug. "Truth is elastic. Most of these people are not spacefarers. They don't understand the balance we strike."

The Blood leader seemed honestly perplexed. Or he

was a good actor. "Have you not explained it to them before bringing them here? That space is dangerous?"

"I didn't 'bring' them. They came of their own choice, each for his own reasons."

"And you choose not to tell them, then? To hide the truth?"

A dare if ever there was one.

Stepping a little closer, to create an illusion of privacy despite all the eyes on them from around the bridge, Kirk spoke slowly.

"You're visitors here. You could easily become prisoners. We're not all that sure of your story. The investigation is still going on. We're analyzing weapons, attack strategy, your wounds . . . we'll find out about you. Until there's a reason to do otherwise, you're being treated as guests. We're in a stressful situation. Food, energy packs, medical supplies are running short, largely because you attracted a hostile force to our supply barges. Limitation might be normal for your people, but it isn't for most of these passengers. They're edgy and frightened. I want you and your men to stop adding to that fear. For now, I'll give you the benefit of the doubt. But we'll be keeping our eyes open."

"I see." Shucorion pressed his palms together thoughtfully. "And while you have your eyes open on us, Captain . . . what do you see?"

A fair question. Kirk was in one of those open moods, the kind that could go either way.

"I see admirable workers," he admitted, "who don't really know their way around space. Despite our asking you about the local spacescape, you don't seem to know things that spacefarers should know. So why were you so far out?"

Though he paused as if unsure of an answer, Shucorion's eyes never flinched. Ultimately he claimed, "We were chased out."

Vague, but at least consistent with the rest of his story.

"You will be chased out too," he added, "if you tempt Kauld."

Was that a threat? Warning?

Or was it some kind of promise? Shucorion had been pushing for the Expedition to turn back, spinning tales of horror and destruction, strain and suffering, yet there was something fatalistic about the way his people told their stories. Struggle seemed to be all he and his people had ever known. They couldn't imagine any other way of life, and thought the chance to get out of it should be taken. They didn't understand why the Expedition wouldn't turn around and get out while they had the chance.

Spock thought Shucorion was telling some version of the truth. Scott didn't like him, but no surprise. Scott didn't like anybody at first. McCoy hadn't weighed in yet, opting to wait until the lightship keeper woke up and told his story.

That was one fact in Shucorion's favor—they hadn't killed the lightship keeper. An attacking force, certainly those making as ferocious an assault as had been made at the lightship, would've eradicated the one eyewitness.

They hadn't. In fact, even though they assumed they would all die in space within days, they'd taken steps to keep him alive. Kirk wouldn't dismiss the gesture, and as he stood here surveying Shucorion with a spice of doubt, he forced himself to hold back, to treat the other man like a captain until there was reason to do otherwise.

"We'll just continue keeping our eyes open. However, you'll have a talk with your men about restraining their conversations."

Was that a nod? Or had Shucorion simply raised his head in some kind of wariness or defiance?

Hard to tell.

Kirk didn't wait around for an agreement. His word would have to be the law, not a request. Dismissing any protest or compliance by turning, he came back to McCoy.

"All right, Doctor, I can see something broiling under your surface. Say what you have to say."

Self-conscious now that there were so many high-ranking people here watching him, McCoy fidgeted briefly before finding complete confidence in what he had to say. The doctor was as unpolitic as anyone Kirk had ever known, but he didn't like to make trouble unless there was a good reason. There must be one.

"Jim," he began, "on behalf of all the medical personnel on this convoy, including the senior physicians and commanding officer of the *Brother's Keeper* and the chief coroner, I recommend turning back before this expedition falls victim to a major catastrophe."

Everyone on the bridge reacted in some way, if only in a jolt of tension, a flinch of posture, or a sudden frown. The medical staff represented a stern barometer of attitude on the Expedition to the Stars. This couldn't be ignored. More than any other single force, the doctors affected everybody, on every ship. On the port side, Michael Kilvennan drifted down to sit on the rail. Near him, Evan Pardonnet did the same, sinking into one of the chairs at the engineering console. The silence was agonizing.

"We already played that card," Kirk rejected. "It didn't work."

McCoy's expression hardened. All at once he and Kirk were the only two men in the universe. "Then you'd better make it work. We're coming into a war zone. You know as well as I do the Federation Council would never have allowed the Expedition to launch if they'd known we were flying into somebody else's war. My staff and colleagues are unified in the opinion that the Surgeon General of the Federation would not approve forward movement."

"Doctor, nobody knew there was a war going on!" Pardonnet held out. "Our initial reports were that there was nothing out here. Nothing!"

"That was because there wasn't anything—yet," McCoy pointed out. "Then those planets cycled back close to each other, and there's suddenly a whole new war. Now somebody's given them warp drive and the cycles don't matter anymore. This area's not only a war zone—it's a war zone forever now. How can we settle a planet, establish a spaceport, and keep the peace when there's none to be kept? A spaceport in a war zone becomes an instant target. You *know* that, Jim."

"Doctor, as usual you're ignoring the potentialities," Spock contested. "There is more at stake than this one colony. A considerable investment has been made not just by these people, but by a vast infrastructure back home. Cultures on a thousand planets are watching, betting on success, planning trade and expansion to the Sagittarius Star Cluster based upon the Belle Terre project." An unexpected defiance came into Spock's voice. His features gave way to passion of his own. "If the Belle Terre project fails, it may sound the death knell of Federation trade and development for a hundred years. We must not turn back."

McCoy pointed an accusing finger at him. "It'll do

the same damn thing if they end up dead in somebody else's war! Better to say, 'We didn't make it over the mountain, let's try again later,' than have pictures of sixty thousand graves broadcast all over the galaxy. Don't you think our enemies will use that against us?"

"Our enemies will also see any retreat as squeamishness," Spock defied. He motioned to Shucorion, standing only a few steps away. "To the Blood and Kauld, we are unknown quantities. The Klingons will not be forgiving of retreat."

Abandoning him, McCoy crossed to Pardonnet. "Governor, you and these people have enjoyed prosperity and peace all your lives. You don't really know what a war is like, never mind war in space, with advanced destructive forces on you and on you, again and again, until—"

"Doctor," Kirk snapped, "leave him alone."

The doctor pivoted to him. "Jim, you should be explaining this to them! This is exactly why the military goes first into unknown territory, why it's a mistake to send the families out to carve the paths. You of all people here *do* know what war is like. Do you want the deaths of sixty thousand civilians on your conscience? Haven't you had enough death in your career?"

The scornful question, blurted with such vicious concern, got Kirk by the throat. Anger heated his face. Only with great bitterness did he cling to the tiny thread that this was what he counted on McCoy to do, this kind of seething honesty that burned every decision down to its core. Kirk depended upon the doctor's natural dissent to read the handwriting on every wall.

But McCoy was right—was it Kirk's responsibility to make sure the colonists stayed alive, or that their dream stayed alive? At this juncture, the two had gone off on forked roads. Was he obliged just to these people, or to the whole Federation and colonies of the future?

What was his job today, different from yesterday? What was his duty?

Just as Kirk parted his tight lips to order the doctor to end this protest, Michael Kilvennan spoke up with a quiet " 'Scuse me." When they all turned to him, he submitted, "The real question is, with our barges destroyed, could we even make it all the way back if we turned around? Turning around here is a lot different than turning back two months ago."

Faltering suddenly, McCoy drew back. That *was* the real problem. Kirk hadn't even thought of it, because he hadn't entertained any ideas about retreat.

Soulsick, Evan Pardonnet gazed at Kilvennan, digesting the impact of those words. If there was no turning back, his noble ideals may have led sixty thousand people to die in space. Body bags. Rows of coffins. Whole families wiped out.

"They're all looking to me for answers," he mourned. "I never thought about being stranded in the middle of a conflict. . . . We all wanted so much to come."

From Pardonnet's left side, Montgomery Scott gazed down with that sage expression of his, almost a smile, almost a beam, and Kirk saw in Scott's face the appreciation lauded upon Evan Pardonnet by everyone who listened to him speak of these things. Even the wizened, unpersuadable, untrusting Scott was caught up in the wonder of crazy chances for the right reasons. That sight mellowed Kirk considerably as he watched, and he glanced around at the other people to measure their reactions too.

"I've got my flaws, I know," Pardonnet simmered on.

"But I also know in my heart that this is good, it's best. Best for the whole Federation. Best for the galaxy, the people who aren't part of the Federation and need to see the possibilities if they get freedom too. How can something that's best for everybody be so hard to make happen?"

"I think you'll find that's usually the case, Evan." Kirk scanned the people around him, upon whom so much would depend as the Expedition nosed into the unknown.

He turned, so that he was partially facing Shucorion, in order to include him in what was about to be said.

"No matter what tales of hardship confront us," he said, "we're going to Belle Terre. It's important for the Federation that we succeed. We've settled hostile space before and dealt with angry cultures and seen good come of it. I believe that more Federation in the galaxy is better than less. I've laid my life on the line many times to move the philosophies of freedom and justice forward, and I'll do it again. I'm asking everyone on this expedition to do it with me. If this attempt fails, the Federation will have a damnable task mustering any others in the future. It's critical that these people actually get to Belle Terre, and that they live and build. It's our job to get them there. From now on, we prepare for the worst. Whatever happens, I intend to embrace challenge."

The bridge fell to its version of silence—a certain pax electrica, lights blinking, circuits beeping softly as they went about their business. Kirk held his position, aware of the effect he had on his little congregation. McCoy relaxed some and clasped his hands. Shucorion was studying him, learning.

Michael Kilvennan stood up and faced Pardonnet. "We're still with you, Evan. I'm here with my wife, two little kids, my mother and her husband, my sister, my brother, and my shipmates. That's all I've got. That's everybody who means anything to me. Everybody except you and the captain here. Me, I got nothing to turn back for."

Pardonnet gazed up at him miserably. "I feel like I painted a picture without any corners. Now we might all fall off the edge."

Kilvennan bothered to put a hand on the governor's slumped shoulder. "You never lied to us. Think we're stupid? We didn't come because you told stories. We came because we want to make our own stories. You're so much one who believes in the decisions of individuals, but you sit here trying to make up a decision for all of us, like we're kids or something. Yeah, maybe we'll die out here. But maybe we won't. Captain Kirk's right. I'm sticking with you, and I'm sticking with him."

"Michael, are you sure?" Pardonnet beseeched. "Because that means things have to change."

"I'm sure. Go ahead—change things."

Taking a grip on Kilvennan's arm in a gesture of unity, Pardonnet stood up. He drew a long breath, steeled himself, and turned to Kirk.

"There's a way to defend ourselves, Captain, and it's somewhere in your mind. If you can figure it out, we'll do anything you say from now on."

Deeply touched, Kirk sincerely murmured, "Thank you . . . very much for that. Governor, I can order Starfleet people to face the cannons. I can even order them to die in the line of duty. I can't order civilians. The only way to do this will be for everyone on this Expedition to become Starfleet. Accept Starfleet officers, use Starfleet weapons, take Starfleet orders without second-guessing. Do everything we say and nothing we don't. If we're going to have the freedoms you want, we'll have to back them up with structure, vigilance, and strength."

A tall order, he knew. But Evan Pardonnet buried a shudder and put out his hand to grip Kirk's. He nodded, unable to respond with words, and gave his solemn agreement in front of all these witnesses.

Kirk held the grip a few seconds longer than necessary. Then he faced Kilvennan. "I need to know the privateers agree," he added.

Kilvennan's catlike eyes penetrated any lingering gap in their causes. "We've seen what you'll do for us. We're going on with you. *With* you."

Warmed to the core, Kirk found himself controlling a hopeful smile as he turned to the whole bridge complement. "Very well, that's how it'll be. We all have new jobs to do. The decision's been made. All hands . . . carry on."

Uhura positively beamed with pride. Pardonnet was pale with acceptance. Shucorion lowered his chin, his eyes unreadable. Spock nodded once, and turned back to his station, a longtime cue for everyone else to do the same. Scott snapped his fingers at two completely stunned junior engineers, who flinched and got back to work.

The machine of the *Enterprise* had just come on line. There would be nothing but toil and wariness from now on.

As the crowd dissipated and the bridge became quiet again, Leonard McCoy folded his arms again, pressed a knee against the rail, and surveyed the man in the middle.

"Wild Bill Hickirk," he drawled.

# Chapter Twenty-two

"EMBRACE THE CHALLENGE . . . *embrace* it? Why would anyone want challenge? I hate it."

Grumbling to himself, Shucorion backed deeper into the unused cubicle on the coroner ship *Twilight Sentinel*. This was the only place he could go in the Expedition and be certain that no one was monitoring him. These cubicles were sacred, he had been told, or private—some kind of meditation place for those who came here to contemplate the dead. He didn't understand that completely. To honor the dead in his culture, no one would simply sit and think. The only honor was in work, in using the wreckage of sacrifice to build new things.

No one else was on this ship, except a crew of three in the piloting compartment. There were many tubes filled with the dead of prior accidents and a battle they had fought. He had avoided collecting details, fighting the urge to be sympathetic toward people he might have to destroy.

"Dimion," he murmured into the device given to him by Billy Maidenshore. It was another two-band vocal broadcaster, they said, focused to so narrow a frequency that only Orions could detect it. "Dimion . . . Dimion . . ."

*"Avedon."* Dimion's voice was broken and faint, but welcome.

"Are you hiding successfully?"

*"Yes, Avedon. We have hidden and are shut down, as you ordered."*

"Restrict all movements until the Blind. Maidenshore was right. They can detect very little then."

*"Have you succeeded? Are they turning back now that they know about Kauld?"*

"They have 'embraced the challenge.' "

*"Embraced it? I don't understand."*

"Neither do I. For Blood, challenge has always meant struggle and suffering. Who chooses to struggle? Suffer? They crave excitement! It's a venture into the insane."

*"Who makes such a decision? Couldn't you change his mind away from such a path?"*

"The leader," Shucorion supplied. "A general named Kirk. I even asked that they share their food with all my men, hoping he would feel the pinch of struggle. These people consider it immoral to let others starve even as you starve yourself. They accepted, but still Kirk will not turn back. Somehow he makes them believe that they can go on. What kind of man is this? No matter what terror rises before him, he orders them onward! And they do what he says. He's ahead—he will get to that planet well before Vellyngaith at this rate."

Dimion was suddenly silent. Understandable—he didn't know whether to agree or not, why it should be a bad thing for the Kauld fortress to be halted before it was begun. Shucorion had cautiously kept from explaining it to him. A mistake perhaps. Poor Dimion deserved trust, yet that would be an unnecessary risk.

The silence hurt them both. *I will explain all this to you soon, old friend. Keep believing in me until then.*

"I'm willing to sacrifice myself," Shucorion began again, "and all I control to make sure Vellyngaith builds that fortress and moves his forces there. As for these Federation people, I would rather they turn around. If Kirk wanted to help his people, he would take them home!"

*"What is it like there, Avedon?"*

"You should see it all! They have enormous ships, filled with food and comfort, yet they spend time in leisure and sleep many hours every day when they could be learning or working. How did they build all this, wasting so much time? Imagine having time!"

*"I can't imagine liking it. Have you discovered anything we can use? Found any of their secrets?"*

Shucorion rubbed his bruised face, touching sore spots he had inflicted himself. "They keep no secrets. It's pointless to spy on them. They tell everything freely. The problem becomes figuring out which is the better knowledge."

He paused to think, and felt for a moment that the cubicle was spinning around him, that he was about to be flung into space and that he must hang on tightly.

"I must stop them from taking that planet before Vellyngaith establishes his fortress and moves his forces there. We have the chance, Dimion, to maneuver Federation into seeing Kauld as enemies. Then Kauld will be forced to deplete themselves against Federation, instead of Blood having to do it."

He paused, and closed his eyes. The image of success lingered in his mind, just out of reach. Did he dare to hope? To stretch out his hand for the prize?

As if speaking to himself, he murmured, "I am truly chosen. I will throw all of Federation and all those people and ships into the pit, if I must, to save mine. For the first time we have a chance for things to go our way. We always barely survived—we never won. This time we have a chance to *win!*"

His voice echoed briefly through the huge chambers of the ship of mourning.

*"If you cannot change the minds of the people,"* Dimion attempted, somewhat hesitantly, *"perhaps you can change the mind of this general."*

Shucorion slumped sideward, to lean against the cubicle wall. How naive Dimion could be at times. "Change the mind of Kirk . . . I see great experience in him. He is strong in his mind."

*"Kill him, then?"*

"No," he decided. "Death in space is a nightmare . . . I regret to cause it."

*"What are you ordering, Avedon? What about you and our men? How can you come back—"*

"Forget about us, Dimion. None of us is important. You have only one concern now. Think about the work and do it. You must summon Vellyngaith. Give him the information from the Orion ships that Maidenshore said would tell about Federation weapons and tactics. You and our Blood navigators must swallow your meal of disgust and lead the Kauld battlefleet. You must come here, to me. When you find us, you must destroy everything."

*"Avedon . . . what about Maidenshore and the Orions?"*

"I don't care about them," Shucorion said. "I care only about what must happen in our favor. All Kauld will not have us for dinner because they are the beast and we are the bird. Bring Vellyngaith, and strike. Strike! Annihilate the Federation fleet!"

# Chapter Twenty-three

## *Enterprise*

### Captain's quarters, Gamma Night

HE'D PUT ASIDE the title of admiral, yet that was what he again must be. A captain's mantle had not protected him from the conflagration of responsibilities involved in moving a fleet of ships from here to there. Though Governor Pardonnet thought James Kirk wanted, hoped, connived to micromanage every detail, in fact Kirk had hoped to avoid just that. He had seized C and C of operations before the Expedition embarked, hoping to make things start out smoothly so they'd continue to run smoothly all the way across the gulf of space into unknown tracts. His hopes had been early dashed. No mission ever went perfectly, but he'd hoped . . .

Now those nagging awarenesses were playing out.

Like it or not, he was Admiral Kirk again in everything but name. More than seventy ships lay beneath his hand, caught to him by invisible strings that made up the scaffold of command, slowly strangling him from deep within. McCoy had been right—he was holding in that hand the lives of sixty-four thousand civilians and the future of Federation influence in the galaxy. He loathed the former, was devoted to the latter. More Federation than less.

He flinched like a teenager stealing somebody else's homework when Spock hurried into his quarters without even keying the door chime. Must be important. Spock was scrupulously courteous.

"Captain—" the Vulcan urgently began, then was forced to pause when McCoy jogged in before the door closed.

The doctor quickly said, "I'm here too! Go ahead, Spock, I want to hear this."

Spock actually seemed glad that McCoy had barged in. "Mr. Chekov and I have the results of our analysis of the bombardment patterns and residue on the barges. Much of it is indeed alien, unrecognized by the computer—"

"Much of it?" Kirk asked. "How much of it?"

This time both eyebrows went up. "Sixty-nine percent, sir."

Kirk swiveled his chair away from his desk to let Spock slip a computer cartridge into the desktop unit and cue up the information. "What's the additional thirty-one percent?"

The screen flickered to life with mechanical eagerness, and Spock immediately pointed to particular wavelengths and diagnostic bars. "You see here . . . and here. Spectroscopy, chemical analysis, and isolated tracings indicate a recognizable intermix formula."

With McCoy peering over his other shoulder, Kirk leered at the screen as it passed hazy blue and red lights over his taut face. "Well, I'll be damned . . ."

McCoy stood back and slapped his hands on his thighs. "Orions!"

Swinging to look up at him, Kirk smoldered, "Billy."

"Jim, he must've done an end run around us!"

Thumping his fist on his desk, Kirk stretched back in his chair. "I *knew* I wasn't quite done with that traitor."

"Apparently," the doctor commented, "he wasn't done with us either."

"Then what of Shucorion, Captain?" Spock wondered. "Is he working with the Orions?"

McCoy looked at him. "How could he? They couldn't have been out here—what's their maximum warp? They would've had to swing damned far out to avoid our long-range sensors, wouldn't they? I suppose they could've moved across our path in Gamma Night, but still, they wouldn't have time to court allies, would they?"

"Maximum warp can be fairly high if they opted to burn their engines out completely. They may have bet on return aboard any ships they managed to capture from the Expedition."

"Would they take that risk? Orions aren't the type to come out very far. They hardly leave their own space."

"What's the risk," Kirk explained, "if your superiors are going to kill you anyway, when you come home empty-handed?"

Kirk stood up and paced across his quarters. Upon the bunk lay his uniform jacket, cast off casually sometime earlier today. He wore only his trousers and white undershirt. The ribbed collar was somehow comforting, like a chenille muffler during a sleigh ride. If only the sleigh weren't rushing downhill. "Go ahead, Bones, tell me what you're thinking. I can hear the clicking."

The doctor held up his hands in feigned innocence. "I think the same as I thought yesterday. This whole expedition was a lofty dream, ultimately cursed. They did too much dreaming and not enough scouting, the Federation saw its expansion beginning to shrink in on them and they were willing to take a crazy chance for publicity reasons, and we'd better turn around before we end up smeared across space on somebody else's hull." He held up a hand when Kirk snapped him a glare. "No, no, I'm not arguing. You've made up your mind. You know I'm with you no matter what dragons rise in my own head."

"Add it up," Kirk appealed. "Shucorion wants us to stay here or turn back. The Orions no doubt want us to turn back, giving them a second crack at our Conestogas. The Kauld, if they're out there, would probably prefer to have us come about. To me, those are reasons to continue forward. Never give your enemy what he wants."

"Then you consider Shucorion an enemy?" Spock asked, evaluating every nuance of the Kirk barometer.

"Depends. If he and his men were attacked by Orions and mistook them for Kauld during the darkness of Gamma Night, he could be completely innocent."

"Or he might be working with the Orions," McCoy reminded.

Kirk shrugged. "You said yourself, how loyal could he be to them? They just got here. All we know for certain is that at least two forces want us to stop moving forward. Might be Blood and Orion, might be Kauld and Orion."

"But it tells us Shucorion's lying, doesn't it?"

Spock tilted his head. "It tells us he's being manipulated."

"We don't know that," Kirk pointed out. "We won't know until we run into the Kauld face-to-face. If their attack patterns and residue are the same as the unidentified alien residue you picked up, then Shucorion's proven innocent and the Orions are working with the Kauld. And we've got a hell of a problem."

McCoy settled back to sit on the edge of the vanity. "I think it's a hell of a problem either way."

Folding his arms, Spock casually added, "I would tend to agree."

"Mmm," Kirk grunted. "I always know I'm in trouble when the two of you agree. Spock, how's the officer distribution going?"

"A bit clumsily at first, sir, but as the governor promised, all ships are complying. All first, second, and third officers from *Enterprise* and *Beowulf,* with the exception of myself, have been reassigned to Conestogas. All private vessels are stationed with lieutenants or ensigns. Unfortunately, that bleeds the Starfleet ships of most of our officer complement. Twelve Expedition ships are still without a Starfleet advisor on board. We could tap the *Beowulf,* if you prefer."

"No, leave the CST alone. All their people are trained to work together in emergency repairs and we may need them for exactly that. Send our yeomen and midshipmen instead. Get an Academy-trained advisor on every ship, if you have to send the cooks."

"Very well, sir."

McCoy rubbed his elbow, bruised from a fall on board *Brother's Keeper.* "I still think you should put Starfleet officers on the privateer ships, Jim."

Kirk's brow tightened. "Something about that rings wrong for me. I have to trust Kilvennan to keep them in line."

"Captain . . ." Spock paused, then plunged in. "I request reassignment to one of the other vessels. The other first officers are reassigned. My effectiveness is limited here."

Enjoying a moment of personal admiration, Kirk smiled briefly at him. "Don't be insulted, Spock. Flexibility could be critical. We have to maintain every option. If you leave, and Scott and Chekov aren't here, and Sulu's—"

*"Bridge to Captain Kirk!"*

Even before he hit the comm, he knew that tone in Uhura's voice. "Kirk here. You've spotted something?"

*"Yes, sir—"*

*"Sulu here, sir. Unknown number of vessels on an attack vector, coming in at high speed, proximity distance! They came out of sensor darkness, we never even saw them coming!"*

"This is it. Spock, get to the bridge. McCoy, beam to the mercy ship immediately, take your post. Uhura, sound general quarters, fleet-wide red alert, and call Mr. Shucorion to the bridge. Mr. Sulu, break formation! Sphere the ships!"

By the time Kirk and Spock charged side by side onto the bridge, the Expedition was already taking fire.

Taking it, and repelling it. Spock broke immediately for his post at the science station.

On the main screen, supported by a dozen auxiliary monitors all over the bridge, a vista of attacking vessels shot past, firing some kind of globular salvo that looked like streams of phosphorescent gel, but erupted violently on the shields of the Expedition ships. The gels came out in red streams, then erupted in milky white blast circles like pond ripples, then skittered across the shields in unpredictable directions, as if seeking the weakest energy output rather than running with the flow of the blast. Not bad.

"Keep calm, everyone." Kirk slid into his command chair, still assessing what he saw on the screens. Something about sitting down at first would help settle everyone's stomachs. He looked to his left, at the tactical displays. There, a clear graphic showed the movements of all the Expedition ships.

Sulu, at tactical instead of his usual post at the helm, busily analyzed the position of each vessel, tugging, pushing, pulling, shifting, until a formation began to take shape out of the gaggle of Expedition ships. At his side rather than at her communications post, Uhura was using her fabulous knowledge of signal-sending shortcuts to funnel the coordinates and fine-tunings to specific ships in the complex formation. All around the Expedition, seventy-plus helmsmen were sweating themselves into little puddles right now, just the fingers and eyes left floating.

With amazing quickness, though, the string of ships drew together in the middle and turned into a swarming mass, then began to shift and morph, further organized from "them" into an "it." Under the attack from incoming vessels, the convoy gathered into the shape of a hollow ball with a second ball inside, like a marching band morphing from long ranks into a predetermined and recognizable formation. In minutes the fleet became a double-hulled sphere five kilometers in diameter.

"Sterns to the core, Mr. Sulu," Kirk reminded.

"Aye, sir." Sulu was polite enough to answer the unnecessary order. He was already doing that. Each ship, as it found its place in the inner or outer sphere, turned as quickly as its own maneuverability allowed, to point its prow outward and its stern inward. The smallest profile now faced enemy fire, as well as the strongest phaser ports.

Kirk watched with surging joy at the sight of the defensive sphere as it took shape. The giant geodesic came into shape with satisfying grace, and bristled with defensive power. In the center, Montgomery Scott was stationed with Captain Graymark on the roundhouse ship *Colunga*, holding position beside the Tugantine *Norfolk Rebel* and the combat support tender *Beowulf,* all prepared for battle repair duty.

As shots rang in from the attacking ships blaring around the sphered Expedition, young crewmen on the bridge glanced uneasily at Kirk. Other than Spock, Sulu, and Uhura, the bridge was staffed now with ensigns and midshipmen, all that was left after bleeding the complement dry of command-trained lieutenants and several ensigns. The arrangement was clumsy and desperate, but it meant that every ship out there had at least one Starfleet-trained officer on its bridge.

Kirk noticed the attention, but ignored them. They were expecting him to bark orders, shout, snap, demand. The time hadn't come for that yet.

"Sphere formation completing, sir," Spock reported, bent over his readouts. "Outer shell vessels taking fire at random stations."

"Inform them to open fire as their phasers bear. Inner ships should stand by." As Uhura repeated his orders to the spheres, Kirk kept his eyes on the forward screen. "Attacking vessels, Mr. Spock?"

"Vessels are of unknown design, tribernium-carbide

hulls with additional trace elements . . . approximately two hundred vessels of fighter proportions, at least twelve of battleship mass, and two flying fortresses. No sign of the Orions yet."

"Helm," Kirk said to the ensign now driving the starship, "bring the ship to position Alpha. Keep aware of the positions of the core factory."

"Aye, sir," the woman said. She seemed young—but all the women on the ships seemed young to him these days.

"What's your name, Ensign?" he asked.

Surprised that the captain would bother with personal details at a time like this, the girl glanced around, her blond hair bouncing at her ears. "Austin, sir, Gina Austin."

"Any relation to—"

"Yes, sir, I'm Captain Austin's daughter, from *Beowulf*."

"Welcome aboard. Keep your eyes forward. Don't take your eyes off the helm."

"Aye, aye, sir!"

That could be a problem. The CST's captain's daughter at the helm of the *Enterprise*. Would she be watching her father's ship more than her own? Did she have the experience to ignore watching her dad die if it came to that and still do her job? Kirk didn't want this to be the time for any more experiments, but there was nothing to be done. He had no legitimate reason to dismiss her. She hadn't *not* done her job yet.

He was glad to be distracted when the turbolift hissed and emitted Shucorion. The alien leader, in a restrained manner that had become quickly typical, stepped down to the lower deck but said nothing. Kirk watched him carefully, noting his reaction as he looked at the screens, the swarm of attacking ships firing randomly at the outer sphere shell.

"Mr. Shucorion, are these your Kauld friends?"

Shucorion actually flinched, then brushed Kirk with a glance. "Yes, they are Kauld."

"What are those two large vessels?"

"Battlebarges. Quite formidable in their ability to destroy. You would not be thought weak for retreating in face of two Kauld barges."

"Thank you, I'll file that away. Sulu, roll the outer shell. Keep at least one privateer to bear on the battlebarges at all times if you can."

"Aye, sir."

"Uhura, warn Captain Kilvennan about the barge firepower. Make sure all ships hold position no matter how much fire they're taking. They *must* hold their positions. No one break formation, no matter what. Is that clear?"

"Aye, aye, sir. *Enterprise* to *Hunter's Moon*—"

"What is this sphere of ships?" Shucorion asked. He placed his hand upon the rail and turned to the portside monitors which showed the graphics of the sphered ships.

"It's an old defensive tactic," Kirk said. "Circling the wagons, only in three dimensions instead of two."

Shucorion turned to him. "Why would you do such a thing? It leaves you no chance to run."

The starship vibrated around them from the wash of enemy weapons pummeling through two spheres of vessels.

"Does your ship shoot?" Shucorion asked.

"That's not in the plan yet."

Charged with the electricity that makes a captain tick at the right pace, Kirk pushed out of his chair and stalked around the command center, back, forth, back, forth. Around the starship, the geodesic of ships shimmered and struggled to hold position under a conflagration of enemy fire. Each ship was part of a five-ship star joined to other stars, each defending a wedge of space and protecting the flanks of four other vessels. The two hundred Kauld fighters obviously knew what they were doing, buzzing around the sphere, shooting at each stationed vessel as they passed by.

"They're confused," Kirk murmured to himself, barely audible over the whine of shots and strikes. "They didn't expect the sphere tactic. . . ."

He watched almost as if spectating as damage communicated itself through the surprised and scattering Kauld fleet. Stiffening suddenly, he got a sharp idea, as if he'd been stuck with a needle.

"Signal the Expedition to hold their fire," he ordered.

Uhura turned. "Say again, sir? Cease fire?"

"Not cease, but hold fire all around."

"Aye, sir." Befuddled, she passed on the odd order.

Even Spock cast him a questioning glance. Wisely he made no protests.

The outer sphere, flashing with weapons fire, crackled a few times before going quiet, now freely taking unchallenged shots from the Kauld ships as they raced past. Kirk imagined several dozen bridge officers calling him something other than pal right now. Even Shucorion was eyeing him with alarming suspicion, complicated by the simple fact that Kirk still didn't know what Shucorion really wanted to happen.

"Uhura, coordinate all weaponry officers to fire on my mark."

She looked up again. "All weapons officers, stand by for coordinated firing sequence!"

"Both spheres, Uhura," Kirk added. "Mr. Sulu, be ready."

"We're ready now, sir!"

Sweating now around the collar of his white undershirt and under the padded shoulders of his jacket, Kirk let his stomach muscles tighten to their worst, egging him on as he watched the sphere take waves of salvos from the Kauld onslaught without shooting back. It was blistering, painful to see.

Kirk held his breath, ticking off seconds until the Kauld ships changed their tactics. Moved in . . . a little closer . . . took advantage of the cease-fire—

"Mark!"

Uhura relayed, "Mark!"

Both spheres, inner and outer, fired at once. The ball of ships bristled with destructive energy. At Kirk's single word, the sphere turned into a spiny urchin spitting venom in every direction. The inner sphere of ships, perfectly positioned, fired between the outer ships, creating a double strike.

Nearly perfect, the strike rang a single percussive blast into the enemy waves. Almost every Kauld ship within range suffered a direct or grazing hit. Wave upon wave of Kauld fighters floundered and fell away, some spewing leakage, others trailing shimmers of flotsam.

"Beautiful!" Sulu cried out. "They were completely surprised by the maneuver, sir!"

Spock, beaming at Kirk in that personal undergirding way he had, turned. "Obviously they've never encountered such an assault before."

"Sir!" Austin called. "They're slinking back into the woods!"

Spock shot back to his readouts. "Sensor darkness is giving them cover."

"Will they come back?" Austin asked.

"I think we can assume that was a first wave," Kirk said. "Damage report?"

"Coming in now," Spock responded. "Starfleet advisors report heavy damage on twenty percent of the outer perimeter, minor damage on other vessels . . . shields down on at least seven ships. The combat support tender is moving in to effect repairs on critical vessels. *Norfolk Rebel* is maneuvering two vessels to the *Colunga,* and the Conestoga tender is supplying two ships with replacement mules."

"Mr. Sulu, shore up positions. Replace critically damaged vessels with fresh vessels from the inner sphere. All ships prepare for the next wave. We'll only have seconds here."

"Aye, sir. All ships, this is *Enterprise* . . ."

Completely stunned by what he had just seen, Shucorion gripped the rail that circled this ship's command area and physically trembled. They were taking a stand!

He had assumed they would turn back once the facts of conflict were known to them. No one with sense would settle in a war zone, any more than build on a floodplain, yet these people stood fast despite everything he had told them. He had come here today regretting the sixty thousand deaths that might be the price of Blood future, but against the Blood billion? Some prices were high.

Those assumptions had come too soon. He had expected them to do what he would have done. He had done what he promised himself he would not do—he had underestimated them.

"I can't read the Kauld ships anymore," Sulu warned. "They're hidden in the sensor blind."

"Position the ships," Kirk said. "Let me worry about the sensor blind."

"Yes, sir," Sulu responded jubilantly. He was actually smiling, proud of what they had just done.

Shucorion stared at them. His idea had been to cut the string of Federation ships into three units, then hammer them to pieces and give Billy Maidenshore the prizes he had bargained for. The Orion files of information about Federation ships had provided technical information and tactical habits. This wasn't one of them. James Kirk had made it up.

By pulling into the sphere arrangement, Kirk had denied his enemies their chance. But it gave him no option of running!

Could it be they had no intention to run? Fight here, win or die here, and no other alternatives? Such thoughts were foreign, bizarre, even mystical! Being weaker, the Blood had always fought by stealth—sneak, hit, fight, run, come back later.

Instead, James Kirk had made one huge battleship out of his fleet of many, causing them to work in special arrangement with each other, no straggling allowed, and combining the firepower in such a manner as was unimaginable in the cluster.

Vellyngaith was out there somewhere, hidden in the Blind now, contemplating whether or not Shucorion had betrayed him with this strange turn of events.

"You mean to go forward, Captain?" Shucorion asked bluntly. "Continue onward into the cluster?"

Kirk didn't look at him, but continued to study the screens. "That's right."

"How will you live, caught between us as you will be?"

'Maybe your war will have to stop. You said your-self, things are different now that you have star-drive."

"But . . . why would you want to live in such strife when you don't have to?"

"We've survived worse. Humans are a hardy race. We have more to do in life than just live day to day. We have things to accomplish."

Shucorion moved a few steps forward, to bring Kirk's stony expression into clear view. "Your settlers will be forever in our war."

Like darts, the captain's eyes grew slim and speared Shucorion. "I've stopped wars before. I'll do it again if I—"

He started to say something else, but stopped, dis-tracted by flickering lights on the consoles near the man called Sulu, who apparently was arranging move-ment of all these vessels, somehow coordinating the great dance from this one post, and the woman Uhura, whose job was a mystery to Shucorion.

"Here they come, sir!" Uhura warned.

Out of the Blind came a hundred Kauld fighters, formed in ranks of three, spearing directly toward the sphere rather than rushing around it.

Kirk stalked the helm. "Hold fire. Let's see what their attack plan is. . . ."

"Holding," Uhura responded.

Sulu clung to his console through the mortal noise of damage. "They're targeting specific areas of the sphere, trying to break us open!"

"All ships, hold position!" Kirk called out. "Don't buckle!"

# Chapter Twenty-four

ENEMY FIRE blew between the ships and outward from one area of the sphere, cutting through the two layers of defense and scoring the *Enterprise* with mortal noise. The shields crackled, but held. Vellyngaith had learned from his mistake.

"They're concentrating on *Hunter's Moon*," Spock said, "and the five ships surrounding it."

Kirk scowled. "Maidenshore probably told them to target Michael Kilvennan out of some perverse theme of retribut—"

His words were cut short as a diabolical flash on the starship's port side lit up four independently scanning screens. Kirk raised a hand to shield his eyes, but somehow still clearly saw the blistering of the combat support tender, caught between one of the larger Kauld ships and the vessel it was trying to repair.

"They've hit the *Beowulf*," Uhura said miserably.

"Direct rupture to the plasma containment . . . sir, she had her access hatch open. The shot went right inside."

Sulu squinted in empathy and shuddered. "A lucky shot. One in a million."

Helpless, they passed a heart-stopping second of horror as the Kauld's white-hot pellets bounced around inside the support tender, held in by her reinforced hull, freely killing and destroying in a mindless way. It must be a furnace in there. Flashes of greenish yellow rupture from inside gave them the only real clue of the hell vomiting through *Beowulf*'s guts.

Suddenly the Tender valiantly broke away from the other ships, flashed her impulse engine once, suddenly ejected a sprout of plasma, turned down at a sickening angle and floated away to die in the center of the sphere.

"Oh, no . . ." Uhura uttered.

As his innards curdled, Kirk mentally analyzed the nucleization going on inside *Beowulf*, how many hideous deaths among her valuable crew of repair specialists had occurred in that incredibly rare hit. The nearly impossible shot that had now cost the Expedition its last Starfleet ship other than the *Enterprise* herself. *Beowulf* was out of the game. A crippling loss.

He turned to the helm. Only now did he remember about Crewman Austin, standing her post at the helm.

The young woman wasn't watching the screens on the port side, but she'd seen them. Her face was stiff and struggling. Was her father alive? She was doing the right thing—divorcing herself from herself. She fixed her eyes on the forward screen instead, watching the enemy vessel trying awkwardly to veer away after attacking the sphere. Good.

Kirk moved to her side, very close, careful not to actually touch her.

Diane Carey

"All right," he said. "Let's hit them back. Anterior vessels . . . pirouette!"

"Pirouette, aye," Sulu responded as he and Uhura broadcast the order to the appropriate ships.

Apparently expecting the order, half of each sphere of ships, internal and external, swung about to face the cavern in the middle. Shucorion tightened his shoulders, both intrigued and dreading what he saw. If they didn't aim just right, the tenders and the *Enterprise* in the central cavern and the ships on the opposite side of the sphere would be in their lines of fire.

"Careful, Mr. Sulu," Kirk murmured.

"Understood, sir."

"Spock, check the targeting solutions on all the anterior ships."

"Very little time, Captain."

"Take the time."

Kauld ships menaced the *Hunter's Moon* and the ships surrounding it, trying to break a hole in the sphere. Kirk hoped their shields would hold a few more seconds.

Spock straightened. "Ready, sir."

"All ships, fire!" Kirk instantly ordered.

The whole sphere lit up again like a Times Square ball, but this time all the power blasted out of one concentrated area. The spiny urchin turned into a giant devil's eye, shooting a death ray through its pupil. Kirk had succeeded in turning the ball into a cannon.

Out in space, the forward two dozen Kauld ships were simply atomized into a cloud. Another dozen fighters piled into the boiling cloud, while still others suffered to veer off.

"Fire again!"

As Vellyngaith's fighters turned on their wings and

tried to escape, another unified blast bore through the sphere's funnel and obliterated the retreating ships. Nearly half of the attack force, destroyed or crippled! Vellyngaith would be in a rage!

The starship trembled with the sheer power of energy fire blasting past it and from it. Only now did Shucorion fully understand the critical nature of holding position, and why there was no option of running away. This was a defensible formation, but not on the defensive. The sphere shimmered with self-confidence. No matter what percussion rocked the sphere, no ship faltered or fell back, but each bore its damage valiantly. They were depending critically upon each other, and none had betrayed the next. Such action would never be possible without total cooperation. How did Kirk know they would hold their ground? How could he control them all so completely in their minds?

"Rotate the phalanx, Mr. Sulu!" Unmistakable jubilance rang in Kirk's voice.

"Rotating, sir!" his choreographer responded, then sent the appropriate orders.

Confused, Shucorion watched in awe as the two geodesic spheres melted into each other, then spread once again into two, this time with the previously interior ships on the outside perimeter. At Kirk's order, the whole arrangement had turned itself inside out!

"Considerable damage to ten percent of the inner circle, sir," Uhura reported.

"Mr. Sulu, draw the most severely damaged ships into the cavern. Tighten the spheres to fill in the gaps."

Different ships with fresh weapons and shielding now braced the spheres. An amazing stratagem—Vellyngaith's forces could not get a grip on weakness he had inflicted because the ships were constantly shifting. The shrinking sphere became more and more prickly. In the cavern, the feisty repair ships yanked disabled vessels out of formation, sprayed them with sealant or made quick repairs, and shooed them back into the formation, with Mr. Sulu nudging the florets of vessels into adjustment with each change. This was like watching patterns in a kaleidoscope, shifting, changing, chattering—

"Captain! Orions!"

As Shucorion's arms tightened, he hoped his posture would not give away his thoughts as the two Orion ships buzzed out of the Blind and rushed toward the now weak opposite pole of the sphere.

"Well, well . . . turn the anterior ships to meet them, Mr. Sulu. Ensign Austin, full about and skim the interior. Follow those ships! Mr. Spock, turn sensors on those Orion ships. Find the—never mind. I'll do it myself. Mr. Shucorion, stand aside please."

His eyes flaring with seismic delight, Kirk stood over the navigation console and punched and tuned the controls himself. Had he hungered to fire the ship's weapons personally? Had he lost faith in the woman at his side or the men and women on the bridge who were controlling the battle at his orders?

A column of glittering light appeared on the upper part of the deck. Shucorion stumbled back. Had they been struck? The hull ruptured?

The shimmer of light began to settle, to gather into a form.

Shucorion held his breath as he came to recognize the shape, the shoulders, the face. Soon the sound and the lights twinkled away, leaving only the man.

How had Kirk done this? Pluck one person from passing ships?

For the first time, the technology of Federation seemed outlandish and magical. Still more underestimating. Shucorion made his oath again.

James Kirk straightened and faced the upper deck.

"Hello, Billy," he said.

"Gave myself up for dead. Thanks for pulling me off, Jimmy boy. Some pretty foxy maneuvers you've got going here. You want to arrest me now, or should we have a cigar first?"

The irredeemable Billy Maidenshore was somehow both welcome and unwelcome as Jim Kirk stepped to the upper deck and squared off with him.

Kirk leered with a merry wickedness. "The bridge is a no-smoking section."

Maidenshore held his hands out, his wrists crossed. "Go ahead, put me in custody. Shielded cabin, three squares a day, entertainment tapes, court-appointed attorney, and a couple of years of due process. Sounds plenty cushy to me after that Orion stink-box."

"Be careful," Kirk warned. "This isn't Federation space. Governor Pardonnet's new laws don't look kindly on treason. Justice out here involves your being turned over to the people you tried to sell into slavery. No questions asked."

For the first time, a flicker of fear drew down the brow of this man who was so vacant of human conscience. "That's not fair play!"

"Fair?" Kirk echoed, spinning the irony. "It's a new Earth, Billy, with new laws. 'Fair' has yet to be defined."

"Security to the bridge," Uhura smoothly ordered, without waiting for Kirk to say it.

Kirk managed to keep from glinting a silent thank-you at her for her motherly attentiveness. That was her way of telling him she thought Maidenshore didn' matter right now.

She was right, but there was something fun abou this even if the enemy wave was coming again. H would wait a couple of seconds.

He met her eyes. "Quickly, have the Tugantine get a grip on *Beowulf* and tow it into the cavern."

"Sir, I doubt—" Though her expression made the rest of her statement, she clearly didn't want to speak in front of Austin. *Beowulf*'s hulk was hardly worth salvaging in that blistered condition. There might not even by anybody alive on board.

Resolution gritted Kirk's teeth. "I'm not leaving it out here. We'll tow it all the way to Belle Terre if we have to."

"The Orion ships are coming around the sphere, Captain," Spock prodded.

"Mr. Sulu, let's make an example of them. I'm sure our Kauld friends are watching."

With only that, he turned again away from the unexpected prisoner and returned to his command center to use his supreme gifts upon the Orions.

Shucorion met Billy Maidenshore's shameless glower with his best expressionless reaction. Would this false-hearted fool reveal their secret? Use their conniving to save his skin from the retribution offered?

There were no illusions, after what Shucorion had seen here today, that the Orions who dared face Captain Kirk in this mood would ever return to their home. They were no longer simply honest enemies, but playthings, and Kirk a raging child greatly fond of his powers.

He deserved to be. With sheer rigor and cleverness

he had thwarted a superior force. He had taken risks that Shucorion found beyond comprehension—and Shucorion had long believed himself a risk-taker. Yet these roguish, freewheeling acts of risk! These enormous strides!

From the lower parts of the ship, two soldiers ran onto the bridge and in moments Billy Maidenshore was in custody, and being escorted from the bridge. Outside, almost as a secondary notice, the two Orion ships were speared with energy lancets from the starship. Demolished.

Before Shucorion's eyes, the future completely reset itself.

# Chapter Twenty-five

"AVEDON, WE'RE AMAZED to see you alive. I was afraid Federation would not give you up to us."

Dimion stood aside as Shucorion stepped from the Federation shuttle onto his own ship.

The Blood Plume rested not far from the wagon train, just outside of the reaching distance of their transporter beams. A beam blackout had been instituted for the entire wagon train as it rearranged itself and effected its repairs. It was getting ready to go on its way, to pierce the star cluster and find its new home.

"Thank you for 'rescuing' me, Dimion." Shucorion smiled grimly, still nagged by the idea that James Kirk suspected him of more than innocence. "Well, we failed for now, in some things. Is Vellyngaith going to come and kill us?"

"He was furious," Dimion said. "But he wants to

wait, to watch awhile, and contemplate the battle before acting again."

"He is wise after all, then. I shall fear him more from
now on."

Dimion hovered at his side as they hurried through
the Plume to the command area. "Do you think Maidenshore will give us away?"

"I have no guesses," Shucorion told him. "He has
said nothing, yet. He too, I imagine, is waiting and
watching."

He nodded dismissively at the others in the crew
who turned to greet him, though no one really knew
what would be appropriate to say. But they were Blood.
They understood setbacks.

Shucorion came to the visual screens and stood in a
kind of awe, gazing at the picture of seventy ships, all
sizes and shapes, once again driving forward into the
sparkling void. They were on their way again, now with
a formidable reputation as their armor against the phantoms of night.

"We must continue to play our parts, Dimion," he
murmured. "Somehow we must convince Vellyngaith
to continue playing his. How will this end? I cannot
wonder. Either Kirk will vanquish Vellyngaith, destroying a legend and deflating the ego of the Kauld,
or Vellyngaith will destroy Kirk, unleashing the fury
of Federation upon the Kauld. Either way, Blood will
stand by and win. If Federation discovers the truth
and leaves the cluster, Blood will take over the area,
or Kauld will be greatly weakened. If Federation
stays, we will eventually have to deal with them. They
will not allow our conflict to come near them, and we
may get the time to rebuild our strength. No matter
what happens, Blood will eventually be the strongest

force in the sector. Then they will have to deal with us."

Dimion came to stand beside him, physically thinner and weakened from the pressure of his unwanted responsibilities. "We believe in you, Avedon . . . we will follow you, though we still do not understand."

Shucorion nodded gently. "You will understand soon, I promise. I alone know the secret held a Belter . . . at . . . Belle Terre. I will hold it here within me, tell no one, let events play out with their natural intrigue."

As he placed his hand upon his chest, where the secret of Belle Terre would be vaulted, his tone was cryptic, hurtful even to his own ears.

"The travelers have journeyed far . . . only to colonize their own tomb."

Pocket Books
Proudly Presents

STAR TREK®
New Earth

*BELLE TERRE*
(Book Two of Six)

Dean Wesley Smith with Diane Carey

Available from Pocket Books

Turn the page for a preview of
*Belle Terre . . .*

Captain James T. Kirk dropped into the soft sand and leaned back against a large log of driftwood. In front of him the dune slanted down to the beach and the green-tinted ocean beyond. He tried to think back to the last time he had simply sat alone on a beach and relaxed. He couldn't remember ever doing that. But he also couldn't imagine this was the first time, either. He must have relaxed on a beach before, although he had no doubt Dr. McCoy would swear it had never happened. McCoy always said that James Kirk never relaxed.

Kirk supposed that was true. Maybe it wasn't too late to learn. Or more likely, it was time to learn.

He took a deep breath and looked around. There was a slight bite to the ocean breeze coming in over the waves, just enough to take the edge off the heat of the midday sun. The salt and brine smell drifted over the beach, strong enough to be enjoyed by a new arrival, but not overpowering enough to be noticed after the first few moments. The beach sand was almost a pure white, and stretched in a ribbon as far as he could see in both directions.

This planet Belle Terre was everything Governor Evan Pardonnet had said it would be. If this stretch of shoreline near the main colony compound was any indication of the rest of the planet, it was no wonder so many people were so willing to travel so far to get here. Even putting aside the governor's high-minded ideas of freedom of thinking, freedom from government, and freedom from the Federation, this place just might turn out to be the utopia Pardonnet had hoped for.

Below Kirk, ten children, chaperoned by Lilian Coates, played a game a few hundred paces down the beach to his right. The sound of children cut between the gentle slapping of the waves rolling up the sand, then retreating. The laughter and childish shouts of joy were wonderful reminders of the perfect afternoon he was having. As a starship captain, he hadn't had many like this.

He almost stood to go and see how the children were doing, then stopped himself. He had come here to relax.

Alone.

And relax he was going to do if it killed him.

He laughed to himself, the sound carried away on the slight breeze. McCoy would be proud of him. Shocked, but proud.

Kirk took another deep breath and stared ahead. The tinted green of the ocean spread out as far as he could see. The waves were no more than gentle rolling swells. The few clouds in the sky were white, puffy, and nonthreatening.

He took a third deep breath of the clean, fresh air and could almost feel the muscles in his back starting to loosen. It wasn't often that he took a few minutes to himself. And after getting the sixty-two thousand colonists and all their varied ships to this paradise, he deserved the time. If he had his way, he was going to take more time, as often as his Starfleet duties of protecting the colonists allowed.

At the moment a large number of his crew were scattered in twenty different groups over the planet, helping the colonists explore, carve out settlements, and load supplies and equipment to the surface. Every one of his senior officers except Spock had charge of a major operation. And from what he'd been told before he beamed down, everything was going smoothly. At this point, only two weeks after arriving, just about every one of the colonists was living on the surface of the planet, an unprecedented accomplishment.

The *Enterprise* was in orbit, standing ready to defend the colony ships from any more threats from the Kauld or their new Orion allies. A fleet of Kauld and Orions tried to keep the colonists from reaching this planet, but Kirk doubted they'd have much trouble from them again immediately. The *Enterprise* and the colonists defeated them handily, But Kirk had no doubt that the Kauld and their enemies the Blood would be back. The Blood leader Shucorion claimed to be a friend to the colonists, but Kirk wasn't so sure of that: The Blood/Kauld conflict would cause the colony trouble at some time in the future.

Just not now.

At the moment everything was going fine. There

was time enough to get the colony started and get crops growing. And time for him to relish this beautiful new world just a little.

He reached for his communicator to check in with the ship, then stopped himself once more. There was also time for him to take a few moments to himself. They could find him if they needed him.

He ran his hand through the soft sand, then gazed off down the seemingly limitless beach. Belle Terre was just about as close to Earth as a colony could find. The climate here on the major continent was moderate and the growing seasons uniformly long, thanks to this planet's orbit around its sun. Pulling guard duty on Belle Terre for the near future wasn't going to be so bad after all. There weren't many better places he could think to guard.

But he couldn't imagine spending his life here, either, no matter how beautiful the place was. Space was too big, with too many mysteries to explore. He didn't mind guarding this colony for a while, as long as they needed him and the *Enterprise*. It was a challenge unlike any he had had before. But when this was done he wanted to get back into deep space.

Down on the beach a child laughed, drawing Kirk's attention that way. He smiled as the children all piled on each other, kicked up sand, laughed some more, then scattered, playing some game Kirk wasn't familiar with. Lilian Coates, her blond hair loose in the ocean breeze, her shoulders straight, her hands in the pockets of her light jacket, stood between the children and the ocean, watching, laughing along with them.

Kirk was amazed that she could even laugh at this point in her life. Her husband had been one of the many colonist casualties on the way here from Earth. With his death, her husband had left her far from home, alone on a colony world. Suddenly without a family, she had to take care of herself and their nine-year-old son, Reynold, in a very harsh and unfamiliar environment. That would be tough on anyone, and would destroy many. But Lilian Coates had just seemed to keep right on going.

He had met her a few times right after her husband had died. She was a strong woman, of that there was no doubt. She was doing just fine, or so it seemed at the moment. Maybe in a few months he'd make it a point to make sure that hadn't changed. Strong people like her were exactly what this colony needed for long-term survival.

He watched her guard the children for a moment, then settled back against the log, closed his eyes, and let the sun warm his face while the ocean breeze cooled him. If lucky, he just might be able to spend the entire next hour right here, undisturbed by the responsibilities of protecting an entire new world full of colonists.

"Captain?" Spock said from behind him.

It didn't seem as if the luck was with him.

Kirk sat up and opened his eyes. Below him Lilian glanced up his way, noting for the first time his presence, then went back to sharing a laugh with the children.

He turned to stare up at the Vulcan as he approached through the sand. "What is it, Mr. Spock?"

"The results of my tests, Captain," Spock said, handing him the scientific tricorder he carried.

"Couldn't it have waited?" Kirk asked without

looking at the report. "I was enjoying a little time away from reports just like this."

Spock had been concerned about slight communication problems they'd been having when not in Gamma Night. Before Kirk had beamed down, Spock had been focusing his attention on one of the moons of Belle Terre everyone called the Quake Moon, because it seemed always to be shaking with small quakes, more than likely caused by volcanic activity. Spock had a theory that the communication problems came partly from the moon and had been so intent in his project that he hadn't even wanted anyone talking to him.

"I am afraid," Spock said, "that time is not something we have an abundance of, Captain."

Kirk stared into the expressionless face of his first officer, then turned his attention to the report. Two words caught his attention instantly.

"Quasar olivium?" he asked, glancing back up at Spock. "In the Quake Moon?"

"Yes, sir," Spock said. "It seems we have found the first naturally occurring deposits of the material."

Kirk shook his head, trying to clear it, then stood as he tried to remember everything he knew about the material quasar olivium. He knew it was named after the scientist Shultz Oliver, who first theorized that the material existed. According to all rules of physics, the material shouldn't exist. And just a few years ago the Federation had been able to construct minuscule portions of it at huge costs, by using factory-sized warp facilities.

Yet now Spock was saying the material existed inside one of the moons of this planet.

"Quasar olivium?" Kirk asked. "How is this possible?"

"I am not certain, Captain," Spock said. "Olivium is formed in the heart of a quasar and rarely survives the process that creates it. It has never been found to exist in a natural state. Until now."

"Right," Kirk said, still trying to get the idea into his mind. "Until now. How much is there?"

Spock shook his head. "The material is in a constant state of quantum flux. I have no way of measuring the amounts accurately."

"An ounce?" Kirk asked. "A pound? Ten pounds?"

Spock shook his head. "Far in excess of hundreds of thousands of tons, if my readings are correct."

Kirk leaned back on the piece of driftwood he'd been sitting against earlier and simply stared at his first officer.

"Hundreds of tons?" Kirk said. "Spock, do you know what this means to science? To the Federation?"

"I do, Captain," Spock said.

Kirk nodded. More than likely his first officer knew even better than he did what such a discovery would mean. The technological advances that would be possible with just a few pounds of olivium were fantastic. Having tons of the material would change everything. More powerful replicators could be built that could make useless molecular structures into useful ones. Greater holographic technology, advances in medical science, advances in computers, more powerful weapons.

The list of advantages of controlling tons of olivium went on and on, and that was just what he knew about. He had no doubt the discovery would be far more important than he could even imagine.

The Belle Terre colony was just about to become

the richest colony in existence. And the most sought after by every race in the sector.

And the most important colony in all of space for the Federation to defend against anyone who would try to take it. Governor Pardonnet had led these people way out here, in part, to get away from the massive restraints of the Federation bureaucracy. It seemed that now he was going to need the Federation and Starfleet even more just to survive. Kirk had no doubt that when word of this discovery got out, the Klingons, the Romulans, and just about everyone else would all try to gain some foothold in this pristine backwater.

Behind him the children laughed and the waves broke gently on the sand. Those kids didn't know how important to their future Mr. Spock's discovery was.

"There is another problem, sir," Spock said.

Kirk managed to force his thinking away from the possibilities and realities of olivium in that quantity and back to the passionless face of his first officer.

"I can think of about a thousand problems, Mr. Spock. What are you saying?"

"The quasar olivium is, by its very nature, unstable, existing almost more outside our space and time than in it. The center of the Quake Moon that seemed hollow to normal sensors actually holds the olivium in a very contained state."

"The bottom line, Mr. Spock," Kirk said.

"The pressure inside the moon is building and has been for some time. The moon will explode, and in the process will destroy all life on this planet, as well as vast quantities of the quasar olivium."

"Explode?" Kirk asked. "Are you certain?"

"Yes, sir," Spock said.

Kirk nodded. When Mr. Spock said he was certain, the event would happen.

"How did we miss this?"

"The moon's crust and the very nature of the olivium make scans difficult," Spock said.

"How long?"

"So far I have been unable to ascertain the exact time of the explosion, again owing to the nature of the olivium."

"A day? A week? A year?" Kirk demanded. "I'm looking for a range, here." He was suddenly very aware of the children shouting below him in their play.

Kirk stepped closer to his first officer and lowered his voice. "You've got to give me an approximate time when the explosion might happen. I've got over sixty thousand colonists to get off this planet and out of harm's way."

"My data is insufficient to allow me to predict the explosion exactly, sir," Spock said. "But it is logical that at the rate of increase of pressure inside the moon, the explosion will occur between six days and one month from this moment. I might be able to give you a more accurate time frame in a few more hours of research."

"Do it," Kirk said. "Quickly."

Mr. Spock turned and moved away. After a few steps Kirk stopped him.

"Spock, can we stop the explosion?"

"I do not yet have enough information to give you an answer, or a possible method of doing that, sir."

"Then get it."

Spock nodded and moved away through the sand toward the closest beam-down point.

Kirk turned and looked back at the children below. One moment these colonists faced a future of vast riches, the next they faced death and being without a home. All in the same report.

Kirk snapped open his communicator. "Kirk to *Enterprise*. Come in."

"Go ahead, Captain," Ensign Jason said. Ensign Jason was a young kid from Boise, Idaho, fresh out of the Academy. He was filling in for Uhura while she led a party working on setting up a communications base just south of Kirk's position.

"Ensign, find Governor Pardonnet and inform him that I need to speak to him at once."

Pardonnet, on the trip here, had often been hard to work with, but Kirk actually admired the young governor. Granted, Pardonnet's ideas of leading and Kirk's were vastly different. And they had often had discussions about decisions. Actually, they hadn't been so much discussions as Pardonnet talking on and on. But with this emergency the governor wasn't going to have a chance to have one of his discussions. He was going to follow Kirk's orders and be quick about it. They didn't have time to argue too much with the lives of the colonists at stake.

"Understood, Captain," Ensign Jason said. "Where would you like him to meet you?"

Kirk knew that if he had the governor meet him, it might take hours. And right now, as Spock had said, there weren't hours to spare. "Ensign, just get his location and give it to the transporter room. Then tell him I'm coming to talk to him. Tell him it's an emergency."

"Understood, Captain," the ensign said.

"And Ensign—have all the crew report back to the *Enterprise* at once. No exceptions. Kirk out."

Kirk glanced down at Lilian Coates and the playing children. She seemed to be watching him almost more than the children, as if she could sense that something was wrong. Maybe if they survived this, he'd explain to her what he had been doing here.

With one more deep breath of the fresh ocean air, he said into the communicator, "Transporter room, do you have the governor's location?"

"I do, Captain," the answer came back.

"Then beam me there at once."

"Understood."

A moment later, while he was staring out over the ocean, the transporter beam took him. So much for resting and relaxing. He just hoped it wasn't going to be the last time he got the chance to look over this ocean on this beautiful planet they had come so far to find.

## Countdown: 8 days, 7 hours

Lilian Coates watched as Captain Kirk transported away, not even bothering to take the time to go to a normal transporter location. She had a sense that something was happening, and that *something* wasn't going to be good for the colony.

As a child she had called her feelings before something went wrong "the fist." At the moment the fist was working full-time. It felt as if a deep sense of dread had clamped a hand around her stomach and was squeezing so tight that not even the beautiful day and the white sand of the beach could help relax it.

It was the same feeling she'd had just before her father had died of a heart attack. The same feeling just before her husband, Tom, had been killed.

Now it was here again.

She turned and looked out over the calm ocean, trying to let the waves soothe her fears. She was making up problems, she was sure. More than likely the captain had simply been called away by a routine action. This planet was so peaceful, so tame, what could be going dangerously wrong?

Maybe Kirk and Pardonnet were disagreeing on some way of dealing with colony protection again. She usually agreed with Kirk when she had heard both sides, even though Pardonnet was the reason she and Tom had signed up for this colony. And even with Tom dead, she still believed in the dream Pardonnet had for this planet. She loved the idea of less government, more freedoms. She could listen to Pardonnet talk for hours on those subjects.

But when it came to defense and protection of the planet and the colony, she had always agreed with Captain Kirk's ideas.

She stared up at the area near the log on the sand dune where he had sat. It seemed very empty without him there. And the fist holding her stomach wouldn't let go.

She focused her attention on the children.

Her son, Reynold, was playing with them. Since her background was in education, she had offered to watch the group of same-aged kids while their parents worked on setting up the colony. In a few weeks, they might even start some sort of formal school for all the children. But for the moment, she was just a glorified baby-sitter, and happy to be doing that much to help.

The children were done with their game, so she started them back up the beach toward the path to the main colony. Another hour and it would be dinner break and all the kids would join their parents.

Maybe by then she would find out what was happening. And why Captain Kirk had to leave the beach so fast, before she had even had the chance to say hello.

In her stomach, the tight feeling of dread squeezed even harder.

**To Be Continued
in
New Earth
Book Two
*BELLE TERRE***

# OUR FIRST SERIAL NOVEL!

## STAR TREK®
## STARFLEET: YEAR ONE

### A Novel in Twelve Parts®

by
**Michael Jan Friedman**

### Chapter Eleven

'I know," said Matsura, "this comes as a surprise to you." He glanced at his fellow captains, Dane included. 'To *all* of you."

In their places, Matsura would probably have been surprised as well.

He was an Earth Command officer by training as well as inclination, not one of the research types Clarisse Dumont had foisted on the Federation's new Starfleet. And at that moment, with every Earth colony in the Oreias system threatened by a mysterious fleet of alien marauders, his military skills were needed more than ever.

But this one time, Matsura felt compelled to pursue a different course of action.

"Listen," he told the others, "I may be on to something. I was studying the Oreias Seven colony back on the *Yellowjacket* a little while ago, and I noticed there were two hills at the edge of the colony."

"Wait a minute…" said Shumar. "There were two hills outside the Oreias Five colony as well."

"I'm aware of that," Matsura replied. "I got the information from your first officer a few moments ago."

"Two hills," Stiles repeated quizzically. "And that *means* something?"

"It sure as hell might," said Shumar.

"So what did you see when you went to examine the terrain for yourself?" asked Cobaryn.

"I'm not sure," said Matsura.

Zipping open the front of his uniform, he delved into an interior pocket and pulled out a handful of what he had found. They were fragments of something, each piece rounded, amber-colored, and brittle.

"I did some digging with my laser," Matsura told the others, "and this is what I came up with. The hill was full of it."

Cobaryn held his hand out. "May I?"

Matsura deposited his discovery in the Rigelian's silver-skinned palm. Then he watched Cobaryn's ruby eyes glitter with curiosity as he held the material up to the light.

"Any idea what it is?" asked Shumar.

Cobaryn made a face. "Something organic, I would guess."

"I'd say so too," Shumar chimed in. He glanced at Hagedorn. "Can we bring up a scanner?"

"Absolutely," said Hagedorn.

Before two minutes had elapsed, one of the *Horatio*'s security officers produced the device Shumar had requested. Shumar hefted it, pointed its business end at the stuff in Cobaryn's palm, and then activated it.

"What is it?" asked Matsura.

Shumar checked the scanner's readout. "It's a polysaccharide." His brow creased. "One that we found in great abundance in the hardest hit area on Oreias Five."

"So we have a pattern," said Matsura.

"So it would seem," Cobaryn responded.

"Though it's one we don't understand yet," Hagedorn pointed out.

"True," Shumar conceded. "But if one of the other colonies is near a couple of hills, and the hills happen to have this stuff inside them, there's a good chance that colony will be a target soon."

Stiles scowled. "And if it is? You think we ought to sit in orbit and wait for an attack?"

Shumar shook his head. "No, because the aliens might go back to Oreias Five. Or Oreias Seven, for that matter."

"So what *should* we do?" asked Dane, who, in Matsura's memory, had never posed so earnest a question before.

"We use our five good ships to hunt the aliens down," said Shumar, "just as Captain Stiles proposed. That's the best approach to keeping *all* the colonies from harm."

"But at the same time," Matsura added, "Captain Shumar and I pursue our hill theory...and see if we can figure out why the aliens decided to attack Earth colonies in the first place."

Cobaryn smiled. "A reasonable strategy."

Hagedorn regarded Matsura. "You're certain about this? I could always use an experienced hand on my bridge."

"Same here," said Stiles.

Clearly, thought Matsura, they didn't think his services would prove critical to the research effort. Still, he shook his head. "Thanks," he told his former wingmates, "but you'll do fine without me."

Hagedorn seemed to accept Matsura's decision. "Suit yourself. We'll hook up with you when we get back."

"After we've plucked the aliens' tailfeathers," Stiles chipped in.

But Matsura had engaged the triangular ships, and he knew it wouldn't be as easy as Stiles was making it out to be. Not by half.

"Good luck," said Matsura.

It was only inwardly that he added *You'll need it.*

Alexander Kapono had been overseeing the spring planting on Oreias Eight when he was called in from the fields.

As he opened the curved door to the administrative dome, he felt a breath of cool air dry the perspiration on his face. It was a welcome relief after the heat of the day.

"What is it?" he asked Chung, one of his tech specialists.

Chung was sitting on the opposite side of the dome behind his compact communications console, a smaller version of the one used on the bridges of Earth Command vessels. "You've got a message from Starfleet."

"Captain Dane?" asked Kapono.

Dane had said he would be in touch when they figured out what had prompted the attack on Oreias Five. However, the administrator hadn't expected to hear from the captain so soon.

The technician shook his head. "It's from a Captain Matsura. He says he's on his way to take a look around."

"Doesn't he know Dane did that already?"

"He says he wants to visit anyway."

The administrator grunted. "I guess he thinks he's going to find something that Dane missed."

Chung chuckled. "I guess."

To Kapono's knowledge, Earth Command captains had never worked this way. It made him wonder if Dane, Matsura, or anyone else in Starfleet had the slightest idea of what he was doing.

Cobaryn peered over his navigator's shoulder at a pattern of tiny red dots on an otherwise black screen. "Are you certain?"

"As certain as I can be, sir," said Locklear, a man with dark hair and blunt features who had navigated an Earth Command vessel during the war. "This is almost identical to the ion concentration that led the *Horatio* and the *Gibraltar* to the aliens."

The captain considered the red dots. They seemed so innocent, so abstract. However, if Locklear was right, they would steer the *Cheyenne* and all her sister ships into a clash as real as flesh and blood.

"Contact the other ships," Cobaryn told his navigator. He returned to his center seat and sat down. "Let them know what we have discovered."

"Aye, sir," came the response.

The fleet had spread out as much as possible to increase its chances of picking up the enemy's trail. However, it would only take a few seconds for the *Cheyenne*'s comm equipment to span those distances.

"They're responding," said Locklear. "The *Horatio* is transmitting a set of convergence coordinates."

During the Romulan War, Hagedorn had led Earth Command's top *Christopher* squadron—the one that had secured the pivotal victory at the planet Cheron. It made sense for Cobaryn to defer to him in tactical matters. Anything else would have been the height of arrogance.

"Chart a course," the Rigelian told his navigator.

"Charting," said Locklear.

"Best speed, Mr. Emick."

"Best speed, sir," his helmsman returned.

Cobaryn sat back in his chair and regarded his viewscreen, where he could see the stars shift slightly to port. They were on their way to a meeting with their sister ships.

And after that, if all went well, they would attend a different kind of meeting...along with their mysterious adversaries.

\* \* \*

Bryce Shumar wiped some sweat from his sunburned brow and considered the hole he was standing in—a ten-foot-deep burrow that descended into the heart of a tree-covered mound of red dirt.

Oreias Eight's sun was a crimson ball of flame, its sky an immense vast blue oven. The colonists who had come to watch Shumar work—a collection of children and their caregivers, for the most part—didn't seem to mind the relentless heat so much.

But then, they had had a few months to get used to it. The captain had been on the planet's surface less than half an hour.

Training his laser pistol at the unusually thick tree root at his feet, he pressed the trigger. The resultant shaft of blue energy pulverized the root and dug past it into the rocky red ground below.

"Why don't I take over for a while?" asked Matsura, who was sitting on a grimy shelf of rock at the level of Shumar's shoulders.

The former Earth base commander cast a glance at him. It was true that his wrist was getting tired from the backlash of all his laser use. However, he hated to admit that he was in any way less physically capable than Matsura, who was a good several years his junior.

"I'm fine so far," said Shumar.

"You sure?" asked Matsura.

"Quite sure," the older man told him. Setting his jaw against the discomfort in his arm, he continued his task.

Suddenly, the ground seemed to collapse beneath the onslaught of his laser beam and Shumar felt his feet slide out from under him. Before he knew it, he was sitting in a drift of loose red soil...

With something hard and amber-colored mixed into it.

"Hey!" cried Matsura, dropping down from his perch to land on a ledge of dirt that was still intact. "Are you all right?"

Shumar took stock of his situation. "I'm fine," he concluded, though not without a hint of embarrassment.

The younger man reached down and picked up a molded piece of amber-colored material about a third of a meter long. "Look at this," he said.

Shumar's eyes narrowed as he considered the object. It was the substance they had been excavating for, but in aggregate form.

"Same stuff?" asked Matsura.

"Looks like it," Shumar told him.

He poked through the dirt with his fingers and dug out another fragment. This one had a molded look to it as well, and it was even bigger than the first piece. As he brushed it off, he came to a conclusion.

"It's part of a shell," he said.

"How do you know?" the other man asked him.

"It's too regular to be a random accretion," Shumar pointed out. "And it's not strong enough to be part of an internal skeleton."

Matsura nodded. "So how do you think it got in here?"

Shumar frowned. "Good question."

"If the shell belonged to an animal," the younger man speculated, "the thing could have burrowed in here and died."

"But, remember," said Shumar, "we found evidence of similar remains in and around all those other mounds. So burrowing would have to have been an instinctive behavior for this animal."

"And it would have to have been in existence on Oreias Five and Oreias Seven as well."

Shumar nodded. "Which means it was transported here by an intelligent, spacefaring civilization."

Matsura looked thoughtful. "For what purpose?"

*For what purpose indeed?* Shumar asked himself.

He turned the piece of shell over in his hands, watching it gleam with reflected sunlight . . . and an alternative occurred to him. "On the other hand," he muttered "maybe it wasn't an animal at all."

"What do you mean?" asked Matsura.

But Shumar barely heard the man's question. He was still thinking, still following the logic of his assumption. Before he knew it, the mystery of the Oreias system had begun to unravel itself right before his eyes.

"Are you all right?" Matsura prodded, concern evident in his face.

"I've never been better," said Shumar. He turned to his colleague, his heart beating hard in his chest. "Have you ever heard of Underwood's Theory of Parallel Development?"

Matsura shook his head. "I don't think so."

"It encourages us to assume, in the absence of information to the contrary, that species develop along similar lines. In other words, if an alien has a mouth, it's likely he's also developed something along the lines of a table fork—even if his mouth doesn't look anything like your own."

"And if you find buried shells...?" asked Matsura.

"Then you have to ask yourself why *you* might have buried them—or more to the point, why you might have buried *anything*."

Suddenly, understanding dawned in the younger man's face. "Then that's it?" he asked. "That's the answer?"

Shumar smiled, basking in the glow of his discovery. "I'd bet my starship on it."

In fact, that was *exactly* what he would be doing.

Aaron Stiles shifted in his center seat. "Anything on scanners yet?" he inquired of his navigator.

Rosten shook her head. "Nothing yet, sir."

The captain frowned. It had been clear from the increasing integrity of the ion trail they had been following that the enemy wasn't far off. It could be only a matter

f minutes before they picked up the triangular ships and
got a handle on the odds against them.

Not that it mattered to Stiles how many aliens he had
to fight. This time, there was no retreat. One way or the
other, he and his comrades were going to put a stop to the
attacks.

"Sir?" said Rosten.

The captain glanced at her. "You have them?"

"Aye, sir," his navigator assured him.

Stiles got up from his seat and went to stand by Rosten's
console. Studying it, he could see a series of green blips on
the otherwise black screen. He counted six of them.

Good odds, he thought. *Excellent* odds.

He returned to his seat and tapped the communications stud on his armrest. "Stiles to Hagedorn."

The captain of the *Horatio* responded a moment later.
"I know," he said over their radio link. "We just noticed
them. I'll contact the others."

"Bull's-eye formation?"

There was a pause on the other end. "You know me
too well, Captain. Bull's-eye it is. Hagedorn out."

Stiles smiled grimly to himself, then turned to his
weapons officer. "Power to all batteries, Mr. Weeks."

"Power to all batteries," Weeks confirmed.

"Maintain speed," the captain told his helm officer.

Urbina checked her instruments. "Full impulse."

Darigghi came over to stand by Stiles's side. "It would
appear a confrontation is imminent," he observed.

The captain resisted the temptation to deliver a sarcas-
tic comeback. "It would appear that way."

"I realize I was not very helpful in our last clash with
the aliens," the Osadjani went on. "If there is something
more I can do this time, please let me know."

Stiles looked up at Darigghi. It wasn't at all the kind
of statement he had expected from his first officer.

"I'll do that," the captain assured him.

Darigghi nodded. "Thank you."

Stiles leaned back in his chair. Maybe a leopard could change its spots after all.

"Navigation," he said, "any sign that we've been spotted?"

"None, sir," Rosten replied. "It'll be—"

The captain waited a moment for his navigator to finish her sentence. When she didn't, he turned to her—and saw that she was focused on her monitor, her brow puckered in concentration.

"Lieutenant?" he prompted.

Rosten looked up at him. "Sir," she said, "I've received a message from Captain Shumar and Captain Matsura. They're asking all of us to return to Oreias Eight."

Stiles felt a spurt of anger. "Are they out of their minds? We're on the brink of a battle here!"

His navigator's cheeks flushed. "Yes, sir."

The captain hadn't meant to chew her out. It wasn't *her* fault that Shumar and Matsura had gone insane.

"Sorry," he told Rosten. "I should know better than to shoot the messenger."

The woman managed a smile. "No problem, sir."

"Why are we being recalled?" asked Darigghi.

Rosten shrugged. "They say they've discovered something that makes it unnecessary to confront the aliens."

His teeth grinding angrily, the captain opened a channel to the *Horatio* again. "This is Stiles," he snapped. "Did you receive a message from Shumar and Matsura?"

"I did," Hagedorn confirmed.

"And what do you think?"

"I think we've worked hard to track the aliens down. I also think we've got an opportunity here to end their activity in this system."

"Then we're on the same page."

He had barely gotten the words out when another voice broke into their radio link. "This is Captain Cobaryn."

Stiles rolled his eyes. "Go ahead," he said.

"I cannot imagine that the recommendation we received sits well with you. After all, we are close to engaging the enemy."

"Damned right," Stiles replied.

"Nonetheless," said the Rigelian, "I trust our colleagues' judgment. I do not believe they would have sent such a message unless the value of their discovery was overwhelming."

"Same here," a fourth voice chimed in.

Stiles recognized the voice as Dane's. It was just like the Cochrane jockey not to follow protocol and introduce himself.

"Ever heard the one about the bird in the hand?" Stiles asked. "Right now, we've got the aliens where we want them. We may never get another shot like this one."

"This isn't just Shumar talking," Dane reminded them. "It's Matsura too. He knows how you feel about stamping the aliens out."

"And despite that," said Cobaryn, "he is asking us to turn around."

Try as he might, Stiles couldn't ignore the truth of that. If it had just been Shumar trying to rein them in, he wouldn't even have considered complying. But Matsura had an Earth Command officer's mentality.

For a moment, no one responded, the only sound on their comm link that of radio buzz. Then Hagedorn spoke up.

"I hate to say this," he said in a thoughtful, measured voice, "but it sounds like we don't have much of a choice in the matter. If there's a chance to avoid bloodshed, we've got to take it."

Stiles felt his stomach muscles clench. They were on the verge of completing their mission, for crying out loud. They were *this* close to showing the aliens that Starfleet wasn't an organization to be taken lightly.

But he couldn't argue with Hagedorn's logic. Even i war, one had to seize the bloodless option if it becam available.

Stifling a curse, he said, "Agreed. *Gibraltar* out."

And with a stab of his finger, he severed the link.

He was about to give Urbina instructions to com about when Darigghi saved him the trouble. As the cap tain looked on, doing his best to contain his bitternes: he saw the stars swing around on their viewscreen.

One thought kept going through his mind, over an over again: *Shumar had damned well better know who he's talking about.*

Hiro Matsura could feel a bead of perspiration trace stinging path down the side of his face.

"Let me get this straight," said Stiles, who was studyin the amber-colored shell fragment that Matsura had jus handed him. "You dug this out of a mound of dirt and de cided to call us back from an imminent confrontation wit the enemy?"

He didn't sound impressed. But then, Matsura re flected, Stiles hadn't heard Shumar's theory yet. Neithe had Hagedorn, Dane, or Cobaryn, who looked a little be fuddled themselves as they stood by a gutted mound i the blazing light of Oreias.

"It wasn't just what we found," Shumar responded pa tiently. "It's what it all represents."

"And what *does* it represent?" asked Hagedorn, wh seemed inclined to exercise patience as well.

Matsura picked up another of the orange-yellow frag ments that he and Shumar had laid on the ground besid the ruined hill. This piece was more rounded than som of the others, more obviously designed to fit the anatom of a living creature.

"We asked ourselves the same question at first," h told Hagedorn. "What was it about these shells that com lled someone to bury them? And who did the burying? hen Captain Shumar came up with an explanation."

Shumar picked up on his cue. "There's a scientific the-y that alien species exhibit remarkably similar behavior, en when they're separated by many light years."

"I believe I've heard of it," said Hagedorn. "Under-ood's Theory of Parallel Development, isn't it?"

"Exactly right," Shumar confirmed. "And with Under-ood's thinking in mind, I asked myself why I would ve buried these shells—why I would have buried any-ing, for that matter."

"To honor the dead," Cobaryn blurted. He looked ound at his fellow captains. "I am quite familar with man customs," he explained.

"Captain Cobaryn is right," said Shumar, smiling at s colleague's enthusiasm. "We demonstrate our respect r our deceased friends and relatives by burying them."

Dane looked perplexed. "But I don't see any bodies ing here. Just a bunch of shells."

"True," Matsura conceded. "But maybe that's where e resemblance to human customs ends. Maybe this ecies sheds its shells, like certain insects on Earth— d feels it has to bury them, because their shells were ce a living part of their anatomy."

"And if it's true," said Shumar, "that these shells have me spiritual value to this species, is it any wonder that would object to offworlders intruding on its burial ounds?"

"In other words," Cobaryn added, following his iend's logic, "the aliens who attacked Oreias Five and reias Seven...did so because we encroached on their cred property?"

"It looks that way," said Shumar.

The captains exchanged glances as they mulled what humar and Matsura had told them. No one was out-ardly incredulous.

"Makes sense, I suppose," said Dane, speaking f
everyone.

"But we're not certain this is the answer," Hagedo
reminded them. "We have no conclusive proof."

"Scientists seldom do," Shumar pointed out. "Ofte
they have to go with what their instincts tell them. A
right now, my instincts are telling me we've hit the mark."

The sun beat down on the six of them as they a
sorbed Shumar's comment. Matsura, of course, had a
ready accepted his colleague's explanation. He wa
thinking about the next step.

"So," he said, "what do we do now?"

Matsura had barely gotten the words out when h
communicator started beeping. In fact, *all* their comm
nicators started beeping.

He took his own device out, flipped it open, and spo
into it. "Matsura here," he replied.

"Captain," said Jezzelis, his voice taut with appreher
sion, "there is an alien armada approaching Oreias Eight."

Matsura's mouth went dry. "Exactly what constitute
an armada?" he asked his first officer.

"I count fourteen ships, sir. And according to our ser
sor readings, their weapons have already been brought
full power."

Matsura looked at the others, all of whom seemed
have received the same kind of news. Their expression
were grim, to say the least. And it wasn't difficult to fig
ure out why.

With the *Yellowjacket* all but useless, they were ou
numbered almost three to one. Not promising, Matsu
thought.

Not promising at all.

**Star Trek: The Next Generation®**

## Star Trek® Books available in Trade Paperback

Omnibus Editions

Other Books

# STAR TREK
## THE EXPERIENCE
### LAS VEGAS HILTON

Be a part of the most exciting deep space adventure in the galaxy as you beam aboard the U.S.S. Enterprise. Explore the evolution of Star Trek® from television to movies in the "History of the Future Museum," the planet's largest collection of authentic Star Trek memorabilia. Then, visit distant galaxies on the "Voyage Through Space." This 22-minute action packed adventure will capture your senses with the latest in motion simulator technology. After your mission, shop in the Deep Space Nine Promenade and enjoy 24th Century cuisine in Quark's Bar & Restaurant.

- - - - - - - - - - - - - - - - - - - - - - - - - - - -

## Save up to $30

SIX CENTURIES,
TEN CAPTAINS.
ONE PROUD TRADITION.

# STAR TREK®
# ENTERPRISE LOGS

## INCLUDES STORIES FROM

Diane Carey
Greg Cox
A.C. Crispin
Peter David
Diane Duane
Michael Jan Friedman
Robert Greenberger
Jerry Oltion
and
John Vornholt

.STAR TREK_

**AVAILABLE NOW FROM POCKET BOOKS**

ENTL